REDEEMED

DIRTY AIR SERIES BOOK FOUR

LAUREN ASHER

REDEEMED

Editing: Erica Russikoff

Cover Designer: Books and Moods

Interior Formatting: Books and Moods

To those who dare to dream
even in their darkest days.

PLAYLIST

REDEEMED - LAUREN ASHER

Older Than I Am — Lennon Stella	3:02	+
Lonely — Justin Bieber	2:29	+
Bad Child — Tones And I	3:41	+
Modern Loneliness — Lauv	4:12	+
Lie Like This — Julia Michaels	3:38	+
At My Worst — Pink Sweat$	2:50	+
Love Songs — Sarah Barrios	2:24	+
Wonder — Shawn Mendes	2:53	+
Take Care of You — Ella Henderson	3:29	+
Golden — Harry Styles	3:40	+
love language — Ariana Grande	3:00	+
What a Man Gotta Do — Jonas Brothers	3:01	+
Wildest Dreams — Taylor Swift	3:40	+
Lie to Me — Tate McRae & Ali Gatie	2:57	+
Hold On —Chord Overstreet	3:19	+
Stay — Gracie Abrams	2:57	+
Last Time I Say Sorry — Kane Brown & John Legend	3:15	+
XO — John Mayer	3:34	+

PROLOGUE

SANTIAGO

THREE YEARS AGO

rowds of fans roar in the distance, fueling the adrenaline building up inside of me. The Silverstone Prix lights reflect off the hood of my red Bandini car. Sweat trickles down my back from the heat of the vibrating engine behind me.

I take a deep breath and hold it as each of the five Prix lights shuts off.

Vamos. I press down on the throttle. My car squeals as it rushes past the first straight. Noah, my brother-in-law and the best F1 racer, leads the group of drivers. His rear bumper stays within touching distance as I turn past the first corner behind him.

The post-rain humidity makes my helmet's shield foggy as we race lap after lap. Slick roads challenge my skills and my tires. I lift the protective visor an inch, allowing the hot air from my mouth to escape through the gap in the helmet.

My lungs tighten with each heavy breath. I push through exhaustion and attempt to get around Noah's car. He keeps to the center of the track, making it impossible to take over his first-place spot.

"Get better control of your car on turn four. You're driving sloppy because it's wet out there," James Mitchell, Bandini's team principal, speaks into my earpiece.

"Got it." I grip my steering wheel tighter, focusing on the road.

Turn after turn, I match Noah's speed. Although he's family and my teammate, we both crave beating each other as often as we can. But together, we work as an unstoppable Bandini force competing against everyone else.

Noah enters the pit lane in need of new tires, leaving the track and his first-place spot open for me. It's my moment of opportunity.

Everything counts. Every breath, every wheel rotation, every damn second ticking away.

The pace of my heart increases as I pass another blurring Grandstand filled with cheering fans. My body hums with a rush of energy. It's a feeling unparalleled to anything else. I've never been high a day in my life, but I assume it feels like this—exhilarating and untouchable. I smile behind my helmet as I drive by the crowds.

Noah returns full force and speeds around me at the latest straight. His tires shriek as he presses on the brakes at a corner.

I jab the button to switch gears. "Bastard. Always trying to steal the spotlight."

"Our computers show that there's a light shower coming

in. For fuck's sake, watch for the wet patches and don't crash into Noah." James's voice echoes through my ear.

"Are they going to let us switch to wet tires?"

"I think the call should be coming in soon. Hang in there." James mutes himself.

A sheer mist from Noah's wheels shoots through the air. Visibility becomes difficult as Noah's tires cause more water to splash against my helmet. I swipe my gloved hand across my visor, wiping away the condensation.

With my visor clear of water, I grip the steering wheel with both hands. My breath catches in my throat as I run over a slick patch of pavement.

One breath. One tire rotation. One second to lose it all.

Control escapes my grasp. My car speeds past the corner I should be turning at. All hell breaks loose as I clutch onto the useless steering wheel.

"Shit. Shit. Shit!" I smash my sneaker against the brakes, but nothing works to slow my car down fast enough.

"Santiago, fuck! Brace!" James yells out something else, but I can't hear him over the blood pounding in my ears.

Everything blurs as the car propels across the gravel at over two-hundred miles an hour. My car speeds toward the protective barrier without slowing. The front right wing of my car smashes into the tires lining a concrete blockade. Rubber tires fly, doing little to shield my race car from the drastic impact.

My teeth snap together and my body jostles from the hit. Blinding hot pain shoots up my right leg. My heart races in my chest, and short, ragged breaths escape my lungs. Every part of my body aches. I blink back tears as my hands shake against the steering wheel.

"Santiago, are you okay? The safety team is on their way!" James calls out. The tremble in his voice gives away his fear.

Fuck. The world spins on its axis as I gaze at the damage. My front bumper resembles a mangled metal ball, with the right side taking the most damage. Smoke billows from behind me, clouding my vision.

I lift from my seat. A sharp pain shoots through my body, forcing me to bite down on my tongue. "Need a medic. Now." My words come out as a moan.

James curses into the mic. "Can you get out of your car and get behind the safety barrier?"

Safety barrier? What a joke, seeing as it did a shit job of keeping me protected.

I attempt to remove my harness, but another rush of pain elicits a groan from me. "No. Fuck. I can't get up." I attempt to wiggle my toes, but my right one stays numb. "I can't move! *Ay, Dios.* Fuck, fuck, fuck."

Negative thoughts fuel the rush of panic building inside of me. *Why can't I move? Why can't I get out of this fucking car? Stand up! Do something!*

Everything I try to do is met with a sharp stab of pain. My vision blurs and acid crawls up my throat.

"Santi! The safety patrol is almost here." My sister's voice booms as she rushes up to the broken barrier. A metal fence rises above the barricade and keeps us apart. Her crazed brown eyes latch onto mine as she frantically grips the chain links.

"Maya. *No te preocupes!*" I try to calm her worries as I remove the steering wheel from my dashboard and throw it on the front wing. The move jostles my body again, sending another shattering pain up the right side of my body.

"They'll get you out! Stop moving!" Maya's voice rises as she calls out for any medic to help.

"I couldn't get up even if I wanted to." My body grows hot as sweat trickles down my face. Everything around me slows as I try to comprehend the pain in my leg. *Is this what shock feels like?*

Adrenaline escapes me like a deflating balloon. My vision darkens as I attempt to remain conscious. Maya tugs on her brown hair, trying to catch my attention, but I don't respond. Processing her words takes effort, and my body wants to give out.

The safety team rushes onto the scene. They ask rapid-fire questions that add to my growing unease. I struggle to explain my situation, and they work on getting me out.

Maya comes up to my side and clutches onto my hand. "It'll be all right. The ambulance is on its way now." Tears escape her eyes.

"It hurts so fucking bad. I think I might pass out."

"*Quédate conmigo.*"

I can't stop the panicky sensation building inside of me as the medics pull me out of my car.

"Maya," I croak.

Someone forces her to let go of my hand as they move me onto a spinal board.

"It'll be okay. They'll take good care of you!" she cries over the yelling crew and blaring sirens.

The lights of the ambulance flash around me. I don't want to give into the darkness, but the mind-numbing ache in my leg has other plans. It steals away my consciousness and my dream of winning another Championship along with it.

The smell of antiseptic hits me first. My nose twitches at the mix of alcohol and pine needles, and my eyes burn as the bright ceiling lights come into focus.

It takes me a few moments to register my surroundings. Beeping machines match the accelerating beat of my heart. An IV needle pricks my hand, attached to bags of fluids.

I blink, forcing my eyes to adjust. My foggy brain doesn't want to comprehend why I'm in a hospital bed.

"*Ay Dios, ya estas despierto.*" My mom gets up from a chair across from me and pulls my hand into hers. Her brown hair is thrown up in a messy bun, and the wrinkles in her clothes match the ones etched into her face.

Maya and my dad walk up to the other side of my bed. Noah stands behind my sister, wrapping his arms around her body.

"*Mami? Papi?* What are you doing here?" I rasp.

My dad runs a hand through his gray hair, making the strands go everywhere. His brown eyes reflect the same concern as everyone else's.

What's happening?

My mom's brown eyes glisten as she looks at me. "*Mi carino.*" She sobs as she throws herself on top of me. The sudden movement jars my body.

What the fuck? My mom never cries like this. Not when she could barely pay the bills, or when she had to work during my birthday every year. Not even when my dad lost his job, making it almost impossible for me to compete in a kart race. She's always been a warrior.

I lift my free arm and wrap it around her shaking body. "*Estoy bien, Mami.* I'll be fine. It was just an accident."

Maya places a trembling hand on my shoulder. "Santi—" The way she looks at me has the beeping machine kicking into overdrive. Her stare sets off every internal alarm, and I struggle to understand why.

My brain moves at a snail's pace to catch up on everything. "What's going on—"

An older doctor walks into the room, interrupting me. He flips through a few papers on his clipboard. "Oh, good. I'm glad to see you're awake, Santiago."

"Who are you?"

He smiles. "My name is Dr. Michaelson. We are relieved that you're up and talking. We were all worried about you, especially your family. You've been through a traumatic experience."

"Why am I here?" My brows draw together.

His smile remains bright and warm, but it does nothing to calm my erratic heart rate. "You're recovering from a surgery. I'm the doctor who was assigned to your case and I plan on helping you through this whole process."

"Surgeon? Why do I need you?"

Whatever I said makes my mom grip onto my shoulder, her nails biting into the hospital gown covering my body. Another sob escapes her, and the sound hits me right in the chest.

The doctor clears his throat. "You've been through a lot within the last twenty-four hours. I can tell you're a strong man. Are you in any pain right now?"

Pain? Everything inside of me feels...numb. Nothing like

how I usually am after a crash with my limbs aching and my head hurting. It's as if someone hit a reset button on my body, and I'm still booting up.

"No. I don't feel anything." I bristle when I meet the doctor's gaze.

There's that look again. Something in his eyes doesn't sit right with me.

The doctor scans my body before offering me another reassuring smile. "I'm sorry we have to meet under this kind of circumstance. I'm a huge fan of your driving."

The heart-monitoring machine's tempo increases as the doctor's eyes flit from me to my family. "If it's okay with you, Santiago, I'd like to speak with you privately for a moment."

No one says a damn thing. Not one single person makes a move to leave the room. It's so damn silent, the IV drip makes more noise than the people surrounding me.

Whatever the doctor has to say can't be good. *Fuck. Is it cancer? A ruptured organ? Why would I need a surgeon in the first place?*

I fist my trembling hands, unsure if I can do this on my own. "Anything you need to say can be said in front of them."

Doctor whatever-his-name-is's brows draw together as he takes a deep breath. "You're currently heavily medicated, so I apologize for any confusion you might be experiencing at the moment." The doctor walks up to the end of my bed. His warm smile drops a fraction, becoming something I don't want to see. Growing up poor and an underdog allows me to recognize pity instantly. It's written all over the doctor's face. It catches me off guard because I haven't experienced it in some time. Not since I made it and became someone. Not since I started living my dream and proving everyone who doubted me wrong.

A bead of sweat drips down my forehead. "Just get on with it. You're making me nervous."

The doctor's frown becomes more pronounced. "I'm very sorry, Santiago, but you had an extremely traumatizing accident."

"No shit. Get to the point," I bite out.

Maya takes in a sudden breath. "Santi."

"It's all right. I can imagine this is stressful and I'm not helping. Not to mention, mood changes and fogginess are expected with the amount of morphine they gave you to combat the pain." His eyes move from my face to the lower half of my body.

I tense.

He releases a shaky breath. "I want you to know that the accident wasn't your fault. There was absolutely nothing you could have done to change what happened today. I'm very sorry to tell you that we could not save the bones below your right knee. They shattered on impact, along with the cartilage, to the point that there was nothing left for us to work with in the operating room. We were able to conduct the emergency amputation to ensure the rest of your leg could be saved..."

Everything around me stops. The whooshing of the machines. My family's cries as they break down in front of me. The whole damn world fades to a gray so dark, it borders on black. One word hits me like a battering ram to my skull.

Amputation.

Amputation.

Amputation?

I clutch onto the sheet covering the lower half of my body. My stomach twists at the cry my mom lets out as she turns toward my dad.

I consider telling my family that the doctor must be wrong. He *has* to be wrong. But something stops me as I lift the sheet with shaky fingers.

It takes one second for my world to crumble around me. One second to realize my life has ended before it ever truly began. One second to wish I could take it all back.

I stare down at my body. My right leg is bandaged and wrong. So fucking wrong I can barely look at it, with acid crawling up my throat. I gag and look away. Someone places a plastic container on my chest as bile escapes my mouth.

I've never experienced pain like this before. The emotional kind that borderlines on physical, as if someone set off a bomb inside of my chest.

I'm not sure who shoves the sheet over my body, but I'm grateful for it. I shut my eyes and tell myself how none of this is real. Except my mind has other plans, not allowing me to think past anything but my leg.

Everything below my right knee is missing. The foot I use to press against the pedal. The calf muscles I work on daily in the gym to make me stronger. The very part of me I depend on during every race is gone, like it never existed in the first place.

Tears escape my eyes. I hate the feel of them sliding down my cheeks. I'm quick to brush them away, not wanting anyone to see me break down. Everything remains eerily silent as my world is destroyed around me. A hollow space takes up the spot in my chest where my heart once belonged, matching my missing appendage.

The doctor's voice breaks the quiet. "I'm very sorry, Santiago. I'm hopeful that we can help you have a speedy recovery. With our patients, it's normal to feel overwhelmed from the shock—"

"Shock? You know what's shocking? Finding out my sister was dating the one man I didn't want in her life. Or maybe learning I would sign with the best F1 team after only a couple years of racing. This? *This* is fucking catastrophic," I hiss. "So don't pretend it's anything but a death sentence." I stare at the doctor with every amount of hate I can muster. Hate feels better than the numbness seeping into my blood, erasing everything I once was. Hate is something I can hold on to. Hate is something I can remember when all else fails me.

"Santiago." My dad speaks in a meek voice, lacking his usual assuredness.

I can't find it in me to care and apologize. I can't find it in me to do *anything*.

"I want everyone out," I say it low, yet the sentence carries a sense of finality.

Mami's cries become louder. *Papi* tugs her into his chest, muffling her sobs.

"You shouldn't be alone right now." Maya's small hand clutches onto my shoulder.

Noah looms behind her like the fucking shadow he is. I can't look him in the eyes. Acknowledging his presence reminds me of everything I've lost. My whole life's work down the drain in the matter of twenty-four hours.

"It's all gone. One wrong move and my entire life is done. One stupid fucking move of driving on the wrong part of the pavement." I hide my face behind my trembling hands. I don't want anyone to see my pain or my tears because it feels like another thing stolen from me. My pride. My manhood. My dignity. All of it robbed after one mistake. One devastating, career-ending mistake.

Fuck that.

Life-ending. One *life-ending* mistake.

"Your life isn't over. We're going to fix this," Maya says loudly over my heavy breathing.

Noah places his palm on top of hers, giving my shoulder a tighter squeeze. "Your life isn't over because I won't let you give up on yourself. This isn't the end."

I refuse to look up at him. My family ignores my protests and stands by me as I lose my shit in silence, giving in to the emotional and physical pain.

CHAPTER ONE

Chloe

"Hey, Mom. This is a surprise. Brooke isn't coming home until eight." I open the door to my apartment.

She walks into the space, running her shaky hands down her disheveled clothes. Her dark, greasy hair sticks to the sides of her head, emphasizing the paleness of her skin. Everything about her resembles a corpse. From her jutting collarbones to her hollow cheeks, it's as if someone vacuumed the life straight out from her.

The way she stares at me sets me on edge. It's the same look she had every time the social worker tried to have us reconcile, only to have Mom screw it up again. Most people have a devil and an angel on each of their shoulders. My mom was stuck with two devils who support her preferred vices—drugs and bad decisions.

"Sweetie. I've been meaning to call you." Her sickly-sweet tone sends goosebumps across my skin. She gazes at me with bulging blue eyes. "I know we had plans for tonight, but I need to cancel. I'm not feeling well."

More like she's not feeling *high*. Crossing my arms, I lean against the kitchen counter. I might as well make myself comfortable for another round of disappointment. I thought it would be different this time between us. I thought *she* would be different.

Stupid Chloe. When will you ever learn?

She rattles on, taking my silence as acceptance. "I'm in a tough spot. See, I owe Ralph some money, and you know how he gets when I don't pay him."

"Rough and handsy?"

Ralph is the reason my social worker revoked my mom's custody. When my mom's boyfriend wasn't heavy-handed with Mom, he was creepy with me. The social worker pulled me out of the house and determined Mom could try again in a few years if she worked on herself and ditched her boyfriend. Mom decided Ralph being her usual drug supplier served a greater benefit than the fat check she received from the government for half-ass parenting. That is if someone could call leaving me to fend for myself in a roach-infested apartment *parenting*.

She scoffs. "I wouldn't ask you for money if I didn't need it."

"No, Mom. You *would* ask. That's our problem. Every time I give you money, you promise to pull yourself together." *And every time you say you'll get clean, I fall for it because I still can't move past my stupid hopeful mindset.*

She tugs her cracking lip between her teeth. "I'm sorry. You know how I am."

"A liar?"

Her laugh borders on cackling. "Oh, Chloe. Don't be that way."

"Truthful?"

It seems like her mood appears to take a turn for the worst as her eyes darken. "Snappy comments are cute for picking up boys, but they lose their charm when used against your mother."

I release a tense breath from my lungs. "I don't have money."

"You're lying. It's the end of the month. You're the responsible type with your bills."

Of course, she would come on payday. How could I have been this dense to think she wanted to actually see me on my birthday? "No. I'm not lying."

"Just give me three-hundred dollars and I'll leave. That's all I need." She chews on a ragged nail.

"*No.*"

My mother's eyes dart from me to my purse hanging on a hook by the door. The very purse that houses my monthly rent payment.

"Don't even think about it." I mean to snap, but my voice is nothing but a hoarse whisper. *Please, don't think of stealing from me. I'm your daughter, for God's sake.* My throat tightens at the idea.

"You don't understand. The spasms are getting worse without my stuff." She makes her addiction to opioids sound like a casual need for ice cream. It's always been this way, with her craving her *stuff* more than she craves being a mother.

"You promised to quit." My voice rasps, sadness eating away at my faux coldness.

She sneers, her patience apparently thinning. "Yeah, well, I lied. I'm sorry. I did try, but it was terrible. I can't live without it."

Even though I spent most of my life listening to sweet lies and empty apologies, the words still sit heavy in my chest every time she says them. It's like I'm taken back to the time I was a little girl.

I'm sorry I didn't show up for today's session with the therapist, Chloe. I'll come next week, I swear.

I'm sorry Ralph walked in while you were showering. You know how he forgets to knock on the door.

I'm sorry I missed Christmas this year. I got tied up, but I'll make it up to you next time.

Mom takes advantage of my distraction and rushes toward my purse. I grab onto the hem of her shirt to pull her back, and she spins around. The crack of her palm hitting the skin of my cheek echoes off the paint-peeled walls.

She actually fucking hit me. Me, a goddamned adult. I step back and press my palm against my stinging cheek. The rush of pumping blood fills my ears, making it hard to hear her.

Mom searches my purse like a woman possessed. She whimpers as she finds my wallet and snatches the bills in her bony fingers. Her greedy hands clutch onto more than three-hundred dollars, but I do nothing to stop her. I'm too stunned at the animal she reverts to when she doesn't get her drugs. How does she stand looking at herself in the mirror? I'm surprised her skin doesn't crawl off her body in a repulsive rebellion.

Mom drops my wallet on the floor. "I'm sorry, baby girl. I wish it didn't have to be this way. I'll pay you back one day, I promise." She looks over at me with an empty stare, just like her words.

I hate myself for wishing she showed an ounce of pity about how she treats me. The hate molds into something dark and ugly inside of me. A toxic anger building up within, threatening to explode on her. "We're done. Don't ever bother coming back here. Do what you do best, and forget I exist. *Forever.*"

"You don't mean that." She has the audacity to frown.

"Get out of here!" I lunge toward her.

She scurries out of my apartment. The door shuts with a soft thud in her absence.

I turn toward the kitchen and search for a cold pack to soothe my burning cheek.

As I ice my face, it hits me that my mom didn't even wish me a happy birthday. It was the whole reason she was supposed to stop by in the first place. The only stupid reason I invited her in years.

This is what I get for thinking with my heart rather than my head. Now I'm two cents away from being broke again because all my rent money is gone.

My mother brings nothing but destruction into my life, and this time it's worse because it's my fault. I believed her when she called and told me how she wanted to change. How she started attending a free rehab program because she was ready to be a better mother.

A fresh wave of sadness douses my anger. The first tear falls down my face, silent and mocking. I rush to erase it from my skin because I hate how pathetic I become when my mom enters the picture. I'm not that desperate child anymore, begging for Mommy's attention.

The thought produces more tears instead of extinguishing them. Before I know it, my face becomes blotchy and my nose clogs. Refusing to give her betrayal any more of my attention, I redirect my energy.

While positivity keeps me going, perseverance is what gives me the courage to fight for another day. To move forward and start a new life for myself pursuing whatever makes me happy.

I grab my wish journal off my bedroom nightstand. The thick notebook is the one item I've kept with me over the years, following me through random foster homes. Every time I make a wish, I write it down. With a random pen, I scribble the first thing that comes to mind.

I wish to find someone who appreciates my presence instead of destroying it.

Brooke's scowl makes the golden skin above her brows wrinkle. She grabs her thick brown hair and pulls it into a messy bun.

I cringe at the gesture. Brooke only does that if she's upset or working on her latest project for school. She's the type who doesn't usually fuss over the waves she inherited from whichever unknown parent. And after everything that went down with my mom earlier, it's hard not to envy Brooke right now not knowing who her parents are. It would save me a load of pain.

Okay, that's shitty of me to say. I know how upset Brooke

gets about her deadbeat parents. Not that I blame her. At least my mother had the decency to give birth to me. Brooke wasn't as fortunate. She was ditched as a newborn on the cold steps of a Brooklyn fire station with a note written in Tagalog—the only hint we have about her Filipina heritage.

Brooke's brandy-colored eyes assess my face. "Promise me you won't see her anymore. She's toxic."

I lower my head. "I know. You were right. She wasn't ready for a relationship with me after all."

"I hate being right about this, but you deserve better than her. You always have and you always will."

My lip quivers. "I promise to let her go this time. For real. Today was awful and not what I was hoping for. She's always been verbal or neglectful, but she's never gotten physical before. Lesson learned." The words sound as pathetic leaving my mouth as they did in my head.

Here I am, officially twenty-four years old and still taking shit from my mom. I thought me aging out of the system would've pushed her to change. Like a hopeless fool, I expected something different from our relationship as I grew older.

"None of this is your fault. She took advantage of your hope, but it's her loss." Brooke tugs me in for a hug.

"What would I do without you?"

"I don't know. You'd probably get bored. I'm told I can be rather stimulating."

I laugh and step out of her embrace. "Gross."

"Perv." Brooke sticks her tongue out at me. "Do you know what you want to wish for?" She passes me a plate with a single cupcake that has one candle in its center. It's a tradition we have kept since we roomed together in our foster home all those years ago.

"Yes." I smile.

"Same old wish?"

Brooke knows me better than anyone. We clicked the instant we met once I was placed in the same foster home as her. She was abandoned as a baby and grew up within the system, which gave her the opportunity to show me the ropes. Awful parents aren't something two teens should bond over, but our survival instincts called for it. And together, instead of allowing our circumstances to ruin us, we supported one another through the darkest times.

With Brooke's friendship, I did what others didn't dare. I made wishes. Whether it was a birthday wish or a late-night entry scribbled in my wish journal, I dared to wish so freaking big, Walt Disney himself would be jealous.

Every single birthday, year after year, I make one wish. Despite the same result time and time again, I always gather a new hope that this will be the year I find out who my dad is. I never give up on my wish. Not even after my mom confessed one year how she had no idea who my dad was since she was drugged out of her mind at the time of my conception. While some girls are the product of two people who love each other very much, I'm the result of someone who cared more about the drugs in her system than protecting herself from an unwanted pregnancy.

To counteract the ugly thoughts inside of me over the years, I made up a grand story about who and where my father was. He became this hero in my head who had no idea I was born in the first place. If he knew about my existence, he would stop at nothing to find me.

Brooke lights the candle, pulling me back into the

moment. "Dream big, Chloe."

I shut my eyes and pull back my dark hair, not wanting to burn a strand with the flame. *Please let this be the year I find some new clue about my dad.* I release a gust of air and blow out the flame.

Brooke claps her hands. She grabs a knife and cuts the cupcake in half before sliding my half across our cracking Formica counter. Some people might turn their nose up at our fifties-inspired, closet-sized apartment. Brooke and I worked our butts off to afford a place in New York City, so we are proud of it. I work two jobs to cover my half of the rent. My mornings consist of taking care of kids at a daycare while I spend my evenings working as many shifts at a restaurant as I can. Meanwhile, Brooke has her life mapped out since she is a few semesters away from graduating with a degree in Fashion Journalism. Unlike Brooke, I can't seem to think of next month, let alone what I want to do for the rest of my life.

Brooke pulls a wrapped present out of the spice cabinet.

I lift a brow. "Really? You decided to hide it in there?"

"Since you can't cook to save your life, it seemed like an appropriate place to hide this bad boy." The package rattles as she shakes it once for good measure.

"I hope you didn't buy anything—"

"Expensive. I know the rules." She bobs her head in a mocking way.

I smile up at her. "You're the best. You know that, right?"

"Open it!" Brooke cries.

I rip at the paper, revealing the last thing I'd expect.

"Oh Brooke, I thought we said we wouldn't." I run a trembling finger across the ancestry kit packaging.

"No. I said *I* wouldn't. You only went along with my plan because you wanted to make me happy. But I decided to take your fate into my own hands."

We both considered doing the genetic test last year but chickened out after we both considered the potential disappointment if the results didn't work out. Brooke was adamant against it, and I agreed because I didn't want to do it without her.

Leave it to my best friend to know me better than I know myself.

"You shouldn't have." This is the burden of being a dreamer. It's all fun and games until Cloud Nine turns into a torrential downpour. And the reasonable side of my brain says this dream can morph into a category five hurricane.

But seeing the kit in my hands makes the dream of meeting my dad attainable. *No, Chloe. It's another dream that could break your heart.*

Brooke grabs a bottle of cheap vodka from the top of the fridge. "There's no time like the present. What do you say? Spit into the little tube, ship it off, and then we can get drunk off our asses to celebrate?"

This whole plan has the potential to explode in my face. I could either end up with an empty ancestry tree or find out that my father is some terrible human who knew about my existence this entire time. But—the irrational part of my brain intervenes—I could end up finding a father who didn't know I existed in the first place. Someone who wants to get to know me and take me in as his family. A dad who wants to love me and make up for lost time, not because he has to, but because he wants to.

The latter reasoning wins, beating back my worries.

I take a deep breath. "Let's do this."

CHAPTER TWO

SANTIAGO

The blades of the ceiling fan spin above me, blurring together in one big circle. I check the time on my phone again. Only five minutes have passed since the last time I looked.

This is my life. Uneventful. Isolated. *Gloomy*.

I've become a shell of a person because it's easier than facing my pointless future. Anything is better than that, including debilitating sadness.

I should call my therapist again and make another appointment.

I should go on a road trip and visit my parents.

I should do something—anything really—but I can't find it in me to beat back the mist taking over my brain.

My therapist calls it depression. I call it my life post-accident.

I shouldn't have read the article last night. The one that

gave a detailed report of my three-year anniversary since my accident. It was a mistake. Any hope about returning to my previous life is extinguished with every negative sentence or article headline. They don't talk about my successful recovery. Or how I'm able to walk like a normal man, even though I look anything but.

Although I'm physically fit, I'm mentally not. Even after three years, I still cling to old ghosts of my past. That's what happens when I have all the time in the world to think. But with overthinking then comes my escape into numbness because it's easier to slip into the mental space where I don't need to care—to shut off my feelings toward my situation. Apathy is my battle armor in my harsh new reality. Because if I cared, then I'd have to embrace the awful articles published about me.

Santiago Alatorre's new maid gives a tell-all about his disability.

Read about Santiago Alatorre's struggle with morphine addiction, alcoholism, and depression.

Santiago Alatorre visits his therapist for the first time in months. Exclusive reports say he is actively suicidal and was rushed to the hospital.

Headlines blur together, with one essential bottom line: everyone wants to watch me fail. I thought success was what people were interested in, but in reality, they're more invested in my downfall. Defeat sells headlines while success sells sponsorships. Not that I deal with the latter anymore. I went from being treated like a god to being nothing but a whisper of a headline once a year.

In the end, reporters are right. I'm not the same person.

I can't drive a car faster than the average speed limit without getting nauseous and paralyzed with fear. So, yeah, I'm the last racer who belongs back on the F1 grid.

My trauma gives me the perfect excuse to hide. It's just me and my massive house, sequestered in some small lake town surrounded by Italian mountain ranges. I call it my personal hell, surrounded by paradise.

My phone's alarm rings again. I press snooze, ignoring the tiny voice in my head pleading with me to get out of bed. The sane part of me urges me to drive my car down the winding coastal road. To shave off my beard because it's a physical reminder of my lack of motivation. To reach out to my family and ask for anyone to visit me because I can't stand the silence in my house for another day.

No. Everyone has moved on, and you're just a loser stuck living in your past memories.

The hopeful thoughts scurry as the darkness takes hold again. I turn over in my bed, allowing the afternoon sunlight to warm my back. Colors drain around me as I shut my eyes, forcing myself to hide in my gray world for another day.

CHAPTER THREE

Chloe

I stare at the log-in screen of the testing company. The mouse hovers over the sign-in button, but I pull back.

"Are you planning on looking at the screen all day or…" Brooke leans on the counter next to me.

"I'm scared," I whisper as if the computer can detect my fear.

"I'd be afraid too. But think about how you've spent the last six weeks anxiously waiting for this." She bumps her hip into mine. "Is it easier if I press the button?"

I nod my head, shutting my eyes. "Yes." There's no use lying to myself. While I might be optimistic, I'm not delusional. I half expect the test to come back empty with meaningless information. That I can handle. The alternative option—the hopeful one—now *that* seems unrealistic.

"Okay. You got it, dude."

My heart lodges itself somewhere in my throat as Brooke clicks the button.

"Oh shit! It worked!" Brooke's scream makes my ears pop.

"What?" My eyes fly open.

"You have a match!" She jumps up and down, clapping her hands together. "Yes!"

I blink at the screen. The results in front of me make it difficult to produce any words, let alone a reaction. Much to my shock, the test linked me to a man I share almost fifty percent of my DNA with.

Oh my God. It actually worked.

It feels like after all the hard breaks I've had in life, I finally won the genetic lottery.

"You have a dad!" Brooke grabs my hand and spins me in a circle.

We laugh up to the ceiling, allowing hope to fill our tiny apartment to the point of bursting.

"Hey, Chloe, would you mind covering the rest of my shift? You can obviously keep the tips. I hate to do this, but my mom forgot to pick up her seizure meds. I need to rush to the pharmacy before they close for the night." Teri, one of the older waitresses, looks up at me.

I'm tempted to say no. The bottoms of my feet ache after running around the daycare all morning. My head throbs from a permanent headache, forcing me to squint every time I enter the brightly lit kitchen. All I want is a nice shower, enough Tylenol to knock out an elephant, and my bed. The simple things in life.

But…I need the money. Any dollar counts toward flying

to Italy and my father faster. According to a Google search and Brooke's social media FBI skills, Matteo Accardi, AKA my long-lost father, lives his best life in some small Italian lakeside town. Flights cost about the same as donating one of my kidneys. Sadly, I checked on giving one away, but Brooke warned me against it. She said to be patient and save up money. But it's easy for her to say that. Who can think, let alone save up money, when my dad is literally *alive*?

Brooke is the realist in this relationship, and she burst my dreamer bubble before it got out of control. She's right. Kidneys are like twins. They shouldn't be apart. So, sadly, I have both and I'm stuck working grueling hours to save up every single dollar.

The DJ in my head plays "Work" by Rihanna, clearly approving of the decision to push through my fatigue for extra money.

I nod my head. "Sure."

"Great! Thank you! You can check with Jamie for my table numbers." She rushes out of the room.

Look at me being such a giver.

I find out Teri's tables from Jamie before I take my minuscule five-minute break. People think I'm a smoker, but I like to stand in the alleyway behind the restaurant and breathe in the stale air of New York City. It's my moment of quiet in a day filled with noise.

I step out into the alley and halt. *Ugh.* There's a random couple defiling my dumpster oasis, with the man practically inhaling the girl's face. *Gross.* But something about the way the guy gropes her has me nodding my head in weird fascination. What kind of couple can hook up by the trash?

The kind that are so desperate for each other they couldn't wait to get home.

I wouldn't know that kind of passion. The only thing close to that is my commitment to working hard to afford the basics in life. Boyfriends are only a distraction, and they require a lot more attention than watering plants. I don't have the time or energy for a relationship. That's why I stick to some meaningless hookups every now and then to satisfy an itch. Plus, I sure as hell don't have the ability to trust someone to that degree. My mom made sure of that. She might have been awful, but she taught me some important lessons.

Don't do drugs.

Don't have sex without a condom.

Don't have kids unless I'm absolutely, positively, five-hundred percent ready because they can't be returned at the nearest mall or grocery store.

And most of all, don't fall in love. It's messy, blinding, and bound to be a disaster.

I turn back toward the door to give these two lovers privacy. My old sneaker squeaks and the man turns to yell at me.

"Hey! Go away, you creep!"

Me? I'm not the one hooking up next to yesterday's trash. I look over my shoulder to apologize. My jaw drops at what I find.

That no-good liar. Teri isn't picking up her mom's medication. How can she be, when she's too busy choking on this guy's tongue? I scowl. Teri officially sucks and if I didn't want her tips, I'd ditch all her tables in revenge.

Why do people need to lie to get their way? Doesn't

she realize she could've told me she wanted a date with Mr. Dumpster Kink and I would've still said yes? There was no need to lie about her mother needing medicine.

People suck. Well, people have always sucked, but they suck times ten thousand right now.

Breathe, girl. You want the money. Who cares if someone you barely know lied to you?

Because it squashes the hope that there are still decent people out there with morals.

Teri doesn't bother explaining, and I don't stick around waiting to hear an apology. There's only two months left before I bust out of this city. And thanks to Teri, I'll be a few bills closer to my end goal.

Someone cue queen Riri because this girl is about to work, work, work, work, work, work.

CHAPTER FOUR

Chloe

After arriving yesterday in Lake Como and knocking out from an intense case of jet lag in the run-down bed-and-breakfast near the center of town, I finally walk the main road of the village.

Lake Como is a beautiful lakeside town surrounded by mountain ranges. The village truly is something stolen straight out of history, with old stucco buildings and cobblestone roads. My charming temporary home has a population the size of La Guardia airport on a Tuesday. Seriously, Google told me less than two thousand people live here. Not to mention George Clooney has a house here.

Yes. I'm talking about *that* George Clooney.

Did I take a gamble by never messaging Matteo before to let him know I was his long-lost daughter who wanted to meet him after all these years? Probably. But I couldn't risk him shutting himself off to me and claiming I was some scammer. So instead, I took a risk and decided to introduce myself the old-fashioned way—in person while shitting bricks. But first, I need to find out where he lives.

Small shops line the streets, with people waving at each other and children running around. It comforts me to see the locals caring about one another. It's like a fairy tale, with people stopping to have a conversation. Their kindness makes me hopeful that someone knows who Matteo is and where I can find him. Unfortunately, Brooke's stalking abilities only go so far. Matteo's address wasn't public information, much to our frustration.

Like a bad salesman, I visit different shops trying to find out where he lives. I attempt the same awful Italian conversation in four different shops before I hit the gold mine.

"*Sto circando signore Accardi.*" I gesture toward the latest prop in my hands and ask about Matteo. Brooke suggested impersonating a food delivery person.

"*Signore Accardi e morto.*" The store owner frowns.

Accardi is dead? I laugh to myself. That's not right. The man updated his profile picture on Facebook yesterday. I don't know what Accardi she is referencing, but I guess it's a popular last name here. "*Morto?* No. *Sto circando signore* Matteo *Accardi.*" I emphasize his first name for good measure.

Her lips form an *O.* She apologizes in Italian and scribbles Matteo's address on a piece of paper.

Italian people. So kind. So trusting. The true unsung heroes of *Expedition Find My Father*.

I exit the store and dump the empty paper bag in a nearby trash bin. The entire walk back to my bed-and-breakfast is spent with me grinning like a madman at the townspeople.

It's time to meet the man I've spent my entire life wishing for.

The screech of the car brakes pulls my attention away from my thoughts.

"Here we are." The driver speaks in a heavy Italian accent.

My eyes slide from my lap to the car's window. A quaint house sits at the top of a winding path, with high walls and a front gate covered in ivy. The yellow stucco walls stand out against the backdrop of the beautiful lake. It's a house I wish I had grown up in.

I release a shaky breath and sift through the front pocket of my backpack to grab my money.

The driver accepts it with a grin. "*Grazie.*"

I exit the car. A quick scan of the street reveals only two houses. One belongs to Matteo and the other looks like it's something straight out of the latest horror film. The dark mansion sits at the edge of the lake, surrounded by tall trees. Dark brick spires shoot into the sky, reminding me of a villain's evil castle. A rotted wooden fence reveals unkempt bushes and an overgrown yard.

I turn away from the abandoned house back toward Matteo's. "You can do this." With legs resembling Jell-O, I walk toward the huge iron gate at the base of Matteo's property.

Loud music plays from somewhere on his property. I stick my head through one of the gaps in the gate and check his driveway, finding multiple cars parked. *Shit.* Stupid me for thinking my father would be by himself.

I text Brooke to let her know I arrived at his house but he's not alone. This moment makes me grateful that she insisted on paying the ridiculous service fee for two weeks while I got situated in Italy. I need her advice on what to do.

A car revving down the road pulls my attention away.

Do they know Matteo? Are they going to ask me what I'm doing outside, lurking by the gate? Or worse, what if they drag me inside and out me as some kind of stalker in front of Matteo? All the options would blow my chance at making a good first impression.

Logic escapes me as I panic about Matteo's newest visitor catching me creeping outside of the property.

Maybe I wasn't ready for this family reunion after all. My eyes flit toward the gap in the fence of the house next door. I run toward it as headlights bask the road in a glow. Branches from the bushes scrape my face and arms, but I push through the pain. Curiosity pushes me to go deeper into the property.

A howl in the distance makes me shiver. *Are there wolves in Italy?* "Shit. If I die tonight, I'm haunting Brooke for the rest of my life. This idea is going to hell."

Using my phone's flashlight, I walk through grass rivaling Africa's Serengeti plains. I follow the stone wall dividing my father's property from this one. My sneakers catch multiple times on thick roots, and I curse into the night.

After five minutes of avoiding fallen branches and scary-looking thorns, I make it to the part of the wall where the music sounds the loudest. Laughing and people talking forces my heart rate into overdrive. An urge to check out the other side feeds my bravery. I search the wall for any purchase to climb, but the stones are slick to the touch.

"Not even the wall could be easy?" I eye the large tree next to the fence. It looks decent enough to climb. "Just like old times, Chloe."

My phone chiming in my hand startles me. "Shit!"

I listen for any changes in the music or conversation just in case they heard me. Nothing seems amiss, with laughter bouncing off the cement wall.

I swipe the glass to answer the call. "Brooke. You won't believe what I'm up to right now." After placing Brooke on speaker, I stuff my phone under my bra strap so I can hear her better while I climb.

"I'm almost afraid to ask."

"Well. I'm currently scaling a tree like when we snuck back into our room past curfew." I speak low as I grab onto a close branch and prop my foot on the trunk. My arms wobble, but I push through with gritted teeth.

"You always sucked at climbing trees so this can't be good." She snorts.

"Don't remind me."

A twig snaps nearby. My arms tremble as I halt my climbing.

"But remember the time you fell on that pile of dog poop?" Brooke breaks the silence.

Ignoring the noise, I grab onto the next branch. I pull myself up a couple of feet higher off the ground. "It's not something I can exactly forget."

"Care to explain why you're climbing a tree?"

"Do you want the legal or the illegal story?"

"By all means, share the illegal one." A new growly voice breaks up the conversation.

I let out a shriek. My fingers slip, and I fall onto my back. An audible *oof* escapes my lungs as something sharp in my backpack pokes my spine. "Ouch."

"Chloe! What happened? Oh, God, please don't be dead somewhere in Italy. I'll never be able to afford the plane ticket to find you," Brooke's voice calls out from far away.

"Brooke, I'm alive!" I search my bra for my phone but come up empty.

"For now."

A chill spreads across my skin at the stranger's voice. His words steal my attention away from finding my phone.

He lingers near the base of a tree, cast in a dark shadow. "Care to tell me what you're doing trespassing on my property?"

I squint, trying to make out his face. The scary idea I imagine isn't doing wonders for my heart rate. Goosebumps explode across my skin as he lurks in the shadows, never stepping into the moonlight.

Like an idiot, I remain lying on the ground, petrified and unmoving. "I…umm…well…you see…"

"If this is how long it takes you to say a few words, we'll be here all night." The words come out short and agitated, with a hint of an accent.

Well, shit. This guy is an absolute asshole.

"*Who* sent you?" he snaps.

Who sent me? What does this guy think I am? A hitman?

Something rustles as his silhouette moves into my direct eyesight. A gust of wind carries his scent. It's crisp and mouthwatering, and I attempt to get another sniff.

"I'm calling the police. They can deal with you like the others." He lifts his phone to his ear. The light from the screen casts his sharp eyes in an ominous glow.

I jolt from my stupor, rushing to stand on shaky legs. The last thing I need is a run-in with the cops. A memory of the last time I saw them causes me to shudder. I hold up my hands to show him they're empty of any weapons. "Don't! Please! I come in peace." *I come in peace? Who the hell do I think I am? E motherfucking T?*

He steps into my personal bubble. The shift in the clouds

has the moon illuminating his face. Shadows dance along his sharp cheekbones, emphasizing his rough edges and plump lips. His strong jaw covered in stubble ticks, and his dark eyes narrow at my face. They have a wild look to them, scanning me in the same way. Thick, dark hair brushes the tops of his shoulders, shifting from the gust of wind.

Damn, the stranger has a rugged look I need to stop and appreciate for a second. I itch to reach out and touch his short beard, but I refrain.

"Are you done gawking?" He scowls.

His snappiness shocks me, pulling me out of my inappropriate thoughts. *Great. Lusting after an unhinged man who wants to call the police on you. We have stooped to new levels of low, Chloe.*

"No. Yes. Kind of?" I squeak out.

His jaw clenches. "Give me one good reason why I shouldn't press the button right now and have them dispose of you."

Holy shit. Dispose of me? The unfairly beautiful man holds the phone to his ear as he steps closer. Everything about him screams intimidation, from his height to the snarl in his voice.

My brain kicks into fight-or-flight mode. Flight is what I'm comfortable with. Flight is all I've known. Flight is what's going to save me from being sent back to Brooke in tiny, cut-up pieces.

"Because..." I dart to the left, but he catches me in his strong arms. *Very* strong based on the way they tense as I try to escape him. And oh do I try. I thrash. I kick. I knock my head back, only to be met with air as he evades the hit. I even pinch his arms with everything my small fingers can muster, hoping he lets go. He doesn't even flinch. It's as if he's made of stone to match his personality.

Chloe. Think. You're one move away from ending up on the evening news.

He turns me into his chest and locks my arms behind my back. "Oh no, you don't. I'm sick of people like you trying to get a story."

"A story?! What are you even talking about?!" My scream turns into a rasp as his arms tighten around me.

Is it stupid to hope that Matteo hears a woman yelling bloody murder and saves me from the clutches of a maniac? This man is absolutely paranoid. It's the only explanation for his erratic behavior and his insistence on me being someone I'm most definitely not. I don't know what kind of ghostbusters come creeping onto his property, but I'm not one of them.

His body stiffens as I attempt to wiggle out of his grasp. Something that shouldn't be hard pokes into my stomach, and I go full-blown survival mode.

Hell. Fucking. No. I kick the stranger in the leg, hoping to incapacitate him. Another scream erupts from my mouth as my toes smashes against something that felt like the human equivalent of a cement wall. "What the hell! You've got to be kidding me. What are you even made of? A fucking rock?!" My big toe throbs to the crazy beat of my heart.

He grunts, but his grip remains tight. "More like who the fuck are *you* and what drugs are you on?"

"Me on drugs? You're the one who is on the worst trip of your life, asshole." Instead of allowing any tears to fall because of the pain in my foot, I let instinct take over. I knee the fucker in the balls with all the strength my body can manage.

He lets go with a string of curse words as he keels over.

No use checking out the damage. I run toward the direction of the main road, not bothering to look back at the psychopath who tried to call the cops on me and got a boner from the entire situation. I've watched a decent amount of horror movies. The girls who look back always get murdered first.

I don't stop running until I'm at the entrance of my hotel. Sweat clings to my clothes as I take in large gulps of air. Leaning against the wall, I sift through my backpack for my phone. Brooke is probably freaking out after everything.

My search comes up empty. Like a cold shower, realization dawns on me.

Shit. Motherfucking shit. I forgot my phone by the tree after I fell.

I thought my experience with psychopaths ended once I left America. New country, same craziness. Except instead of running away from legal issues, I'm heading straight toward them.

But hey, breaking and entering is only considered a crime if I get caught.

CHAPTER FIVE

SANTIAGO

I f it weren't for the ringing cell phone on my nightstand, I would've considered last night the weirdest dream I've had in a long time. A dream starring a dark-haired trespasser who kneed me hard enough in the balls to leave a lasting impression a day later.

I've had a handful of people break in since I moved here a few years ago. Reporters and heartless paparazzi can't resist sneaking in to get a peek at my reclusive life. They're like sharks in bloody water, desperate for a taste.

The trespasser's phone rings again for the third time in half an hour. Someone must be desperate to get in contact with her. At first I thought it was a worried boyfriend, but Brooke is the only person texting and calling the mysterious woman. When I answered her call, Brooke screamed into the phone about how torture is still legal in 141 countries and I better pray she doesn't find me in one of them. At least after that phone call, she stopped calling me.

Hopefully, the woman returns for her phone and reveals

her identity. I need her arrested and taken care of. Holding people like her accountable sends a proper message to everyone else who wants to attempt the same shit.

The ringing stops before starting up again. A random Italian number flashes across the screen, piquing my curiosity.

I answer. "Hello."

A raspy voice releases a stream of curses away from the phone before returning. "*You.*"

Ah, we meet again. "It's me."

"I see you stole my phone."

"You're confusing the word *stealing* with *saving.*"

A mumbled *fuck you* on her end makes me smile like an idiot.

"You're welcome," I probe.

"While I'm being so uncharacteristically grateful, thank you for scaring me with your erection yesterday. As charming as it felt against my stomach, it's a hard pass for me."

"Blame the arousal on adrenaline from finding a criminal on my property."

She scoffs. "Right. Let's get two things straight. First, I'm not a criminal. Being detained isn't the same as being arrested. And two, if that's what you feel like from adrenaline, I'm afraid of you in the bedroom. That was..."

The ridiculousness of her comment has me laughing to the point of my lungs burning. "Are you seriously complimenting me right now?"

"Does it win me the points I desperately need to get my phone back? Guys love it when you hype up their dick size."

My good mood is washed away with the reality of her goading me to get what she wants. *Typical.* "No. Finders, keepers."

"You've got to be joking."

"Not about this."

"Why do you need a phone with a sparkly case?"

I place her on speaker and check out the clear case with glitter water and sequins inside. "It complements my eyes."

Her scoff sounds more like a laugh. "You're being impossible."

"Better than being someone who's already been arrested once. Ready to add a second stint to your record?" The unfiltered words leave my mouth in a rush.

"*Cool.* I was actually *detained*, not arrested. And to be honest, I'd rather be someone who got wrongly accused of a crime than an asshole who needs to steal shit to feel like a man. I hope you like my shitty five-year-old iPhone. Bye." She ends the call.

Fuck. With my phone, I call the number back. Someone picks up the phone, asking what I would like to order from a random restaurant in town.

Damn. She's smart, not leaving a trail for me to follow. I smile, captivated by her ingenuity. Somehow, I came across someone who doesn't bother fitting the status quo of my life lately.

Instead of my usual moping, I grab my laptop and research how to hack someone's cellphone. I hope to find out some information about my mysterious trespasser. Using someone's detailed directions from a Reddit board, I attempt to unlock the phone. All I end up doing is forcing her phone to shut down after it takes a photo of me with the Face ID.

My phone buzzes from an incoming call, interrupting my next Reddit hack. I grab it and answer. "Hey."

"So...don't be mad," my little sister coos into the phone like I'm a child.

I grunt in disapproval. "What did you do?"

"Well remember how I told you I wanted to visit you soon?"

"No, you must've forgotten that tiny fun fact in all three times we have talked over the past two weeks."

"Well, I do call, but you don't answer."

I wince at the hurt in her voice. It's not like I try to ignore her calls, but some days I can't force myself to move, let alone speak. My reasoning doesn't ease the guilt growing in my gut.

She lets out a nervous laugh. "Well, I miss you and want to visit. It's been a month since I saw you last."

"That's because you're traveling with Noah while he races." *Try harder to be nice, you irritable idiot.*

She sighs. "You know he plans on retiring in a season or two."

"Great. He deserves it after all his success." I try with everything in me to not sound bitter, but the words come out like that anyway. It's not Noah's fault. He worked his ass off, competing and winning against the youngest talent year after year. Unlike me.

"You're not being fair to yourself."

"Life isn't fair. Just because we've protected you from that lesson doesn't mean the rest of us survive unscathed." *Shit.* My mouth keeps getting me in trouble today. Maya doesn't deserve my bitterness, no matter how much life pains me at times. "Maya, I'm sorry. I didn't mean it like that. You know I would take on anything to make sure you were okay."

She stays quiet for a few seconds before she sniffs.

Fuck. Not the sniffles. My chest tightens at upsetting the one person who means the most to me. "I'm sorry. You didn't deserve that."

"It's okay. There are some lessons you can't protect me from, no matter how much you want to." Her voice cracks.

Something rumbles on the other side of the phone, and Maya protests before her voice fades away.

"If it isn't the dickhead of the decade. How are you doing? Not that I should care after you upset Maya," Noah snaps.

My life has become so fucked up that I've come to appreciate his dickishness toward me. It reminds me of how I'm very much still a grown-ass man. Anything is better than my parents who treat me like I'm made out of porcelain or Maya who hides stories about Noah and Marko because she doesn't want to upset me.

"I would say good, but since I'm talking to you when you're angry, I'll go with regretful."

He huffs. "Good idea. If you're going to be a grumpy asshole, save it for everyone *but* your sister right now. Think you can manage such a small request?"

I grind my teeth. "Most definitely."

"Good. I'll save you the shock from our surprise since I know how much you *love* them. We will be at your house in an hour. Don't make this an issue. We need your help, so strap on your fakest smile and drop the grumpy asshole routine for your sister." Noah hangs up, leaving me slack-jawed and staring at my phone.

Shit.

My nephew, Marko, squeals as I throw him in the air. His dark hair flies around his face with the rush of air.

"Again! Again!" His blue eyes light up.

I carry him like an airplane, noises and all. Spending time with Marko is like chugging a glass of liquid sunshine. The little four-year-old takes away the darkness, and I love him more because of it.

"Look at that. The beast has a soft heart after all." Noah smirks at me.

I switch Marko to one hand to flip Noah off.

Maya's eyes widen. "No, Santiago! He copies everything."

Marko looks at me with a wide smile, showing his tiny teeth. He attempts to flip me off with his index finger.

I chalk it up to coincidence. "You should protect him from your husband, then."

"It took some work but I've kiddie-proofed Noah's mouth." Maya smiles.

"It's forking hard, but I try my best for you." Noah grins before placing a soft kiss on Maya's head.

I sit down on the couch and place Marko on my knee. My sweatpants hide my leg, but that doesn't stop him from lifting the hem and checking out the matte metal.

My body tenses. I try my best to cover up my leg when I'm around others. The visual reminder sours the mood, so unless I need to, I hide that nasty fucker. It's taken years to perfect my walk and conceal any kind of limp.

I'm not ashamed of my leg.

I'm ashamed of my *life*.

"*Tío* Santi is Iron Man." He taps the leg, looking up at me with the cutest smile ever.

The constricting feeling in my chest lessens at his innocence. *See, liquid sunshine.*

Marko is the only one I'd ever let call me Iron Man. With my nephew, it's as if I'm his hero, rather than the washed-up has-been the media makes me out to be. It feels good to be the hero in someone else's story, even if it's only for a few hours. And because of that, the little kid has me tied around his pinky finger.

Maya plucks Marko's hand away from my leg and lowers the fabric of my sweatpants. "Marko, what did I say about touching other people without asking?"

He tucks his chin into his chest. "No touching."

Maya shoots me a wobbly smile. "I'm sorry. I told him not to call you Iron Man anymore, but he must have forgo—"

"Let him do what he wants. And stop handling me with kid gloves, Maya. While I love that you care, I think raising one kid is enough for you, don't you think? No need to baby me too," I snap.

Maya stiffens.

Noah rises from the seat parallel to mine. "Outside. Now."

The lethality in his tone has my spine straightening. He doesn't bother looking back to check if I follow him.

Regret hits me instantly, and I face my sister. "I'm sorry about what I said. I need to control myself better." I pull Marko off my lap and place his feet on the floor.

Maya nods, looking away from me. She swipes at her face with the sleeve of her sweater.

"Maya, don't cry. I'm sorry." I tug her into a hug.

She pushes me off after a few seconds, still not looking me in the eyes. "It's fine. I'm just hormonal. Go talk to Noah."

I deserve her brushing me off. My sister is the last one I want to make cry, but I can't avoid the surge of anger exploding out of me every time I feel weak and babied. It's not easy going from being the provider to someone everyone coddles. It makes me feel less than. And most importantly, it reminds me of everything I lost.

I walk outside my house, finding Noah standing by the lake's shore.

"Hurry the fuck up! My patience is thinning," Noah calls out and turns his back toward me.

Noah's anger makes me instantly regret losing my cool with Maya. No one messes with his wife. Not even me.

"I'm coming, asshole." I walk toward him with ease. After my excruciating journey through physical therapy, I can walk like a normal person. So normal, if I wasn't wearing pants, people wouldn't know I was missing a key component. It's one of the reasons I choose to wear sweats in the scorching heat. I prefer pretending. It keeps the darkness away enough for me to function around my family.

I stop by his side but remain quiet. His anger hits me like a wave as he focuses on the lake in front of us.

"You act like that around Maya again and I'll rip off one of your balls to match your leg." He doesn't bother looking my way.

I wince. "I'm sorry. I didn't mean to snap like that and make her cry."

His shoulders drop. It's subtle, but the change in his demeanor sets me on alert. Noah isn't one to look defeated.

"What's wrong?"

He stays silent.

"Why did you both decide to pop in unannounced? That's not like you two." The words tumble out of my mouth.

"We're having a hard time."

"Trouble in paradise?" I elbow him in the ribs, trying to lighten the mood. These two are crazy about each other. Noah dotes on Maya every chance he has, and she makes him happy in return. I can't imagine them having marital issues.

"No. Nothing like that." Noah sighs. He looks over at me. His eyes cloud in a way I've never seen before on him.

"What's going on, man? You're worrying me." I stay rooted to the ground, staring wide-eyed as he covers up a sniffle with a grunt.

"Maya and I…" He curses under his breath. "Maya and I need you to take care of Marko for a couple of weeks while I'm on summer break from the Championship."

Acid rolls in my stomach. "Why? You always spend summer break prepping for the back half of the season."

"Something more important came up. So, Maya and I need some time to connect and take a break from everything. Go off the grid."

"And you want *me* to take care of Marko? Why not my parents?"

"They were our first option, but they're leaving for a two-week Caribbean cruise today and Maya doesn't want to stop them."

Ouch. I don't know what's worse—not knowing my parents were going on a vacation or being a second-best choice. "Okay…"

"Maya was pregnant." His voice breaks.

He's got to be fucking kidding me. No…

Noah can't tear his gaze away from the lake. "The baby…"

I place my hand on Noah's shoulder and give him a reassuring squeeze. "You don't have to say anything else."

He brushes away a stray tear with the back of his hand.

Fuck. My poor sister. She hasn't stopped talking about wanting another baby since last year. To know she is hurting from losing a child…it makes me ache in ways I didn't know possible.

She was right after all. There are things I can't save her from, and this is one of them. It must kill Noah to feel this kind of helplessness, too.

He coughs. "We need to take a little vacation. *She* needs one. I doubt I can convince Maya to stay away from Marko for the full two weeks as it is, but I want to try. She just needs some time to…"

"I got it. No need to explain." I raise my chin.

Noah looks at me with red eyes. "I kind of do. If you keep acting like an asshole, she's going to end up canceling the idea. She thinks you can't handle Marko on your own."

"I can do it." The fact that my sister thinks I can't take care of my nephew for two goddamn weeks makes me more sad than angry. I'd never do anything to put him in jeopardy.

Noah shrugs. "I mean, feel free to take offense, but you don't exactly scream capable."

I narrow my eyes, the anger from earlier returning with vengeance.

Noah rolls his eyes. "Not because of that, idiot. Because of how you don't take care of yourself." He points with his index to my stubble and grown-out hair.

"You're telling me that Maya needs a vacation, but the

only way she will go on one is if I convince her I can take care of Marko?"

"Yes. So can you turn down the attitude for a day? We plan on sleeping over tonight, that way she can test you out and see if you're up for it. That means you need to buck up and put on your best babysitter act. I don't care what you have to do, but your sister needs this trip. She wants to think of every reason she shouldn't go, so prove her otherwise."

"No problem. I'll be so convincing that even *you* will second-guess my capability." I smile.

"God help us all."

CHAPTER SIX

Chloe

slip through the same warped wooden plank as last night. Dark clouds hide the moon, which makes my journey through the overgrown yard difficult with only a small flashlight. My mood takes a dive when I trip over a group of exposed roots. I land on my knees, scraping them in the process. Wet dirt clings to my legs as I stand, and I'm pretty sure my shirt ripped down the back based on the breeze tickling my skin.

"Has this man ever heard of a lawnmower?" I mumble under my breath as I brush a clump of dirt off my shin.

I somehow make it through the maze of trees and bushes without any more accidents. My neck cranes as I check out the ominous mansion this man calls home. It's about as welcoming as a nap in a coffin.

"I've officially made an enemy out of Count Dracula. Good to know." I scan the front entryway, not finding any cars in the driveway. Like a desperate fool, I search nooks and crannies for a spare key but come up empty.

I follow the perimeter of the house and peek through a few windows. The rooms are dark enough for me to catch my reflection in the glass. My confidence grows as I praise God for helping me out and making sure the house is empty.

I come up to the back porch. Testing my luck, I try the knob only to find it locked. The standard deadbolt is easy to break into based on the information I gathered earlier from YouTube's crash course on picking locks. I'm not entirely proud of how many times I watched it until I mastered the movements.

I pull out a special screwdriver I scored from a local shop from my backpack. Holding my mini flashlight in my mouth, I replicate the motions I practiced on my own bathroom door this afternoon. After a few failed tries because of my nerves, the door opens with a click.

Darkness cloaks the house in shadows and random shapes. My tiny flashlight does a poor job of guiding my way through the kitchen. Nothing stands out on the counters, so I continue moving forward.

"Okay, think. If I was an unhinged man, where would I hide a phone?" I stumble out of the room.

I make my way through a wide hallway before I'm spit out into a large room. Everything is going fine and dandy until I trip on something I didn't see with the flashlight. I let out a scream as I fall forward, landing on my hands and scuffed-up knees. My eyes water as something embeds itself into my hands.

My fingers brush across lots of small rectangular shapes with ridges. I pull one up to my eyes and analyze the foreign object. "A fucking Lego? This place really is owned by the

Devil." I crawl through the Lego warzone, brushing the pieces aside.

I make it to a grand staircase lit by the glow from a dangling iron chandelier. I'm halfway up the stairs when the front door opens with a groan. All hell breaks loose in the lobby of the house, and my ears ache from a female screaming.

My heart gets stuck in my throat. "Seriously. Why can't I catch a break this week?" I whisper under my breath. All that effort for nothing. In a rush, I tuck the flashlight into my back pocket and turn on my heel, hitting the guests with my best smile. With my knees threatening to buckle, I clutch onto the railing for support.

A few overhead lights turn on, revealing a brunette in a billowing skirt and a T-shirt. "Oh my God. Santiago, who is that?" She screams again for good measure.

I'm tempted to cover my ears but stop myself.

"Hmm. I didn't expect you to show up unannounced." The same rough voice from earlier sends a shiver up my spine. How exactly did he want me to show up?

"The welcoming committee and marching band were busy tonight, so I couldn't announce my arrival." I smile at him, hoping my eyes scream *fuck you*.

I take a moment to get a good look at the grumpiest man I've ever met. Of course, *Santiago* has to have a sexy name to match his looks. Lighting from the chandelier illuminates his warm golden skin, making his brown eyes shine. The asshole happens to be the most attractive man I've had a chance to look at in my short life.

I feel cheated by the moonlight last night because Santiago looks sexier in the light. He makes rugged seem attractive in the best kind of way with a thick, short beard and long hair grazing his shoulders in a wavy mess. His dark shirt highlights bulging muscles, and his gray sweatpants show off strong thigh muscles.

Damn. Seriously, this man should not be running around in public. He's a danger to society and women everywhere for multiple reasons. The first starting with the instant attraction I have in his presence.

The woman grips onto Santiago's arm. "Is this your girlfriend? You've been holding out on us! No wonder you haven't answered my phone calls." She speaks with such delight at the idea.

Oh God. No. My face must say everything words can't. Santiago smirks like he's in on a joke I've yet to catch onto.

I speak at the same time as him. "This isn't what it looks like—"

"My *girlfriend* wasn't supposed to be here."

Girlfriend? Excuse me?

The asshole has the nerve to smile at me. At least he has plump lips to distract me from the cunning lies he spews.

Maya frowns at me. "Are you okay? Your knees are covered in dirt."

My cheeks flush as I brush random clumps of dirt off me. "Oh, yeah. I was gardening."

Her brow raises. "At night?"

"My fair skin tends to burn easily so I like to work at night." Well, that's not a *total* lie.

Another guy appears, cradling a small child to his chest. *Okay, seriously, what is in the Italian water and where can I get some?* His dark hair and penetrating blue gaze has me wanting to pinch my arm to make sure I'm not dreaming.

Santiago's eyes narrow at me. "She was supposed to come over tomorrow to help me babysit. That is, *if* you agree to letting Marko stay of course." He looks at the woman before his eyes meet mine. "She must've mixed up the days."

Well, I can't let him win this round. I'd rather outplay him at his own game than let him have the upper hand.

I walk down the stairs with as much Julie Andrews' *The Princess Diaries*' energy as I can gather under tense circumstances. "I've heard so much about Marko. I can't wait to help babysit. I actually spent years working in a daycare before coming to Italy."

"Oh, that's great! I'm Maya, Santiago's sister." An overly excited Maya offers her hand. Her assessing brown eyes make me nervous.

"Chloe." I shake it with a fake smile.

"Chloe—" The way Santiago says my name has my toes curling in my sneakers. Screw this mission to hell and back. Would he think I'm weird if I ask him if I can record him saying my name a couple of times? For mindfulness meditation activities, obviously.

Santiago tilts his head in the direction of the other male. "This is Noah, my sister's husband." He says it in a way that makes me feel like I should recognize his brother-in-law.

I blink at Noah, trying to place him. *Nope. Drawing a blank.* "Santiago talks about you all the time." *Well, that sounded like the right thing to say.*

Noah smiles wide, looking way too handsome for comfort. "Oh, does he now? I'm flattered."

"Yeah. It's not my fault your ugly face is always on TV,"

Santiago offers, saving me.

I have no clue why Noah's face is on TV, but based on how he looks, Hollywood would suit him well. "I've heard a ton about you." I move toward the front door. "Well, it's pretty late, and I have an early morning. It was great to meet you both."

"Oh no." Maya's bottom lip wobbles.

"Don't go yet." Santiago, in his typical *don't mind me, I'm secretly a psycho* way, grabs me and tugs me into his body. His strong arms wrap around my body, basking me in his enticing scent and warmth. I'm tempted to rub my face into his shirt like a creep.

Bad Chloe. This man is anything but stable. Not to mention he stole your phone.

"Yes, please stay for a few more minutes." Maya clasps her hands together. "So... Santiago didn't mention you today."

"You know him. He prefers to have a life full of secrets in this big castle of his."

Everyone laughs. *Interesting. The plot thickens.*

"I see why he hid you from us." Noah's blue eyes lighten.

Santiago's hand slides up my side, singeing my skin. "Chloe had me pegged from the first night she met me."

"Yeah, it seems like only yesterday."

The way Santiago laughs, loose and rough, has Maya and Noah looking at us with wide eyes. Something about their reaction tells me Santiago doesn't laugh that way often.

Can I make him do it again? I've always dreamed of having a superpower.

Marko stirs in Noah's arms.

Maya brushes his head with a tenderness I'm

unaccustomed to seeing. "We'd love to have breakfast with you before we leave tomorrow. I can't believe Santiago has kept you a secret for this long. I need to know *everything* about you. He hasn't had a girlfriend since he was a teenager."

I'm eating up all these clues about Santiago like discounted candy after Halloween.

"Oh. Chloe can't have breakfast with us since she has to visit her friend." Santiago speaks for me.

Right. My friend. AKA the father I traveled thousands of miles for but haven't gotten the courage to meet yet.

Maya's smile drops.

Noah's eyes move from his wife's face to mine. "I insist you join us. I'm sure your friend wouldn't mind rescheduling."

"Well…" I bite my bottom lip.

"We don't visit often," Noah says.

"More like ever," Maya mumbles under her breath.

Shoot. "Umm…"

Santiago's arms tighten around me in a way that says *don't confess our lie or else I'll kill you.* At least, that's what I assume from the way his body tenses behind me. I go along with it because I honestly wouldn't put it past him to have a graveyard somewhere on this property.

"Sure. I can just meet up with my friend later," I offer.

Maya's face brightens again. She forces Santiago to let me go and wraps her arms around me in a hug. "I'm beyond excited to spend some time with you! I didn't realize Santiago was creating a life over here."

I freeze, unused to this kind of affection from someone I barely know. Actually, I'm unaccustomed to this affection from people I *do* know. She releases me after one last squeeze.

She and Noah say good night and retreat upstairs with Marko.

I wait for them to disappear before I turn and stare Santiago down. "Girlfriend?!" I whisper-shout.

He shrugs. "It was the best thing I could come up with under pressure. It sounded better than calling you my little criminal, or was I wrong?"

I want to ignore the possessiveness of his nickname for me. It shouldn't get me all tingly in my chest, but here I am. Now is not the time to realize I've got a thing for killers and creeps. I want to blame binging too many episodes of *Dexter* at a young impressionable age, but there's no use denying the pull I have toward Santiago.

I clear my throat, recovering. "Of course that's better. But now I need to have breakfast with your family and pretend I know who the hell you are."

He rolls his eyes. "You can stop pretending. The innocent act was cute in front of them, but you can give it up now."

"I'm sorry, what? An innocent act? You're the one who's acting, forcing me into pretending I recognize some Hollywood actor and his wife. It's not like I'm exactly the type to flip through *People Magazine*, seeing as I have to work all the time."

Santiago's eyebrows draw together. "Hollywood actor?"

"Yes. *Noah*. The guy we 'watch on TV together.'" I offer with air quotes. "I've never seen that man on any show before. So, is he a D-list actor or something?"

Santiago's frown turns into a smug smile. "Or something like that."

The way his eyes glow with something unknown has me bristling. "You're up to something."

"That's funny coming from the woman who broke into my house."

I can't stop the laugh that bubbles out of me. It's hard to remain serious based on the ridiculousness of our situation. Seriously. What the hell has my life become? Here I am arguing with a man I met less than a day ago about a fake relationship.

Santiago stares at me with such intensity, my stomach muscles clench. "Well, you better get some rest before breakfast tomorrow." He opens the front door for me.

My jaw drops. "Wait. What about my phone?"

"You'll get it tomorrow after breakfast. Consider it collateral."

"You really are a psycho." I huff under my breath.

"Funny, I'd say the same about someone who would trespass not once, but twice on the same person's property. Speaking of—which window did you break to get inside? I'm assuming you won't cover the bill based on the state of your clothing." He runs a finger down the ripped back of my shirt. His touch sets off a bodily reaction I have no time to comprehend. I can only describe it as fireworks shooting off my skin, forcing every cell inside of me into overdrive.

I suck in a breath and turn on my heel, facing him in all his handsome glory. "I'm more talented than that."

"I apologize for underestimating your abilities after yesterday's shitty display of sneaking around."

I rub my heart like his words hurt me. "One: I wasn't sneaking around. And two: I don't like you."

"Okay. Sure." He scoffs. "I don't need you to like me. I just need you to show up and pretend for a little longer. See you in the morning." He shoots me a tight smile before shutting the door in my face with a soft thud.

The audacity of this man. I want to hate it, but I end up respecting him for acting unapologetically himself.

Santiago whatever-his-last-name-is seems like the kind of man to trap people into giving him what he wants. And like an idiot, I willingly fly straight into his web of lies.

CHAPTER SEVEN

SANTIAGO

’ve made a handful of stupid decisions over the past twenty-four hours. After my accident, I swore off impulsivity like the plague. Reckless choices ruined everything I had set up for my life, and I refused to fall into the same trap again. Yet here I am, making stupid decision after stupid decision ever since Chloe entered my life forty-eight hours ago.

I didn't anticipate Chloe breaking into my house while we took Marko for a walk by the lake. She has turned out to be a rather unexpected whirlwind in my painfully mundane life. I don't like it one bit. The simplicity of repetition means I can't fuck up my life anymore. My days usually include waking up, exercising, cooking, and working on whatever car I decide to restore next. As long as I'm not sinking into the dark place of my mind, I push myself to keep busy.

Chloe threw everything to hell once my sister laid eyes on her. Her breaking and entering forced me to make up a lie that has Maya practically foaming at the mouth in excitement. So much so, Maya woke up at the same time as me to question me about *Chloe*. I entertain her curiosity because she has had enough shit happen to her lately. If this conversation makes her happy, I'll give it to her.

"Chloe seems nice." She bats her lashes.

Chloe seems like a criminal who needs to be locked up, but I refrain from fact-dropping. "That she is."

"What's she like?"

"Sneaky and cunning."

Maya laughs. "Reminds me of you, seeing as you kept her a secret for how long?"

"A year?" It seems like a solid amount of time.

"A year?!" Maya screeches to the ceiling. "How could you keep this from us for that long?"

I lift a brow and wave my hands at her reaction.

She laughs. "Okay, true. But still. Keeping secrets from me is so not cool."

I survive another ten minutes of Maya's questions. So far, I've made up Chloe's hobby for restoring cars with me, our bond over horror movies, and her preference for chocolate over candy. I've basically created a female version of myself that my sister gushes over. She's so enthralled, she doesn't realize the unlikely similarities.

"Why haven't you ever mentioned her before?"

"Because of the way you're acting now." *Good save, Santi.*

"*Mami* is going to freak out when she hears about this."

"Don't tell her yet." I don't want my mom to grow attached to my fake girlfriend. The same girlfriend who has absolutely no clue who the hell I am, let alone about my family and Formula 1. That information in itself adds to my interest in her. And interest is bad. Interest leads to infatuation, and I can't bother entertaining either.

"I'll give you two weeks to tell her yourself. She's on a cruise anyway so she won't be able to rush over and bombard Chloe like I'd want her to. But if you don't tell her, I will because there's no chance I'm letting you get out of them meeting each other."

I swallow back the lump in my throat. "Deal. Does that mean you are leaving Marko with me after all?"

"Yup. I think he'll be in good care with you and *Chloe*." She offers in a singsong voice.

I suppress the urge to groan. "You made that conclusion about Chloe from the one conversation with her?"

"She worked at a daycare. That's a glowing recommendation letter if I've ever heard one."

"You're too trustworthy. Thank God Noah keeps an eye out for you and Marko."

Maya opens her mouth to speak, but the doorbell chiming pulls us from the kitchen. My sister opens the door like she owns the place. She pulls Chloe in for a crushing hug and welcomes her to the house.

I now understand why Noah invited Chloe to breakfast because Maya's happiness makes this crazy plan worth it. I'd do anything to banish the sad look in her eyes whenever I catch her daydreaming.

Chloe gazes at the two of us with denim blue eyes. I take a moment to appreciate how she looks in daylight for the first time. Her white dress makes her appear rather innocent, but her ratty sneakers say a different kind of story. One that shows she probably runs around and gets in trouble on a daily basis.

She's on the taller side, and I like the way she reaches my chin. Her loose, black locks sway as she moves, resembling the night sky, with hints of navy when they shift in the light.

God. She's gorgeous. She probably gets away with a ton of illegal shit because her beauty has the power to distract a man.

I take back what I said about this crazy plan being worth it. I'm instantly tempted to shoo her out the front door based on the way my body responds to her nearness. Blood rushes to my cock as she licks her bow-shaped lips.

Is it too late to say we broke up?

She walks up to me and offers a bouquet of flowers tied together by a tattered ribbon. The array of flowers ranges from orange to purple, mixed together with random tufts of white and green. Her smile brings my attention toward a small white scar crossing diagonally from her cupid's bow through her top lip. "I picked these from the forest you call a front yard."

Why the hell would she pick flowers from my yard? Is she some kind of delusional princess who walks around with a team of singing animals?

Seriously, where is this girl from and what's the return policy?

"Interesting choice. Thank you." I move to grab them from her hands. Our fingers graze one another, heating my skin like flames.

She rocks back on her tattered sneakers. "I thought it could liven up the place."

Noah laughs as he walks down the stairs with Marko in his arms. "You're going to need more than a dozen flowers for that. This guy is so doom and gloom, he needs an injection of serotonin to survive the week."

"I think they're lovely." Maya fawns over Chloe.

I look down at the bouquet. The wildflowers remind me of her, beautiful in an untamed and understated kind of way. I grip them harder, forcing some stems to snap by accident. A couple of petals fall to the floor and Chloe stares at them in horror. My sister plucks the bouquet out of my hands and scowls at me.

Shit. "Are we going to keep chatting or does someone want to eat the pancakes I made?"

"Pancakes!" Marko squirms in Noah's arms.

"With chocolate chips." I grab Marko from Noah's grasp. "What do you say, little guy?"

He screams *yes* as I throw him in the air.

I sneak a peek at Chloe, finding her mouth gaping open. "Hope you like pancakes."

"You don't know if your girlfriend likes pancakes?" Maya looks at me with narrowed eyes.

Fuck. I need to try harder to fool everyone. "We usually miss breakfast because we have other priorities," I blurt out.

Chloe groans, covering her eyes with her hands. "Oh my God. You didn't just insinuate what I think you just did."

Noah's stare unsettles me. "He used to love embarrassing others. Glad to see that charming trait is back."

"Used to?" Chloe raises a brow. "I'd believe you except I've found him quite embarrassing in all the time I've known him."

She doesn't realize how in the forty-eight hours I've known her, I've acted more like my old self than in the past three years. It's disarming how much I like messing with her. I don't even know who she really is, but I enjoy the way her cheeks flush from embarrassment.

"I'm glad to know he acts like his usual self around you." Maya smiles at Chloe in a way that has my stomach turning.

I hate lying to my sister, but what is a white lie in the grand scheme of things? *Okay, more like a* few *lies.* Starting with the fact that I'm hiding how famous Noah is and my connection to him.

Chloe walks through my house, barely attempting to hide her surprise as she takes in her surroundings. Maya distracts Noah, giving Chloe the opportunity to gape.

I get it isn't what people expect. While the castle has a gothic look on the outside, I chose comfortable furnishings for my prison. Plush couches and fluffy carpets set a welcoming tone despite the asshole who lives here.

"Not what you expected?" I walk beside her, holding a squirming Marko.

She runs a finger across the back of a velvet gray couch. "It looks different in the daylight."

I chuckle. "I imagine with your line of work that you don't get the chance to appreciate it all."

Her eyes narrow at me. "I want to punch you right now."

I put Marko between us, pretending to cower. "No violence in front of the child."

Her scowl turns into a small smile as she tickles Marko, making it challenging for me to hold on to him as he wiggles around.

"Clever."

Chloe falls in line with everyone else, grabbing a plate and serving herself before sitting next to me like we do this all the time. Noah cuts Marko's food while my sister nurses her cup of coffee.

"So Chloe, I hear you like restoring cars." Noah looks up from Marko's plate.

Leave it to Maya to share everything about Chloe with Noah. Where did she find the time? My sister's eyes dart around the room, not landing on anything.

"Oh, I do. It's my absolute *favorite* hobby." Chloe looks at me with pinched brows.

I don't bother restraining my enjoyment. A loud laugh escapes me, which results in Noah staring at me for a few seconds.

"What's your dream car?" Maya props her elbows on the table.

"Umm. A 1967 Chevy Impala. If you throw in Dean Winchester too, I wouldn't be opposed." Chloe doesn't even stumble as she comes up with that response.

"I love *Supernatural* too!" Maya swoons.

"You love the guys on *Supernatural*. There's a difference." Noah smirks.

Chloe listens to Maya and Noah go back and forth, tugging at her bottom lip with her teeth in a way that isn't meant to be sexy. The move has my body aching in ways I haven't felt in a long while. So fucking long, instead of enjoying it, I'm wary of the attraction I feel toward her.

You know nothing about her, and everything you do know is a lie. And letting my guard down isn't something I'm keen on doing anytime soon.

"And you said you worked at a daycare before coming to Italy?" Noah asks.

"Yes. For about four years."

"What's your middle and last name?" Noah eyes her.

"What is this, an interview? Do you want her social

security number while you're at it?" I interfere before Noah gets out of hand.

"That would make this process easier." Noah shrugs.

Chloe rolls her eyes, ignoring me. "My full name is Chloe Arabella Carter. Born and raised in New York City."

Noah pulls out his phone and busies himself.

My sister chats with Chloe, battering her with question after question. Chloe plays her part and answers every question with grace. According to her, she's never been to a Broadway show and she had an imaginary friend until the crazy age of eight years old. Her favorite hobbies include napping because apparently, she doesn't get enough sleep.

"Why did you file a restraining order against Ralph Williams?" Noah looks up from his phone.

I clench my fists. "What the fuck, Noah!"

"Santiago! No bad words!" Maya admonishes me.

"Fuck!" Marko offers excitedly. "Fuuuuck!"

Maya shakes her head at my nephew. "No! That's a bad word."

"Sorry, Mommy." Marko shoves pieces of pancake in his mouth.

Noah frowns. "I'm not going to leave my kid with just anyone, especially if Chloe here is in danger herself. If she can't tell me who Ralph is, then we'll take Marko with us."

My skin heats as my irritation grows at Noah's dismissiveness. "So you dig into someone's life without any semblance of privacy? Are there any lines you won't cross?"

"You'd do the same if you were in my shoes," he counters.

"It's okay." Chloe gives my hand a squeeze under the table. The contact has my skin prickling in a new way I'm afraid to give more attention to. "Ralph is my mother's boyfriend… He isn't a danger to me anymore, especially since I'm this far away from home. When I was a teenager, my social worker insisted on filing an order after he was caught doing something he shouldn't have. But he never bothered me again after that. Based on how lazy he is, I think he's more of a danger to himself." Her laugh fails to make light of the situation.

What does that even mean? What sad fucks has she hung around because of her mother? I'm stuck staring at her like a surprised idiot. The exact kind of idiot I shouldn't be if this is my actual girlfriend. I school my features, ignoring the urgency to pester Chloe for answers.

She and Noah lock gazes. Neither backs down as he reads her face like the emotionless robot he tends to be around anyone who isn't family.

Chloe raises her chin and rolls her shoulders back. "If you're concerned about Marko being with anyone, it should be Santiago. He might teach him every bad word while you're away. And he also has terrible people skills, so I'd feel bad for Marko."

"Hey, that's not nice." I pinch her side, smiling when she laughs and pushes me away.

I'm tempted to touch her again. I like the way her eyes light up and her skin flushes because of me.

Everyone joins in to laugh, and the tension dissipates.

"Please tell us how you met. Santiago didn't bother sharing this morning." Maya claps her hands together.

Jesus.

Chloe taps her lips with her index finger. "One day I was in a…"

"Park," I finish for her.

"Right. A *park*. And I was climbing a tree." She stalls.

"To help that stray cat," I offer.

"Yes. That poor cat. She was missing clumps of hair and had one blind eye." Chloe's lip wobbles in an impressive way.

I'm absolutely captivated by her performance. Damn.

Maya leans toward us, grinning like a madwoman. "Tell me more!"

"Well, I fell out of the tree because your brother scared me."

I withhold my laugh by sheer willpower alone. At least that part of her story is the truth.

"No!" Maya reels back.

"And then what?" Noah smiles at Chloe, clearly pleased after his little test. *Asshole.*

"We saved the cat and took her to a vet together. Santiago cradled it like a little baby, which was beyond cute. He definitely had my attention after that." Chloe demonstrates the motion, making her perfect tits hike up an inch.

Fuck. Me. And she definitely has my attention after *that*. It's official. Chloe needs to get the hell out of here. She's a danger for my self-restraint, which says a lot because I have endless amounts of it when it comes to women.

"I'm surprised Santi left his little castle to go visit a park in the first place." Noah wipes syrup from Marko's fingers.

"Now that I know him, I'm surprised he did too." Chloe nods. Everything she spews is absolute bullshit, yet oddly accurate. "I guess he couldn't resist coming to my aid."

I shouldn't enjoy this charade as much as I do. "The shorts she wore made the rescue mission worth it."

Chloe smacks my arm. I let out a loud laugh, enjoying the way her cheeks turn pink.

Maya and Noah stare at the two of us. Noah crosses his arms and grins at me while my sister openly gapes.

I look away, not liking the weight of their stares.

The rest of breakfast goes off without an issue. Chloe and I make a show of domestic bliss, with her drying the dishes I wash.

I jump in place when Marko sneakily lifts the leg of my sweatpants while I put away the dishes. My first dirty secret I've kept from Chloe comes out as Marko begs for Iron Man to help him fly.

Chloe stares at my leg. The way she blinks a few times has my stomach churning. It's a look I immediately interpret as aversion. I hate it. But most of all, I despise how lesser than it makes me feel. This is exactly what I try to avoid by not allowing new people into my life.

Maya walks into the room and grabs Marko. "What did I tell you yesterday about *Tio* Santi's leg?"

My temple throbs from the pressure. I clutch onto the counter, trying to soothe the frustration building inside of me. It's not as if I can flip a shit in front of my sister since my *girlfriend* should know this basic fact.

Chloe's gaze snaps from my leg to my face. She smiles at me in a way that has something twisting in my chest. I don't know what to make of the expression on her face. It's a look I want to label as appreciation, but that doesn't make sense. But is that surprising when nothing about her makes sense?

A tiny part of me—a part so small I forgot it existed— questions if she can be physically attracted to me like I am to her. A flicker of hope fills me. It's microscopic, yet strong enough to overwhelm me.

Chloe the criminal has devastation written all over her, and I need her to run in the opposite direction. Because now that I've been around her, I don't know who's more dangerous—her or me.

CHAPTER EIGHT

Chloe

For the second time in two days, I find myself trapped. Marko holds me hostage beneath a pillow fort he built with a random blanket as the roof. I tried to escape when Maya and Noah announced they were leaving, but Marko forced me to stay by promising cookies. While I could've said no to the sweets, his crooked smile convinced me to hang out for a full hour after his parents left for their couple's trip.

"Marko. It's time to let Chloe go home." Santiago speaks from somewhere outside of our imaginary castle. The way his accent comes out heavier when he calls Marko's name has me smiling. Who knew a Spanish accent could sound this sexy?

Marko covers my mouth with his fingers, staring at me with blue eyes similar to his father's. "Shh. The tickle dragon hears us. I save you."

I suppress my laugh. A tickle dragon is a new one, even for me.

Marko waves his spoon in the air, nearly whacking my face. "You don't steal the pretty princess. You can't eat her!"

I always wanted a man to defend my honor. But I didn't expect it to be Marko, a four-year-old with a wooden spoon for a sword. The thought makes me giggle.

Marko's hand muffles my mouth. "Be quiet!"

Santiago roars. Marko's face lights up with excitement as the blanket is snatched from above our heads. "'Run, Chloe! Tickle dragon!"

Marko abandons me as he runs away from the fort. So much for being my savior. Santiago darts after him, making a whole ordeal of trying to wrangle him. I find myself entranced by his lightheartedness with his nephew. Laughter bounces off the walls of the house as he chases Marko through the halls as if his metal leg isn't a problem.

Santiago doesn't bother looking back to check if I follow them. It's to be expected, seeing as he avoided me after his nephew revealed his "superpower."

At first, I was shocked by Santiago's leg. But after the initial surprise disappeared, I looked at him in a new light. The perfect idea of him was shattered in the best way. It made him more down-to-earth. Because while he looks handsome, he's still a human with flaws. It has me interested in learning more about his story, even if he is ashamed of his leg.

The latter weighs heavy on me. His shame is obvious in the way he carried himself after the reveal, standing straighter and pretending as if I never saw his leg to begin with.

I follow them toward the front entryway where everything began last night. Santiago stands over Marko who lies on the floor, giggling from the tickles. It's the most precious sight. My heart melts a bit more for the disheveled man.

This is how we get in trouble, Chloe. Resist the man with a damaged past and a heart to match.

Santiago catches me staring. His smile drops into something flat and empty. A sense of loss takes over me, wishing he smiled at me like before.

He pulls Marko up off the floor and leads him toward the front door. "Marko, it's time to say bye to Chloe." He pulls my phone out of the pocket of his sweats and shoves it in my hand. "Here you go."

My skin warms from the contact. I'm tempted to drag his hand back to mine and test the connection, but he's back to his unapproachable self. Whoever made breakfast and joked with everyone about us dating is long gone. It doesn't take a genius to understand I'm the issue and the reason behind his change. Now that his family has left, the facade isn't needed anymore.

The sense of rejection grows into something big and ugly in my chest, feeding off my insecurity of being unwanted. A ruthless demon, popping up at the worst time.

He opens the door. "Thanks for helping me."

"So that's it? No more need for a fake girlfriend?" I cringe at the tinge of sadness in my voice.

"Well, my sister isn't coming back for—"

"Chloe. Please stay!" Marko clings to my legs with both his arms and legs.

"I've got to go home, little guy." I pat his head.

"Will you come back tomorrow?" His lip wobbles as he stares up at me. "*Tio* Santi is taking me on his boat."

This man has a boat, too? The closest thing to a boat I've been on is the ferry I took to visit the Statue of Liberty. To be real, I would love to go out on a boat and see Lake Como from a different view.

I crane my neck back, searching for approval. Santiago's height makes anything eye-level challenging. My smile drops as he shakes his head, answering my question.

I don't know why I expected more from him, but disappointment sits heavy in my chest. "I'm sorry, bud. I have a lot to do tomorrow."

Marko detaches himself from me and lets out a puff of air. "Fork me."

My eyes bulge. "I'm sorry?"

"Fork me. Daddy speaks it when he loses races."

Oh. Kid talk for *fuck me*. Got it. Noah must take games of tag with his son seriously.

Santiago unleashes a laugh. It's unrestrained and makes his face light up. I wish he did it more often, and I remember to save that thought for my journal later. *Look at me making wishes for other people.* I'd count that as my selfless act of the day.

"Will you come back?" Marko smiles again.

"Don't worry. I believe I'll see you soon." I wink.

"How do you know?"

"Because I make wishes and lately, they've been coming true."

"And you wish to see *me* again?" Marko's eyes become as large as two quarters.

"Of course. Who else would protect me from the tickle dragon?"

Marko gives me a tight hug before running away, claiming he needs to guard the castle.

Santiago rubs the back of his neck. "So…"

"This has been the weirdest forty-eight hours of my life." I step out onto the porch.

"I want to agree, but I've had weird shit happen to me." He leans against the door jamb.

My eyes flit to his covered leg before realizing my mistake.

Santiago's demeanor changes to something unrecognizable and borderline terrifying. His eyes darken and his jaw tightens, casting his cheekbones in a shadow. "I wasn't referencing *that*, but thanks for the reminder."

"I'm sorry. I didn't mean it like—"

"It's fine. Everyone has the same reaction. Pity, disgust, and everything in between. You're not some unicorn who's immune to my disability." He spits the last word out with such distaste, it coats the air around us.

I don't bother allowing him to have the last word. Instead, I step toward him, closing the distance and rising onto my toes. I wrap my hand around the back of his neck and pull his face toward mine.

Our lips smash together. His body stiffens at the kiss, and his arms remain plastered to his sides. *That reaction can't do.* I run my tongue across the seam of his lips to tempt him. The softness of his lips has my spine tingling. He relaxes and allows instinct to take over as he tugs me into his body. His mouth opens and his tongue lashes out against mine.

It's messy and chaotic. Unplanned and unhinged. Something unlike anything I've experienced before, with my toes curling inside of my sneakers and my head growing lightheaded. One of his calloused hands holds my head in place while his other roams down my body. It's everything I didn't realize I was missing when I kissed boys in the past.

My body shivers from his touch, and I moan when his large palm grips one of my ass cheeks. An overwhelming sense of attraction invades my head, the chemistry building between us like electricity.

Kissing him is a different experience altogether. Santiago kisses me like a man who found an oasis in the middle of a desert. It's nothing I expected but everything I want more of. And that thought terrifies me, especially with our situation.

I pull my mouth away with a rush despite everything inside of me wanting to continue. His arms fall by his sides, releasing me.

I swipe my swollen bottom lip with my tongue.

He looks like he wants to continue, but somehow restrains himself. *Good.* I don't think my body could handle part two.

I take advantage of his silence. "Next time you *think* I looked at you with disgust, remember that kiss. I'm not a unicorn because I'd much rather be a dragon in the story. They're more badass anyway."

His jaw drops open. I don't bother letting him answer me. Backing away, I shoot him a smile I hope expresses how that was the best kiss I've ever had in my life. Even if I never see Santiago again, he can remember that parting gift. "Enjoy your time with your nephew, Santiago." I slide toward the area in the fence I snuck through before.

"You could go through the front gate like a normal person!"

"I'm anything but normal, so why bother pretending?" I yell out, ignoring the bushes scraping me.

The laugh he releases as I fade into the background sends a shiver up my spine.

I smile during my entire walk back to my hotel with his laugh replaying inside of my head.

"Where the hell have you been? It's been forever since you called me from that sketchy Italian restaurant!" Brooke's raised voice makes the speaker on my phone crackle.

"I'm so sorry! I was doing my best given the circumstances." I throw myself on my bed, the springs creaking at the sudden assault.

"What happened? You left off at the part where the guy stole your phone and you planned on breaking into his house to steal it back. But I thought you got caught since you never called me last night."

I snort. "You're not going to believe what's happened."

"Oh, now this has got to be good. Don't skimp on a single detail."

I dive into one of the wildest stories of my life. Brooke listens, not bothering to ask much as I explain the series of events that led to this moment.

"Holy shit," she whispers.

"I know! It was crazy."

"And you kissed this random man after only knowing him for barely a weekend? That's so…"

"Unlike me. I know! But he started to close himself off again, thinking I found him ugly because of his missing leg. It was written all over his face."

"Wait! You didn't mention anything about a missing leg. Tell me more."

"Well, I think everything below his right knee is missing. I couldn't see much else because his nephew was in the way."

"He sounds hot in a damaged kind of way. I'd do him."

I groan. "Brooke!"

"What? You think he's sexy and you kissed him. It's not

like you're going to marry the man. No harm, no foul."

"Yes, foul! Big forking foul."

"Forking?"

Shit. "I couldn't curse in front of Marko."

"Look at you going all *Disney Channel* on me. Cute."

"Anyway, your plan sucks because even if I wanted to kiss him again, I don't even have his number or full name."

"I'm going to light a candle for you."

"That only works in churches."

She scoffs. "Nonsense. The power is in the will. That and the highest quality Jesus candle a dollar can buy."

I roll my eyes. "You're crazy."

"Right back at you. So in this whole story, you missed out on a big part."

I purse my lips considering what I could've missed.

Brooke fills in the silence. "Have you introduced yourself to your dad yet?"

"Oh." *Yes, Chloe, the whole damn reason you came here in the first place!* "I was a little preoccupied."

"Right, too busy playing house with Santiago, whose name is unfairly sexy, thank you very much." Her laugh cackles through the tiny speaker.

"I plan on stopping by Matteo's house tomorrow since I know Santiago won't be there."

"Atta girl! Are you planning on scaling a tree again?"

"No." I snort. "But seriously, I'm not sure what I'll do. The idea of speaking to him face-to-face terrifies me."

"Understandable. But I believe in you and your wishes. This was meant to be."

The more people say it, the more I believe it. But there's

a reason people say be careful what you wish for. I just haven't figured out why yet.

I stare at the same gate I walked up to three days ago. This time I don't see any cars in the driveway or hear any music pounding from the backyard.

I eye the speaker box next to the entrance. No matter how much I yell at my limbs to move toward it, I stay glued in place. Questions flood my head every time I consider speaking to Matteo. How should I introduce myself? What if he says he knew about me this entire time and didn't care about meeting me? What if he asks me how my life was up until this point, and my honesty scares him away?

My confidence drains with every new question that pops up in my head. I dial Brooke, desperate for support.

She picks up on the second ring. "What's up, betch? I was wondering where you have been all morning."

"It's still nighttime there. What are you even doing awake right now?"

"Finalizing the last details for my project. What are you *not* doing right now since you called me for a distraction?"

"I can't do it."

"You can't have sex with the hot guy who lives in the creepy castle?"

"*No.* I can't find the courage to speak to Matteo. My body tenses up anytime I get the courage to visit his house."

"Maybe you're worried it won't be a natural introduction."

"I'm not sure how anything along the lines of 'Hi, I'm the

daughter you didn't know existed' can ever sound organic."

"What are you thinking?"

"What do you mean?"

"Come on. I know how you are. You tend to be impulsive and I want to see how I can talk you out of whatever new plan you've thought up."

"What if I applied for a job at the coffee shop he owns?"

"How do you know that he owns a coffee shop?"

"Umm… I followed him around yesterday after our phone call."

Brooke whistles. "Damn, girl. You're breaking all kinds of laws now. First, you were a peeping tom, then you got accused of some good, old-fashioned breaking and entering, and now you're stalking someone? Where was this rebellious streak when we were sixteen and I begged you to sneak out to Jack Gibson's party with me?"

"I didn't want to get kicked out of another home."

"Yet now you're on a path to a more permanent house. The big house, if you get me."

I laugh. "Well, it's done. I'm putting my illegal past behind me. I'm not that girl anymore."

"Wow, you have a quick turnaround time for changing yourself."

"Brooke…"

"Okay! God, you're really serious lately. So back to you working at the coffee shop."

I tap my foot against the ground. "How does that plan sound?"

"Awful. You don't like coffee."

"Well, working at a coffee shop doesn't require 'liking

coffee' as a prerequisite. All I have to do is sell it."

"And make it."

"That's nothing YouTube can't fix."

Brooke giggles. "So I gather that you plan on staying there a lot longer than the original two weeks we planned."

I bite my lip. "Yes. I can set up an ad for someone to sublease my apartment that way we're not struggling to pay the rent while I'm gone."

Brooke clucks her tongue. "Don't worry about it. I'm sure I can find someone from school who needs a place to crash."

"Thank you."

"You can thank me by sharing all the dirty details of this adventure. I seriously can't wait for future developments of how you try to sneak in your real identity while working for your dad."

I sigh, pressing my head into the cool metal of the gate. I can't remember the last time I second-guessed myself like this. And I'm not sure if I'm capable of achieving the one thing I always dreamed of.

A family to call my own.

CHAPTER NINE

SANTIAGO

There are certain things I want to forget about my life. The first is what it felt like to walk with two normal legs. The second is the feeling of adrenaline pumping through my veins as I raced in a Prix. And the third is the way Chloe kissed me like she needed to resuscitate the damaged part of my heart I thought was long gone.

The third memory is the one that keeps troubling me no matter how busy I get taking care of Marko. It assaults me at the most inconvenient times. And it's not like my nephew helps with my cause of trying to move past the kiss. He doesn't stop talking about Chloe as he protects his castle, claiming he needs to wait for his princess.

It seems like she not only has my nephew enraptured but me as well. The woman is an enigma. Everything from the way lies flow past her lips about our "relationship" to how she shatters the preconceived notion I had about her finding me repulsive.

It's not even the way she kissed me that has my brain going haywire. More like it's everything that kiss meant to her and what she wanted to prove. Chloe challenged me and my idea of her being disgusted by me and my impairment. She took a gamble, and it worked. It worked so damn well, I respect her more because of it. In fact, I wish I could ask if she wants to repeat it under a different circumstance without my nephew nearby. But like the idiot I've been around Chloe, I realize I never got her number.

Instead of allowing disappointment to settle in my gut, I take the issue for what it is. A sign to not pursue her. Fate has a way of intervening in my life without my consent, and it's about damn time I listened.

"Where's my Monkey?" Maya calls out through the FaceTime call.

Marko giggles behind the couch.

Noah smiles into the camera. "I don't know. I hear something that sounds like Marko, but maybe it's someone else. Santiago, did you lose Marko?"

I shrug. "I don't know. The tickle dragon might've eaten him."

Marko's giggles stop. He jumps up from behind the couch. "Boo!"

Maya gasps and Noah hoots for Marko like he achieved the biggest award.

"What did you do today, Monkey?" Maya asks.

Marko rambles on, explaining how we worked on a car together.

"And have you spent time with Chloe?" Maya bursts with excitement.

"No." Marko frowns.

Little shit. I thought we were in this together.

Noah looks at me. "I thought she planned on helping you? Trouble in paradise?" Noah's mocking voice matches his smirk.

I take his smugness without complaint because he doesn't need any more of my shit. "She has been dealing with some personal stuff."

"Marko, go get your race car. I can't remember if it's red or blue, and I want to see which one I need to buy you next," Noah orders.

"Silly, Daddy. Red like yours!"

"But I want to see it too!" Maya does a great job feeding Marko's excitement.

He runs toward his room.

"Is she okay? It's not that Ralph guy, is it?" Noah's eyes darken.

I shake my head. "No. She just had something unexpected come up at work." The lies come out easier the more I pretend Chloe is actually my girlfriend. "You know...not everyone has a job that entails traveling around the world."

Noah takes advantage of my slip-up. "You could have one too if you reviewed the emails I sent you. You'd be able to race—"

My answer will always be the same. "No."

"But the Formula Corp will agree to hear your case if you just try. There's nothing stopping you anymore." Noah's brows pinch together.

I gesture to the biggest obstacle between me and racing again. "Really? Please explain how that's possible because last time I checked, I didn't grow another leg."

Noah's jaw ticks. "The new proposal addresses that. You'd see that if you read it."

No one has tried and succeeded in coming back to the F1 grid with a disability. Getting burned or breaking a major bone might stop a racer for a handful of races or a whole season. But no one bothers to return after something like what happened to me. Too many obstacles. Too many adjustments. Too many people doubting my ability to achieve anything close to what I did in the past. Hence, my stance on the matter.

"You promised you'd stop trying." I look away.

"And you promised to return back once you got a handle on your situation."

I shouldn't have done that. Noah mistook my hopefulness during the first few months of my recovery as everything but what it actually was: *Denial*.

"Yeah, well, I lied."

"Then, so did I. I'm not going to stop trying." Noah crosses his arms.

Maya's gaze flickers between her husband and the camera. "Noah... just give him time to think about it. The proposal isn't going anywhere, and neither is Santi."

"Yeah, well, if he continues to wait, his best years will fade away before he gives himself a real chance. And that's not only stupid, but selfish."

"Selfish? Please enlighten me on how *I'm* being selfish," I snap.

"Because, rather than choosing to be a role model for other

people in similar situations as you, you've become a public example of what happens when you let life break you. And as your brother-in-law and best friend, I simply can't accept that. If our roles were reversed, you wouldn't let me do half the shit we let you get away with, so I don't understand how you expect me to. I can deal with you avoiding the media and wanting a fresh start somewhere new where no one bothers you. But what I can't wrap my head around is how one of the most badass people I've met—the very guy who threatened *me* of all people—let his circumstances destroy who he is. So yeah, I'll keep sending you proposals and updates on a car I can only hope you drive one day because *I fucking care.*" Noah rises from the couch and places a kiss on Maya's head. He steps out of the camera frame, followed by a door clicking shut somewhere on Maya's end.

Her eyes reflect the truth Noah laid out in front of me. Except she won't say anything. She never says anything, and it drives me crazy. "Listen, Noah's been more irritable and protective lately…"

The last thing I want is for Maya to worry about my relationship with Noah. He obviously does everything from a place of love. That's what makes it harder than anything to reject his hope time after time.

I lift a palm up at her. "It's fine. I get that he cares, but I can't race again. It's just not possible."

She shakes her head. "I don't think you understand *how* much he cares. Noah's been developing the hand controls himself with Bandini. He's committed to making your return as easy as possible, including clocking in hours during his busy schedule to make sure the throttle pad and steering wheel is perfect."

"Are you serious?" The words leave my mouth in a whisper.

"He's spent the past two off-seasons visiting the warehouse working with engineers and James on a car configured specifically for you. You're the missing piece he needs, Santiago. He can test everything himself, but he can't face the Formula Corp by himself, and you know that. They'd never accept the proposal without proof of your recovery."

Holy shit. I had no idea Noah wanted me to return this much. I hate how I'll only end up disappointing him with my decision to not race. No matter what he does, I can't face that lifestyle again. The thought of living in the shadow of the racer I was has me solidifying my decision.

I open my mouth, but she stops me.

"I hope you know we believe in you. You'll get back out there. I'm sure of it. And one day, you'll show the world the same role model I had growing up. And I can't wait to be there to cheer you on."

The thought alone has me wanting to end the video call and hide from the emotions they both stirred up inside of me. Rather than express my feelings, I lock them up in a box and bury them deep within me.

I'm not racing. Not now. Not next season. Not ever.

CHAPTER TEN

Chloe

lean against a wall around the corner of the coffee shop. "You can do this, Chloe. This is the moment you've been waiting twenty-four years of your life for."

After enough deep breathing to clear anyone's sinuses, my nerves return to a somewhat acceptable level. A bell chimes above me as I enter Matteo's coffee shop. The aroma of espresso beans hits me in the face and a machine whirls in the distance.

I stop moving as my eyes land on my father for the first time. He focuses on steaming a cup of something, which gives me time to gather myself and get a good look at him. His dark hair appears as black as mine, with the faintest gray at his temples.

His brown eyes catch mine. Two dark brows pinch together as his eyes scan my face. Something passes over him, but he shakes his head.

Does he recognize me? Do I look like my mom? Maybe I expected too much when I created a scenario in my head about him immediately recognizing me as his long-lost child.

"*Ciao. Che cosa vuio bere?*"

Yeah, I definitely expected too much. My mouth parts open before shutting again. Unexpected tears prick my eyes, but I take a deep breath and chant to myself how everything is okay. I'm here now, and that's better than never.

His lips turn down, showing off some deep-set wrinkles near his eyes and mouth.

"I don't speak much Italian," I blurt out.

He nods his head. "I can speak English too. My mom was born in New York." He smiles in a way that makes my knees weak. The whole experience of meeting him is something indescribable, with my chest tightening and hopes I long gave up on filtering through my head.

I rub my damp palms down my cotton dress. "Oh. Nice. New York." *You can talk the paint off a wall, but now you lose the ability to speak when it matters.*

He chuckles to himself. "Yes. Did you come here for coffee?"

"Well, actually, I was wondering if you were hiring a barista." All right, my approach was about as smooth as sandpaper.

He looks around the nearly empty shop, his eyes bouncing from the one customer in a corner to me. "Since we don't get many customers here, I handle all the orders."

I'm getting the brush-off by my own dad. I mentally dig my feet in and raise my chin. I did not go through hell to get here only to give up at the first sign of trouble. "I can help with *anything* you need. Accounting, the ordering of supplies, checking stock." I list off everything I have no experience with. If I learned how to pick a lock on YouTube, then the world is my oyster.

His brows lift. "Well, I could use help with one thing, but the pay isn't great."

I attempt to keep my nod to a normal level of enthusiasm. I'd accept working for free at this point because I'm willing to do just about anything to spend more time around him. "Sure. What is it?"

He explains the pay and how he needs help cleaning the shop every day because he messed up his back a few years ago. My excitement doesn't falter when he passes me a rag and window cleaner. Spending time with Matteo is what I traveled all this way for. Who cares if I'm sweeping floors or making terrible coffee for unlucky patrons? As long as I get to be with him, I couldn't care less about my job.

I plan on taking advantage of every second with him, even if it means living out a Cinderella fantasy. Who needs a fairy godmother when I have myself?

It takes two days of wiping windows, cleaning a gross bathroom, and mopping the sticky tile in silence before Matteo breaks the awkwardness.

"Where in America are you from?" He asks the simplest question, but it has my heart racing in my chest nonetheless.

"I was born in New York." Maybe if I sprinkle facts here and there, he will get the hint.

"Ah, just like my mom. I used to go there every summer with my brother to visit her." He clears his throat, focusing back on cleaning his coffee machine.

I can barely hear my own voice over the sound of my blood pounding in my ears. "So, what did you do in New York?" I wince at the desperation in my voice. *Smooth, Chloe, smooth.*

Matteo laughs. "Just about everything. My mom moved back to the States after she and my father divorced, so when my brother and I would visit, we tended to make the most of it."

Does he remember sleeping with my mom? Will he be shocked to realize he has a child? I force my thoughts to slow down.

Matteo carries on with his business, ignoring how I'm stuck in place, staring at him. My brain screams to attack him with more questions. But something tells me to hold off because I don't want to make him suspicious of me.

"And is this where you lived the other parts of the year?"

"Yeah. My father was born and raised here. He started this shop himself." Matteo looks around the store, smiling.

"Wow. That's incredible." I appreciate the shop in a new light, knowing it's been passed down by each generation.

"Well, I know this town is smaller than one New York city block, but I love the people and the quiet."

"You've got that right. I'm still getting used to walking past the same people every morning and having them smile at me. In New York, if I smiled at a stranger, they might call the cops on me for suspicious behavior."

Matteo laughs. It's a full and hearty sound, with his eyes crinkling.

My jaw drops open, and a sudden urge hits me to confess who I am. I could drop this disguise and spend some real time getting to know him in a daughter-father way. But I rationalize that our relationship needs to be taken slowly rather than me plunging headfirst. I recover from my temporary lapse in judgment and solidify my need to hold back.

He collects himself. "Do you like it here?"

I consider his question and how the past week has been the wildest thing out of my imagination. From crashing into someone else's life to working for my father without him knowing it, nothing about my experience has been typical. Even the ancestry kit working itself out has me questioning where all this good fortune was throughout my life. It's like turning twenty-four meant all the parts of my life would align after years of loneliness and disappointment.

I settle on something a little more subdued. "It might make me sound crazy, but this town feels like it has a bit of magic." Him. The people. Santiago.

Matteo nods his head. "Magic is everywhere and in everything. People only have to believe in it for it to work. If you notice it, then embrace it because that's what makes us dreamers."

My dad speaking about *us* as a duo has my lungs burning from a sudden inhale of breath. I want there to be an us so freaking badly, I'm willing to bottle up all the magic in this damn town and hoard it. But not everything is meant to be contained, and magic isn't the exception to the rule.

CHAPTER ELEVEN

SANTIAGO

I spend a whole week somehow keeping Marko entertained within the confines of my house. To be honest, my sister failed to warn me that the kid is cute but a human wrecking ball. I've never spent this long babysitting him and I'm starting to see why. By the eighth day of his stay, he's already painted my walls with every crayon in his arsenal and pissed more times outside of the toilet than in. I've been doing laundry around the clock to keep up with all the food that lands on his body, and my couch has become a prime example of what happens when kids are given adult glasses instead of sippy cups.

Desperate to help Marko expel some energy after dinner, I take him on a much-needed visit to the lakeside park. I could also use something to calm myself down too because I can't put my mind to rest lately. If I'm not considering checking the email with Noah's proposal, then I'm thinking about Chloe and what she's up to during our time apart. It's like the two of them worked together to wreak havoc on my head over the past couple of days.

Marko entertains me, not allowing my thoughts to slip too far into the deep, dark pits of self-loathing when I consider what Noah said. My nephew shows me how there's still good for me to look forward to in the world even if I don't exactly feel that way often.

"Look who it is! Princess Chloe!" Marko's hand slips out of mine as he runs down across the grass.

I stop and stare across the lawn at her. She sits on the grass with her legs crossed, holding on to a circular object. Like an old bad habit, I tug my hat lower down my face to hide myself from anyone who passes by us. I'm not too worried about any fans finding me based on how empty the park is at this time of day.

"Hey, you!" Chloe laughs as she throws whatever she was doing on the grass. She spreads her arms and Marko launches himself into them. He wraps his arms and legs around her, proving why he was nicknamed *Monkey* in the first place.

My curiosity peaks at the object she was working on. It's a half-finished embroidery circle. The design is impressive and extremely detailed, with the bright mix of random flowers standing out against the white linen material.

I point at her work. "I'm seeing a trend here. Do you like wildflowers?"

"There's something beautiful about chaos."

"They remind me of you." The words escape my mouth before I can stop them.

Where the fuck did that come from?

Her cheeks flush. "Some people would be offended about being compared to a bunch of weeds."

"I have a feeling you don't fall in the same category as those people."

"Why?" A hint of a smile crosses her lips.

"Because those who see beauty in chaos also see flowers instead of weeds, and that's a gift in a world like ours."

"That's rather poetic of you." The pink in her cheeks deepens.

I smile at her reaction. She makes it too easy, and I won't deny how I look forward to making her blush. Flirting with Chloe invigorates me in a way I haven't felt in some time.

Marko lays a sloppy kiss on Chloe's cheek, stealing her attention back. "I miss-ed you." He crawls off her lap and sits by her side. His tiny hand pats the grass next to him as he looks up at me.

Come on, Marko. You're supposed to be my wingman. I stare at the grass with such hatred, I'm surprised it doesn't catch on fire. Getting up and down off the floor was always one of my least favorite physical therapy activities. Not because it was hard, but because it made it so damn obvious that I have an impairment to begin with.

Chloe laughs, soft and carefree as she brushes a strand of hair out of Marko's eye. "Aw, I miss-ed you too."

"Really?" He smiles in that infectious way of his. His eyes narrow at me as he pats the ground again. "*Siéntate, Tio.*"

I avoid Chloe's gaze as I take a deep breath. I've practiced this move hundreds of times in rehab but executing it around Chloe has me feeling another sense of dread. Just because she kissed me doesn't mean she is interested in anything more. And the kiss was a way to prove her point rather than to make me feel good. Based on the way she doesn't look in my direction, I'm the only idiot who can't get it out of my head.

Ignoring the acid rolling in my stomach at making myself look any less of a man in front of Chloe, I put my left leg forward for balance and then fold my right leg. My prosthetic hits the grass at the same time as the palms of my hands. Transferring my body weight to my arms, I pull my legs forward and in front of me. It's awkward and disjointed, with each second ticking by at a snail's pace.

Chloe focuses on tickling Marko's stomach. Her indifference fills me with a new wave of appreciation. It's as if she knows what to do without me having to ask, and that's something I've yet to experience around anyone. Not even my own family knows how to act when I take longer to do what used to be second nature.

Her tickling leaves Marko breathless and red in the face.

"He just ate, so unless you want him to become a vomit launcher, I'd stop." I place my hands behind me as I take in the sunset reflecting off the lake.

Marko makes a *bleh* noise.

"Gross. We don't want that." She wrinkles her nose in the cutest way.

Marko abandons his spot in between us and runs around in circles, making retching noises between giggles.

"I'm curious. What made you want to take a walk in the park? I thought you didn't leave your castle much." She drags a finger underneath the bill of my cap, lifting it.

Her blue eyes darken as they focus on me licking my lips. *Hmm. Maybe she does think about our kiss, too.* "I wanted to make sure there weren't any cats who needed rescuing."

She drops her head back and laughs. "I didn't hear any

crying in the trees, so I think we are good."

"That's great. We can't have you checking on them and falling again."

"I wouldn't have fallen if it weren't for a big, brooding shadow of a man who scared me in the middle of the night."

"It's not every day I have a trespasser wanting to climb a tree on my property."

She scoffs. "The fact that you have to specify what kind of trespasser you have speaks volumes."

I shrug. "People are weird and invasive."

"Maybe they're interested in checking out if your house is haunted."

It's my turn to laugh. "What?"

Seriously, how can this girl not know I'm famous? I can't remember the last time I've been completely anonymous. By the time I was eighteen, I already had over a hundred-thousand followers on my social media accounts.

"Your house. Have you seen it? It's like Luigi's Mansion but less fun."

"Are you a Nintendo fan?"

"Are you not? Be careful how you answer. I might have to end this friendship before it has a real chance."

Friendship? She's got to be kidding me. I'm not about to get friend-zoned by a woman who kissed me like she might die without it. No way. Fuck that.

"Of course I like Nintendo. I grew up using Mario Kart as practice."

"Practice for what?" Her brows scrunch together.

Shit. I ignore the urge to reveal my racing past. "For actual driving. What else?"

"I wouldn't know. I never learned how to drive."

"What? You don't know how to drive?" I try to wrap my head around the concept. I've been driving karts since I was four years old.

"No! I grew up in New York. No one knows how to drive."

"Whoa. That needs to be amended."

She laughs to herself. "And you're going to be the one to sacrifice yourself for the cause?"

"It's not a sacrifice if I'm willing." I grin.

Marko, cockblocker extraordinaire, interrupts us, squeezing my neck with his sweaty arms. "Time for gelato?"

"Hmm, I don't know. You already had gelato yesterday."

"Please!" He squeezes my neck tighter. "You're the bestest uncle ever."

"Thanks. It was a tough competition with myself, but I'm glad I won."

Chloe giggles and I want to hear more of it.

"So yes?" Marko whines.

"Why don't you go run around some more?" *Go run. Go hide. Go rip grass from the ground like I did when I was your age.* Anything to give me an ounce of privacy with Chloe.

"Then I get pukey." He fake retches.

Chloe's deep laugh has my dick waking up like it's time to play.

"Then sit." I pat the grass. If it worked on me, maybe it'll work on him.

He moves onto Chloe, crawling into her lap and holding her face with his pudgy hands. "Princess, can you take me? Tickle dragon is grumpy."

The little shit.

Chloe looks at me with a raised brow. "I don't want the tickle dragon mad at me."

"Please." Marko pouts.

"Fine. We can go." I exhale.

"Yes!" Marko claps and stands up, offering his hand to Chloe. "You coming?"

Chloe opens her mouth, clearly wanting to reject Marko.

I jump in. "You don't want to disappoint a four-year-old because they tend to hold grudges. And this little guy is the worst at them. He forced me for an entire week to dress up as Elsa because I didn't want to watch *Frozen* with him."

She chuckles to herself as she packs up the few items she had strewn out on the grass. "Sure. Why not? I don't have anything else to do tonight." She rises from the ground with ease.

I make a move to get up before remembering I can't do it the same way anymore. The vein above my eye throbs as I prep myself.

Fuck. This was a terrible idea. Getting up is way worse than going down.

"Hey." Chloe bends over, hitting me with two sapphire eyes. "Marko calls you Iron Man, right?"

I raise a brow, ignoring the clenching of my stomach muscles from the fresh wave of nerves. "Yes."

The scar above her lip twitches as her lips part. "And do you know what makes Iron Man special?"

"His suit?"

She laughs and leans into my ear. The hot air from her mouth sends sparks down my spine. "No. Iron Man is special because he owns who he is, no matter what people think of him. He is unapologetic and people are drawn to him like a magnet. Personally, I don't care if it takes you a minute or an hour to get up. All that matters is that you *do*."

How the hell did life throw this girl in my path? I'm destined to destroy her before she has a chance to get away. She's too good for the likes of me.

I swallow back the lump in my throat. "Is this your game-day speech?"

"This is my *get your head out of your ass* speech. I reserve game-day speeches for special occasions like sex marathons and getting out of bed on Sundays."

My dick is interested in both options with her. Chloe is the perfect blend of sweet and sexy, giving me a hard-on from her presence and words alone.

She moves away from me, taking her warmth with her. Marko asks her to watch him race across the grass, and she walks over to him.

I do what Chloe told me to and push aside the idea of her staring at me. Instead, I focus on the motions of getting up. I grab my prosthetic and cross it over my left leg. Rolling onto my knees, I bring my left foot forward and press it into the ground before standing.

I brush the dirt clinging to my hands. No one pays me any attention, and I enjoy the warmth spreading through my chest at my accomplishment. Instead of my usual hatred toward myself, I feel stronger. Not only because I could get up, but because I found someone whose first instinct isn't to baby me or avoid talking about my injury. Honestly, it seems like Chloe doesn't give a shit about it. She treats me as an equal, which is more than I can say about many people. It has me wanting to get to know the real her rather than the lie I created in my head. And I'm not exactly opposed to it anymore.

I can't tear my eyes away from Chloe licking the chocolate gelato off her spoon.

Why did I think inviting Chloe to this was a good idea? My body is out of control, reacting to anything and everything Chloe does. I shouldn't find licking a spoon erotic. Clearly, I've stooped to new lows during my time in isolation. Lows that include one visit already to the bathroom for me to readjust myself.

It's not like I'm bringing women back to my house to fuck me. The last time that happened was over a year ago, and the woman only had sex with me out of pity. I could tell by the look in her eyes after I stripped out of my jeans. Rather than remove my leg to be comfortable, I kept it on and went along with the act anyway. The hopeful part of me believed it would make me feel better about myself if I was sexual with someone. It didn't. I never bothered again after that occasion because I felt worse than I ever have in the bedroom.

By now, I'm practically a born-again virgin. So, yeah, watching Chloe lick her spoon is like viewing live porn for me at this point. Sad but fucking true based on how my dick threatens war against the zipper of my jeans.

Chloe pushes her cup of gelato away, and my cock weeps.

"Well, that was so good. Thank you." She looks over at me before turning her attention toward Marko. "I loved seeing you again."

"Will you come tomorrow on the boat?" He bats his lashes in a way I recognize as something Maya did as a kid.

"Oh. I have things to do."

"What things?" I blurt out.

"Um…work."

"Where do you work?"

"The coffee shop next to the bakery on the main road." Her eyes fall to her lap.

"We swim tomorrow. You can come!" Marko demands.

It's a sad moment to realize my nephew has more pull with women than me and he's only four. No doubt he will be a real charmer when he's older.

Chloe's head snaps up, her eyes searching mine for help.

I shrug. "Saying no to him is exhausting." *Right.* "What time do you get out of work?"

"I'm done at noon."

"Does one o'clock sound good, then?"

"Sure." Her voice sounds anything but sure, but her face remains calm.

I ask for her phone number, just in case anything comes up. She rattles off the digits before leaving the two of us behind.

"I've got to hand it to you, kid. You've got your dad's skills for getting what you want." I offer him my hand to smack.

"Hell forking yes." He shoots me a huge smile and slaps my palm.

Hindsight truly is twenty-twenty. Inviting Chloe swimming was a bad idea. The thought kept me up way too late last night after Marko went to bed.

I've officially voted my nephew the worst wingman ever.

Neither one of us can recognize when our ideas suck, and that's a deadly combo.

Like an asshole, I text Chloe while she's at work about postponing our plans because Marko came down with a nasty cold. It's the oldest trick in the book, but I'm fresh out of ideas. This is the last thing I want to do but I have to. I can't bear her seeing the real me without any pants or barriers hiding my leg.

No amount of counseling or physical therapy I've completed makes the feeling of inadequacy go away. I can't do it, no matter how much I want to spend time with Chloe.

My stomach sinks as Chloe texts me back.

> **Chloe the Criminal:** Oh no :(Poor guy. What's he feeling?

Yeah, Santiago, what is he feeling?
One look at Marko jumping across couches yelling something about not touching lava makes my chest tighten.

> **Me**: Sore throat and the sniffles.

And a case of bullshit inherited by yours truly.

> **Chloe the Criminal:** No worries. I hope he gets well soon. Maybe we can go another time when he's feeling better.

I can't find it in me to respond.

Marko asks me to take him for a walk by the lake. We spend an hour trying to skip rocks across the water. He claps and does a victory dance when one of his rocks skips across the flat water. It reminds me of Noah and me winning on podiums together, chugging champagne to blasting music.

The memory has my body tensing before I can push it away. I do my best to keep those hidden away but spending time with Marko brings back the oldest ones.

Marko's voice snaps me out of my daze. "What's that?"

"What?"

He runs up to a paper bag laying on the ground about twenty feet away.

My mood goes from bad to worse as I walk up to it. I analyze the contents, finding different kid's medicines and a Tupperware of hot soup. The get-well package lacks a message, but it's obvious who would bother showing up with one.

Guilt hits me, with my stomach tightening to the point of unease. I tug my phone out of my pants to find a new message.

> **Chloe the Criminal:** Glad to see Marko's feeling better.

Thank God being a lying dick isn't contagious.

My palms shake as I think up a way to explain myself. To make her understand why I made the decision I did because of my insecurity with myself, not her. I type out my first message, wanting to send something, and buy myself a second to think.

> **Me:** It's not what you think.

I keep typing. The dots on her side of the message come and go as fast as they appeared in the first place. I don't have time to send my next response before my phone pings again.

> **Chloe the Criminal:** You're right because here I was thinking you were someone you clearly aren't. I should've known better the first time you lied about us to your family. Do us both a favor and lose my number.

> **Me:** You don't understand. Give me a chance to explain.
> **Chloe the Criminal:** Compulsive liars are a hard limit for me. I'll pass on your offer.

Marko looks at me funny when I groan. All I have done is lie in front of her, around her, with her. Everything we have done together has been a show for someone else. Well, everything but our private conversations and yesterday. That was all us.

Except you're hiding your true identity, and that's still a lie.

> **Me:** I'm sorry.
> **Chloe the Criminal:** Sorry. This number is no longer in service. Get a hint like I did and forget I ever existed.
> **Me:** But what if I don't want to?

I stand by the lake with Marko for another ten minutes, waiting for a reply that never comes. It's obvious that I fucked up. Period. It doesn't matter what my reasoning was in the first place.

The worst part about all of this is knowing she'll never accept me. If this is how she reacted from a small lie, I can't imagine how she will feel after I tell her I'm actually famous. Or was.

My list of flaws continues to grow while the redeemable parts of myself shrivel into nothing but distant memories.

CHAPTER TWELVE

Chloe

"What a dick." Brooke speaks over the beeping horns of a busy morning in New York. It's unlike her to call me on her morning walk, but I entertained her since Matteo left the shop already.

"Tell me about it. I can't believe he would lie about a child being sick. Who even does that?" I swipe the mop across the coffee shop's floor.

"Someone who's used to lying to get his way?"

I scrunch my nose. "*Ugh.* I should have known better."

"What are you going to do about him then?"

"Well, I'm hoping we never run into each other again."

"Speaking of running into someone…"

I suck in a breath. "What happened?"

"I ran into your mother."

"No. When?"

"Yes. She stopped by our apartment again this morning. I didn't see her when I ran out the door, so I ended up spilling my coffee all over my favorite blouse when our bodies collided."

I wince, mentally noting that I need to cover Brooke's dry-cleaning bill. "You're joking."

Brooke sighs. "Sadly not. While I stood there, soaked with burning hot coffee, she had the audacity to ask me if you were there. I told her you were in Europe."

"You what?!"

"Fuck. I knew it was the wrong thing to say." She groans. "I'm sorry. My bad. But to be fair, I wasn't thinking straight. All my coffee had landed on my shirt rather than in my mouth."

I sigh. "You don't need to apologize to me. She's not your problem."

"But I still feel guilty."

I hate putting Brooke in this position. She shouldn't have to act as a buffer between my mother and myself, especially when I'm not there to help. "Don't. Please. She's the one who was in the wrong. What did she say when you told her I was out of the country?"

"She asked if you were now working as a flight attendant because that's the only way you could afford to travel."

"What a bitch."

"I agree. I told her to fuck off and have a nice day."

I lean against the counter, brushing my loose hair out of my face. "Should I call her and tell her to stop coming to our place? I don't want her to bother you while I'm not there."

"No. Don't give her any attention. If there is anything I've learned from my creepy ex-boyfriends, it's that attention only reinforces their behavior."

"Really?"

"Yup. I tested it time and time again. First, they get upset because you aren't giving them what they want, but eventually they give up and find someone else to harass."

"And it works?"

"Eventually. It's not like she can get money from you if you're not even here."

"You're right."

She laughs. "As per usual."

"Thank you for dealing with her and putting up with me. How will I ever make it up to you?"

"Find me a husband. All I ask is for someone with a big—"

"Brooke!"

"Heart! A big *heart*."

I giggle, erasing any anxiety about my mother. She can't bother me when I'm thousands of miles away. And in the end, I'm the one who gives people permission to hurt me. Finally, I'm taking my stand against her and leaving that part of my life behind me.

My cell phone rings, startling me awake. I groan as I sit up and grab the phone from its holder. "Hello?"

"Chloe. Thank God you answered. I need your help. Please." Santiago's voice comes out as a half growl.

I haven't bothered answering any of his texts since yesterday's lake incident. Instead, I ignored his apology like it never happened. Giving him a chance in the first place was a mistake. I should've known better with how easily he lied to everyone else in his life. If someone can lie to their own sister, they can lie to anyone.

I hate to admit I enjoyed faking our relationship in front of Maya and Noah. It was fun and I felt like I was part of a family for a solid thirty seconds. But in the end, lying isn't right and it's something I avoid at all costs.

Well, lying isn't something I usually do with anyone but Matteo. But that situation is acceptable. I can't exactly storm the castle and confess who I am without him knowing me.

Marko cries on the other side of the line, snapping me out of my thoughts.

"Shit." Santiago groans.

"What's going on? Is Marko okay?" I throw the covers off my body and stand.

"I need your help because Marko is actually sick this time. I swear I'm not lying. He's puking his guts up and I don't know what to do and I desperately need your help. He's crying for his mom and she's halfway around the world right now, so you're the next best thing I can think of right now."

"Did you give him any fluids?"

"Just water, but he can't keep anything down."

Marko's wails carry through the speaker.

"Fuck, I've got to go. I wouldn't ask this of—"

I ignore the urge to stand him up. It's what he deserves after what he did to me. But Marko crying out for his mom on the other side of the line has me shelving my anger toward Santiago.

"Don't worry about it. I'll be there in fifteen minutes."

I use the side gate like a normal person this time and

enter Santiago's house. Crying from down the hall guides me to a bedroom on the first floor.

Marko squirms on the mattress. His PJ shirt is a crumpled mess on the floor, covered in vomit.

"Chloe!" Marko cries out the moment he sees me.

Santiago stands by Marko's side and clutches his hand with a steel grip. He looks over his shoulder, and relief instantly floods his face. "Thank you so much for coming. I'm so grateful that you're here."

I push aside the fluttering in my stomach at his sincerity. *Pull yourself together, Chloe. This man is bad news. He's the human equivalent of the newspaper's obituary section.*

"No problem. Let me check him out." I place my hand on Santiago's shoulder and give it a squeeze. The muscles tense under my touch.

"Seriously. I owe you. I have no clue how to fix this or how to help." The wrinkles in Santiago's forehead lessen. He steps back, giving me some room.

I smile down at Marko. "Hey, little guy."

"Hi," Marko rasps, sitting taller.

"What's up?" I brush his damp hair away from his forehead and press my hand onto it. "At least he doesn't feel hot. That's good news."

"I go *bleh*." Marko scrunches his nose.

"I think his fever broke after he threw up the second time." Santiago's breath heats my neck, making me shiver.

Chloe, focus on the child, not the hulking figure behind you.

"I miss Mommy. She kisses me better," Marko mumbles.

"I know. Mommy wishes she could be here, too. Will you drink some water? It might make you feel better." I grab the plastic bottle off the nightstand and pass it to him.

Marko snatches it from my hands and sucks on the straw.

I turn to Santiago. "What did you both eat today?"

"Nothing out of the normal. I made our usual pancakes in the morning, pasta for lunch, and then chicken and rice for dinner."

"And you ate all the same food? Are you feeling okay?"

"Yeah, and I feel fine. The only difference is the snacks he eats, but he's been having those the entire time he's been here. He never got sick before."

I think back to my daycare training. "Any food allergies?"

He tugs at his thick hair. "No. He can eat anything and everything."

"Then he must have a stomach virus."

"Uh, Princess?" Marko taps my shoulder.

"Yeah?" I turn to him.

"I don't feel good again." His face, even in the dim lighting, loses some of its coloring.

I freeze. "Oh, no! Where's the bucket, Santiago?"

"Bucket?"

Ugh. Maybe I can get him to the bathroom before—

The water Marko chugged makes a return appearance, and I am not a fan of the encore. It saturates the comforter.

Santiago mumbles something under his breath.

My chest tightens at Marko crying again. I throw the duvet off Marko's legs and bundle it up on the corner of the mattress.

I cringe as Marko's wails become ragged coughs. "If he keeps this up, we might need to take him to the hospital."

"My sister would freak out and rush back here. If you have another idea, I'm all for it." Santiago's voice hits a new level of panicky.

"Okay, it's fine. Relax. Let's see what happens over the next hour. We should move him to your bed so you can keep an eye on him." I step out of the way to give Santiago room to grab Marko. Each step he makes is followed by a heavy thud.

I check out the hardware attached to his leg. I've never seen anything like it before. His right leg is strapped into some kind of device where he can kneel on a pad attached to a stabilized pole. His knee and stump lie comfortably on the padding, covered by some kind of protective sock.

Marko crawls into Santiago's waiting arms.

I sneak another peek at the special kind of walking crutch. "Do you want me to carry him instead?"

His back tenses.

Way to go saying the wrong thing.

His back rises and falls as he takes a deep breath. "Don't do that."

"Do what?"

"Don't start treating me like I'm different now," he whispers.

My body locks up at the broken rasp in his voice. Even after he lied to me, my heart aches for him in a way I've never felt before. He makes it impossible to stay mad at him. Not with him looking defeated, plagued by whatever thoughts eat away at him.

"I carry him like this every night after he falls asleep in my bed. It's not a big deal." He turns toward the door, not bothering to look at me.

How can I make the sadness in his voice disappear?

Think, Chloe, think.

"No one should look as good as you do while carrying a

kid. You're a risk to women's ovaries exploding all across the world," I call out as I imagine a swarm of brunette face-palm emojis floating around my head.

What can I say? There's no better way to break the awkwardness than to compliment a man. Their egos are like starved plants in need of sunshine.

I catch his smirk before he turns out of the room. *Boom*. Achievement unlocked.

I'm not lying either. Watching Santiago carry Marko is the ultimate eye candy. Forget abs and corded arms. After this display, I'm all about men cradling little kids and kissing their foreheads. Santiago officially made the top of my sexy list.

Okay, who am I kidding? He *is* the list.

I follow behind the two of them, fascinated by the way Santiago moves on his device. Santiago walks slower, with the sound of the stabilizer echoing off the walls of his house. He still remains agile with the crutch-like device, clearly comfortable in his environment. To be honest, he's more graceful than me, and I have both legs firmly planted on the ground.

He stops walking. "I can practically feel your eyes on me."

"Sorry. I'm too curious for my own good." I blush. I'm grateful to be standing behind him because the last thing I need is to show him how flustered I am.

"Trust me, I'm well aware."

"What do you call it?"

"An iWalk. It's what I like to wear when I don't want to go through the hassle and discomfort of the leg." He continues walking.

Something tells me the simple admission about his pain and discomfort took a lot out of him. It's the first time he's addressed his disability to me in a matter-of-fact way rather than something to be ashamed of. I find myself wanting to encourage more of that out of him.

Ugh. He's right. I'm too curious and I'm bound to get hurt by it.

I cover up my surprise. "It's the coolest thing I've ever seen. Marko is right. You *are* Iron Man."

Santiago's back shakes from silent laughter. "You should check out my other gadgets and gizmos."

"I don't know if that's an innuendo for something not PG rated."

Santiago grumbles something I can't hear before speaking louder. "You don't want anything but PG from me." He enters his bedroom, leaving me in the hall.

I take a moment to catch my breath. Why is this man so infuriating? And worse, why do I care about changing the way he perceives himself? *He lied, Chloe. You're only here to help Marko, not learn more about his uncle.*

This is how I get in trouble every single time. I think I can fix damaged people when they end up like my mom— disappointing and chronically allergic to stability.

I walk inside his bedroom. The light from the full moon beams through a large window, guiding our movements. Santiago carries Marko to the bathroom and helps him brush his teeth.

The aesthetic of the room fits the owner, with dark colors and few mementos. His space lacks anything to help me understand the man who lives here. It's honestly rather sad. I find Santiago's room nothing like my bedroom at home that bursts with everything I love in the world. Growing up in a foster home made me appreciate every inch of space, making every place I live in a home.

A masculine four-poster bed dominates the middle of the room with its huge mattress. I resist the temptation to jump on it and test the springs.

"Sleepover?" Marko mumbles, his eyes drooping.

"You're sleeping with me tonight." Santiago helps him get settled into the middle of the bed, the dark covers swallowing him.

"Chloe. Stay." Marko pats the bed next to him.

My eyes snap from the bed to Santiago. He doesn't bother looking at me, instead choosing to focus on his hands. *Thanks for nothing.*

"Uhm. I'm going to sit on the living room couch for an hour just in case you need me." I move to make my exit.

"No," Marko whines.

I struggle to resist. Damn kids with their tiny frowns and sad eyes. How can anyone ever say no to them?

"Do you mind?" I look over at Santiago.

Please mind. Say this is a bad idea and let's call it a night.

He shakes his head.

Bastard.

I grumble to myself as I tug at the laces of my sneakers and rip them off. Climbing into Santiago's bed is nothing short of an experience. The mattress is made of a foam voodoo, and I sigh as my body sinks into the cushion.

Santiago is going to have to hire a crane to lift me out because I'm never leaving this bed.

Marko snuggles into my side and places his head on my chest. "Mommy holded me like this." He plucks my hand and places it on his back. "*Tio*. You too." He does the same patting of the bed that sucked me in.

Santiago stares at me and visibly swallows.

I grin. *How do you like it now, traitor?*

His hands clench in front of him, forming two tight balls.

"*Tio*," Marko speaks louder, his voice croaking.

Santiago drops his head, letting out the longest breath.

"It's fine. This bed is big enough to fit a whole family," I offer, hoping to ease his discomfort.

He climbs onto the bed and turns his back toward us. Distinct clicking sounds break the silence as he works to remove the straps of his iWalk. He places his sock covering on the nightstand with a shaky hand.

My heart aches at his distress. I want to say something to make him feel better, but I'm not sure how he will react.

Santiago's muscles strain as he gets situated under the covers. I keep my eyes focused on his face to offer him some privacy, but not enough that he thinks I'm turned off by him. I refuse to go down that path again because I won't survive kissing him again. The only one we had is forever ingrained in my memory, with my lips tingling at the idea.

Marko grabs my hand and links it with Santiago's. An electric feeling spreads across my skin from the contact. Santiago flexes his hand before tightening his grip on mine. *Does he feel the same kind of connection between us?* How can he not? It's like sparks shooting off our skin whenever we touch.

"All better. Like Mommy and Daddy when I is scared." Marko pats our united hands.

I crack a smile at Marko trying to recreate what makes him comfortable.

It doesn't take long for Marko to fall asleep on me. He eventually lets out soft snores as he breathes in and out.

"Thank you for coming to save the day. I don't know what I would have done without you." Santiago's eyes remain focused on the ceiling.

"You're welcome."

It feels like ten minutes before he says anything again. "You could've said no."

"I know I might have some cons, but I'm not exactly evil."

"Just lethal." A faint smile crosses his lips.

I let out a low laugh.

Santiago turns his head toward mine. "I'm sorry I lied to get out of going on the boat with you."

My eyes find his. A spectrum of feelings pours out of him from one single look. Pain. Sadness. Regret. It's the same look I recognize in myself throughout the years. Seeing it on someone else hits me in a different way, forcing me to empathize with him.

I shelve the desire to say something snappy back at him about liars always apologizing. Instead, I let out a heavy sigh. Marko doesn't flinch when my chest moves.

"I regret lying to you," he whispers. "In the end, it was all for nothing. I let my own insecurity rule my behavior, and it didn't even matter. I upset you by wanting to prevent you from seeing exactly what I showed you tonight. Except this version is way worse."

"Why?" One word, a bunch of different questions that need an answer. I attempt to pull my hand out from his grasp, no longer needing to pretend for Marko's sake.

Santiago holds on. "I was nervous for you to see me in

nothing but a swimsuit and my leg." He pauses. "No one sees me that way except my family. When I invited you to go swimming, I didn't realize my mistake. Everything felt so…"

Natural. I want to fill in the word for him, but I stop myself. My heart cracks for this man who struggles to come to terms with himself. Low self-esteem is a tough battle. His confession hits me differently because he looks like an Adonis in every sense of the word. Yet again, Santiago reveals another layer of himself I can't help appreciating.

How can someone who looks so perfect be so flawed?

"I don't care about something like a prosthetic leg, but you refuse to accept it. Your injury doesn't define you. Your decisions do." I shut my eyes, wanting to escape his gaze. Yet everything about our proximity has my body aware of him in ways I wish weren't possible.

Silence cloaks the air. His grip on my hand loosens, and I slip out of his grasp.

I stay awake and wait for a reply that never comes. Eventually, I fall asleep to Marko's steady breathing.

Marko thankfully slept through the rest of the night with no more stomach issues. Somehow, I didn't suffocate Marko with my usual habit of cuddling someone to death. Santiago kept to his side of the bed, and Marko rolled over to lie on top of his uncle in the middle of the night.

Santiago looks peaceful and unplagued by the worries that force his face into a permanent scowl. It takes everything in me not to watch him snooze, stuck between being a creep and offering the man some privacy.

I pull myself away from the bed, grab my sneakers off the floor, and exit Santi's room without making a noise. While his confession last night about his reason for lying touched my heart, I can't find it in myself to speak more about it today. Not when I need time to decompress from the whole experience.

As I walk down the main road, my eyes land on my father's house. I hate the stupid gate standing between us—a physical barrier as much as an emotional one. It reminds me of my failure and lack of confidence to approach Matteo and be honest.

Here I am getting angry at Santiago when I'm just as much of a liar. A stupid, cowardly liar who can't face the one obstacle getting in the way of what I want.

But I have a good reason to lie. I'm afraid of being rejected by another parent.

I turn away from the gate, unable to face any more feelings for the day. I've reached my limit of bullshit, especially when it comes from my own self.

CHAPTER THIRTEEN

Chloe

I clutch onto the handle of the mop as I swipe it across the floor of the shop. The bell above the door chimes and I turn to face the newcomers.

"Hi, Chloe!" Marko waves. His headphones match his Iron Man costume.

I turn in time, dropping the mop as Marko runs into my arms for a hug. "Hey! I'm happy to see you're feeling better."

"No more pukey." Marko makes a funny face.

"I like your suit. Reminds me of someone I know." I look at Santiago. He wears a ball cap, hiding his eyes beneath the bill. His T-shirt and jeans mold to his firm torso. *Sigh*.

He smirks when my eyes connect with his. "Hey."

Busted. How does one word out of his mouth make all the nerves in my body fire off in unison?

My cheeks heat. "Hi."

His lip twitches. He sets Marko up at an empty table with his iPad before walking back toward me. "I didn't get a chance to say thank you again before you snuck off this morning."

He came all the way over here to say thanks? My heart betrays me, racing in my chest. "Yeah. I didn't want to be late for my shift."

"I see." Santiago looks around the empty shop. Matteo is working in the back office, counting supplies since it's a slow day.

"So..." I rock back on my heels.

"Well, I actually need to tell you something. You fell asleep last night and..." His voice trails off. His eyes slide down my body, and I feel every second of it.

"Well, to be fair, you didn't say anything for a while and I kind of knocked out."

He smiles, small and hesitant. "Yeah. About that... I don't want to have more lies between us. It was fun—and a bit messed up—pretending in front of Maya and Noah about us, but that's not how I usually am. I swear you've seen the worst parts of me."

"Are you sure there's a good part?"

He laughs. "Maybe. But really, my sister was excited about the idea of you so I just went along with it. She's going through a rough time, and I did the first thing I thought would take her mind off things. And to be fair, a fake girlfriend was the first idea I could come up with to explain why there was a stranger in my house. But either way, it's not right, and I plan on confessing the truth to her once—"

"You don't have to do that. It's fine. We can make something up instead. But it should be your last lie."

"Okay." Santiago clears his throat, bringing my attention to his thick neck and the muscles bulging out of the back of his shirt. He removes his cap and runs his hand through his roguish hair. The muscles in his arms twitch, attempting to say hello.

Seriously. Can he please be less appealing?

My eyes slide from his body to his face. "Was that all you needed to tell me?"

"No. I don't want you to be mad, but there's something else you need to know about me. I'm hoping my honesty about the situation makes up for the dishonesty in the first place because I like hanging out with you. For real. So, please don't be too angry, okay?" His voice carries a hopeful note, but his words make me apprehensive.

"It's not fair to ask someone not to be mad before you—"

"*Oh, mio dio, sei Santiago Alatorre!*"

Santiago's eyes widen. "I thought you were alone." He curses under his breath.

I look over my shoulder to find Matteo's mouth opening before closing again.

Matteo catches himself. He walks up to Santiago and offers his trembling hand. "You're here! In my shop! Wow! My family has always been a huge fan of racing, and when we heard you were living here, we couldn't believe it. Especially since no one has seen you in person. But here you are in my shop of all places!" Matteo's cheeks turn bright red.

I turn toward Santiago. I look so damn hard at him that I wonder if my eyes will turn into lasers. Who is he and why does Matteo recognize him? And what does Matteo mean about *racing*?

"A fan?" My voice croaks.

"Let me explain." Santiago's eyes snap from me to Matteo

and back to me again.

My stomach churns at the look on his face.

Matteo pushes through, clearly not reading the room. "Of course. We've been Bandini loyalists for decades." His face looks like a kid on Christmas morning. This is the most excitement I've seen from my father, and it happens to be toward the one person I clearly don't know much about.

The only thing I do know is Santiago Alatorre is a liar. A big, fat, impossibly handsome liar.

"My son is a huge fan of yours and your brother-in-law. He says you guys were the best duo in years." Matteo smiles.

A powerful wave of jealousy hits me. Matteo has a fucking son? My knees tremble, and I lock my legs to prevent myself from falling over. Jealousy coils around my heart and gives it a squeeze.

"Your son?" I choke on the words.

Matteo nods. His eyes scan my face, and his lips turn down. "Are you okay? You look pale."

"I didn't know you had a son. He's never come by here before."

"Oh, yes. He's living in Milan, doing a summer internship hosted by his university."

I attempt to get a hold of myself, but the world spins in a way that has me stumbling. Never during all of Brooke's research did she find information about a son.

Santiago wraps an arm around me and pulls me into his side. I want to rip his hands off me for lying about something that seems pretty damn fundamental, but I'm also grateful for his presence. Matteo keeps dropping too many bombs for me to process them all at once.

Matteo's eyes snap from my face to Santiago's arm. "Wait, Chloe. How do *you* know Santiago?"

Somehow, I gather my wits and plaster a smile on my face. Out of the hundred responses I could say, I settle on the one I hope gives me better access to my father's inner circle. If the way to his heart is through his son, I'm willing to take a few hits.

I stand taller. "Matteo, meet Santiago Alatorre, my boyfriend."

The way Matteo's eyes light up has me excited about my choice.

Sorry, Santiago Alatorre. He might be the King of Lies, but I'm the Ace of Spades. And that only means one thing for him.

Game over.

CHAPTER FOURTEEN

SANTIAGO

Her boyfriend? *What. The. Fuck.* That's all my brain can come up with as Chloe pats my hand covering her hip. Is this how she felt when I did the same? I've got to give it to her—this round of payback is a whole other level of crazy.

Matteo's phone rings from some back room and he frowns as he rushes to answer it.

I move to take back my hand but Chloe's palm presses against mine. "Don't."

One word has me freezing. Does she understand what she just did?

Of course, she doesn't. You didn't bother telling her who you were last night and now this is karma.

Yeah, karma, well fuck you. No one likes the asshole who says, "I told you so."

Matteo rushes back into the main dining area. "I'm so sorry, but I have to go pick up my friend. I hate to leave." He frowns at me.

Chloe's face brightens. "Oh! That's okay! What if we invite you over for dinner next week?"

I grind my teeth together. Now she's inviting random people over to my house? I want to interrupt and cancel these plans before they have a chance to flourish, but the smile on Chloe's face has me second-guessing myself. Maybe playing her fake boyfriend for a couple of occasions in front of her boss isn't the worst thing ever. It's not like I have much else to do once Marko leaves. Plus, I don't mind her brand of positivity. It beats living by myself, counting the days from my bed.

Matteo's frown morphs into a smile. "Really?"

Chloe nods. "Sure. I'd love to spend time with you."

I raise my brows. Something about the way Chloe trips over her words throws me off. No one acts *that* excited about dinner with their boss.

Matteo's enthusiasm makes him blind to the meaning behind Chloe's words. "Great. We can set a date when you come in for tomorrow's shift. I can't wait. Here's the spare key for you to lock up the shop." He places it on the counter. "Santiago Alatorre! Wow!" He beams at me before walking out the front door of his shop.

When Matteo disappears, she steps away from me.

"Who the hell are you?" The happiness she had toward Matteo slips away as she stares at me with narrowed eyes and reddened cheeks.

I'm desperate to have her smile at me again. Anything but this angry version of her would do.

"How badly do you want to know the truth?"

"More than I want to hear a lie," she bites.

I look up at the ceiling, praying for the right words. "Remember when you thought Noah was an actor?"

"Yes."

"Well…he's not."

"You don't say," she spits out with heavy sarcasm.

"Have you heard of Formula 1?" I can't believe I'm asking someone this question. This is most definitely a first for me.

"Kind of? Is that the one where they drive around in circles like the movie *Cars*?"

A laugh bursts out of me. "No. That's NASCAR. Please don't insult me again by comparing F1 to that."

Her scowl deepens.

Okay… "Why don't we take a seat?" I point to an empty table across from Marko. The kid hasn't bothered looking up since we got here because he's immersed in whatever movie is playing on his iPad.

I fumble, pulling out a chair for Chloe. "So, my brother-in-law is probably the best Formula 1 racer of the decade. Hell, maybe the whole sport."

"Okay…" She sits. "And you are?"

I take a seat across from her. "…I *was* his teammate." My eyes drop to my lap. "Before my injury."

Her mouth pops open at the same time as her eyes widen. "You mean to tell me that you're some famous race car driver, and you kept that a secret from me this entire time?"

I lift my hands up in submission. "To be fair, I didn't have much of a chance to tell you. Between pretending we were in a relationship—"

"Oh, you mean the lie of a relationship you started?"

I swallow, hoping to ease the dryness in my throat. "Right…between that and everything else, I kept going with it."

"Don't give me some half-assed excuse. Own up to what you did because you had plenty of time after to explain who you were."

Damn. I enjoy her form of bluntness. I'm not one for reading between the lines anyway.

"I'm sorry that I lied. It's my fault, and I'm not excusing that part. But you have to believe me when I say I didn't do it from a malicious place. Not at all."

"Then why do it in the first place? Why not come clean once your sister left? You pretended to be someone you're not in front of me for two weeks."

"Because you didn't look at me like I was *that* guy. You treat me like the man I am *now*, rather than the one I once was. And that was something special to me that I wanted to hold on to for a bit longer. My reasoning was purely selfish, but I didn't mean to hurt you. I came here today to admit the truth to you because I couldn't stand lying to you anymore about it. Because you value honesty, and I value the way you act around me." The words pour out of me, raw and earnest.

There it is. The god-honest truth that made me desperate to keep my secret from Chloe.

Her eyes soften, and her grimace turns into a flat line. "And how do I act around you?"

"Like you want to get to know who I am without the fame, fortune, and baggage associated with my name. And that's something that doesn't happen to me anymore."

"That's because I didn't know it existed in the first place."

I shake my head. "No. After spending time with you, I know you wouldn't have cared about it either way. It was stupid of me to think you'd change by knowing what I did before."

"I honestly still have no idea who you are." Her laugh comes out a bit panicked.

"You know more than I've shared with anyone since my accident. How many people do you think I've let see me with my iWalk?"

"Umm…a handful?"

"None. Besides you and Marko, that is."

Her brows raise. "Really? Not even your family?"

I shake my head from side to side.

She rears back. "Why?"

"Because I don't like showing any kind of weakness. *Especially* to my family."

Chloe frowns. "It's not a weakness to need something like that. Iron Man would agree." She nods her head towards Marko.

My lips twitch, fighting a smile. Seriously, she has this ability to erase the ice in my veins whenever I speak about my injury. "I'm sorry about lying and taking advantage of the situation."

"I'm sorry too. It's not like I'm completely innocent either. I went along with it all and lied to your family. And I just lied to my"—she stares off into the distance—"to Matteo."

"Who is he to you anyway?"

"Someone important."

"Does he know that?"

"No." She looks down at her hands. "He doesn't."

"Why?" I speak low, without judgment.

Her head lifts. "He's my dad. But he doesn't know that I exist in the first place." She goes off, explaining her ancestry kit experiment and how she ended up in Lake Como.

She wrings her hands together. "After I saw how he reacted around you, I kind of freaked out and said the first thing I thought would keep him interested in seeing me outside of here." She waves a hand around the coffee shop. "I've tried multiple times to get him to go to lunch after my shift and he always has something else to do. I was getting desperate. But I'm sorry for using you like that. I wouldn't have done it if I had known you're actually some celebrity."

No wonder she pretended I was her boyfriend. He practically tripped over his feet to meet me, and she took advantage of the opportunity. I can't blame her when I basically did the same with my sister.

"It shouldn't matter who I am. You told him I'm your boyfriend, and I doubt you can go and take that back. Plus, there's no reason to."

"Why? I'll just pretend we broke up." Her eyes drift away from mine. "Honestly, it's probably for the best. I don't want to lie to him either. That makes me a big hypocrite."

"Do you feel ready to tell him who you are?"

She shakes her head from side to side. "Not at all. Today was honestly the first time I saw him animated like that. He's nice and all, don't get me wrong, but he treats me like an employee."

I feel like shit. Here she is trying to connect with her dad, and I'm stealing his attention after a few minutes. An instantaneous flood of guilt hits me, wanting to make amends. "Then no. You can't tell him the truth yet. Lying be damned, you should spend some time around him," I blurt out.

"Why don't you want me to tell him the truth?"

"Because you can spend some more time with him, using me as a way to keep his interest." God, I hope that's not the case. It's sad enough that she traveled all this way to find him, only to be hiding. It must be lonely for her.

Just like it is for me.

Her brows lift. "Why on earth would you want me to use you?"

"Let's say I have my own selfish reasons for wanting you around."

And in all honesty, I do. I like the way Chloe makes me feel normal again. It's something I need more of, and this sacrifice seems like a small price to pay. I can build my confidence around her while she uses me as a prop.

"I feel like I'm getting the better end of the deal here."

I shake my head from side to side. "I can assure you that you're most definitely not."

"Well...If you insist, I suppose it's not the worst idea out there." Her blue eyes brighten as they land on me.

I sit taller in my chair and lean in. "I'll only ask for one favor in return."

"What?"

"Join Marko and me for dinner tomorrow. It's his last night before he leaves, and he hasn't stopped talking about you since he first met you."

"Why?"

"Because it's about time we get to know each other. The real us."

"For consistency. Smart."

She wants consistency, I want someone to ease the loneliness I'll feel once Marko leaves. This solution is the best of both worlds.

And with a nod of her head, I know I've got her trapped. She gets to spend time with her dad because of me, and I get to feel like a better version of myself.

It's a win-fucking-win.

CHAPTER FIFTEEN

Chloe

"Let me get this straight: Santiago is famous, you lied to your dad and told him that Santiago is your boyfriend, and you plan on hosting a dinner like a happy couple to spend more time with said father who still doesn't know your true identity?" Brooke's voice echoes through the phone.

"Yes." I pinch the bridge of my nose and fall onto my mattress with a loud thud. "On a scale 0 to 10, how bad is this idea?"

"You broke the rating system in the best kind of way. Imagine how fun this will be." Brooke's fingers typing across a keyboard echo through the speaker. "Wait. Santiago is *really* fucking famous! Oh my God!"

I pull the phone away from my ear. "Brooke! Stop googling him!"

"But he's worth over 100 million dollars! How the hell did you trap this guy?"

"It's fake, so I didn't exactly trap him."

"Well, damn. It's never too late to try. You should charge him for your 'girlfriend' services. He can spare a few thousand dollars. *Trust me*. I'm checking out the layout of his yacht right freaking now! You know, because your *boyfriend* had *GQ* interview him."

"He's the one who should be charging *me*. I'm the one who needs his help now."

"Ugh, you're no fun." Her mouse clicks in the background. She mumbles something about a private car collection and a house in Spain before I stop her.

"Can you quit prying into his life?"

"No. This is the most fun I've had all year! Have pity on a small-town girl who needs a little romance in her life."

"You were born in New York City."

"Excuse me, Little Miss Buzzkill. Fine. I was born with a small-town heart. Plus, it's not every day your best friend dates someone famous! Give me a break. You'd be disappointed if I didn't google him for you."

"*Fake* dating. And I don't want to know what the internet says about him."

"What about the reports on how he's hung like a horse?"

"No! Not even that!" I screech. The memory of his impressive erection pressing against me on the night we met is permanently burned into my brain.

Brooke giggles to herself. "How about the story about how he eats pussy like a seven-course meal? Or that his favorite position happens to be cowgirl because the view from below is worth the lack of dominance."

"Oh my freaking God, where are you getting this

information? Stop it!" My skin heats from Brooke's gossip.

Nothing I chant to myself erases the images from my head. They play on a loop, reminding me why I can look but can't touch. Been there, kissed that. Anything with Santiago spells trouble in two different languages.

Brooke rambles on. "I have my sources on the dark internet."

"Reddit doesn't count as the dark web."

"Okay, fine. But it's a good site for this kind of shit. How else would you know about his dick size?"

"Uhm, by touching it?"

She scoffs. "Please. You wouldn't remember your way around a dick if an anatomy book hit you in the head."

"I hate you. Just because it's been a long time since I had any kind of intimate relationship, doesn't mean I don't remember how to please someone else."

"No, you love that I call you out on the lack of male company lately. If you don't orgasm on the spot by touching his nine-inch cock, then I'm banishing you from our apartment. Don't bother coming back."

A laugh erupts from me. "What has gotten into you?"

"You're fake dating someone who's rumored to tongue-fuck pussy like he doesn't need oxygen to breathe."

I ignore the way my skin prickles, hoping the rush of blood through my body settles. "Do people truly share that kind of info? About his—" I wince. "That's such an invasion of privacy."

"What do you expect? He's *famous*. You lose all rights to being considered human the moment TMZ features multiple stories about you."

"What do I do? I shouldn't have agreed to dinner tonight with Marko. Shoot, I shouldn't have agreed to any of this. Fake dating is my worst idea yet."

"Relax and enjoy it. All you've done in your short life is grow up way too fast and work until you drop. I'm telling you to strap on your cowgirl boots and go for a ride. After dinner, that is, because you don't need to scar the little kid, no matter how tempting the dining table looks for some good fucking."

"You're the worst support system. You should tell me this is a terrible idea and I should cancel."

"It *is* a terrible idea, which is exactly why you should do it! What's the harm in faking it in front of his family and yours a couple of times? You both get something out of it."

"I don't like using people." The idea alone makes me feel icky.

"You're not her."

Resembling anything close to my mother is the last thing I want in life. I can't deny how everything spiraling out of control reminds me of her. "Yeah, well, lately it feels like that with the lies piling up."

"Listen, it's normal for you to worry about turning out like your mom, but this is different. Santiago is a willing participant."

"Yeah, but—"

"No buts. Didn't he agree to hosting a dinner with your dad next week once Marko leaves and things settle down?"

"Yes."

"Okay. Does that sound like someone who is being forced?"

I bite into my bottom lip. "No."

"Would a normal person agree to be used?"

"Not a sane one."

"See! It's mutual then. You help him, he helps you. Now... if you want his help in the bedroom, I'm sure he'd be happy to oblige as well."

"I can't anymore with you!"

"Holy shit!" Brooke gasps.

"What?"

"You didn't tell me his sister is Maya Slade! She's YouTube famous. I watched her vlog last year when I was manifesting a trip to Switzerland."

"What?" With every new piece of information that comes to light about Santiago Alatorre, a year is shaved off my life.

"She does a bunch of travel and lifestyle videos. I didn't connect Santiago's name and hers when you mentioned him! Oh my God. Noah fucking Slade!" Brooke screams a string of words into the phone. "That's it, I'm packing my bags. You need a partner-in-crime, and I straight up just need a partner. They have to have some hot, famous friend for little old me."

I laugh up to the ceiling, loving Brooke for erasing my concerns about seeing Santiago tonight. "If you come here, you'll never leave."

"Don't tempt me."

CHAPTER SIXTEEN

Chloe

Tonight is nothing like my last visit. For starters, Marko abandons me the moment I step into the house. He sits on the living room couch with his eyes glued to the television. His absence makes Santiago's presence that much more daunting, like a dark force swallowing me whole. I, for one, am afraid of some unsupervised time with the tall man who checks all my boxes and then some.

He leads me into his luxurious kitchen. The smells coming from the stove and oven have me salivating. It's nothing I'm used to.

Santiago knowing how to cook completely disarms me in a new kind of way. I lean against the counter, captivated by him cutting up onions like he's a hot Spanish version of Gordon freaking Ramsey. His arms flex with every movement. The five minutes I spend drooling on the counter solidifies my commitment to binging every cooking show available on TV. Screw *Love Island*, I'm here for the kitchen island.

Thank God I have him locked down as a fake boyfriend. He shouldn't be allowed in the dating world with talents like his.

I laugh to myself at my possessiveness over something unreal.

He looks up from the cutting board. "What's so funny?"

"Oh, nothing," I say to his straining bicep.

He tightens his hold on the knife, forcing the muscles in his arm to flex.

My cheeks warm as I lift my gaze, catching his eyes. "I didn't know you could cook. Like *really* cook, you know, with fancy knives and real vegetables."

"I'm almost scared to ask what you mean by 'real vegetables.'" He fake shudders.

"Hey, don't judge. I'm not talented in the kitchen so I make do with the frozen stuff."

"Frozen stuff? Why would you do that?"

"Here's a rough summary: I burn bread."

The laugh he lets out makes goosebumps spread across my skin. "That's like my sister. She couldn't find her way through a kitchen if you gave her step-by-step instructions and a video tutorial."

"I'd burn the guide and call for takeout. It sounds like the safest option for everyone involved."

"Are you willing to learn?"

"To cook?" I ogle him while licking my bottom lip. The idea of Santiago teaching me something domestic has me practically panting.

His eyes darken as they drop to my tongue. "Can you stop doing that? It's distracting." He drags his thumb across my bottom lip, drying it.

I choke on my inhale of breath. My fingers clutch onto the counter as I fight hacking up a lung. "What?"

"Do you want to help me?" He ignores my question and points to the ingredients covering the counter.

"Really?"

"I'll consider it my duty to society. We can't have you out in the world eating frozen vegetables and risking the lives of others by burning bread." He smirks.

I flash him a smile, enjoying his lightheartedness. "If I went back to America knowing how to make anything besides instant Mac and Cheese, I think my best friend, Brooke, would personally send you a gift basket."

Santiago chuckles, rough and warm. "Do you know how to peel potatoes?"

I nod. "Brooke and I attempted a few too many unsuccessful holiday dinners."

He passes me the peeler and the bowl of potatoes. "How about you do that while I finish up here?" He resumes his chopping.

I work at the pace of an arthritic grandmother, not wanting my time with Santiago to end. The way he completes tasks takes the definition of food porn to a whole new level. He moves along, working on different ingredients with such ease. I'm seriously tempted to fan myself with an oven mitt.

I grab another potato from the bowl and get to work. "What are you making for dinner?"

"Empanadas because they're Marko's favorite, and other tapas for us."

Seriously, this man is a whole other level of irresistible. He cooks, he babysits, and he's grumpy. My kind of kryptonite.

"Wow. Most kids like pizza and chicken nuggets, yet he likes fancy-sounding Spanish food."

"Empanadas are anything but fancy." Santiago laughs.

Way to make yourself sound classy to a millionaire, Chloe. "Oh. Right." I ignore the heat crawling up my neck, hoping Santiago misses it.

Based on how his smile grows larger, I can't count myself as that fortunate. His stare zaps my skin to life. "I can see why you think that based on how many ingredients we need. It's my mom's recipe. She taught me this one when I was a little older than Marko."

"Really? Your mom is a smart woman, training you from a young age to be ideal husband material." The words escape me before my filter intervenes. I'd smack myself if I didn't have my hands occupied.

"More like I would beg *Mami* to teach me so I could steal pieces before dinner. But I won't lie, it does come in handy though when I'm trying to impress a beautiful woman."

Of course he cooks to lure in unsuspecting women. Why would I think I'm such a special snowflake that he cooks with?

"Has anyone told you that you have an extremely expressive face?" He points the tip of his knife in my direction.

If I had any sense of self-preservation, I'd consider it serial killer scary. "No. Why?"

"Because your smile dropped after I spoke. I should be clearer. I'm impressing *you* through empanadas, tapas, and good wine."

My heart goes into overdrive, racing in my chest. "Really?"

He winks. I blush. The cycle repeats itself.

I clear my throat. "So, where is the wine you speak of because I could use a glass right about now?"

He shakes his head with a smile. "Not until after the pointy objects get put away."

We work side by side, with Santiago explaining each step of the process. Together, we make a batch of empanadas. The ones I created are a bit wonky and stuffed to the brim, but Santiago laughed and cooked them anyway.

Santiago works on a couple of his tapas while I chug a glass of wine.

Marko comes when Santiago calls his name. The three of us sit together and eat, acting like some happy little family I have only experienced in Santiago's presence. My youth didn't include anything close to this. But instead of the typical coldness seeping through my veins at the idea of my past, a shot of something warm spreads through my chest.

Oh God. Don't go getting attached to something you can never have.

I push aside the thoughts and focus all my attention on Marko. He distracts me with his babbling about all the fun stuff he did with his uncle today before I showed up.

"What are you doing next, Marko?" I look over at him.

"Mommy and Daddy take me racing." He makes a zooming noise resembling a car as he flies an empanada into his mouth.

"Racing? Wow!" I laugh at the sight of him. The kid is so stinkin' cute, I want him to stay for another week.

"They're off to the next Prix once Maya picks him up tomorrow and joins Noah. They'll spend the summer traveling around with the team before Marko starts school again."

"That's fun! Where are they going next?"

"Monza for the Italian Grand Prix." He speaks low.

Marko claps his hands. "Yes! Italy! Daddy wins!"

I smile. "How do you know?"

"He's the bestest."

Santiago's smile drops. The change is dark and unmistakable. Memories have a way of torturing us all, no matter the time or place.

I hate the look that crosses his face. Thinking with my heart rather than my brain, I blurt out something crazy because I want his sadness to disappear. "So, Santiago, what are your plans next week once Marko leaves?"

A couple of wrinkles mar his forehead as his eyebrows pull together. "Nothing much besides our dinner on Tuesday. Someone is delivering a new car for me to restore, so I guess I'll work on that over the next few weeks."

"Oh really? Do you remember that I love fixing cars? It's a new passion of mine."

His frown disappears as he cracks a smile. "Yes. I remember that fact about you. Vintage cars, right?"

"Oh, yes. The older the better." *That sounded like the right thing to say.*

His smile turns into something downright devious. "Weird. I love vintage cars too."

I press my palm into my chest and fake my shock. "Would you look at that? Who knew we had that in common! I'm sure you wouldn't mind if I joined you then to repair whatever car you picked?"

His guarded eyes meet mine. "Why would you want to do that?"

Yeah, Chloe, why? I remain calm and collected despite my racing thoughts. My actions barely make sense to myself, seeing as we never discussed spending time together outside of the ruse. But I can't resist wanting to remove the sad look in his eyes when he thinks about his family racing without him. Even if it means letting my guard down.

CHAPTER SEVENTEEN

Chloe

"I guess I better head out." I intertwine my fingers and rock back on my heels.

With Marko asleep in his bed and all the dishes put away, it seems like the right time to go.

"Do you want to stay a little longer? I can open another bottle of wine?" Santiago rushes to get the words out, his voice hesitant yet hopeful.

Oh God. Is he nervous? I attempt to get a word out, but nothing passes my lips. Me, speechless. Brooke would laugh her ass off at the idea.

"No pressure. If you can't because you have to go to work early tomorrow, then don't worry about it," he rambles on.

Screw him for crawling under my skin and making himself at home. I can't resist nodding my head, agreeing to some one-on-one time with him. It's as if he emits pheromones, trapping me with muscles, a sexy Spanish accent, and timid smiles.

Santiago leads us back into the living room before he leaves to grab a bottle of wine. My eyes land on the label when he enters the room again. It's the same brand I fawned over during dinner, claiming I've never had anything that good since I usually purchase anything with a "buy one, get one free" label. The fact that he grabbed another of the same brand has me nearly falling over from swooning too hard.

Santiago takes a seat on the couch, saving a bit of space between us. I'm thankful for it because I'm seriously doubting my self-control around him tonight. He's acting too sweet for my taste.

He passes me a full glass of wine. His hand brushes mine, sending a current of energy up my arm.

I rip my hand away. "What car do you plan on restoring?"

"A 1951 Jaguar C-Type." He smiles to himself.

"Sounds...luxurious?" The only thing I know about cars is how the ones with the loudest muffler usually signal how there's a man with a small dick nearby.

He laughs in a way that has my toes curling inside of my shoes. "Based on how it looks now, you wouldn't say that."

"Really? Why buy it then?"

"Because the fun is in fixing it up."

"How long have you been doing this hobby?"

He looks away. "Since I could afford it."

I try to hide my surprise. "And when was that?"

"When I made it with racing. Before that, it was a struggle for my family to make ends meet. All of this"—he waves around the room—"took hard work. My parents weren't exactly financially set in life. At least not until I fixed them up with enough savings to live the rest of their lives comfortably."

"Oh. Wow. I didn't know that about you." That small fact about himself has me looking at him in a new light. Maybe we have more in common than I initially thought.

"If you google me, it's probably one of the first things that shows up." He shakes his head. "Wait. Don't google me. That's never a good idea."

Well, technically *I* didn't google him.

His eyes narrow as he scans my face. "You did, didn't you?"

I glance away, melting under his scrutiny. "Umm...not me. Brooke did though. But she didn't tell me much."

"What *did* she say?"

I look everywhere but the source of my embarrassment as if his eyes can detect my thoughts. "Just that you have a net-worth comparable to a small country."

"That's it? Okay, that's not too bad." He scrunches his nose in an adorable way. Good God, adorable? *Chloe, please rein in your ovaries. They're wreaking havoc on your brain.*

"Mm-hmm." I grip my wine glass and chug half of the contents in one go.

His head tilts, and a ghost of a smile crosses his lips. "I like how you can lie to everyone but me. It's rather endearing."

"What?" I sputter.

"I'll give it to you. You're impressive at lying. To my sister, my brother-in-law, your father. It's something that caught my attention about you. But when I have you on my own, you give everything away. So, I'll ask you one more time. What did your roommate say?" The authoritative tone in his voice has my lower half clenching.

"Brooke told me that you have a huge dick worthy of poems."

Santiago's head drops back as he lets out a roar of laughter. "Actually, I've changed my mind. Google me all you want. The naughtier the articles, the better, please."

I lean over and give him a shove. My hand lingers on his forearm before I tug it away, chiding myself for being touchy. "Hey. I didn't research you. Brooke did."

"Brooke is my new favorite person. Maybe I'll be the one to send her the *thank-you* basket, instead."

My eyes flick from his face to his jeans, curiosity eating away at my politeness. "So, you're not denying it then?"

"A man would be stupid to deny those kinds of claims. Especially if they're true."

Oh. My. God. I squirm in my seat. Now I have an idea of what he's packing under those jeans and it has my mind reeling.

He pours himself a bit more wine before topping my glass off. "Now that you know a secret of mine, it's your turn."

"A secret? You're the one boasting about having a steel pipe for a dick. That's not a secret. That's a fact."

Santiago's face turns red as he laughs harder than I've ever heard him before. "Tell me a secret anyway. I feel like I'm at a loss here."

"Secrets take trust, and I don't trust you." My smile drops.

"What would it take you to trust me?"

I sigh. "That's a loaded question since I don't trust people easily. Skip."

His brows furrow. "Why don't you trust others?"

"Why don't *you* trust others? You're the one who lied to me about your identity for two weeks. That decision doesn't scream trust," I snap.

Santiago's eyes widen.

Shit. I mentally sheath my claws. "Sorry, I—"

"It's fine. I'll admit that wasn't my finest moment. As far as trusting others...I've met some of the nastiest people who feed off fame and failure. Seeing the worst in humanity has me understanding the value of people who I can trust."

His answer is far-fetched compared to mine, with his life in the limelight, yet we have similarities I can't deny. Ones that are fundamental, no matter one's circumstance.

"I've seen the worst in people too. And they tend to have a way of disappointing me. Instead of getting my feelings hurt by trusting the wrong person, I'd rather not do it at all."

"What about Brooke?"

"Exception to the rule."

"So, you're willing to break yours about trust then?" His eyes take me prisoner as a smile graces his lips.

"Maybe. Depends on the person."

"That's good enough for me. Plus, maybe you learn how being around bad people gives you the ability to appreciate the good ones." His gaze lingers on my face in a way that makes me feel uncomfortable.

I don't like the easygoing feeling spreading through my body from his words. Nope, nope, nope. I survived years of foster care because I didn't fall for flowery words and empty promises. I'm the one who likes to be in control of how much I share about myself.

His eyes soften. "You might not trust me now, but you will eventually."

"That's quite the claim coming from you."

"I'm not one to state things I don't mean. If it takes you

some more time to open up, that's fine. I'm not exactly going anywhere." He points to his iWalk. "Plus, we have a car to fix up together. You already offered your services."

My heart warms at the notion. It's the first time he's openly addressed his injury without an ounce of contempt. His reaction has me smiling.

"Why do you even want my trust anyway? That's not a requirement of fake dating."

"Because some people in life are worth the extra effort."

My breath catches at his words. I thought it would be fun to drag the hermit out of his shell, but it turns out he's working his own magic on me.

He has me hoping that he proves me wrong. And that in itself is the most concerning thing about him.

"Chloe. I need you to come to my house right now and save me. My mom is on her way," Santiago whispers into the phone.

That's not exactly what I expect to hear come out of Santiago's mouth the moment I answered his phone call.

"Huh?" I rub the sleep from my eyes after my afternoon nap. Work today completely wiped me out because Matteo finally asked me to help him with some rush orders after a swarm of tourists showed up at his shop.

"My mom is coming to my house right now and she's asking for you."

"What?" I rise from the bed. "You didn't mention your mom visiting! And what do you mean 'she's asking for me'?

This was not part of the plan."

"Trust me, you're not the only one who's surprised. But she wants to meet my *girlfriend*."

"Is that even normal for her to show up unannounced?" What kind of family does this man have?

"No," he grumbles. "But I'm guessing Maya's little story got her all kinds of excited. I'll get to the bottom of that issue after."

"Fuck."

"My thoughts exactly."

"This is getting out of control. I'm not ready to meet your mom. I barely know anything about you!"

"You know enough about me to survive meeting my mom. I swear I wouldn't put you in this situation if I didn't think you could fake it. Plus, she's going to want to batter you with questions about yourself, not me."

"Oh, God." So much for Santiago giving me time to open up. This is a total nightmare.

"But I should warn you. My mom can smell a lie from a mile away. Hell, she knew about Noah and Maya liking each other before I did."

I drop my head against the pillows and throw my arm over my eyes. "What do you want me to do? Everything about us is a lie!"

"Well, not everything." His voice drops low.

Goosebumps rise across my skin, reminding me why hanging around him more than necessary is deadly. "How am I supposed to pretend in front of a human polygraph machine?"

"She's going to be busy getting to know you, I doubt she'll

ask you much about me. I'm not the reason she came to visit. So, don't worry. She'll love you."

"Easy for you to say," I grumble under my breath.

He chuckles. "Come and fake it for a few hours until I say you have to go to bed early because you have to work tomorrow. It'll be easy."

"Fine. What's a few hours of questions and your mom?"

This is the moment Morgan Freeman, the narrator of my life, interrupts me to say how this is a very bad idea.

Screw you, narrator. Screw you.

CHAPTER EIGHTEEN

SANTIAGO

"**Y**ou told me you wouldn't tell her anything until I did!" I run both hands through my hair, tugging at the thick strands.

Maya and I both whisper in the kitchen while Marko plays with his toys in the living room. She came by herself to pick up Marko today while Noah busies himself at Bandini's headquarters in Milan, prepping for his Monza race.

Maya throws her hands in the air. "It wasn't me! Marko mentioned her to *Mami* when they talked on the phone this morning after she landed in Madrid. What did you expect me to do? Rip the phone out of his hands and hang up?"

"Is that too much to ask?"

She smacks my shoulder. "Yes. He's a little kid. It's not like he knows what he should or should not say. Plus, once Marko told her the news, she said she was booking a flight and joining me for the next week before Noah's race. Well, that and how she wanted to meet me *here* so she could say hi to you."

"Hi? More like she wanted to interrogate my girlfriend."

I still can't believe my mom is coming here in the next hour to visit.

Maya winces. "Sorry."

"How did she orchestrate this plan in less than a few hours?"

"That's *Mami* for you. I'm pretty sure *Papi* was already driving her back to the airport while she chatted with Marko. She's quick. I'll give her that."

"Great. Just great," I groan. This is the repayment I get for taking care of Marko for two weeks. The last thing I need is more obstacles in my way, especially if it's my mother.

Maya shrugs. "Try not to worry about it too much. She seems very excited about Chloe. Especially after Marko told *Mami* all about how Chloe took care of him when he was sick."

I can't exactly get mad at my nephew for not knowing any better. "Whatever. It's just for one day."

Maya's eyes focus on something behind me. "Well..."

"I'm afraid to ask, but I don't have much of a choice. Spit it out."

"You didn't hear it from me, but *Mami* wants you to attend the Prix with us next weekend."

I release a stream of curses, switching between English and Spanish. The air in the room thickens as the walls around me inch closer. A swell of something ugly and weak blooms in my chest, feeding off my anxiety. Returning to the one place that I promised myself I would avoid at all costs brings about a new wave of panic. I try to gain control over my breathing, but short breaths escape my lips.

Shit. I run a shaky hand through my hair.

Maya's eyes grow wider. "No one expects you to go! Just tell her you can't because you're busy."

"Busy doing what? Watching my investments add up and taking a stroll by the lake? Yeah, amazing lie, Maya. I'll tell her to ask me in another thirty years when my busy schedule frees up from watching the clock tick by."

She looks down at her sneakers. "True."

I pace across the room. "Why does she want me to go?"

"Probably because it's Noah's last Italian race with Bandini. You know that's a big deal."

"He's retiring after this season? What changed?" Holy shit, everyone is going to be after his F1 seat. Noah's been racing with Bandini for over a decade already.

"He was planning to retire after next year, but things… well… He wants to focus on his family, and that's hard when we're moving around all the time. Marko's getting older, and he's starting school and all. We want to grow our family somewhere that's a bit more stable than a private jet or a motorhome."

Damn. I guess Noah plans on retiring early because of her and everything that happened. He gains another ounce of respect from me at this latest admission.

Now I have to go to this race. Monza is a huge deal, and if it's Noah's last one, I'd be the biggest dick on the planet if I stayed home. The selfless notion doesn't sit right with me because it's the last thing I want to do, right up there with getting a colonoscopy or becoming a vegan.

"I'm fucked, aren't I?" I whisper to the ceiling as if it can respond back to me.

"Well, if you're set on going, you could always bring your

girlfriend along with you to make it more bearable."

Now, that's an idea I can work with. Taking Chloe could ease some of the anxiety I have about showing up at a racetrack again. If I concentrate on her and our fake relationship, then I won't have time to harp on the past.

Sorry, little wildflower, but I'm not sure you'll survive my deadly storm.

"Chloe, tell me about America." My mom links her arm with Chloe's. Maya and I follow behind them, hugging the curve of the lake's shore.

"*Mami* is seriously going to pretend she's never been to America?" I mumble under my breath.

Maya elbows my side. "She's being polite. You remember being that way, don't you? You know, back when you did more than growl at people?"

I glare at my sister. Maya laughs and focuses her attention back on Marko.

"Well, New York is way more crowded than this town," Chloe offers.

"Oh, yes. But other parts of Italy are pretty crowded. Have you been to any other cities in Europe yet or has my son been hiding you away from the world?" *Mami* smiles at her.

"Oh, no. I was—I didn't have time yet. I've been working and stuff." Chloe stumbles over her words.

Yup. I'm screwed. Chloe is way too nervous, and my mom isn't helping the situation.

"Wow. I'd expect my son to treat his girlfriend with a

bit more care. It's a shame he hasn't bothered taking you anywhere else, especially since he has been to tons of places himself. He used to love traveling."

"Well this town is pretty great, so there hasn't been a reason to leave yet." Chloe smiles over her shoulder, winking at me. The small gesture distracts me and I trip over a rock.

She laughs before facing my mom. *Mami*'s eyes bounce between Chloe and me, her smile expanding at whatever she finds amusing.

Damn. I take back my last statement. With one smile at my mother, I know Chloe has her wrapped around her pinky. How can she not, when she works the same magic on me?

"Do you know what else is great?" *Mami* grins in a way that has the hairs on my arms rising.

Shit. *Mami* is going to go for it, with or without my approval. I'd be impressed by her sneakiness if I wasn't on the losing end of it.

Chloe's eyes dart from my mom to me. "What?"

"How would you feel about going to an F1 race? My son-in-law is driving and it's his last one."

"In Italy! He still has plenty more." Maya awkwardly laughs and shakes her head.

I appreciate Maya trying to give me an out, but it's not necessary.

"Oh." Chloe bites her lip as her eyes find mine. Whatever she sees has her cheeks tinting to a rosy shade. "Uhm, I don't think I can. We have plans."

Mami's lips purse. "Plans? Like what?"

"Like fixing a car." Chloe nods her head.

I pinch the bridge of my nose. We lost the battle before it even began.

"And...um…" Chloe stammers.

"Well, my son can hold off on fixing one of his twenty-five cars. Right?" *Mami* looks back at me. Her eyes tell me if I say no, I'll be regretting it for quite some time.

"Right." I nod.

I hope Chloe makes this trip tolerable like Maya suggested because I can only imagine the shit show it's bound to become. The idea of revisiting my demons has me sweating and my hands trembling. I haven't seen an F1 racetrack since my accident, let alone been near old fans and coworkers.

Chloe stops in her tracks and holds her hand out to me. She looks like a dark angel, tempting me with a wicked smile and bright eyes. "I'm sure we can make the most out of the trip."

I grab onto her hand, indulging in the energy crackling between us. "Who can resist showing her off to the world?"

She shakes her head. "Well, maybe skip the 'prancing me around in public' part. I don't do well in the spotlight."

"How would you know?" I quirk a brow.

"I threw up on stage during my part in a middle school play."

"It's normal to be nervous during those kinds of things," my sister offers.

"I was a tree. I didn't even have to speak." Chloe's cheeks flood with color.

I pull Chloe into me, relishing in the feel of her. Might as well enjoy her nearness under the guise of pleasing my family. "Oh, that's okay. I'm sure you'll get used to the attention after the first hundred paparazzi questions."

"What are you doing?" she whispers under her breath.

"Having fun for once." I wink, brushing aside a loose strand of her hair and tucking it behind her ear.

Mami and Maya whisper to each other, creating a peanut gallery of two behind us.

Her eyes narrow. "Consider us even after this trip. That is if I survive the heart attack I'm bound to have."

I owe her for more than a weekend outing with my family. She revives a part of me I've neglected over the years, pushing me to be a better version of myself.

Chloe Carter has me hooked, and I can't exactly say I'm sorry about it.

CHAPTER NINETEEN

Chloe

"**A**re you serious? You can't be serious." Brooke stares wide-eyed into the video chat camera.

I bob my head up and down. "I'm about to be announced to the world as Santiago's girlfriend next weekend."

The thought alone has my stomach churning like a washing machine. Why did I agree to this? *Because he did you a solid, and you owe him one back.*

"OH MY GOD!"

"I know. I KNOW!"

Brooke smirks. "You're going from privately pretending in front of each other's families to the red carpet real quick, my dear. Now that's what I call a *glow up*."

"Don't remind me."

"How do you plan on surviving something like that? They don't exactly have garbage cans lining the velvet ropes for you to throw up in when you get nervous."

Glow up and *throw up* are becoming synonymous in my head right about now.

My eyes narrow. "That happened one time."

"Only because you magically became sick every time we had a school play after! Some people thought you hated Christmas because you never were a part of the production."

What kind of monster did my classmates take me for? "I plan on taking a shot before I even get to the event. That should cure any stage fright."

Brooke nods. "Moving along to my next question about this train wreck of a plan. How nervous do you think he feels about returning? If you're scared, I'm sure he's shitting bricks."

It's *all* I can think about. How will Santiago handle that kind of pressure? What will it be like for him to return to the one place he swore he would never be a part of again? Will he crumble under the pressure? My list of questions grows as the days tick by.

"Trust me, I do think about him. I still can't believe he agreed to do it in the first place. I mean, he's only going for Noah, but still."

"There's nothing I love more than a good old-fashioned sacrifice."

"That came out very wrong, just so you're aware."

Brooke cackles. "All right. Walk me through your plan for the weekend. And if it doesn't include touching his dick, I'm unfriending you and selling all your shit on Facebook Marketplace."

"You wouldn't dare."

"Try me." She smirks.

"Chloe, I hope you don't mind me asking this question, but I can't hold off anymore." Matteo closes the drawer to the cash register.

I pause my swiping of the glass window. "Yes?" Somehow my voice remains calm despite my escalating heart rate.

What could he possibly want to ask me? Is it too much to hope he recognizes me finally after working around each other for this long? We have the same hair color and both agree the eighties was the best decade ever. It's not exactly twinning, but it's close enough.

"Why are you working here if you're dating Santiago? Not that I'm not grateful for your help, but..."

Disappointment taints my excitement. Rather than stew in my negativity, I say the first thing that comes to mind. "I'm interested in opening a coffee shop myself, so I thought the best way to learn was from someone who has one."

Nice. A+ response. I swear, I'll stop lying once I reveal my identity to Matteo. Until then, I plan on weaving a web of lies with my hypocritical fingers because I can't bear facing the truth.

I hate myself a bit more each day I work here. It's draining to pretend I'm not dying to learn everything personal about him and give our relationship a real chance.

He purses his lips. "Ahh. I didn't know you were interested in that."

Yeah, neither did I. "I've spent time visiting different shops and learning about them." Okay, that's true. I tend to visit a

Starbucks from time to time when I run out of coffee for the week.

"What have you learned so far from me?"

"That you love your shot of espresso with a dash of milk and you sing ABBA's 'Take A Chance on Me' when you're thinking about something." I mentally face-palm myself at how stalkerish I sound.

"You pay attention."

That's one way to reframe my psychotic behavior.

I smile. "Yes. Plus, I've been watching you make different drinks and learning for myself."

He pats the counter with a smile. "If you're interested in learning more, you can start working behind the counter with me."

"Really?" The question leaves my lips with a squeak.

"Sure. Come in tomorrow an hour earlier and I'll teach you some of the basics."

"Yes! I'd love that! Sure!" I cringe at my desperation.

"If only my son was as excited as you are to learn about the family business." Matteo chuckles to himself.

My chest tightens. It's such a casual statement, but it has me grinning to myself. I don't want to be petty about my supposed little brother. It's not his fault he wants to go to a university and live his best life in Milan. The selfish part of me wants something Matteo can be proud of me about, and this seems like my way in. If it means learning all about coffee and posing as someone I'm not, so be it.

"How is your son?" I offer to ease some of my guilt.

"He's good. I've been actually meaning to ask you something about dinner tomorrow."

"Do you have to reschedule?" *Please don't reschedule.*

"No." He shakes his head furiously. "The opposite. I don't want to intrude, but the moment I told my son about meeting Santiago Alatorre and being invited to dinner with him, he was excited. He begged me to come along. See, we heard the rumors of him living next door. We even saw some reporters occasionally, but we never had the chance to meet your boyfriend ourselves. So, I wanted to ask if my son could come with me to meet Santiago, but I understand if you both don't want to."

The panic building up inside of me is replaced by a sense of disappointment. He wants to bring his son to dinner with us? All because of Santiago? What the hell am I supposed to say to that? *Sorry, no, your offspring shouldn't come along because I want to get to know you all by myself.* I can't exactly say no when Matteo clearly wants to be a cool dad to his kid.

Instead of yelling an obscenity, I nod my head. "Sure. We'd love to meet him."

Santiago's going to hate the plan even more than me. A little brother crashing our dinner party wasn't part of the agreement, especially someone who seems like a huge fan. Instead of getting upset, I shelve the feelings. It's probably normal for a son to beg their parent to join us. If I were in their shoes, I would do anything to meet my idol.

I need to focus on my end goal. Choosing the easy path isn't an option, so I go with my gut. If Matteo and his son want a superstar, I'll give them one. I only hope Santiago doesn't kill me for it.

"Why would you say yes to something like that?" Santiago passes me the salad supplies and a step-by-step guide on a sheet of paper.

"Seriously, a how-to-create-a-salad manual?" I snatch the piece of paper and give it a once-over.

He frowns. "You could've said 'no.' Ever heard of the word?"

"Based on how I said yes to your crazy plan of spending a whole weekend with your family, I can see why you'd think that."

"Be serious for a second. Why did you agree?"

I let out an agitated breath. "I was afraid he would get upset if I denied such an easy request."

"The whole point of this dinner was for *you* to get to know *him* outside of the cafe."

"Yeah, well, not everything can be perfect. I'm making do with a shitty situation."

"I don't like this plan."

I shrug. "You don't like many plans unless they're about you secluding yourself in your giant lair of a house."

"*Hilarious.*"

"What's the worst that can go wrong?"

He groans. "Don't say that out loud. It's bad luck."

"Fine." I huff dramatically.

Santiago and I work together, prepping the food. He spends the entire time testing me with questions about him. My answers have him switching between laughing and scowling, but the game distracts me.

I appreciate him a bit more for going out of his way to make me comfortable. No matter how many times I warn myself about Santiago, I can't help the draw I have toward him. This man is beyond likable, and I don't know what to do about it.

CHAPTER TWENTY

Chloe

"They're coming!" I call out to Santiago as I adjust the wine glasses for a third time.

"Relax." Santiago's arms wrap around me. His warm breath heats up my neck and tickles my ear.

Whoa. This is the first time he's initiated touching me without an audience, and I am not exactly opposed to it. Honestly, I want more of it. I'm tempted to cling onto him like a baby koala and make myself at home.

He presses his thumb to my pulse point. "You're going to have a heart attack if you keep this up."

No, sir, I'm going to have a heart attack if you *keep this up.* I let out a shaky breath. "Time to get this show on the road."

"Quick lightning round of questions. What's my favorite movie?" Santiago steps away from me.

Cool air replaces his warm embrace, and I sense the loss immediately. "*The Shining* because you're clinically certifiable."

He laughs. "Name something I'm talented at."

"You have a talent?"

His eyes darken as they land on my mouth. "You can think of one thing, I'm sure."

Umm, okay. Excuse me while I choke on my own saliva. "Such a naughty mind."

"Naughty insinuates the things I want to do to you are wrong. I can promise you they'll feel *very* good." His wink has my lower half giving a standing ovation.

I try to think of something to say besides staring at him like I want to give his dick a ride, but he interrupts me again. "How many World Championships have I won?"

"Two."

He smirks. "And am I a morning or night person?"

"Night because the sunshine kills your pissy attitude."

"You should try standup comedy. I feel like you're missing out on a viable career option here."

"Noted."

He nods. "It seems like you're about as ready as possible for tonight, but..." His voice drops off.

"But?"

"But we have to prepare better for a trip with my family."

"Why?"

He reaches out and runs his knuckles down my cheek, sending a current of energy down my spine like a shooting star. "Because you're supposedly my girlfriend, yet still act surprised when I touch you."

"That's because I am."

"Well, it needs to be amended."

"Joy," I squeak out.

His smile goes from sweet to seductive. *Dear Lord,*

someone please ask him to put away his pearly whites. They make me blind to the dangerous man standing in front of me.

His lips brush against my temple, making my skin tingle.

The ringing doorbell pulls our attention away from each other. Santiago motions for me to open the door. I grab the handle and pull, finding Matteo and my brother on the other side, grinning.

My new sibling looks a few years younger than me, rocking a mop of dark hair and light brown eyes.

"*Merda*. Santiago Alatorre!" My brother's brown eyes widen as his mouth drops open.

Merda is right. Matteo introduces his son as Giovanni. My brother looks similar to me, with the same faint splatter of freckles across his nose and pale skin.

I can't think of anything to say besides a welcoming hello. Matteo and Giovanni ignore my lack of words, focusing all their attention on the giant next to me. Giovanni drops a bunch of mumbled *fucks* as he hits Santiago with a few questions. Santiago's jaw ticks with each one. I appreciate him forcing a smile despite how much he hates this. It can't be easy to answer questions from a fan after years of hiding from the world. A tiny surge of guilt hits me for putting him in this situation in the first place and making him vulnerable. If we were the real deal, I'd offer him a blowjob for this round of torture.

Santiago ushers us into the main dining room, keeping his hand pressed against my lower back. I shiver at the possessiveness of his touch. Addiction must run in my family because I'm hooked on his touch, craving our connection to keep me grounded.

Except this is all fake, Chloe.

Giovanni and Matteo sit beside each other at the table. Santiago pulls my chair out to help me sit. I take a seat and Santiago pushes me in before sitting beside me. He goes above and beyond with his display, even offering to serve me my food.

Ugh. He cooks, he puts up with me, and he acts like a gentleman. If I hadn't met his mother, I would have thought he came from outer space.

Everyone else takes turns dishing themselves, and the bright smiles around the room tell me Santiago's cooking is a hit. I preen at everyone eating my salad.

"This food is amazing." Giovanni closes his eyes as he stuffs another piece of chicken in his mouth.

"I've never had anything like it." Matteo stabs a piece of lettuce.

Santiago grins at me. I blush and look away, focusing back on my family.

"I watched some of your cooking videos with your sister. YouTube doesn't do your food justice." Giovanni smiles in a boyish way. He's absolutely starstruck and I find it somewhat endearing.

"Right. I almost forgot those were out there." Santiago's gaze drops to his plate.

"You forgot? They have millions of views! How can you not remember something like that?"

Santiago clears his throat, a light blush creeping into his cheeks. "Things like that are easy to forget."

"Why haven't you done one in a while?" My brother, who lacks appropriate people skills, carries on.

"I don't want to be filmed anymore. I'd rather stay away from any kind of attention like that." Santiago's fists clench under the table.

"I don't like the attention either." I clutch onto his fist closest to me and force his fingers apart. They intertwine with mine, and he holds them to his thigh. The intimate gesture feels so right that it scares me.

"Obviously Santiago's been hiding you from the world. I've never seen you before," Giovanni says.

"Just how I like it." Santiago's hand tightens around mine, cutting off all circulation. Ouch.

Giovanni's gaze moves from me to Santiago. "Do you think you'll ever go back?"

"Gio… Smettila." Matteo frowns at his son.

This night is going terribly wrong, and I don't know how to stop it. Santiago cuts off any hope of blood circulation to my hand.

I clear my throat. "Giovanni, Matteo told me you're finishing up your degree at a university in Milan. How do you like it?"

My brother stares at me with a raised brow. "It's fun and I have lots of friends."

"That's great. I always saw happy students when I passed by NYU on my way to work. What's it like?" My head bobs enthusiastically.

Santiago tilts his head at me, his eyes scanning my face. The weight of his attention is the equivalent of having hot coals run over my skin.

"You didn't get a degree?" Matteo frowns at me.

I shake my head. "No. I had other priorities sadly. But I

accepted that some people aren't meant for college."

"My uncle said the same thing." Giovanni laughs.

"And look how he ended up." Matteo's eyes narrow at his son.

Okay, I'm guessing Matteo's brother is a sore subject. I try not to pay much attention to the contempt in Matteo's voice about not attending college, but it's easier said than done. The icky feeling takes over, making me feel lesser than because I don't have an expensive degree.

Those kinds of opportunities aren't for people like me. They're for those with money or people who can afford lost time and countless loans.

It's like a thundercloud rolled in over my head, darkening my mood.

As if sensing the shift, Santiago releases my hand. I attempt to pull it back but he traps it against his thigh. His index finger drags across my knuckles, sweeping over the goosebumps spreading across my skin.

I don't know what to concentrate on anymore—his touch or the bomb of a conversation with my family. I decide on the latter and gesture to my knife with my left hand.

Santiago huffs and releases my hand from his sensual torture. He smiles at the show I make of stretching my fingers. "Giovanni, what are you studying?"

"Engineering." Matteo answers for him as he sits taller in his seat, preening like a proud peacock about his son.

"Oh, that's awesome. What kind?" I pluck my glass of wine from the table and take a sip.

"Mechanical. I'm interested in working in the racing industry." Giovanni's gaze moves from me to Santiago again.

Oh, boy. Here we go again. His tampered down infatuation was fun while it lasted. Someone needs to teach my brother the art of not coming on too strong. I don't want to imagine him picking up women in a bar.

The conversation turns toward racing and cars again. Giovanni steers clear of asking Santiago anything too personal, focusing more on his car collection and other hobbies he enjoys like boating.

Matteo and Giovanni seem to forget I sit beside their favorite racer. Santiago attempts over and over to include me, answering in a way that should bring their attention back to me. Nothing works.

I hate the look of concern Santiago sends my way. It's one I've spent my entire life seeing on everyone else's faces. He might as well call me out on being the poor foster kid who found her family, only to realize they're not interested in me at all. Trust me, I see it. I don't need Santiago's awareness adding to my embarrassment. It's obvious Matteo didn't come here for me. He came to collect his "Dad of the Year" award after he introduced Giovanni to the next best thing since the invention of the iPhone.

Unease sits heavy in my gut, growing larger by the minute. Everything about this is fake—from my relationship with Santiago to Matteo coming here to spend time with me. It's a sad fact to realize the most genuine thing here tonight is Giovanni's infatuation. The uncomfortable thoughts batter against me.

My eyes sting, and I stand in a rush. "I'm going to go grab us a bottle of wine!"

Matteo's eyes land on the full bottle of white wine in

the middle of the table. I come up with some half-ass excuse about a different kind I prefer after dinner. My neck heats as I turn on my heel and bolt to the kitchen.

Ragged breaths escape my lungs. I open a cabinet door that hides the wine cellar, properly dubbed by me as the *bat cave*. My sneakers echo off the stone walls as I take the stairs two at a time.

I press my back against one of the glass refrigerator doors and slide down, hugging my knees to my chest. It takes everything in me to not release frustrated tears.

Nothing about tonight is going my way. Every choice I've made up until this point with Matteo has gone terribly wrong, making my life a mess. And for what? A father who already has a family and doesn't even know I exist?

I'm a joke. A fraud. Nothing better than my mother, lying to get my way. The realization brings about the tears I fought against before. I swipe them away, hating the evidence of my distress.

"You have two choices. You can go out there and show them what they're missing out on, or you can hide in here and I'll tell them to go." Santiago's low voice bounces off the walls. A pair of sneakers stop in front of me, his body casting a shadow over me.

My heart lodges itself somewhere in my throat. "Holy shit! How are you so damn quiet all the time?" I press my hand against my chest as I tip my head back.

"Practice." His smirk drops into a scowl as his eyes flick over my tear-stained face.

He lets out a breath as he gracefully squats.

My heart warms at the idea of him pushing himself to

his limit to meet me where I'm at. I lean my head forward, avoiding his gaze. "Tonight sucks."

He tucks a thick, calloused finger under my chin, forcing me to face him. "Ehh. *They* suck. There's only one person at that table making everything bearable." He smiles in a way that makes me want to shake him.

Screw a penny for his thoughts. I'd offer my firstborn child if it means gaining access to a piece of his mind.

"I made a mistake, didn't I?"

He shakes his head. "No, you didn't. And I can't exactly blame them either because fame makes people stupid. They think the way to make me happy is asking me questions about myself, but they couldn't be any more wrong."

"Why?" The words leave my mouth in a whisper.

"Because obviously the way to any man's heart is through his girlfriend."

"Fake girlfriend." I mumble half-heartedly. Fake girlfriends shouldn't feel how I do about him, but here I am, lusting after a damn hermit.

He shakes his head, fighting a smile. "How do you feel about playing a game?"

"A game?" My jaw drops open.

"Yes. A game." He nods, his grin growing. "Whoever makes up the most ridiculous story about our relationship wins whatever they want."

I laugh. It's loud and unrestrained, echoing off the walls. "Why would we do that?"

"Because I'd rather see you smile than cry."

I suck in a sharp breath. His sweet words sink in, repairing the damage from tonight. It scares me to rely on someone like him. But at the same time, I can't ignore the security he offers.

"What do I get if I win?" My smile widens.

"The real question you need to ask is what do I get when I win?" His smile turns mischievous, liquifying my insides.

Oh. Shit.

I'm willing to lose if it means I get another smile like that. I might as well wave my flag of surrender now because Santiago looks like the type to not take any prisoners.

CHAPTER TWENTY-ONE

SANTIAGO

Not thinking out my plans is becoming a pattern, ever since Chloe stumbled into my life. Catching her crying on my cellar floor made my heart twist in a way that had me acting first, thinking later.

The night is everything I expected, which adds to my concern. I should have trusted my instincts and rejected this plan. My gut feeling was right. Chloe's family is completely starstruck. It was written all over their faces the moment they entered my house. Originally, I chalked it up to my doubts about others' intentions, hoping they wanted to get to know my girlfriend too. Instead, they steamrolled over every comment centered around Chloe tonight, focusing back on me.

Chloe is putting a lot of stock into Matteo accepting her once she admits her identity to him. I'm afraid she will only be disappointed if he rejects her. And worse, I'm nervous she won't have a reason to stay here anymore if he breaks her heart.

He's the one person tying her to this town, and I can't have him screwing it up. I enjoy her company too much to lose it now.

I was hoping to be wrong about Matteo and his son, but everything that happened tonight proves I'm probably right. And fuck them both if it makes Chloe miserable. So hence, my stupid game. The same one that reignited the fire within Chloe, banishing her tears. Like a champion, she marched through my house and took her seat next to me.

I clutch onto her hand, holding it hostage against the tabletop. She raises a brow at me, and I smile. The tiny voice in my head whispers how lines are blurring and feelings are bound to get hurt. But for once in the past few years of my isolated life, I don't bother listening to it. I've spent far too long being numb. I'm so damn tired of it, I'll play all these games with Chloe and enjoy our private stakes.

Matteo stares at our hands joined on the table. "How long have you two known each other?"

I blink at him. The asshole finally asks a question about us, rather than just me.

Chloe takes advantage of my silence, shooting me a telling smile. "Oh. Ever since childhood. It was a slow-burning romance of the ages." She bats her lashes.

Oh, this ought to be good. I lean in closer to her, taking a deep breath of her flowery scent before whispering in her ear. "Whoever gets the most questions out of them about a story wins. Let's keep it fair and unbiased."

She sucks in a sharp breath, her body shuddering as hot air escapes my mouth. Her nod of approval starts our game.

Giovanni smiles. "Oh, really? I remember hearing about Santiago's ex on one of his sister's vlogs. But no other information came out about her."

I wince. Everyone was always curious about my ex-girlfriend, but I kept that story locked away with some others. During interviews, I preferred to keep my life private, and reporters took it as something salacious instead of innocent.

Chloe shrugs in a faux-shy way, her long lashes fluttering. "Well, it's me. This big guy was secretive about it all."

"Why?" Matteo takes a sip of his wine.

"He was ashamed to tell others how he lost me after I broke his heart."

I force my laugh into a ragged cough.

"No freaking way! You broke his heart? Why?" Giovanni's eyes threaten to pop out of their sockets.

"Back when I knew him, he was just a boy with a dream of racing one day. But fame changes people, and I was afraid." Her lip wobbles.

Everyone becomes enthralled by her story, including myself. We hang on to each new piece of information she shares. I keep a mental tally of each question, with her story of us breaking up earning a total of eleven questions. That's going to be a hard one to beat.

Chloe gloats like she's on top of a podium, shooting me a taunting smile. She mouths *beat that* when her family isn't looking.

Matteo excuses himself to use the restroom. Giovanni follows him, claiming he needs to go as well. It's a fitting intermission for our dinner and a show.

I reach out toward her, grazing her bottom lip with my thumb. Her smile drops as her eyes widen.

There's no reason to get close to her, but I can't help

it. And more importantly, I don't want to. "Don't plan your victory parade just yet."

She rolls her eyes, but her breaths become shallower as my thumb rubs back and forth across her bottom lip. "I can't see how you'll beat eleven questions. You count grunting as a second language."

I laugh, low and rough. "If you knew the old me, you'd take back that statement. I don't like losing."

Her eyes soften. "I don't need to know the old you."

"And why is that?" My thumb moves toward her cheek, stroking the soft skin.

None of this is fake now. Her reaction, my interest, the way both our bodies respond to each other's touch. It's all so fucking real, I can practically taste the attraction between us both.

"Because I find this version of you intoxicating enough." Her eyes flutter shut as she leans into my touch.

"What if I said I really want to kiss you right now?"

"Then I'd tell you to take what you want before you lose the chance."

Blood rushes through my body, and my dick twitches beneath my jeans. I press my lips to hers, and Chloe releases a breathy sigh.

Some kisses stoke a passion. Some kisses heal the soul. Kissing Chloe is a combination of two—the sweetest medicine that leads to a lifelong addiction.

I run my tongue across her bottom lip and get a taste of her favorite wine. Her body shudders, and her lips tremble beneath my onslaught. A yearning builds within me to pull her closer. To piece myself back together with her help.

The clapping of shoes against the marble floor has us pulling away from each other. I have a strong desire to pull her back, but our company stops me.

Chloe's eyes bounce between my lips and my eyes. "That was…"

Real. Incredible. Fucking undeniable and if you friend-zone me again I swear to God I'll kiss the word straight out of your vocabulary. "Only the beginning." I brush my thumb across her lower lip one last time, the plumpness easily becoming my favorite distraction.

Matteo and Giovanni enter the dining room, stealing our attention away once again.

I turn away from Chloe despite the urge I have to steal her away and call it a night. "Chloe reminded me of a funny story while you both were in the restroom."

"Oh, hell yes!" Giovanni claps his hands together.

"I'm not sure if you read anything in the papers about the time a desperate fan was escorted off the F1 property after they snuck into my suite to confess their love?"

Chloe's laugh echoes off the walls, solidifying my choice. I like the way it sounds way too much.

"No! Wow. How long ago was this?" Matteo smiles.

One question down, eleven more to go.

I might have stepped away from the F1 podiums, but that doesn't mean I stopped craving a win. And I'm ready to beat the competition into submission.

"We're going to die. It's official. God save us," Chloe mumbles, looking up to the car's roof. She does the sign of the cross incorrectly, and I laugh as I show her how it's really done.

"Relax." I scan our surroundings. The street is empty and flat—the perfect place to teach someone how to drive.

"When you won last night, I didn't expect you to waste your win on this."

"Well, I did say we needed to amend your issue of not knowing how to drive. That's illegal in my house." I rub the leather dashboard of the Jeep. I'm offering Chloe the sturdiest of my vehicles to learn how to drive.

"There's three pedals. Why are there three pedals?" She moans.

The sound sends a rush straight to my cock. I take a deep breath, easing the ache that's become familiar around Chloe. "Because automatic cars are for grandmas."

"Okay, that's fine. I'll own up to being a grandma because I barely go out anyway. I mean, I embroider as a hobby. I'm practically one year away from fostering cats and living the rest of my life attached to an oxygen tank."

I offer her a blank expression, denying my urge to laugh.

She offers me the praying hands. "Please don't make me do this. You're no John Cusack, and this isn't *Say Anything*."

"What are you even rambling about?"

"Have you ever seen the movie?"

"No."

She looks up at the ceiling. "It seems I have two things to pray about now. It's no wonder you've been single for so long. Do you even know how to woo a woman?"

I blink at her. "I do not need to *woo*."

"Everyone woos. You're breaking my eighties-loving heart."

"Really? How many men have you wooed?"

Her cheeks flush. "Uhm…I don't woo. But that's different." The words rush out of her mouth.

"Of course it is. Double standards tend to be oddly convenient."

Her mouth parts. "*Excuse* me? There are no double standards. I just was never interested in wooing someone before! That's totally different."

"Because your eighties-loving heart set your standards for love too high?"

"Exactly. You'd understand if you grew up around my mother and her crappy boyfriend. I'd rather have high standards than that dumpster fire mislabeled as a romance."

"Wait. Have you not been in love?" I don't know why I'm shocked. I've never been in love either, but Chloe…she's different. Someone should've snatched her up by now. At least for a little while.

She focuses on the steering wheel. "No. Have you?"

"No," I answer honestly.

"See, maybe if you wooed a girl, you'd be in love already." She flashes me a grin.

I shake my head and return my attention back to the task. "Stop distracting me so I can explain how this is done."

I go through each step with her, explaining the gear shift, the pedals, and all the other basics she needs to know.

She grips onto the gear shift and tries to move it. Her brows pull together as she releases an exaggerated sigh. "Well, I guess since the car is broken, we should just quit now before anyone gets hurt. Better safe than sorry."

"You forgot to turn the car on." I cover my smile with my fist.

"You're enjoying my struggle way too much. I knew you were demented, but this is a whole new level of fucked up, Santiago Alatorre." Chloe rolls her Rs perfectly.

My dick perks up at the way she says my name. I've yet to share my nickname with her, which is new for me. I kind of like how Chloe's one of the few people to call me Santiago rather than Santi. Might as well keep it that way. I shimmy in my seat, adjusting myself while explaining how to turn on the car.

I pluck her hand from the gear shift and show her the movements. The addictive smell of her invades my nose as I lean in. I want to stay in the position, with my dick throbbing and her driving my car becoming an erotic dream.

Yeah, I'm a horny fucker. I got it. Anyone would be after being in a relationship with their right hand for as long as I have.

"Did you just sniff my hair?" Chloe's incredulous voice snaps me out of my fantasy.

"No."

"Oh my God, you totally did!" Her giggles become a full-blown belly laugh.

"You're delusional. I was trying to check for any gas leaks."

"*In my hair?*" She turns toward me. Her chest brushes against my arm, reminding me of everything I'm tempted to touch. "You're shy." She traces a finger across my heating cheeks.

Her touch ignites a fire in my veins, forcing more blood into the very cheeks she strokes.

Fuck. Since when have I been shy?

Since you became a freak to the public, the small yet effective voice in my head offers.

I cover up my dark thoughts with an eye roll. "No. Men like me aren't shy."

She pokes my chest before dragging her finger down the muscles of my stomach. "You totally are. Tell me, why do you like sniffing my hair?"

"Truth or lie?"

Her gaze meets mine. "Truth. Always the truth."

"Because you smell annoyingly good and I wanted more, okay? Are you happy now?"

"Absolutely thrilled. Sniff away, you creep." Her laugh drowns out the car booting up.

Her mood is infectious. I absorb it, allowing her positive energy to pulse through me. I'm growing to enjoy Chloe's presence as we spend more time together. And honestly, part of me wonders what more I can do to have her stay a bit longer around me.

CHAPTER TWENTY-TWO

Chloe

I mindlessly sweep the coffee shop's floor.

What am I supposed to wear this weekend?

What am I supposed to say?

But, wait, how am I supposed to live in the same hotel room with Santiago for days and keep things between us solely platonic?

"Chloe, I've been meaning to talk to you."

I jump at the sound of Matteo's voice. The broom slips from my hands and clatters against the floor. "God. You scared me!"

He chuckles. "I'm sorry. I called your name a few times, but you didn't hear me."

Oh. *Stop daydreaming on the job.*

I turn toward him. He gestures for us to have a seat at one of the empty tables.

Is he going to fire me? He's never this formal, and after our dinner from hell, things between us have been a bit tense. I try not to hold it against him, but I'm still slightly bitter.

"What's up?" I keep my tone casual despite the loud thoughts battering my head like a marching band.

"Well, I feel like things haven't been right between us."

Wow. This man really *is* my father. How else could he sense my annoyance?

He continues. "You have been pretty quiet and not like your usual self ever since our dinner the other day."

Someone give this man an award. He understands women and seeks them out to make things right. This town truly is magical after all.

"Yeah. About that…"

He lifts his hand. "My son and I… We were embarrassing. I realize that now."

My mouth pops open. *Whoa. All right. I can get behind this kind of self-awareness.*

"No, you both were just excited."

"We were both rude, and don't try to cover it up as something else. Save me my dignity here."

A laugh slips out of me. "Well…"

"We've never been around someone famous, and we acted like fools. You must be used to Santiago since he's your boyfriend, but for us—it was like meeting our idol for the first time. Santiago Alatorre is one of the greatest, along with his brother-in-law. Your boyfriend is right up there with Michael Schumacher."

Michael Schumach-who?

"Right." Well, that sounded a lot safer than asking more questions about the boyfriend I should know everything about.

"You invited us there to spend time with you outside of

work, and we hogged it by pestering Santiago. Please forgive us for acting like bumbling fools in front of you both. I'm embarrassed I reacted that way."

If I had a glass of water, I would choke on it right about now. His apology is sincere, and I can't help forgiving him. It's not like I can hold it against him. If someone told me I was about to have dinner with Michelle Obama, I'd be freaking the fuck out too.

Wait, could Santiago help me score a dinner with the Obamas? Now *that* piques my interest about his fame.

I assure Matteo that everything is fine between us, and we get back to work. I'm not the kind to harbor grudges because life's too short to spend it angry at people who genuinely care. Matteo could've not apologized and left things how they were. But his bravery and honesty has me appreciating him in a whole new light.

"Will you pass me the screwdriver, please." Santiago rolls out from underneath the car, hitting me with his brown eyes.

He stands out against the gray cement flooring of the garage. Is there such a thing as being too pretty? Asking for the male staring up at me with a grin that should be illegal in whatever country I reside in.

I grab the tool and pass it to him. Thank God he taught me the names of all his thing-a-ma-jiggers because I would've been screwed after he mentioned the auto jig and dent puller.

I look around his garage. It's something straight out of a *Fast and Furious* movie, with tons of cars from various generations. I'm tempted to pull off a grand theft auto and snag the red convertible when he's sleeping.

Tempted being the key word.

"What's that look about?" He points up at me with the screwdriver.

"Thinking about what it would take to steal one of your cars."

"I knew you were a criminal."

"Criminals get caught." I shoot him a mischievous smile.

He rolls back underneath the car. "Are you ready for this weekend?"

"About as ready as one can be for the apocalypse."

His laugh carries over the clicking noises of his tools. "It's not that bad."

"Oh, really. Then it's a true wonder how you stayed away from it all for this long." I imagine him rolling his eyes at me.

"You know why."

"Fine. What did you do during all your time away from the land of the lavish?"

The noises underneath the car pause. "Why are you asking?"

"Oh, I'm just curious to know more about you."

He snorts.

I grin. "You do understand I need to know more about my fake boyfriend than the fact that he likes cars, he used to race, and he enjoys short walks where no one bothers him, right?"

"Emphasis on the no-one-bothers-me part, please."

I laugh up to the ceiling. "Come on. What's something no one knows about you?"

"Why would I share something like that with you, only so

you could tell a reporter?"

My, my, someone is grumpy today. "I'm not going to tell anyone. But I do want to have an idea of who you are as a person. You know, for when I need to make up stories that require some consistency."

"I used to play the guitar every night before I went to bed."

"Stop. No way!" I lean over and peek under the car, only to be met with the top of his head. So much for getting a read on him.

He grumbles something I can't understand.

I somehow lift my jaw back up off the floor. "You seriously play the guitar?"

There he goes pausing his work again. "Acoustic."

"Oh my God! You need to play for me."

"No."

"Come on," I whine.

"Still no."

"You're such a spoilsport."

"I never claimed otherwise."

I roll my eyes. "Back when you raced, did you used to bring your guitar with you?"

The screwdriver clatters against the ground.

Ugh. Wrong question.

"Never min—"

"Yeah. I always traveled with my guitar during the racing season. It made the bad days bearable and the good days memorable."

I lean against the hood of the car to stop me from falling over. Swooning can do that to a girl. "Do you still play?"

"No."

"Why not?"

"Because music is food for the soul, and mine feels like it's missing."

Whoa. His heart calls out to mine, begging me to help him. He might look beautiful on the outside, but he's nothing but broken on the inside. It has me absolutely enraptured.

I have a feeling Santiago loves too hard. Whether it's his family, or racing, or even the music he plays, he loves unapologetically and with everything in him. And how does someone move past the level of heartbreak he experienced when he lost his leg and gave up racing?

"I hope you play again one day." I mean every word.

"Me too, Chloe. Me too."

CHAPTER TWENTY-THREE

SANTIAGO

I swipe my towel across the foggy bathroom mirror. My ragged face stares back at me, with my beard growing out and my hair looking rough around the edges. I've never had it this long before. I run a hand through the locks, my fingers catching on a few knots from my shower.

Is this who I want to show the world this weekend? The guy who let his circumstances break him to a point where he barely recognizes himself? And more importantly, is this the guy I want to be in front of Chloe? I want to impress her, not make her want to run in the opposite direction.

One look at myself has me wondering why she didn't run the first chance she had. I look like someone who has seen way better days. Hell, someone who has seen a way better *life*.

I tug open one of the vanity drawers and pull out my supplies to trim my beard. It might only be a cosmetic change, but it's a change nonetheless.

It takes me what feels like forever to remove all the excess facial hair. I run a hand over the stubble and smile. "Now, what the fuck am I going to do about my hair?"

"Honey, I'm home!" Chloe calls out from the front door.

I walk into the entryway, eyeing her suitcases which look one trip away from falling apart. How those ragged bags lasted all the way here from America blows my mind.

"Holy shit!" she gasps. "Who are you and what have you done with Santiago?"

Based on Chloe's reaction, the major haircut was worth it. My head feels a hundred times lighter, with the strands styled how I used to like it.

"Hey." I rub the back of my neck.

Her eyes move from my face to my hair to my face again. "Wow. *That's* what you were hiding under that beard and hair? It's like *The Devil Wears Prada*, but manlier. And definitely hotter by like a thousand degrees."

I laugh under my breath and tilt my head toward her bags. "You're bringing all that for a weekend trip?"

"No. I was planning on moving in here afterward. What do you think?" She speaks in a singsong voice as she bats her lashes in a way that screams everything but innocence.

"*Cute*," I offer in a dry voice.

"I checked out of the bed-and-breakfast for the weekend because money doesn't grow on trees around here. Do you mind if I store some of my bags here?" Her eyes drop to her ratty sneakers.

I hate how the topic of money seems to embarrass her. Obviously I can't hide the fact that I have plenty of it, and her struggles add a gap between us that I hate. I want to tell her how, at the end of the day, a bank account can only make someone so happy. After a certain threshold, dollar signs become meaningless, like the people who flock to me because of it.

I choose against it, not wanting to embarrass her more. "You can keep them here. For a second I thought you were way more high maintenance than I pegged you for," I tease, wanting to rid her of her nervousness.

"God no. I'm about as high maintenance as a pet goldfish." She pushes her luggage toward me.

"The one I had growing up died, so I don't have a good baseline to compare it to." I grab it from her and roll it into the closet underneath the stairs.

"Seeing as I never had a pet to begin with, it's not like I can either."

I laugh again, and she grins. It's a beautiful look on her, with her eyes shining under the bright light of the chandelier. I'm tempted to kiss her. Right here, right now.

Her lips part as her eyes analyze my face. I inch closer, moving to wrap my hand around her neck.

My mom's custom ringtone interrupts us. I groan, rubbing a hand down my face. "I better go answer that. Make yourself at home while I grab my bags."

Her shoulders drop a centimeter. It's subtle, but the move has my pulse quickening. I like making her want me. It brings a hopeful part of me back I stored away long ago. One I'm afraid of letting loose in the first place, not because I don't want to, but because there's no stopping it once it starts. And that's a dangerous game with someone who only plans on being here temporarily.

I make my way into my bedroom and grab my phone off the nightstand. A voicemail from my mom pops up on the screen. She rambles about packing extra clothes just in case we end up attending multiple activities in one day. Even after moving out at eighteen, she still babies me.

I move toward my luggage on the bed, shuffling my clothes around until it all fits. As I drag my luggage off the bed, it slips from my hands and slams on the ground. A shot of straight agony shoots to my right leg. My lungs burn from the sudden inhale of breath I take.

Phantom pains. I thought I had beaten this part of my healing, but another throb tells me how wrong I was. They're one of the worst parts of losing my leg. Messages fire off from my brain, only to be met with a missing limb. It's like a panic attack inside of my body, with my nerves freaking the hell out.

Fuck my right leg to hell and back. Fuck it all.

This pain isn't real. Your leg is long gone. I chant my old mantra, praying the pain away.

Another wave of turmoil has me hunching. I bite back a curse, grinding my teeth to combat the ache. A cold sweat breaks out across my skin as I release a moan.

"Oh my God, are you okay? I heard something fall and was worried." Chloe's voice breaks through the sounds of my heavy breathing.

I hate how concerned she sounds as much as I hate her finding me like this. Weak. Desperate. In unbelievable pain. It's like my demon couldn't let me find happiness even for a couple of days with someone else.

No. My leg needs to be the star of the show, time and time again.

"I'll be out in a few minutes once this passes." My voice cracks.

I fumble with my leg, scratching at my jeans as I lift the hem. Another shudder runs through me as my body interprets an injury where there is no fucking appendage. I can't withhold my groan in front of Chloe.

"You're freaking me out and I don't know how to help you!"

"Go outside. It'll pass in a few minutes." I somehow muster enough energy to reply. Every word takes effort, between my panting and the pain.

"Yeah no. You're crazier than I thought if you think I'm going to leave you here like this." Chloe drags a massive wingback chair from the corner of my room toward me. The scraping noise against the wood has the goosebumps on my arms rising.

The last thing I want is her help, but I can't find it in me to snap something miserable. To push her away before she sees the mess I really am. Everything about us has been this grand fairy tale, with us avoiding the truth and pretending in front of everyone. But it's not real. If she's the princess who picks wildflowers and radiates sunshine, then I'm the beast—scarred with a personality to match. And like the beast, I'm better off left alone. Newsflash to the romantics out there: Belle suffered from Stockholm syndrome. No woman would've wanted that bastard if she wasn't a prisoner.

"Please go away," I rasp.

"No. I'd translate it into Spanish, but it's the same shit, different language. So no and *no*." She lulls the last word in a fake accent.

I want to smile, but I settle on a scowl.

She pushes my shoulders, forcing me to take a seat. "How can I help?"

The deep breaths I take do nothing to ease the ache. "Fuck. Give me a second," I manage to say through my grinding teeth.

"Is it your leg? Do I need to call for an ambulance?" Chloe clutches onto my trembling hand and helps lift the hem of my jeans higher up my leg.

There's my prosthetic in all its glory.

Chloe looks me straight in the eyes and doesn't bother blinking. "Tell me what to do and stop acting like a princess about it."

"Can you help me walk to the mirror over there?" I point to the massive full-length mirror next to my dresser. I kept it after all this time for occasions like this, but the damn thing is too far away.

Her brows draw together, but she doesn't ask questions. She helps support my body as I limp toward the mirror. I try to keep most of my weight on my good leg, but I stumble. Chloe grunts at the sudden shift in weight.

My confidence shrivels up as we stop at the rug. I hang my head low against my chest. "Do you mind helping me to the floor?" I whisper the simple request, disgust settling deep within my gut.

This is the absolute worst thing that could've happened to me with Chloe. I feel humiliated as she helps me get situated up on the fluffy rug in front of the mirror. I tuck my prosthetic behind the mirror, hiding the appendage as I avoid Chloe's gaze. I'm afraid of what I might find lingering behind those blue eyes.

She said over and over how she doesn't care about my leg, but how can she not? I can barely look at it without being disgusted. And in this moment? I absolutely despise myself.

"Can I help you with anything else? Do you need an Advil or something?" Her sweet request has me releasing a cynical laugh up to the ceiling.

"No. What I need is to wipe your memory of the last ten minutes."

"Well, it seems like you're stuck with me now since the Men in Black are busy."

I sigh, hating what comes next. "You can go now."

"Do you want me to?"

"Don't you want to go?" I peek up at her.

Her eyes reflect the same warmth she always has toward me. In fact, there's a sheen to her eyes that wasn't there earlier.

Great, now I made her want to cry. I shake my head and return my focus back on my leg.

"There's nowhere I'd rather be than here with you." She drops onto the rug across from me and crosses her legs.

Another sharp throb echoes through my body, stealing away my attention. I don't have time to concentrate on Chloe's presence. I expel all my energy on the exercises I learned during my time in rehab. Mirror therapy is the cruelest of all the exercises, with me manipulating my brain into believing I have two whole legs.

The pain in my body lessens as I pretend my leg in

the mirror is not my prosthetic. I go through the motions, flexing my foot and curling my toes before moving onto more complex movements. It takes thirty minutes to eradicate the pain. By the end of it, I lay down against the rug, sweaty and spent. Shadows play across the ceiling as the fan above me rotates.

Chloe lays down next to me, the heat of her body warming my side. "Do you believe in wishes?"

The ridiculousness of her question catches me by surprise. "What?"

"Do you believe in wishes? Yes or no?" She turns her head toward me.

Our breaths mingle together from the proximity.

My eyes drop to her lips. "Uhm...No?"

She palms her face. "Figures."

"Why?"

"Because I believe in wishes."

I can't help it. Her response makes me laugh, releasing the tension from my body.

"Hey, it's not nice to laugh at someone sharing a story. I've only told this to one other person in the entire world, and your reaction makes me not want to share it anymore." She pinches my side, knowing the exact spot to make my body jolt.

"You're right. Please forgive me?"

Her smile doesn't match her faux offense. "Yeah. So, I have this thing called a wish journal. And I get it's ridiculous, but I've made wishes ever since I watched *Pinocchio* as a kid."

"But you wish in a journal instead of on a star? How does that work?"

"In New York, the only star you'll find is on Broadway since there are too many lights to see the sky clearly. I was practical and found a journal instead. Plus, it's easier to keep track of all my wishes that way. And boy do I keep track."

"I don't know what's more shocking about this story. The fact that you write wishes in a journal or how you call yourself practical."

Chloe lets out a melodic laugh up to the ceiling. "Okay wise guy, what if I told you some of my wishes came true?"

"Then I'd tell you that you have a flawless case of confirmation bias."

Chloe goes wild from my comment. God. I love the way she laughs—like she might die from oxygen deprivation. I'm tempted to make her laugh again and again. Isolation has made me a sad sap of a man, begging for attention from someone who seems equally lonely.

She rolls her eyes. "Okay, please quit the comedy act while you're ahead. There's only room for one of us in this sham of a relationship, and it isn't you, buddy."

I chuckle. "Fine."

"Anyway, it might seem stupid to *some*"—her eyes narrow at me as she turns her head in my direction—"but my wish journal is really important to me. It was the one thing that was exclusively mine, especially after I was forced to move out of my mom's place and into a foster home."

Her voice lacks the sorrowful note I'd expect from a depressing story like this. I imagine a young Chloe, clinging to a journal, wishing for better circumstances only to be disappointed time and time again. The notion sits heavy in my chest. How does she stay so damn positive after growing up like that? Who would?

She continues, "You can laugh all you want, but one of my wishes landed me here, so I'd say there's a bit of magic in my journal. Don't you think?"

I'm hooked on the story, craving more from her. "What did you wish for?"

"Two things actually."

"Oh, really?"

"The first wish was for me to find my dad and reunite with him."

"And obviously that happened."

She smiles "Yeah."

"And what was your second wish?"

"I don't know if I should share it. I might be suffering from a wicked sense of confirmation bias." She sticks out her tongue at me.

My eyes focus on how her tongue drags across her bottom lip. I'm tempted to roll on top of her and kiss her.

She shakes her head. "Nope. Not going there right now with you."

"Buzzkill." I sigh. "Then tell me what else you wished for."

"I wanted someone to appreciate my presence rather than destroy it."

I frown, hating how she needs to wish for something like that in the first place. "Why did you wish for that?"

"That's a story for another day."

Fuck another day. I want the story now. "Come on."

"Nope."

"Fine for now. But how do you know the wish came true?"

"Because I met you."

Shit. How does her simple statement make my heart pound harder against my chest?

Damn, I like this girl. I expect fear to infect my common sense, but nothing happens. Not a glimmer of anything other than happiness echoes through my body.

"Why are you sharing this with me?" *That's the best you can come up with? The girl is basically telling you she likes you, and you're fucking it up.* I'm an idiot. That's the damn truth.

She laughs again, her smile banishing my thoughts. "I wanted to share the one thing that makes me vulnerable."

"Why?"

"Because we all have weaknesses, Santiago. You believe yours is how you're missing a leg, and I think mine is my crippling loneliness and preference for wishing instead of doing. I make wishes to combat the emptiness I feel from all the disappointments in my life. Wishes are the closest thing I have to magic."

I want to tell her that the magic is within her, not some wishes scribbled in a journal. And I crave screwing over every person who has disappointed her and has threatened to destroy her happiness.

I say nothing, choosing to soak in her words. The hum of Chloe's restorative energy fills me to the brim with something I can't ignore anymore.

I want the real deal with her. The dates, the laughs, and the feeling she brings out of me time and time again.

She describes her loneliness as a weakness, but I only see it as a strength. While people like me shrivel away in the shadows, people like her create their own light. She's like the moon who shines bright despite the never-ending darkness.

And she makes me want to wish that daylight never comes again.

CHAPTER TWENTY-FOUR

Chloe

"**A**re you ready for our road trip?" I open the passenger door of Santiago's G-Wagon. Thank God I have long legs because this SUV is a monster. I grab the hem of my boho skirt and use the step to hop inside the car.

"It's less than two hours away. I drove in races longer than that."

"Oh okay, Mr. *I'm a famous racer, hear me brag.* Are you forgetting I grew up in New York? I never went anywhere!"

Santiago gets into the driver's seat and slides on a pair of Ray Bans. My eighties-obsessed heart sings at the sight. He's a mix-up of every John Hughes' character I love watching.

Please don't get me started on his new look. I knew Santiago was sexy before, but I didn't realize he was *that* sexy under his beard and long hair. Seriously, I don't think I have enough self-control to make it through a car ride next to him, let alone a whole weekend.

Santiago starts the car. "Is this your first time traveling

outside of America?"

"This is my first time out of New York. Period. I've never been anywhere else besides here and the four-hour layover in Portugal. So technically speaking, I've visited two other places now besides New York."

"You can't count a layover as visiting another country. That's just sad."

"No. It's just the truth." I cross my arms and look out the window. It's not as if Santiago means to judge, but it comes off that way.

The air shifts between us as I remain quiet. I can spend two hours in silence as long as he doesn't play jazz music. That's a hard limit.

He clears his throat. "I'm sorry if what I said came out wrong. I wasn't trying to insult you."

"It's fine."

"Uh-oh."

I shift in my seat, turning to face him. "What?"

"'Fine' is code for *I'm not fine and if you ignore it, I'll tell you just how not fine I am a few hours from now and you'll wish you had asked more from the get-go.*"

I snort. "What? Who told you such classified information?"

"I grew up with a sister. She taught me the basics by the time I was a teenager."

"Okay, your comment bothered me a little bit—"

He raises a brow.

"Okay, a lot. But it's not your fault. It just reminds me of everything I missed out on that others have experienced. Growing up the way I did left much to be desired for."

"I'm sorry. I didn't mean to make you feel bad because you

haven't traveled. Especially not because of your circumstance."

"It's okay. No big deal." I smile.

He bites down on his bottom lip in a way that isn't meant to be sexy but is hot enough to break a glass thermometer. "So... What did you used to enjoy doing in your free time besides working?"

Great. He's trying to be polite and I'm here lusting after him. "Besides embroidering? I mean, I don't exactly have much free time to begin with."

"Tell me more about that then."

I rear back in my chair in surprise, banging my head against the headrest like a dork. "What do you want to know?"

"For starters, how did you get into that kind of hobby?"

"Well, I used to have some anger issues."

"I find that very hard to believe." He attempts to keep a straight face but laughs anyway.

"It's true." I punch him in the arm for emphasis.

He only laughs harder.

"So my social worker took me to the hobby store one day after an incident." I shiver at the reminder of the day I lost my mom, my home, and my last ounce of innocence. "She told me I could pick anything from the store, but I had to agree it would be my outlet for my emotions rather than anything physical."

"And what made you pick that?"

"She thought it would help for me to stab something. The needle seemed like a safe option."

Santiago's laugh bounces off the roof of the car. "I would've never guessed you had this much pent-up aggression."

"I was pretty mad at the world as a teenager."

His smile drops. "I'm sorry."

"Don't be. It is what is."

"Why do you do that?"

"Do what?"

"Make everything seem like it's okay?"

I shrug. "Because it is. I can't do anything to change the past, so why continue to let it bother me?"

He nods and focuses his attention back on the road. The lakeside town disappears as we drive through the winding roads toward Monza.

"Are you any good at it?" He breaks the silence.

"Embroidering?"

"Yeah."

"I'm not one to show off, but I'm wearing one of the pieces I made now." I point down at my embroidered T-shirt. It's a basic pocket tee, with a bunch of multicolored dainty flowers designed above the pocket. It was a total nightmare to design, but I love it all the more because of how hard it was to make.

"Wow. I thought you bought that."

I shake my head, hiding my smile. "No. I like designing pieces like this."

"Have you ever thought of selling them to the public?"

I snort. "Not really. I've never had the time or money to start my own Etsy shop."

"Would you be interested? If you had time, that is?"

I pause and consider it. Thinking up designs feeds the creative side I've neglected throughout the years while overworking myself. I love the thrill I get when drawing out my creations on the fabric and bringing them to life. The peace from the process and the sense of accomplishment once the piece is done is another bonus.

I love it all. From beginning to end.

"I mean, in a perfect world where I had limitless money and didn't have to work as much, sure. But the world is far from flawless, so I'll stick to the things I know will support me."

"You should consider making more time for your hobby."

"Why?"

"Because if you love something enough to smile like you are right now, then you should pursue it before it's too late."

I press a hand to my lips. "I don't have the time."

"And you never will if you keep finding reasons not to."

Whoa. Here I've been pushing Santiago out of his comfort zone, only to have him do the same. Santiago is embroidering himself into my skin like the designs I love so much, and I'm not exactly sure what I'm going to do about it.

CHAPTER TWENTY-FIVE

SANTIAGO

I regret agreeing to visit my family at the Monza track. It takes everything in me to step out of my car after the road trip from Lake Como. The valet workers don't leave me with much of a choice as they take over, grabbing our luggage from the back. I pull my cap low on my face as I take a deep breath of the fresh air.

Chloe exits the car with a huge grin plastered on her face, staring up at our hotel with wonder. "Oh my God. Look at this place! It's even cooler than your house, and you live in a castle!"

I never noticed the details of this older hotel when I stayed here with the Bandini team. Looking at it with Chloe goggles, I appreciate the architecture and classic design.

She blinks up at the building. "Wow. It reminds me of the Biltmore Estate."

"The what?"

She lets out a sigh. "Oh, forget it. Sometimes I forget you're not from America."

I open my mouth to respond, but something catches my

eyes. A bystander pulls out their phone and snaps a picture of us. I'm tempted to call them out on their lack of privacy, but Chloe pulls me out of my thoughts.

"Do you think it's haunted?" She pokes my chest.

I release a shaky breath, ignoring the interested onlookers. "No. At least I hope it isn't. We better check in before a mob starts forming."

Chloe scans the entryway, her eyes stopping on the fans who've gathered near the lobby. "You know, there's one thing learning you're famous, but then there's a whole other thing experiencing it firsthand."

"This is nothing," I mumble as I direct her toward the concierge desk.

"They're taking video of you! That's so creepy."

I'm thankful for the jeans covering my leg. Nothing about my fans' scrutiny makes me feel good, but I can't do anything about it while we are out in the open. "Ignore it. You'll get used to them by the end of the weekend."

"I don't know if that's something I want to get used to in the first place." She purses her lips.

The employee checks us in, her gaze focused on me. She drops our key card twice before I reach over and pluck it from her trembling hands with a thank you.

My skin itches as people's stares heat the back of my neck. "Let's go," I grunt, stealing Chloe's attention away from a fancy painting she was ogling. With fidgety hands, I grab onto our luggage and lead the way toward the elevator.

We enter a waiting car. The doors shut, and I exhale.

"Are you okay?" Chloe tilts her head at me.

"I just want to get to the room and relax."

"Mmkay." She rocks back on the heels of her sneakers.

The numbers change at a crawl as the car begins its slow ascent. I tap my fingers against the metal handlebar.

"Do you want to cancel? It's not too late to turn back now and go home."

Home. A word like that out of her mouth shouldn't make my skin heat with a welcome nervousness, but it does. Something deep within me wouldn't mind taking Chloe home. Anywhere but here.

I shake my head. "No. And based on the amount of photos the fans took, I'm sure everyone will know I'm here by the end of the hour. If I run, then I'll look like a coward."

"Or someone who values their privacy." She shrugs.

Her gesture is sweet, but I couldn't escape this fate even if I wanted to. The elevator stops, and the doors open to our suite.

"Holy shit." Chloe's mouth gapes open as she exits the car, leaving me behind to roll our bags inside.

Lights bounce off the chandelier above our heads, highlighting the expansive space. Chloe runs her hand across a suede couch. I enjoy the look of awe on her face as she takes in everything.

"The only way this weekend can get any better is if you tell me there's free champagne and chocolate in this room." She throws herself on the couch.

Her reaction reminds me of my first time experiencing the lux life of Formula 1. I was lost in the luxury of everything, not realizing how easily it could be taken away.

I frown at the idea. Unfortunately, it was. The psychological wound festers into something tangible, with an ache emanating through my body toward my leg. If a phantom pain happens again in front of Chloe, I swear I'll lose my shit. One time was enough of a blow to my confidence. Two times in one day would be catastrophic.

Inhaling deeply, I turn away toward the door on the opposite end of the room. It takes everything in me not to stumble. "Feel free to make yourself comfortable. I'm going to take a nap."

"Oh, sure." Her smile drops. "I'll keep quiet and explore the palace. I mean *place*." She laughs to herself.

Another pain shoots through my leg. *Fuck.* I grip onto the knob and rip the door open. Without looking back, I enter the room, sealing myself off from Chloe's help.

I refuse to let her see me weak anymore. How can she ever want me if I'm still some struggling cripple who can't function like a normal man? The last thing I want is for her to see me as anything lesser than.

Dark thoughts eat away at my restraint, making me question if this weekend was a good idea. But like everything in my life, my quick decisions lead to drastic consequences.

I work through the phantom pain on my own. Without my mirror, it takes twenty minutes longer than usual for the exercises and mind games to work. And in Chloe's absence, I struggle to breathe easier as the pain fades away. I already miss her coaxing me out of my mental cloud of self-contempt like she did this morning.

A realization hits me. I'm becoming reliant on a woman who has every opportunity to walk away. And damn, I want her to stay, even if it's for a little while longer.

Chloe stares at me, her mouth gaping like a fish. It's cute. Endearing really.

Yeah, you're fucked. You think everything she does is appealing.

"You're telling me that we have to share one bed?" Her eyes bounce between the king-size mattress and my face.

"Yes."

"And one room?"

"That's usually how the one-bed situation works. Yes." I smirk.

"Would it be too much to ask for a second room? You are rich and all."

I shake with silent laugher. She says the word *rich* with such distaste, I end up respecting her more for it. "Because that wouldn't be obvious to my family at all."

She remains silent, but her eyes remain wide as she checks out the room.

"We've already done this once. What's the worst that can happen?"

"Yeah, well, we had a sick child to take care of." Her eyes darken as they roam across my body.

I grin like an idiot. "And now?"

Her throat bobs as she swallows. "Nothing."

"Oh, come on. Are you nervous to share a bed?"

"No."

"Excited?"

She scoffs. "Definitely not."

"Then what's the problem?"

"You look like someone who takes up the majority of the bed."

"The horror." I gasp and press a palm against my chest.

She groans under her breath and grabs her clothes from her luggage. "I'm going to shower."

"Do you need any help?"

She throws a bundle of socks right at my face.

My laughter is met with the soft click of the bathroom door closing behind Chloe. Warmth spreads through me at the idea of sleeping by her side.

Oh, yeah. I'm absolutely, positively fucked.

Chloe slides into bed after her shower. The darkness hides her face from me, but her hesitant movements have me raising a brow.

"Good night," she mumbles under her breath. The sheets rustle as she hugs the edge of the bed.

"If you fall asleep like that, you'll end up on the floor."

"Better than the alternative."

"Which is?"

She scoots closer to the middle of the bed, abandoning the edge. Her hands fumble in the dark, creating a pillow barrier.

The sight of it has me chuckling up to the ceiling.

She sighs.

"Is this the moment you admit to me that you like watching people sleep?"

"No!" She cackles.

"A secret toe fetish?"

"Oh my God. Stop!" Her giggles grow louder.

"Oh, I know. You snore!"

Her body thrashes as her laughs bounce off the ceiling. "I've been labeled a stage ten cuddler."

My interest is doused by a surge of jealousy that catches me by surprise. "By who?" I attempt with everything in me to keep my voice flat.

"Brooke. Supposedly I almost suffocated her in her sleep when we had to share a bed a couple of times. She said I wrapped myself around her like a wet blanket."

"Is that supposed to be a con?"

"That and a red flag."

"Well, when it comes to you, consider me colorblind."

She lets out the most obnoxious laugh that has me grinning. "You're supposed to run for the hills."

A laugh bubbles out of me, uncontrolled and unexpected. "You're strange if you think that's the case."

"Well, I didn't claim I wasn't weird."

I point at the poor attempt of a pillow barrier. "You're also stubborn."

"I prefer the more positive synonym of *tenacious*."

"Okay, Merriam Webster."

"You're going to call me another woman in bed? You really are the worst fake boyfriend." She fake gasps.

I let out a throaty laugh. Something about Chloe makes everything lighter. Better. Happier. I'm tempted to keep poking fun at her just to hear what ridiculousness she spews next.

With each joke between us, her laughs because more unrestrained.

It hits me that playing guitar isn't the only music that feeds my soul anymore. Chloe's laughs are the sweetest melody, a harmony of sounds that can't be recreated by any strings or notes. They fill me with a warmth, banishing the darkness that grew and festered over the years after my accident.

I wake up to a heavy weight against my chest. *What's that?*

I open my eyes, blinking away the blurriness to find a mass of black hair against my chest.

Right. Chloe. Shared bed. A failed pillow barrier.

When Chloe called herself a cuddler, she was not kidding. She molds herself to the left side of my body. One of her legs is thrown over my lower half, uncomfortably pressing against my growing erection. Her hand is splayed on top of my chest and her hair is a mass of tangles trailing down her back, tickling my skin.

She smells like daisies and sunshine, and I'm growing addicted to the scent.

I wish I didn't have to leave, but I can't have her seeing me without my prosthetic. I'm just not ready for that yet. For a few minutes, I enjoy her presence. Intimacy with her is something I've come to appreciate after living many years without it.

Chloe doesn't even stir as I pull myself from underneath her. She sleeps like the dead and looks good doing it.

Not wanting her to wake up and find me in this position, I move quickly through the motions of putting on my leg. I glance over my shoulder halfway through the process. She replaced me with a pillow, and I instantly regret getting out a bed.

I look back down at my leg. One day I'll feel comfortable enough to share this part of me with someone else. But today is definitely not the day.

CHAPTER TWENTY-SIX

SANTIAGO

"**C**hloe, are you sure that you're okay with being filmed for my vlog?" Maya looks over at Chloe with her camera clutched in her palm. Ever since I stepped on the empty racetrack, my skin has been clammy and my heart has been beating at a rapid pace.

Bandini employees work in the pit lane. The crew secures spare tires and checks on car parts after Noah's earlier practice rounds. If I close my eyes, I can imagine the noises and smells of a race day. Besides the occasional crew member looking up at us, everyone keeps to themselves. I didn't realize how much I missed the energetic buzz of the pit on a race weekend. It's become a distant memory after all these years.

"Sure! How hard can a race be?" Chloe checks out the sleek Bandini sports car.

A race?!

"Against Maya? Don't let her fool you. She knows her way around a car better than half the crew." Noah wraps an arm around Maya's waist.

I tuck my hand in the back pocket of her shorts and pull her flush against my side. "Since when did you plan a race?" I whisper in her ear.

"Since your sister texted me this morning asking if I would do a vlog with her. She is very persuasive and I had a hard time saying no."

"How did you even get each other's num—" I pinch the bridge of my nose and take a deep breath. "Forget it. It doesn't matter. You can't drive."

"Why?" She shakes her head in a sassy way.

I'd find it endearing under any other circumstance. Now, her defiance annoys me.

"Maya, Chloe can't drive. She doesn't have a license," I announce to the group.

"You suck," Chloe mumbles under her breath.

I tuck a strand of her hair behind her ear and lean in to whisper, "My goal is for *you* to suck, but this is good enough for now."

Her crimson cheeks are the only response I get.

"Oh. I didn't realize you just learned to drive. We can do something else. How about an exclusive interview? I'm sure my fans would go crazy to learn more about you." Maya's eyes perk up.

Hell no. That plan is somehow even worse than this one.

"That sounds like a great idea." Noah's smile grows larger as he gauges my reaction.

Fucker. The last thing I want is Maya interviewing Chloe. It might put our game at risk, and I can't have that. It's purely selfish of me, but I want to keep faking it with Chloe. It gives her a reason to stay around me.

I step in. "What about a hot laps match? Noah versus me. I'm sure that kind of vlog would interest your fans a bit more than an interview with Chloe. No offense." The words slip past my lips before I have a chance to consider the consequences.

Noah stares at me without blinking while Maya's mouth drops open.

I mean I get it's surprising but come on. There's no way in hell I'm letting my sister interview Chloe, but I'm also not letting Chloe behind the wheel of a car worth a quarter of a million dollars.

Maya laughs nervously. "Oh no. Don't worry about it. We can scratch the vlog and go eat an early dinner instead with Mom and Dad."

I lift a brow. "Are you afraid I'll beat your husband? I know he's old and all but have a little faith in him."

Chloe stares up at me with her lips parted. I'm tempted to kiss the look of surprise off her face, but I refrain. Just because I can't drive an F1 car anymore doesn't mean I can't race against Noah like the old days in a normal sports car like this one. I've practiced with similar cars I own over the past couple of years.

"If you beat me, I've clearly lost my touch." Noah holds out his palm for me to shake.

"May the best man win." I grab onto his extended hand and squeeze.

"I need to go grab my spare camera and car mount! I'll be right back!" Maya runs off, rambling to herself in Spanish.

"I'll grab the keys from the office." Noah walks off.

I walk up to the Bandini car and run my finger across the

hood. It's been years since I've ridden in this kind of sports car. One meant to break every speed limit and look good doing it.

My eyes shut as I imagine the purr of the engine, revving as I press down on the throttle. Uneasiness trickles up my spine at the thought of speeding down a track at neck-breaking speeds. My hand falters, slipping on the hood.

"You didn't have to save me back there. I could've done an interview with your sister." Chloe places her hand on top of mine. An energizing sensation replaces the coldness from my earlier thoughts.

"And risk you making up terrible stories about me to old fans? I can imagine the outrage already."

"I'd only take it to a certain level."

"And what level is that?" My voice drops as I prop my ass against the hood and spread my legs. I grab onto her hips and turn her toward me, securing her in front of me.

"Oh, I don't know." She looks up at the sky. "I'd only reveal a skeleton or two about you."

"Please, by all means, share what you had in mind. I'm curious what dirty secrets you've picked up on during our few weeks together."

"You're a blanket hog." She smiles in a way that snatches the oxygen straight from my lungs. Fuck. It's like my body can't keep it together around her.

"Am not."

"Are to. I almost froze to death last night. You left me with the smallest corner that could barely keep my feet warm, let alone my body."

I chuckle. "Well, that explains why you were cuddled up to me this morning."

She shrugs. "I did try to warn you."

I nod, failing to hide my smile.

She scrunches her nose in distaste. "Well, now that we're here listing flaws—you snore. Loudly, I might add."

I throw my head back and laugh. "Now I know you're just saying that to get a rise out of me."

"Is it working?" She places a palm against my shaking chest. The heat of her hand makes me shudder.

I want to test her touch in a different circumstance, preferably with no one else around.

"You'll have to do a lot more than that to get me ruffled."

"Oh, I have some ideas—"

"Ready?" Noah calls out.

Chloe winces as my hands squeeze her hips. "You don't have to do this if you don't want to." Her voice is nothing but a whisper in the wind.

I shake my head, hoping to wipe the worry from her eyes. "I was born for this."

"I'm going to join Noah in his car. Chloe, if you want to stay in the pit area, we'll be done quick!" Maya focuses on setting up the camera in my car.

"Wait, you're going with him?" Chloe's eyes bounce between Maya and Noah.

"Of course! It's so much fun." My sister beams.

"Oh." Chloe looks up at me with bright eyes, making something in my chest tighten like a coil. "Can I go with you? If you don't mind that is?"

"Sure."

Except I'm very unsure about the whole thing once I take a seat in the car. The fresh leather smell does little to calm my racing heart, and my stomach churns at the purr of the engine starting up. Chloe tugs her helmet on before securing herself in a protective harness.

I stare at the steering wheel, my fist tightening around the leather to stop my hands from trembling. My breaths become shallower as thoughts plague my head.

What if I lose control?

What if I crash and hurt Chloe in the process?

What if I—

"What do you think of us placing a bet?" Chloe grabs onto my clenched hand and releases my fingers one by one from the wheel. She links our hands, holding mine hostage.

I focus on her touch rather than the panic building up inside of me, settling deep within my bones. "A bet?" I croak.

"A bet. I bet Noah beats you."

"You're betting against me?" The audacity of this woman. To think I invited her to a weekend of torture and free alcohol.

"Of course. Noah is the reigning champion and all." She smiles tauntingly.

"What do you win if I lose to my brother-in-law?"

"Hmm. If I win, I get to give you a blowjob."

The breath I take turns into a fit of coughs. "What?" Maybe it's worth losing for that prize alone. But Noah would gloat for days, and I'm not sure any blowjob is worth that special kind of torment.

"Did you hear me okay or are you woozy from the blood relocating itself from your brain to your dick?"

What is it about this girl that has me constantly breaking out deep belly laughs?

She squeezes my hand. "So, is that a yes?"

"Sure, Chloe."

"And what do you want? If you win that is?"

I want to wipe that smug grin off her face. "*When* I win, I get to go down on you whenever I want."

"Whenever?" She wheezes.

"Whenever I want. Whichever way I want. What do you say? Let's make a *bet*."

"Deal." She shakes our already clasped hands up and down.

I push aside my worries because I have a new goal. Beating Noah wasn't enough. Beating Noah while securing a hookup with Chloe has my skin buzzing with a different kind of excitement. One I allow to feed my adrenaline rush.

This is just like driving your other cars. You've practiced these exact moves with your leg before.

Noah and I drive up to the checkered line.

My sister lowers her window and waves from the passenger seat. She presses a button on a remote, and the red light from the camera on our dashboard flashes on and off. "The camera is filming. The first person past the finish line after ten laps wins."

"Good luck," Noah calls out.

"See you in my rearview mirror." I rev the engine once, letting the rumbling soak into me. Energy crackles around me as my confidence grows.

And at the end of Maya's countdown, I surge down the racetrack with Chloe screaming beside me. Tires squeal in protest as Noah and I rush side by side across the pavement. My heart threatens to pop out of my chest, and my hands tremble from the fresh rush of adrenaline.

"Oh my fucking God, this is the stupidest thing I've ever done!" Chloe cries out.

"Oh, Chloe. If this is the stupidest, you're clearly not living." I look over at her, smiling at her.

She's always been beautiful. But her by my side while I battle my demons? It's a look that can't compare.

"Focus on the damn road!"

"I'm confused. Did you expect me to go slow?" I push against the accelerator, surging past Noah's car and cutting him off. I press my foot on the brake and smoke billows from the tires.

"Oh, God. I'm sorry I don't pray to you enough, but now is the best time. Please don't let me die." She presses her palms together.

I chuckle, switching gears to match the curves and straights of the track. "You'll only die when my tongue is fucking you into oblivion. I promise."

"We are on camera!" Chloe's waves at my sister's vlog gear.

"Don't worry. My sister has someone who edits her videos."

"How is that a good excuse?"

I laugh, ignoring her.

Noah zooms past my car at the next straight, pushing me to outsmart him. Back and forth, we fight for first place within the second lap of the race. Every muscle in my body tightens as I force the car to its limit.

I don't have time to second-guess myself, let alone worry about crashing at high speeds.

"I hate you!" Chloe screams again as I turn sharply, the car's tires locking in submission. We drift, leaving behind another plume of smoke.

Laughter explodes out of me. "Have fun with me."

"I'll have fun once you lose this damn race!" she shrieks.

"Is that a challenge?"

"It's a fact."

"Cute little Chloe taunting me." I press on the accelerator, forcing Noah into second place as I pass him once again.

She looks away, failing at hiding her smile. Interesting. She *is* enjoying herself. The little criminal is a pretty good faker after all.

After a few laps, Chloe's squeals shift from fear to enjoyment. Her reactions push me harder to drift at curbs and force the car to a new breaking point.

It hits me out of nowhere that I'm having fun. For the first time in the longest time, I'm enjoying myself while driving. It's such a damn good time, I don't avoid hitting almost one-hundred and seventy miles per hour. It's the fastest I've gone since I was in an F1 car racing.

The real deal feels intoxicating. I forgot how much I was obsessed with the speed and adrenaline. It's like a shot of excitement to the veins, with my heart pumping fast in my chest. Anything I've done since my accident to replace this feeling is only a cheap imitation. I love it. I miss it. And I absolutely want more of it.

Racing today didn't diminish my need, it created a new one. I cross the finish line with the biggest grin plastered across my face.

"You won!" She lifts her arms in the air and laughs.

"Fuck yeah!" I smack my palm into the steering wheel, grinning as I stop the car.

She laughs as she removes her helmet. Her dark hair is a mess of waves and loose strands.

I tug on a piece. "You shouldn't have doubted me."

"I never did."

"Then why make a bet in the first place?"

"Because how can you focus on being anxious if you're too focused on winning something you want?"

My gaze darkens as I focus on her lips. "I won more than a race today."

She winks. "And don't you forget it."

If I didn't already know I liked this girl, today would've sealed the deal.

CHAPTER TWENTY-SEVEN

Chloe

"**G**ood morning." Santiago's rough voice greets me as I exit the room. He sits on the hotel room's couch, shirtless while reading on an iPad.

How does he always wake up way before me?

I scan his upper body, my eyes getting stuck on ridges of muscles across his stomach. Good God. I've never met a guy who actually looks like he belongs on a magazine cover until now. I cough, recovering from my perusal. "Did your shirt get lost somewhere?"

He chuckles. "I don't sleep with one."

"Well, you can always wake up with one."

His smile expands. "And miss the look on your face as you check me out? What kind of man do you take me for?"

"Are you sure you want to hear my answer?"

He laughs. "Maybe it's best I don't."

"Good choice." I grin.

"So, I have a surprise."

My smile disappears. "No."

"Hear me out."

"I don't do surprises. Ever."

"How about if it involves shopping?"

"*Especially* if it involves shopping."

He dares to laugh. "I'm sorry then. Really I am. But my sister and mom want to take you shopping for a dress for the gala tonight."

"*Ugh.*" I throw myself dramatically on the couch. My legs flop over his thighs, and he secures them to his lap.

"I tried to talk them out of the plan, but they're pretty dead set on it."

"You're throwing me to the wolves on day two!"

"I wouldn't ask you if I didn't think you could handle it."

"Right. And let me guess. You're not coming with."

He frowns. "I could if you want me to. It's just that I never go shopping with them, and they seem excited to have some time alone with you."

"This is a disaster in the making. They'll figure out our ruse in an hour or less."

Santiago shakes his head, trying to hide his smug grin. "No. They'll be focused on you and shopping that they won't notice anything amiss."

"Anything I make up about you in front of your family is your own fault."

"I wouldn't expect anything less from you. The more outrageous, the better."

"Oh, I plan on it. I'll start with how you secretly love frilly bath bombs." I smirk.

"If they ask, please only recommend the kind that smell

like lavender or citrus. Anything else makes my skin itchy."

While the grumpy version of him was tolerable, a joking Santiago is rather addictive. One so beautifully toxic, I wouldn't mind overdosing from the experience.

I feel like the biggest fraud, clutching a glass of champagne as we walk through a luxurious store with a name I can't pronounce. My scuffed-up sneakers squeak every time I move across the marble flooring.

We've bounced between stores, with Santiago's mom, who asked me to call her Daniela. She spent the whole morning sharing funny stories about her son while Maya talked him up like a contestant on a love show. It's not as if I need someone to convince me Santiago is a standup guy. I've seen it with my own two eyes and it's not exactly something I'll forget anytime soon.

"What about this one?" Maya hands me a silky dress. The material feels lush and unlike anything I own.

I sneak a peek at the price tag and nearly have a stroke. This dress is worth more than my rent for a month.

"Do you not like it?" Maya's smile drops.

Why does she have to be this wonderful and kind? Can't she have a flaw that would make it easier to run out the door and never look back?

I stutter. "Uhm...no. It looks gorgeous, don't get me wrong, but..."

"Is it the price? Don't worry about it. Santiago slipped me his Amex before we left the hotel."

"He did what?" The first lines of *Pretty Woman* blast in my head as my stomach twists into a tight knot.

"He said to pick out the prettiest dress for you or else he won't attend the gala tonight. I took it as a challenge."

"That's so...sweet," I choke out.

"I don't think I've seen my son this enamored by someone before." Santiago's mom winks at me. Her brown eyes have a lightness to them I can't ignore.

Either we're amazing at faking this relationship or everyone wants to desperately believe Santiago is genuinely happy.

"Oh." That's all I can muster up. The guy offered to pay for my dress for God's sake and all I can say is *oh*. I'm slipping into extremely dangerous territory around him. It's the kind of treacherous waters a girl can drown in if she's not careful.

A dress on the mannequin at the front of the store window catches my eye. The black material shines under the spotlights, making thousands of crystals appear like they're moving. Long sleeves balance the severity of the open back. I don't think I've ever seen a piece of clothing as stunning as that. It's as if the designer captured an illusion of moonlight reflecting off the glittering ocean at midnight.

"Oh, just look at your eyes light up!" Maya calls out to the employee who helps us. "We need that dress, please."

"What? I like the one you picked out!" I stumble over my words.

"But you *love* that one." Maya waggles her brows.

Based on the how dress is part of the storefront display, it must cost way more than the one I hold in my shaky hand. It makes me sick to purchase something like that on someone else's dime. I don't even see a price tag on it which only means one thing.

"Don't bother saying no. When my daughter sets her mind on something, come hell or high water, she is getting her way," Santiago's mom offers.

Maya plucks the dress she chose from my hands. She gently pushes me into a dressing room and the store attendant passes me the black dress.

I can't walk out of the store with this. How could I live with myself when I was barely making enough to cover my rent last month?

I pull out my phone and text Santiago.

> **Me:** Please tell me you didn't tell your sister that you wouldn't go to the gala if she didn't buy me a pretty dress.
> **Santiago:** Can I plead the fifth?
> **Me:** Seeing as you're not American and you don't follow the Constitution, the answer is no!
> **Me:** Seriously. I can't let you pay for something this expensive. Tell your sister to take me to a Zara or something a little more on par with my budget.
> **Santiago:** But I'm scared of her. Why don't you tell her since you're the one opposing this in the first place?
> **Me:** You're afraid of your sister? I wish I could choke you through the phone.
> **Santiago:** Is that your kink? You really are quite the surprise.

I snort.

> **Santiago:** And yes I'm afraid of my sister. She might be small but she's scrappy. I wouldn't mess with her. The one time I tried, she shaved my head in the middle of the night as payback.
> **Me:** You're the most infuriating person I've ever met.

> **Santiago:** Replace *infuriating* with *kindest* and you have yourself a compliment. Try it with me. Things like this take practice.

I huff. My phone beeps, interrupting my typing fingers.

> **Santiago:** You can always pay me back if it really kills you to accept a gift.

The only way I could afford a dress like this is if I worked until the day gray hairs started sprouting from my head.

> **Santiago:** But I'd rather you didn't. That takes away from the fun of it. Just let someone else take care of you for once.

Let someone else take care of you for once. Something about his simple words makes my chest tighten. I can't exactly reject him when he is this honest with me.

> **Me:** Thank you.

I can't think up anything else, and I doubt he expects me to. His words alone already incapacitated my brain for the morning.

"Is everything okay in there?" Santiago's mom calls out.

"Just perfect!" I offer in the nicest voice I can fake.

I remove my clothes and put on the new dress and matching shoes. The material clings to my body, highlighting curves I didn't know I possessed. My feet turn on their own, and the material swirls around me. Crystals reflect a spectrum of colors off the walls.

"Whoa." I snap a picture of myself and send it to Brooke.

"Let us see!" Maya chants.

I exit the stall, doing a little twirl in my heels.

Maya claps. "That's the one! Santiago is going to *die* when he sees you."

Well, Maya doesn't have to try too hard to convince me. I may not be the classiest gal to strut the red carpet, but I'll play the part.

I should be wary of how our performance is becoming much more real by the day. Instead of feeding the mental monster, I chug the rest of my champagne and enjoy my day with Daniela and Maya.

This is the closest thing I've ever had to family bonding, and it brings fresh tears to my eyes. And they're not exactly the happy kind. I traveled to Italy to find my family, but all I've done is throw myself into someone else's.

The worst part is I want more of it. I shouldn't crave more experiences with Santiago's family, but I can't resist. I've been denied a family to call my own for years. And my starved heart will suck up any kind of love it can get, even if it's poison.

I walk into our hotel room after having a spa day with Maya in her penthouse suite. She welcomed me into the life of the rich and lavish with manicures, pedicures, and a private makeup artist before our night at the gala. I never knew joining the dark side meant having champagne and a charcuterie board, but now that I've tried it, I'll never look at pre-gaming the same way again.

"Santiago?" I call out.

No response has me searching the large hotel room. I attempt the doorknob to our bedroom but find it locked.

"Santiago?" I tap against the door.

"Give me a minute," his voice croaks.

Shit, is he having more phantom pains? I press my ear to the door. He mumbles something I fail to catch.

I tap the door again. "Are you okay?"

"Define your meaning of *okay*?"

"Do I need to bust this door down to save your ass?"

"No. But I might need you to save me from myself because there is no way I can go tonight."

"Huh?"

The door opens, and I tumble into his room. His hands dart out to stabilize me.

My eyes flit from his tux to his eyes. Damn, he fills out the material in the best kind of way. He looks regal, with his hair slicked back and his face cleanly shaven.

I love everything about his look except for the frown plastered on his face. "What's the matter?"

"I don't know why I thought I could do this," he mumbles, turning away from me.

"Go to a gala?"

"A gala, seeing coworkers from before, and doing interviews with people asking me too many damn questions. I don't think I can do it." He takes a seat in a chair off to the side of his bed. His eyes avoid my gaze as he puts his head in his hands.

"If there is anyone who can do this, it's you."

He looks up at me, his eyes plagued with a darkness I hate. My breath lodges itself somewhere in my throat as his eyes roam down my body, taking in every detail. As good as it makes me feel to have his attention, it seems like a distraction for how he actually feels.

His chest heaves as he takes a few deep breaths. "Fuck. Here I am freaking out when I should be commenting on how beautiful you look."

I take the seat across from him, halting his assessment. "Eh, you have all night to compliment me. You know, at the gala you probably should attend, seeing as it's honoring your brother-in-law and whatnot. Plus you got all dressed up already. It would truly be a crime against humanity to hide you from the world when you look like that."

He laughs, but the sound is hollow and unlike him.

I tap his knee. "But it's okay to be freaked out. I would be if I were in your shoes."

His brow lifts. "Really?"

"Of course. You're making a huge, scary sacrifice for your family."

"What if I don't want to go anymore?"

"If you don't want to, then we won't go." I shrug. "We can order takeout and binge watch TV until we pass out."

His lip twitches. "After you spent all that time getting ready, you'd be okay skipping out?"

"Absolutely. I'll count us even as long as you take a picture of me for my social media page. I've never dressed up like this before, so pics or it didn't happen." I grin.

"Never? What about prom?"

I shrink back and stare at my hands. "Oh, I couldn't go."

"Why not?"

"Because my foster mom didn't have the money to buy a dress. It wasn't common for kids like us to go to those kinds of things anyway. But it's fine because I didn't plan on winning prom queen or anything."

Wrinkles mar his forehead as he frowns. "Don't do that."

"Do what?"

"Act like it doesn't bother you. It bothers the fuck out of me, and it wasn't even my prom."

"What do you expect me to do? Get mad?"

"Frankly, yes."

"Well, I can't turn back the clock, and I don't want to." The last thing I want to do is relive those years of my life.

"You're right. For the first time in a long time, I don't want to turn back the clock, either." He looks up from his hands, hitting me with a stare filled with mixed emotions.

"Why?"

"Because you make me want to live in the present rather than kill myself by focusing on the past."

My chest tightens to a point of discomfort. There's nothing in the world that can prepare me for having real feelings toward Santiago Alatorre. Feelings are dangerous, and I want to push them away. Very few people in my life have elicited any positive ones. And developing any kind with him gives him an opportunity to break me in ways I've never allowed anyone to do before.

I don't have time to evaluate how I feel toward him. It's messy and convoluted because of our fine line between fake and real. And it doesn't help when he says things that muddle my brain.

I didn't come to Italy to fall in love. And I most definitely didn't come to Italy to have my heart broken. But with all the time I'm spending around Santiago, I'm not sure if the two are mutually exclusive anymore.

The first camera bulb blinds me. I blink away the black spots in my vision, only to be set off by another flashing light. "How does anyone walk the red carpet if they can't see?" I clutch onto Santiago's arm, my fingers digging into the material of his tux.

Somehow my game-day prep speech worked on him while my confidence disappears by the minute. He struts the carpet like he was meant for this life while I struggle to keep up, my attention diverted by reporters yelling out questions.

"I'd say you could get used to it, but I hope we don't have to attend another one of these for a very long time."

My feet grind to a halt at his words. "We?"

His eyes land on everything besides my face. "We. Me. Slip of the tongue."

Right. I scrunch my nose.

A reporter calls out Santiago's name. He grumbles something under his breath as he leads us toward the red velvet rope. "Let's get this one over with and then we can drink until the world blurs."

I laugh as I follow him.

"Santiago Alatorre! What a pleasure it is to have you here at Monza with us!" The reporter beams at my date.

"I'm happy to be here." Santiago offers a half-assed smile.

I elbow him in the ribs and whisper, "Try a little harder."

"And who is your date for tonight?" The reporter moves the microphone from Santiago's face to mine.

"Oh." I suck in a breath. "I'm Chloe."

The reporter looks at me expectantly. "Chloe who?"

"Carter."

"From?" he prompts, his right eye twitching as if he wants to hold back an eye roll.

"America?"

The reporter laughs while Santiago looks like he sucked on a lemon. Am I making myself look like an idiot on live television? If I had a mom who cared, I'd apologize to her later.

The man shifts his attention back toward my grumpy date. "Santiago, will we see you out on the track this Sunday cheering Noah on?"

"Of course. It's Bandini's home race and Noah's last Italian Grand Prix. I wouldn't miss it for the world." Santiago's smile looks more like a wince.

I pat his hand, and he wraps his muscular arm around me, tugging me into his side. My heart speeds up at his touch, and all the nerves in my body go haywire.

"And how long have you two been dating?"

"A month."

"A year." We both speak at the same time.

The reporter's head snaps back and forth between us.

"A year and a month." Santiago squashes the man's confusion.

I turn my laugh into a cough. Somehow my fake relationship has been more successful than my last two relationships combined.

The reporter asks if I need water, but I wave him off. "Sorry. I have chronic allergies."

"A pity indeed, always flaring up at the most inconvenient times." Santiago cracks a smile in my direction.

The reporter carries on, expressing his enthusiasm at

scoring an interview with the enigma beside me.

I learn a few things as we continue down the carpet, answering questions from fellow reporters. People genuinely care about what Santiago has been up to. Their gaze remains sincere as they ask him appropriate questions. But most of all, Santiago brightens as he gains more courage with them.

I don't want to assume, but I think deep down that he misses this. The attention, the race car talk, the whole *don't mind me, I'm really fucking famous* situation.

The curious part of me wonders what it would take to help Santiago realize he has what it takes to come back.

It seems like after this trip, I need to add something new yet essential to my European expedition. I refuse to leave Italy without helping Santiago return to his former glory. Whether it's racing or living a life out of the shadows, I want to help him. And nothing can stop me from accomplishing what I put my mind to. Not even a grumpy, six-foot-something male who seeks to be invisible when he's meant to shine.

CHAPTER TWENTY-EIGHT

SANTIAGO

I survived the red carpet of torture. My head throbs and my palms remain permanently sweaty as Chloe and I make our way through the crowds of people inside the ballroom.

Rather than focus on their obvious stares, I remain laser-focused on Chloe. It's not a hard task in the slightest. I'm enchanted by her. Absolutely, utterly captivated by the brunette beauty who emanates warmth and confidence despite her fear of attention. I'd pay for a hundred more gowns if it meant I could see her dressed like this again. The material flows across her curves like water, changing colors depending on the light.

My attraction isn't even about the dress she wears or the makeup she put on. It's more than that. It's *her*. Before her, I wasn't interested in love, but damn if I'm willing to try it now. Our fake relationship has been fun and all, but I wonder if she wants to trade up for the real deal.

We approach Maya and Noah. Maya wraps her arms around Chloe and snatches her attention away from me.

"I didn't say it before, but thanks for coming this weekend. It means a lot to us." Noah pulls me in for a hug.

"I wouldn't dare miss your Bandini send off before you head to the retirement home."

He laughs as he pats me on the back and pulls away. "Relax. I still have a handful of races left."

"The last few for the rest of your life. How does it feel?"

"I'm ready to spend the rest of my years with Maya and Marko, traveling and enjoying life. I can't exactly take my money to my grave, so I might as well use it."

My sister lucked out finding someone like Noah. He loves her in the way she deserves, and I can't help feeling happy for her. There's no better match for her and Marko.

"Are you ready to party?" Maya waggles her brows.

"You've watched *Bad Moms* too many times," Noah grumbles.

"It's one of my favorite movies." She smiles at Chloe. "But come on, my mom is watching Marko tonight so we can have fun."

"How about we start with one drink and see where the night takes us?" Chloe offers.

"Smart. Don't let my sister trick you into shots. She's more lightweight than a feather." I grin.

"Stop ruining my fun." Maya rolls her eyes. "Let's go to the other bar. The line looks shorter." My sister locks arms with Chloe and steers her toward the opposite end of the ballroom.

"They're getting along well." Noah nods in their direction.

"Great." My throat closes up as I become distracted by everyone surrounding us.

Partygoers look in our direction and whisper to one another. A few of them inch closer, clearly wanting to interrupt. Their attention stifles me. Without Chloe, the weight of the situation hits me. I'm tempted to walk in the opposite direction of Noah because I'm sure he's the reason behind everyone's interest in us. Noah is a bright star who everyone wants five minutes with.

Noah laughs. "Why do you look like you're about to throw up?"

A server walks by and I wave them down, grabbing two glasses of champagne. I chug the first before sipping from the second.

"Aw, you're nervous. How cute." Noah lays a hand on my shoulder.

"Call me cute again and I'll punch you."

He rolls his eyes. "No one will bother you unless you openly talk to them."

"How do you know?"

"Because we're surrounded by people who used to work by your side. These aren't the same people who wrote those nasty articles about you. And if you want me to be real with you, the Bandini crew misses you. They don't want to scare you away before they have a chance to win you over again."

My lungs squeeze as I attempt to take in a few deep breaths. "You can't know that."

He shakes his head. "I do. Me retiring has stirred up quite the buzz. An open seat with Bandini again is a big deal."

"The biggest." I have a feeling I know where Noah wants to take this conversation.

"I want you to fight for it."

Yup. Guessed it. I bring the rim of the champagne flute to my lips and down the rest of the contents in two chugs.

Noah continues. "This is your chance to come back. There's no one else I want to take my spot but you. And there's no one who deserves it more."

I clutch onto the empty glass with a tight fist. "I can't do it."

"You can. You only need to get back in the car and try. It only takes one time to let the rush take over and erase your fears. People like us crave that kind of adrenaline, and it'll never go away, no matter how hard you try. And I've helped create the technology to—"

"I love you like a brother for wanting to help me, but I can't do it. You don't understand."

"Give me a reason why I should drop it. A *good* reason. Not the same bullshit you've been spewing for years."

"Is there a bigger reason than the fact that I'm down a leg and shouldn't be behind a wheel in the first place?"

"Don't you miss it? Didn't racing against me yesterday stir up anything in you?"

Of course it did. The race had me feeling buzzed to the point of feeling drunk without touching an ounce of alcohol. I thought I wouldn't be able to do it, but I accomplished my fear with Chloe by my side. It reminded me how I miss it more than anything in the world. But missing something I can never achieve again doesn't serve a purpose.

Wishing for the impossible is stupid. Chloe would kill me for saying it, but it doesn't make my words any less true. Wishes lead to disappointment, and disappointment leads to depression, and I'm done battling that darkness. It's exhausting fighting an invisible war inside of my head.

"I don't think I can ever race with F1 again."

He nods his head, looking away. "I can manage that."

"What?" I rear back.

"You said 'you don't think.' You've spent years saying you won't, but this is the first time you're uncertain. That you hesitate when I ask. All I have to do is convince you otherwise."

I shake my head from side to side. "You can't."

"Maybe I can't, but now you have someone worth pushing yourself for. Maybe you want to show her and yourself that you can be the man she deserves. The guy who would go through hell to walk out on the other end victorious. And that's enough to get you back behind the wheel. I know it."

I don't try to correct him. It's not like I can reveal that my whole relationship is a farce. And most of all, I don't know if Noah is entirely wrong. I've already accomplished more in the small time I've known Chloe than I have in the past few years. But while she makes me feel good, I can't ignore the feelings growing inside of me.

A hand smacking again my shoulders steals away my attention. I'm spun around, coming face-to-face with James Mitchell. He looks the same since the day I left the racing world. His graying hair is slicked back, and his suit remains as pristine as ever.

"Look who it is!" His green eyes lighten as his smile widens.

"Hey, James."

"It's good to have you back."

My posture goes rigid. "For the weekend."

His smile doesn't falter. "Even better. My old age means I can only handle one of you assholes at a time." He winks.

Noah laughs beside me. My shoulders drop, and I release a breath I didn't know I was holding in. I don't know why I expected James to push me on the subject, but he remains relaxed.

James wraps an arm around my shoulder and pulls me into him. "Relax. We're happy to have you even if it's just for a weekend."

I nod my head and return his hug. After being gone for as long as I have, I didn't realize how much I missed James. I've neglected this part of my life for too long.

He releases me. "How do you feel about saying hi to some of the old crew? They've been wanting to say hi, but they didn't want to cross any boundaries."

Since when have I become an intimidating piece of shit? That was always Noah's job. I look over at my brother-in-law, wondering how I became the grumpy asshole out of the two of us.

Noah lifts a brow in a silent response.

Right.

Is this how I want to be remembered? Even after Noah retires and I never have to show my face at a racetrack again, I'll go down in history as the recluse who let my circumstances ruin me. And no one wants to be remembered as the loser in history.

I nod my head, solidifying my decision. Fuck the consequences. I'm going to say hi, even if a bit of my dignity shrivels up and dies.

James leads us toward some old coworkers. I spend the next ten minutes answering easy questions and listening to stories from the guys working in the pit. Everyone remains friendly and approachable, and no one asks me about the one subject I hate the most.

I hate to admit it, but Noah was right. It really does seem like these guys miss me. It's obvious in their smiles and the way they share stories about race days with Noah. They rag on him, making me laugh at all the times Noah messes up, which isn't very often. No one tries to reminisce about my old days. Instead, they focus on asking me what I've been up to lately.

Something releases inside of me. I don't know what happens, but it's as if something I've kept locked up finally makes its way to the surface. Honesty pours out of me, describing my time babysitting Marko and all the disasters that happened. I share details about the different cars I've restored and how I've finally started enjoying living in Lake Como. Everyone remains interested, and the questions they ask make the conversation easier.

Something sparkling in the corner of my eye catches my attention. Everything fades away as Chloe steps into my eyesight with her beaming smile and halo of positivity. Everyone's eyes snap in her direction as she knocks her head back and laughs at something Maya says. We're all helpless moths seeking her light.

The sight has me frozen in place. My chest tightens as I take her in, letting her breathe a new life into me with nothing more than her presence.

Maybe I should make a wish after all because women like Chloe Carter don't come around often. And damn, she has me wishing for more than driving again or escaping the prison I created for myself. She makes me want to wish for love, and that's the most dangerous thing for someone like me. Not because I don't want it, but because I desire it to the point where I'm willing to do anything to make it happen.

Absolutely anything. Sacrifices be damned.

CHAPTER TWENTY-NINE

SANTIAGO

Chloe's heels click against the tiled floor as we enter the hotel elevator. I press the button for the penthouse, and the car groans as it rises.

Chloe looms in the corner of the car, staring up at the ceiling. I scan her body, struggling to choose between focusing on her face, her tits, or her ass. The dress looks incredible on her, and I'm tempted to buy one in every color.

The air thickens around us, heavy with tension as her eyes focus on me. All of me.

I stand taller, enjoying the way her eyes darken as they run across my body.

Chloe blushes and looks away when her eyes meet mine. She whistles, and I laugh.

I eat up the distance between us. "Are you nervous?"

"Honestly?"

I nod my head.

"Yeah, the way you're looking at me scares me." She swallows and darts her eyes toward the old-school dial above the elevator door indicating we are only on floor ten out of thirty.

I brush my knuckles across her cheekbone. "Why?"

"Because whatever you're thinking about can't be good."

"But it can sure be fun."

I can't wait to get her into our suite because I plan on collecting my win from the race with Noah. Her cheeks flush after I press a soft kiss against her mouth. She sucks in a breath, and I grin.

A loud, screeching sound grates against my ears. I wrap my arms around Chloe as the elevator drops. My stomach matches the sudden descent of the car. The elevator shakes as it falls, the screeching noise reminding me of nails on a chalkboard. Chloe's scream makes my ears ring in protest.

The car stops with a yank, as if it was tugged taught by a cord. I stumble but catch us before we fall over.

Chloe clutches onto me as the elevator makes one last grinding sound. "Oh my God." She presses her head into my chest.

Lights flicker before going out. We both breathe heavy, the sounds of our inhales and exhales matching one another. Pitch darkness surrounds us. I lay my chin on top of Chloe's head, regulating my breathing.

"Did we almost die?" she rasps.

"No. Of course not. Elevators have safety mechanisms for situations like this. Especially in old buildings like this." I don't have the first clue about elevator mechanics, but something about her voice tells me to pretend it's all okay.

The speaker box crackles to life as someone speaks Italian to us. I release Chloe and walk up to the electrical panel.

"*Aiuto.*" It's one of the few words I can muster up as I press the call button.

The person rattles on, saying things I don't understand. The voice disappears as they say something I assume is along the lines of *help is coming*. I check my phone for service, but the lack of bars makes me curse.

"How long do you think we will be stuck in here?" Chloe's voice doesn't carry its usual assuredness. It sounds small and weak, which concerns me.

"I don't know. Could be an hour or more probably? It depends on if we are stuck between floors."

"I can't decide if I feel like throwing up or crying." The tapping of her heel against the floor gives away her agitation.

I'm not sure if the rush of adrenaline or gratitude for being okay has me laughing up to the roof of the small car. "While I'd hate for you to cry, please don't throw up in here. That would make a bad situation way worse."

"This isn't funny!"

"It's a little funny."

"How? We almost died!"

I walk up to her and press my body into hers, trapping her in a corner. My hand has a mind of its own, wrapping strands of Chloe's hair around my fingers. "But we didn't."

"That's *so* not reassuring." Her voice wavers. "Is now the time to reveal to you how I don't like tight, dark spaces?"

"Shit. Are you claustrophobic?"

"Umm."

Fuck. Her breathing quickens. I pluck my phone out of my pocket and use the flashlight. She winces at the sudden brightness. I bend over and place the phone on the floor, illuminating the space enough to make out her shadow.

"Is that better?"

"A little bit." Her voice hits a new high pitch.

Okay, so not better. Think, Santiago.

Everything clicks into place. I use the handle behind Chloe to kneel. The movement is anything but steady and fluid, but the limited lighting conceals my struggle.

Chloe's hand freezes on my shoulder. "What are you doing?"

"What does it look like I'm doing?"

"Well seeing as how I can barely see in the first place... Did you drop something?"

Her reaction has me chuckling. "No."

"Then why are you kneeling on the floor?"

"Take a guess."

"Now's not the time for games." Her voice cracks. It's obvious she's about to flip out at any second.

"Why would I play when I already won?" I run my fingers down her dress before lifting the hem.

"Oh, God." Chloe's panicky voice morphs into breathless pants.

"Not even He can save you from me." I press a kiss against her silk-covered center. The material blocks me, but Chloe gets my message.

"Fuck. Fuckity fuck fuck."

I chuckle under my breath. "Jump onto the handlebar and hold on to the hem of your dress."

"What about the magic word?"

"Orgasm?"

She laughs up to the ceiling. "No."

"Cock."

"*Please.*"

"I knew you could beg if you really put your mind to it."
I trace a finger across the damp material covering the place I
desperately want to taste.

"Bastard."

"I prefer *bastard who's about to make you come*, but we'll get
you there eventually."

Chloe's body trembles as I press my thumb against her
clit. She follows my command, spreading her legs in front of
me.

The shadows give me little ability to memorize how she
looks, and I hate it. But what I do know is she's perfect. So
fucking perfect, I'm beside myself with excitement. It's been a
long time since I've had any kind of connection with someone
like this. I soak it up, enjoying it for exactly what it is. Human
connection. Something so fundamental I've denied myself for
years.

I trace my fingers up her legs with the lightest touch. It's
faint, enough to tell her I'm here. To make sure she knows
I'm the one in control of the situation. Her skin pebbles as
my fingers clutch onto her underwear. I tug the satin strip of
fabric down and tuck it into my pocket.

My confidence grows at her enthusiasm. God, my mouth
practically waters at the sight of her spread in front of me. The
flashlight from my phone reveals the faintest smile on her lips.
I latch onto that image of her, burning it into my memory
as my lips descend on her. I leave behind kisses on her inner
thigh before I trace her seam with my tongue.

The moan she lets out has my dick throbbing in my pants.

I become addicted to every groan and breathless sigh she releases as I pleasure her. It's the best feeling, bringing her to life in the same way she does to me. I'm a lost man, finding bits and pieces of myself again with Chloe's help.

She goes wild as I suck on her clit. My little hellion, unrestrained and needy, begging for my cock with her whimpers. I sink a finger into her, and she clutches onto my hair with a sigh. If I thought I was addicted to Chloe before, I'm a goner now. Don't bother signing me up for rehab.

Touching her is a dream, with her being incredibly responsive to anything I do. Heat trickles down my spine as she takes my next two fingers without protest.

Getting Chloe off is my next favorite thing, right up there with making her laugh. I torture her, bringing her to the edge of pleasure before retreating again.

Her fingers clutch onto my hair, tugging at the root. "If you don't make me come, I swear to God when I return the favor, you'll be begging for way longer than me."

I smile, increasing the tempo of my fingers pumping into her. I suck on her clit and use my tongue to my advantage.

Her moan echoes off the walls as she comes apart above me. I don't stop until her body quits shaking and her fingers release my hair from her death grip.

Her head hits the wall behind her with a thump. "It's official. I discovered the cure to claustrophobia."

"Orgasms?"

She giggles. Her distraction cloaks my struggle as I lift myself up from the ground with the help of the handlebar. I wince at the pressure on my leg, a hiss escaping my mouth before I can catch myself.

Chloe grabs onto my hand. "Are you okay?"

There's nothing I want more than for Chloe to forget that I'm different. I don't need to be coddled because she thinks I shouldn't do what a normal man can. Fuck that. Fuck it all to hell and back because I'm over that shit around her. I'm all man. No injury or metal leg can stop me from proving that to her.

I ignore her question, wrapping my arm around her waist and pulling her toward me. My lips press against hers. Our kiss is charged. Crazed. Needy. Like every cell in my body is on a mission to fire off at the same time.

She wraps her arms around my neck and pushes her body into mine. Her legs wrap around my waist, and I grind my erection into her.

She runs her hand down my chest and lands on the band of my trousers. I drop my head in the crook of her neck and groan as she nears the place begging for her attention. And I mean *begging*. I consider the pre-cum leaking from my tip as tears of joy. It's been too long since I've enjoyed this genuine kind of contact—one full of desperation and lust. I'd beg on my knees for her touch if it didn't make me look like some kind of freak.

I freeze as the image of Chloe being eye level with my prosthetic leg harasses my brain. The thought kills my lust-crazed buzz. I clutch onto her hand and return it back around my neck.

"Why did you do that?"

"Do what?" I move to kiss her again, but she pulls back.

"Stop me."

"Because that's not the point of tonight." I turn her face

back toward mine.

"Cut the bullshit. Any warm-blooded male would let me go through with what I want to do." Darkness cloaks her face in shadows, giving me nothing to go on besides her irritated voice.

"Let's *not* talk about other males while my lips still taste like you."

She growls and pushes my chest. I step away, and she slides off the handlebar.

Her heels click against the floor as she traps me in a corner of the elevator. "You're afraid."

I let out a sarcastic laugh that grates my ears. "What? That's ridiculous."

"Is it because you have a small dick after all, and you're worried I'll call you out on it?"

"You're the one who is actually certifiable. It's a shame I'm realizing this now." Who am I kidding? I'm into the hurricane of craziness that is Chloe Carter. I want to get lost in her storm and never come out.

"Sir, if you didn't realize I was crazy after I broke into your house, then you set yourself up for that kind of disappointment."

Her comment makes me snort in the most unflattering way.

She smooths the lapel of my tux, distracting me with the warmth of her palm. Her other hand palms my dick again.

I shudder, unable to control my body's response to her touch. "I told you tonight isn't about me."

"Please?"

Fuck. The way she whispers the word has my dick

throbbing beneath her hand. Only this girl would ask for the opportunity to suck my cock. Any rational thought leaves my head as her palm moves up and down my length.

I press my hand against hers, halting the motion. "One condition."

"What is it?" Her voice hints at her excitement, and the sound sends another rush of heat through my chest.

"The lights have to be off."

She abandons my erection and fumbles for my phone, shutting off the flashlight in no time.

Darkness hides everything I'm desperate to keep from Chloe in an intimate moment. Nothing says mood killer quite like an up-close view of my stump.

I'm just...not ready for that yet. If I could hide in the shadows during sex for the rest of my life, I would.

Chloe presses a soft kiss against my lips, gaining my attention. "I'm granting your one request because I crave this more than I want to push your boundaries. Don't count yourself free of your fears yet," she whispers, her voice carrying a rasp I find beyond sexy.

I lean against the wall, wishing I could see her on her knees in front of me. Instead of allowing myself the real deal, I imagine it like a vivid dream in my head.

Her hands fumble with my trousers. The desperation in her touch has me groaning up to the ceiling.

She releases my dick from my boxer briefs and rubs her thumb across the tip, collecting my arousal.

I clutch onto the handlebar as her tongue replaces her thumb, flicking across my tip. "Shit."

Chloe teases before the warmth of her mouth surrounds

my cock. She works me into submission, switching between sucking me off and running her tongue along my shaft. It's the best kind of torture. I don't know if I've ever felt anything quite as amazing as her mouth on me.

Whatever noises escape my mouth encourage her, and her movements grow sloppier. My breath comes out in pants. A sudden surge of energy shoots down my spine as my world spins.

Chloe doesn't heed my warning when I tell her I'm about to come. A fire spreads through my veins as I erupt. She swallows my release, not breaking away until I stop shuddering.

God. I thought I liked her, but now I'm not sure what to make of the feelings swirling in my chest. It's nothing like I've ever experienced before, and I can't exactly dissect them. It seems like *more*. Chloe tucks my dick back into my briefs and helps button my trousers.

She rises without my help, and I tug her into a kiss. It's soft, with our lips faintly touching. But somehow, it seems like way more than a simple peck. It feels like she just destroyed the world I created for myself, and I'm not sure what to do about it. How can I ever go back to the person I was before Chloe entered the picture? And most of all, I don't think I want to.

"Thank you," my voice rasps. *Thank you? What the actual hell. Good God, she sucked your dick, man. You're acting like she treated you to coffee.*

Chloe laughs in a way that has the anxiety melting off my body. "You're welcome." She pats my chest.

"I can't wait to get out of this damn elevator and fuck you tonight."

She freezes in my arms. "No." Her voice is faint enough for me to misunderstand her meaning.

"Huh?"

"No." She speaks with more strength the second time around. Warmth seeps away as she steps out of my arms, adding to the distance between us.

"Why not?"

"I can't have sex with you."

"Then what do you call the thing we just did?"

"Something amazing."

I'm absolutely baffled. She has my mind spinning.

She continues. "It was incredible—for me at least. But I don't want to have sex until you're ready to reveal yourself to me. And I mean *all* of you."

My heart rate escalates. "Why?" Reality crashes back down around me.

"Because sex isn't something I'm ashamed about, but it's clear you don't feel the same way about yourself."

"This is who I am. Take it or leave it." I grind my molars.

"That's the thing. I do see who you are, and I want to take it. The real question is if you really are ready for something like that."

Chloe has caught me in her spell. But I don't know how I can go about accepting the version of myself she sees.

Silence surrounds us, accompanied by the shadows. We both sit on opposite sides of the car, our legs grazing one another. My skin itches as the emotional gap between us widens.

I don't want that. Not in the slightest.

"Chloe?"

"Mmm."

"Why are you afraid of small spaces?"

If we were outside, I imagine crickets would fill the silence. She says nothing, and I consider dropping it.

"When I was little, my mom used to lock me inside of my bedroom when her visitors came over."

What the actual fuck?

She prattles on, not realizing my disgust. "My room wasn't big since we were poor. Honestly, it was more of a closet than a room in the first place." She laughs, but it comes off insincere. "But it was a safe place if my mom had whatever boyfriend of the time over, getting high and doing other things. Even as a young kid I knew what was going on because kids at school would talk. Turns out she didn't have the best reputation. So, anyway, my mom didn't want me to get in the way, so she would lock me inside my room until she was done."

Heat bubbles inside of me, building beneath the surface of my skin. "You don't have to keep going. I get it."

"No, it's fine."

It isn't, but I don't bother arguing with her. I doubt this is easy to share.

"The thing is my mom is forgetful, especially if she was high when she locked me in my room." Her voice cracks, and something in my chest tightens at the sound. "That's why I hate small spaces. It's like I'm taken back to those years, and there's some automatic response in my body that protests to get out."

I drag my body across the floor to get to her side. She accepts me wrapping my arm around her and pulling her into my side. "I'm sorry that happened to you."

I want to say more, but the words don't come easy. And I don't want to scare her by revealing how much I'm like her.

"It's all right. There's no reason to get upset. It's in the past."

"Is it? How can anyone move past that?"

"Because then I'd lose sight of what's important."

By this point, I'm sure Chloe can hear my heart pounding wildly in my chest.

"And what's that?"

"Life is about creating the memories that matter, while forgetting the ones that don't."

I want to create new memories. With my family, with racing, and maybe even with Chloe.

I can't change the fact that I lost my leg. But I wonder if I truly have been looking at my life all wrong since the accident. Maybe Chloe is right, and I can't jump into something serious with her if I can't accept myself first.

I want to see what she sees in me. I've lived the past three years in a world of black and white. Depression and isolation ate away at the man I was, creating someone I don't recognize. So, yes, I want to experience the world through Chloe's eyes because it's like seeing color for the first time. It's breathtaking and spectacular, fundamentally shifting life as I know it.

She's my kaleidoscope in a world of gray.

CHAPTER THIRTY

Chloe

Okay, getting stuck in an elevator last night wasn't the worst experience of my life. It took two hours for the maintenance team to free Santiago and me from the small car. After my dismissal of his "let's do it" proposition and my confession about my mom, we spent the better part of the ninety minutes not talking. I took his silence for what it was. Indifference.

He called my bluff. It's not that I don't want to have sex with him. But some issues take precedence, and what's the point of being intimate if he can't be comfortable enough to leave a flashlight on.

After we were freed from the car, we both pretended nothing ever happened. It worked out well since we both went to bed right away.

Except now, after a restless night of sleep, my skin heats from the memory of his lips on mine. Hell, of his lips on other places of my body, bringing about sensations I could only dream of. Brooke would be beside herself because it turns out Santiago really does have the skills to back up those ridiculous articles.

Overwhelmed doesn't cover how I feel at the moment. Bandini mechanics, crew, and reps run around the car garage. Santiago, Maya, and his mom hang around Noah's race car and chat together. I keep to myself, offering very little conversation.

For once, I don't know what to say. It's like all the words I learned in my short life have escaped my brain. Santiago pretends to be unfazed, but I read his body language like a book. His spine is straighter than a rod and his jaw remains permanently locked. He offers about as many words as me, which at this point is zilch.

"What do you think of the race scene?" Daniela looks in my direction.

"Oh, it's umm…a lot."

Santiago's laugh catches in his throat. "That's one way to describe it."

"What do you know about F1?" Maya moves her attention from Marko to me.

"Oh, tons. Santiago loves to chat about his race days."

Santiago stiffens beside me. Shit. Wrong thing to say. *Oh, God. Is it too late to fake a sore throat?*

"Oh, does he now?" Noah raises a brow. "Did he tell you how he beat me for the World Championship title once."

Santiago rolls his eyes.

I grin, praying he doesn't get too mad at the shitstorm I started. "Well, he didn't have to share much because he showed me the reruns. I'd say he's sorry about the crash, but then I'd be lying."

Noah and Santiago laugh together. A few crew members' heads snap in our direction. I can see why. Noah and Santiago enjoying themselves is quite the sight.

Someone calls Noah away for a pre-race interview with a local news channel. Santiago grabs Marko and throws him in the air, switching between helicopter noises and a speeding jet.

Ugh. Why does he have to be so perfect all the time? It's hurting my self-restraint.

A teeny tiny part of me is tempted to call off my stupid bluff and give into our attraction. But then Santiago bristles when a crew member walks by, noticeably checking out his leg as if the worker has X-ray vision to see past his jeans. The way Santiago scowls and shields himself from more scrutiny has me solidifying my choice.

If Santiago wants to have a more serious relationship with me, whether sexual or otherwise, he needs to accept himself. Because at the end of the day, no one who looks and acts like he does should hide themselves from the world. It's such a damn shame right up there with Brad Pitt leaving Jennifer Aniston and ABBA breaking up.

I can't let Santiago cloak himself in darkness and secrets when he's meant to shine, even if it means putting my own agenda aside. Plans don't always go accordingly, and I refuse to give up on helping him. Priorities change and revealing my identity to my dad isn't the most urgent thing in my life anymore.

I'm officially an F1 addict. Today couldn't be any better,

with our own private room to watch the race. There's free champagne and exclusive access to Noah's team radio. I've never been one to lap in luxury, but Santiago had me convinced the moment he passed me a mimosa. A race day is like brunch minus the pricey bill.

Massive TVs play the footage from the F1 cameras and drones. The crew sets the racers up in a crisscross fashion throughout the grid, with Noah's car leading the pack.

Santiago shakes his head. "No one can beat him off his pedestal, even after all this time."

"There's only one man who has the best chance, and he's standing in this room." Maya sips her mimosa.

Santiago scowls at his sister. "Are you trying to get a rise out of me?"

"If I'm getting a rise out of you, that means something about this situation still bothers you. Ever thought of it that way?"

"No. I'm thinking my annoying little sister forgot her manners for a second."

"Santiago," I hiss under my breath. "Cut it out."

Maya waves me off, shooting her brother a glare. "You belong out there."

Santiago looks toward his mother for help, but she shrugs and focuses her attention back on Marko. *Smart woman.* I'm tempted to go over there and join them.

"*Mami's* not going to save you from this conversation. Just be honest with me. Do you miss it?" Maya turns back toward the TV.

One by one, the five lights above the cars shine before shutting off. The cars squeal as they speed past the grid and through the first corner. A dashboard camera gives fans and us the perfect view of Noah's front wing as he passes the first straight. He speaks to his engineers, relaying stats off his steering wheel.

Santiago's eyes remain glued on the TV. His body grows more tense as Noah goes around the circuit again and again. "Of course I do." He speaks low, his voice barely a whisper under his breath.

"Then will you please at least check out the car he worked on? *Please*? If not for him, do it for me." Maya's eyes soften.

Santiago doesn't look at his sister.

I tense as his eyes drop to mine. He clasps onto my hand, hiding the trembling from his family. His jaw tightens as he scans my face before focusing on his leg.

I grow uncomfortable as the silence continues. Giving Santiago some space, I focus my attention back on the race. Noah continues down the track. Everyone's excitement grows, especially Marko's, as his dad fights off the other racers. No one dares pass Noah's car. I clap my hands together as Maya squeals in delight as he passes through the next lap without a problem. I look up at Santiago, expecting him to be watching the race, but his eyes are trained on me.

"I'll test out the car under one condition." Santiago speaks to his sister, but his eyes don't leave my face.

Maya looks up from Marko at her brother. "What is it?"

"I'll try the car if Chloe comes to the track with me."

My mouth gapes open, and I take a deep breath. The sudden motion makes my lungs burn, and I cough. "Come again?"

Santiago's frown grows into a smile as he nods his head.

"I'll test out the car if you come to the garage with me."

Oh, fuck.

I guess Santiago isn't done with me after all. Quite the opposite. This smug male is actually going to try to beat back his fears. And based on the way he's staring at me, I can tell it's more than just because of sex.

Something else lurks behind his eyes. I can't figure it out no matter how long I stare at him. It seems like I was all wrong earlier, mistaking his silence as indifference. Rather, it turns out it was something much more dangerous.

Scheming.

I leave the party room to use the restroom while Santiago's family celebrates Noah's win. During my bathroom break, I connect to Bandini's free Wi-Fi. My phone pings over and over again as Brooke's texts flood my phone. Each has a different time stamp spread throughout today. I lean against the sink counter and open up my missed messages.

> **Brooke:** I was in the shower this morning when I dropped my phone after I saw your face plastered all over the internet! The screen cracked and I stubbed my toe but it was worth the shock factor. Call me ASAP!! I WANT DETAILS.
>
> **Brooke:** Seriously I'm jealous of your legs. They look a mile long. And that dress is a stunner by the way, and the guy next to you doesn't look half bad. New sexy couple alert!
>
> **Brooke:** Why haven't you answered :(Long distance relationships suck.
>
> **Brooke:** I need to digest this information with you. Please tell me you got some action after

> looking like THAT last night.
> **Brooke:** Okay your mom just stopped by while I was icing my toe. I'm kind of scared of how excited she looked when she mentioned your new beau. Call me!!

My stomach sinks. I can't believe my mom stopped by unannounced. I rush to answer Brooke.

> **Me:** Oh no. Did she say what she wanted?
> **Brooke:** Hello to you too, Ms. I'm Too Famous for My Best Friend Now.
> **Brooke:** And no. She kept it very discreet but she said she would be in touch with you. I got straight up shivers after she said that. Mother Dearest looked like a scary, strung-out motherfucker if I do say so myself. Don't answer her if she calls you. Remember, talking to them is a reinforcer for bad behavior!
> **Me:** I can't ignore her stopping by our place again. Your strategy isn't working.

I chew on my bottom lip as I wait for Brooke's reply. The last thing I need is for my mother to stir up some trouble between Santiago and me. She may have fooled me in the past, but I'm not going to chalk up her stopping by my apartment as anything but a coincidence.

> **Brooke:** I don't recommend it because she's a bitch, but if you really feel like you need to, then you should call her and put her in her place. I don't mind shooing her away but the choice is yours.

What option do I have? I run the risk of having her do something stupid, and the last thing I want on this planet is my mother sinking her claws into my new life over here.

My new *temporary* life.

I use the Wi-Fi to call my mom. She answers without letting it go to voicemail, and I count that as a small miracle.

"Hello, Chloe. It's about time you called your mother back."

"What do you want?"

"Now, is that the way to talk to me after all this time?"

"Cut the shit. Niceties don't suit you."

She lets out a huff. "I saw the pictures. I'm proud of you. You landed yourself quite the catch while gallivanting across Europe."

My teeth grind together. "*What do you want?*"

"How much are you willing to pay to keep your little dirty secret under wraps?"

"My what?" I rear back, hitting my spine against the faucet.

"I have evidence of the assault. You know, when you bashed Ralph's head into the shower wall after he walked in on you in the bathroom?"

"Oh, you mean the wall he happened to be jacking off against while watching me shower? That wall?" I can't believe her boldness. If it weren't for the government's various attempts to reunite us, I would doubt she was my mother. How can someone who gave birth to me despise me this much? Are money and drugs worth her soul?

Fuck her. Mothers are meant to protect their children from creeps, and all she did was provide him with nonstop access to me. I shiver at the memory of his beady eyes watching me. Making me feel dirty and disgusting. I shake my head in an attempt to push the memory away.

"It doesn't matter what happened before. What matters is that I have pictures and documentation from the hospital about the condition you left him in."

I didn't think it was possibly to hate her more than ever

before. It's deep-rooted, like a cancerous growth after years of her abuse.

"So what?" I let out a shrill laugh. "You can't connect it back to me and you know it. For all anyone knows, Ralph slipped."

"He slipped after you round-house kicked him in the balls."

"He deserved far worse."

"Oh, really? You want to play with me over something as serious as this?"

"I'm not playing. Go ahead and release whatever you want to whoever you want. I'm not afraid of you anymore. Your evidence is circumstantial at best, seeing as I was a minor. And honestly, it's his word against mine." I'm done with her mind games and deception. I want to snip away my connection to her with a set of pruning shears.

"You can't be serious. You're willing to let the world see you as the gutter rat you are?"

"Sure. Maybe other little girls like me can also wish to escape monsters like you."

"This is disappointing. I gave you the easy option, Chloe."

"That's where you're wrong. The easy option is forgetting you ever existed. I'm blocking your number, and Brooke will never answer the door to you again. This is the last time I let you threaten me or abuse me into giving you what you want. I'm not afraid of whatever *evidence* you have of what I did. The cops dropped the charges, and Ralph is the one with the restraining order against him. So, do whatever helps you sleep at night."

"Chloe, you better listen to me—"

I cut her off. "No, Anne, you better listen to *me*. I'm moving on with my life. You're nothing but a past memory that I have no interest in reliving ever again. I hope you live a happy life, and good luck with Ralph. You're going to need it because I'm done supporting your addiction. Goodbye." I press the red button with a shaky hand.

I'm done hiding from my past. It helped me become the person I am, gutter rat and all. Anne Carter underestimated her power over me. I'll take her down with me, if it's the last thing I do.

I only hope I made the right decision. I'm gambling with someone who is unhinged on her best day, and downright immoral on her worst. But I can't let someone like her control me—my thoughts, my wishes, my happiness. My experiences with her tainted my idea of others, their intentions, and my own future. I've pushed boyfriends away. I've barely made friends, let alone settled down into anything but two jobs I've barely tolerated. After spending time with Santiago, I understand I've been letting my life pass me by as well. It took watching someone else slip into their dark thoughts over and over again to slap me out of my own.

I've been living scared, which isn't really living at all. I'm done experiencing life on pause anymore. I want to challenge myself to be better. To be someone I'm proud of, whether it's pursuing a degree or traveling around the world.

All I know is it's about damn time I focused on the people who matter, rather than the ones who don't.

I do my best to pretend I'm not rattled after the shocking call with my mom. Santiago looks at me a couple of times for a few seconds longer than I'd like, but he doesn't ask me if anything is wrong.

For the rest of the day, I throw myself into playing Santiago's dutiful girlfriend. I support him as he answers questions with reporters and visits Bandini employees. Similar to me, it was as if a switch was flipped inside of him over the weekend. It's the best sight, with him checking in on old friends, asking about their kids and their families. I love every second of it. In fact, phone call aside, I love this weekend way more than I should. I'm sad to see it come to an end.

It isn't until we both enter his mansion hours later that reality hits us. His hands linger on the handles of my luggage, with him not passing them over. They stand out like a sore thumb against his marble floors and luxurious wallpaper.

I move to grab one from him. "Listen, I've been thinking—"

He speaks at the same time. "You should move in with me—"

My eyes threaten to pop out of their sockets. "What?!"

"What if you lived here instead of paying for a place to stay?" His golden cheeks flush with color.

Santiago Alatorre needs to stop surprising me because I'm pretty sure my heart has officially gone into cardiac arrest. *Mayday.* Someone needs to call the doctor because I'm not making it out of this weekend alive.

CHAPTER THIRTY-ONE

SANTIAGO

L isten. I get it. Everyone thinks I'm going crazy after this weekend, with me deciding to test Noah's new steering wheel. Even Chloe looks at me now like I told her I'm an alien. I can't begin to explain my reasoning behind inviting her to live with me. It's crazy and unexpected, but it's for my own selfish reasons. Do I want to help her out when she clearly shouldn't be spending her savings on some shitty bed-and-breakfast? Of course. But I also can't bear the silence anymore. This massive house is lonely, with my thoughts occupying all the square footage.

After my bravery this weekend, I'm afraid to revert back to how life was before. Experiencing Chloe's chaos is a hell of a lot more fun than stewing in my self-hatred. I've grown fond of her choice words and energetic presence. And most of all, I really like her. So, yeah, I'm a selfish fucker who benefits more from having her around than the other way around. Sue me. Life is unfair, and I'll preach that lesson until the day I die.

Chloe blinks at me, her brows drawing together. "You want me to move in with you?"

I nod my head.

"Okay, haha, very funny." She takes a hesitant step toward the door like a scared animal.

I tread carefully because I'm afraid to scare her out of the idea. "Listen. Why bother paying for a room at a hotel when I have plenty of space?"

She stares at her sneakers. "I can't do that."

"Why not?"

"Because that's crazy."

"Of course it is. But since when do you shy away from crazy?"

"Since I ended up breaking into someone's house and faking an entire life to a long list of kind people who don't deserve to be lied to."

Whatever small ground I had to stand on is slipping out from underneath me. "Well, seeing as I have sixteen bedrooms here, it's not a huge deal if you take up one of them. It's free room and board."

She rolls her eyes. "Your head just grew a little larger."

"What do you say? We can be roommates."

"Roommates?" Her lips purse.

Shit. This is going terrible. Everything I say sounds worse by the second. "The reason I'm offering you a place to stay is because you shouldn't be living out of a hotel for the rest of the summer. Think about it. You could stay here, right next to your dad, which could lead to more encounters. And you did offer to help me with my car remodel...and that requires 24/7 on-call service."

God, that sounded about as desperate as I feel.

"24/7, huh?" She smirks.

"Out of everything I said, you pick that?"

She laughs up to the ceiling. "This is the weirdest summer of my life. And you call me crazy! You're asking me to move in with you and I barely know you."

I frown. "You know me."

"Not enough to move in with you. That's not normal."

"Since when do you follow the status quo?"

"Well…when you put it that way." She snorts.

Damn. After our weekend, I definitely can't let her leave. The thought of being on my own here again is…stifling.

"Is that a yes?" My voice sounds pathetic to my own ears, but I don't care.

"No."

My heart sinks. The thought of Chloe leaving me to my silent, empty mansion fills me with dread. I hate the idea more than I should, but I can't help it. Being alone is like drowning in the middle of the ocean. No one can find me, let alone save me from myself.

She rocks back on her sneakers. "But…"

I cover my smile with my hand. "Yes?"

"Maybe I'll agree if you tell me the real reason you want me to move in with you."

I weigh the cost of telling her the truth. Not the flowery words I shared prior, but the real deal.

I'm tempted to call her out on her bluff, but her clutching onto her luggage and rolling it toward her has me stopping myself.

Shit. Will she really leave?

"The past few days in the hotel have been incredible. I don't want to go back to how things were."

"And how's that?"

"Lonely. Without you and Marko, the thought of being on my own again is awful. Absolutely unbearable. It's like I had a gaping hole in my chest that only started being filled over the last few weeks."

Her bottom lip juts out. "Oh, Santiago."

I step up to her, grabbing the handle of her luggage and pushing it in the opposite direction. "And most of all, you make the bad days better. I want more of that. If you go, I'm afraid I'll go back to the way things were."

She runs her hand down my chest before placing it against my rapidly beating heart. "I don't want to be a crutch. You need to fight for yourself because you want to. Not because I'm here, for however long that is."

Something in my chest constricts over her leaving permanently. "I do want to fight for myself. That's the point. And you're not a crutch. You're part of the foundation to help me get where I want to be."

"And that is?"

"Accepting that, while I can never be the man I was, I can become a man you want to be with." I brush my thumb across her bottom lip.

Her eyes widen. "You can't be serious."

"Why not?"

"We don't know each other well enough."

"Give me a chance then. A real chance. No faking. No pretending. Just us spending time together, learning about each other."

She tugs her bottom lip between her teeth. The silence sets me on edge, but I hold out, hoping she will give in.

She lets out a tense breath. "Okay. But there is one house rule."

"Name it and it's yours."

"No sex. Until you work on yourself—for real—I'm not sleeping with you. Bottom line."

Mierda. I nod my head, accepting my fate. If it's a battle with myself that Chloe wants, then it's a battle she's bound to get.

Except I refuse to be a loser this time.

"Please tell me why the fuck some woman called my assistant asking for your number, Santiago." Noah skips the pleasantries, jumping straight into the reason behind his random call.

"Who?"

"Anne Carter called asking to get in contact with you. You know, Chloe's mother?"

Now I have a full name to the horrendous stories Chloe shared about her mother. Edginess creeps up my spine at the deranged woman attempting to infiltrate my inner circle. That stops now. Chloe's spent her entire life escaping the grasps of her mother, and I'll be damned if she haunts her in Europe, too.

"What did she want?" I snarl.

"Beats me. She left a slurred voicemail about needing to speak to you because she can't get in contact with Chloe. I feel the need to warn you..."

Fuck! This is all my fault. I'm the one that pushed Chloe into the spotlight, and now her mother found out.

"Did she leave a callback number?"

"Why don't you ask your girlfriend?"

"Seeing as she has a restraining order against her mom's boyfriend, is that really the best idea?"

Noah huffs. "No."

"Then give me her number."

Noah rattles off the number Chloe's mom left his assistant. A part of me wants to tell Chloe about her mother contacting Noah, but I'm struck with an intense urge to protect her. I don't want to bring up old memories, especially if it's my fault in the first place. Her mother wouldn't bother with Chloe if it weren't for me.

Chloe didn't ask for this kind of attention. Hell, she warned me against it in the first place. It's my responsibility to fix whatever damage has been done and hope her mother crawls back into whatever pocket of hell she came from.

I dial the number. It rings before going to voicemail. My second attempt is a success, with Anne's rasp of a voice answering after the third ring. "Hello."

"This is Santiago Alatorre."

"Well, I didn't think my message would actually make it back to you." Her voice fails to match the soothing one Chloe has.

"I'll start this call with telling you to never call Noah Slade again. Hell, don't contact anyone who has anything to do with me, Chloe included."

"That's a big claim for someone who is hiding an even bigger secret."

"What secret?" *Is she high right now?*

"The fact that you're shacking up with someone who was arrested for aggravated assault charges."

Fuck. I nearly drop the phone before catching it. "Excuse me?"

"Chloe attacked my poor boyfriend, Ralph, when she was in high school. Left him with a concussion, two broken ribs, and a chipped tooth according to the hospital report I have. Somehow her social worker convinced the cops to drop the charges, but it doesn't matter. With your fame, I doubt it's something you want associated with your name. Now is it?"

What the fuck happened inside of Chloe's house when she was growing up? I can barely focus on the vile words her mother shares as I try to picture living in fear like Chloe did. Being forced to spend time inside of a closet while her mother got high with men. Fending for herself against a disgusting man who tried to take advantage of someone smaller than him.

The whole situation makes me sick. Disgusted to the point that I want Anne Carter to disappear forever.

"How much?" I hate making deals with the scum of the earth, but to protect Chloe, I'll do anything. Even if it means supporting a drug addict like her.

"How much do you think Chloe's secret is worth? I have a video of Ralph speaking out against the attack, and it's not pretty." Anne chuckles to herself.

Acid rolls around in my stomach. How much does it cost to keep a drug addict quiet? Fuck if I know. "Fifty thousand dollars."

Anne laughs. The sound elicits the same chill as hearing nails running down a chalkboard. "You'll have to do better than that. I googled you. Everyone knows how much you're packing in that wallet. Do you really want to take a gamble on me revealing who your girlfriend is to the world? Something tells me the crowd you run with won't be as accepting of someone like her."

My jaw clamps down. "If someone doesn't accept her, then they were never part of my crowd to begin with."

"I see why she likes you." She snickers.

I clutch onto my phone with a death grip. "Three-hundred-thousand dollars. That's my final offer."

"I knew you were willing to pay the right price. With all those fancy cars and houses, it's barely a drop in the bucket."

"You're repulsive."

"I never said I wasn't. But I'm also an opportunist. The world is a harsh place, and my daughter happened to find the right kind of guy. I'm proud."

"This is the last time you'll ask for any money."

"Don't worry. That kind of money will keep me happy for a long time." She sighs in a dreamy kind of way.

"Let me be clear. I give you the money and you stay away from my family, including Chloe. That means you disappear from all of our lives. Period. While you have a lousy story and whatever half-assed evidence your drugged-out brain could muster up, I have endless connections to wipe you from the map if you mess with us again. So, if you ever crawl out of the gutter you came from to cause us problems again, I'll have you shipped off to a facility where you'll live the life you deserve. No drugs. No people. Nothing but sobriety and your nasty thoughts to keep you company. Got it?"

"So testy. I see why my daughter is drawn to you."

My jaw clenches. "I want a real yes or no answer. Your offer is disappearing in three...tw—"

"I promise not to contact you, your family, or Chloe." She gives me a number to wire her money to, and I finish the deal without hesitating.

Chloe told me she was done with that piece of trash, and I only helped her solve that problem faster.

CHAPTER THIRTY-TWO

SANTIAGO

Chloe's only moved into my place as of two weeks ago and the energy is already shifting between us. The routine we have fallen into is easygoing, with both of us modeling domestic bliss. Our days with each other include cooking together and movie nights, with restoring the car in between.

Whenever she leaves for work, I grow agitated. A discomfort builds inside of me in her absence and I become desperate to fill the time. Enough so, I spend the better part of my morning working out in the gym. But not even that is enough to satisfy the edge inside of me. I use it as an excuse to buy something stupid while Chloe is away at work.

It takes two days for my latest purchase to arrive. The shipping company sets up my new system in an empty room on the first floor of my house, far away from anyone else.

With hesitant steps, I walk toward the room, clutching onto the package Noah sent me after the Monza weekend. Taking a deep breath, I walk into the room. The F1 simulation system sits in front of massive monitors. My hands tremble as I walk up to the machine and rip off the brand-new plastic wrap.

The pedals mock me and remind me of the way I used to race. I ignore the urge to run out of the room, instead choosing to remove the standard steering wheel and replace it with Noah's custom-made one. Pieces click into place as the new wheel dominates the front of the machine.

"If you don't practice, you'll never get back out there." I hold on to the back of the leather chair and take a steady breath.

I press the power button, and the machine whirs to life. Tension sizzles beneath my skin at practicing with the new wheel.

This could be a disaster. A total and utter failure of epic proportions.

But it could also be the best thing to happen to you in years. Imagine getting back out there.

My dilemma is cut off by sneakers squeaking behind me.

I turn to find Chloe gaping at the machine.

She steps into the room. "Look at this setup! I can hear the nerds all over the world crying tears of joy."

"This isn't for nerds," I mumble under my breath.

"Okay, sure. Whatever you say. But real talk: Can you play Mario Kart on it?"

My jaw drops open. "Mario Kart?"

She looks at the monitors with longing. "What I'd give to throw turtle shells and banana peels at other racers with this setup."

The ridiculousness of her idea has me throwing my

head back and laughing. "I honestly don't know if this newer machine is compatible with it."

"Then what is it for?"

"F1 racing."

Her lips form an O. "Got it. Okay, well sorry to interrupt you. I'll leave you to it then." She walks backward before bumping into a wall.

"Wait."

She halts.

"Do you want to test it out? If I can download Mario Kart, that is?"

Her eyes narrow. "Why do I have a feeling you're trying to distract yourself so you don't have to do whatever it is that you wanted to do in here?"

I grin. "Because that's exactly what I'm doing."

Her smile drops. "Then no thank you. I'll pass."

The last thing I want is to be left alone in this room. "Okay, fine. How about we compete in a Mario Kart match? Whoever has the highest score wins whatever they want."

"Are you sure about that?"

I nod.

"All right, if that's what you want. But just so you know ahead of time, I'm not betting on giving you a blowjob this time."

My skin heats. "Why not?"

"Because if I win, I'm going to ask you to try out the F1 simulation with that fancy wheel you have there." She points to the one Noah shipped.

"I better not lose then."

I'm able to download the most recent version of Mario

Kart without any issues.

Chloe cracks her knuckles one by one. "Step aside, sir. Bowser is here to rock and roll."

"Bowser?"

"Did you expect me to pick Princess Peach? And here I thought you knew me better than that." She sticks out her tongue.

My skin prickles with memories of that tongue on my skin. I cough as I load the screen, trying to rein in my hormones.

Chloe and I take turns competing in a championship against one another. She's a natural, and I find it hard to keep up with her high scores. And worse, I barely put any effort into beating her.

I don't mind losing the bet. As long as Chloe stays by my side, I can attempt the simulation afterward. Honestly, playing with her wasn't about avoiding what I came in here to do. I just wanted to spend time together since she was gone the whole morning, and it seemed like a good idea.

She doesn't leave once as I situate myself in the fake cockpit and start up the latest simulation game. My hands tremble as I get a feel for the throttle paddle. The fake F1 cars line up on the grid, one by one, reminding me of old race days.

Chloe's hand covers mine. "I just want you to know I'm really freaking proud of you right now."

A blush creeps into my cheeks. "It's just a game."

"It's more than that."

"How so?"

"This is your redemption."

Chloe runs the needle through the linen before pulling it up over her head. She sits crisscross on one of the lawn chairs by the lake, seeming to enjoy the early morning breeze.

"What are you making?" I plop down on the chair beside her after my morning workout of mowing the lawn. Could I pay someone to do it? Sure. But could I give up the opportunity to give Chloe a front-row seat to me working the machine while hiding her attraction? Definitely not.

She flashes me the embroidery circle. It's an exact replica of the lake and mountains surrounding us.

"Wow. You are incredibly talented. How did you make it look so real?" I peer over and check out the fine thread details. There has to be hundreds of multicolored stitches recreating the scene.

"First I sketch whatever design I want on the fabric. Then I pick the threads. For an intricate design like this, I split the threads to make it finer."

My eyes widen. "Wait. You drew that first?"

"It's not that hard." Her cheeks flush.

"No. It's incredible. Do you have pictures of other ones you created?"

I didn't realize she was this good at her designs. They're like pieces of art, woven together by thousands of threads. It's a shame she hides this talent from the world.

She pulls out her phone and opens up an album. "Here. You can flip through all of those."

I grab it with greedy hands. The different designs Chloe made range from picturesque nature scenes to quotes and poems. All her designs show up on different objects, from clothes to accessories. I had no clue she was this talented.

"Are you sure you don't want to start up a shop? These are amazing."

She laughs. "You've never seen other designs to know if that's true. What if I'm secretly terrible and you have no clue?"

I roll my eyes and pull out my phone.

"What are you doing?"

"Researching the market."

She snorts. "Why would you do that?"

"Because someone I know speaks from a tall soapbox to others about boosting their self-esteem yet doesn't do the same to herself."

"Burn," she hisses.

I smirk and scroll through Etsy and Pinterest. Spending time with Maya taught me all the tricks of where to purchase certain types of custom items. There are quite a few talented embroidery shops, but nothing compares to the designs Chloe makes. It's like she channels her inner Bob Ross and makes intricate landscapes out of thread and a needle.

"Okay. I've completed my analysis and have the results." I turn toward her.

"And?" She bites her lip.

"Your designs are superior. The end. You need to start a shop, ASAP."

She laughs. "I appreciate your kind words. It's nice."

"But?"

"But starting up a business is the last thing I should do."

"Why not?"

"Well, once I go back to America, I need to pick my jobs back up. This summer has been fun and all, but reality will come knocking eventually. Brooke can't live with some stranger subleasing my room forever."

My stomach dips at her words. "When do you plan on leaving?"

She shrugs. "I'm not sure. I'm still figuring out when I'll tell Matteo about who I am."

Can I cast my vote for never? "And if you tell him?"

"Then I guess I'll see from there. I've never been much of a planner." Her smile doesn't fill me with its accompanying warmth.

"Have you ever considered staying here, even after you tell him? Don't you want to stay with your dad after being apart after all this time?" My voice carries a hopeful note.

Her eyes return to her embroidery circle. She fiddles with the needle, twirling it with her fingers. "Honestly, no, I didn't think it was even an option to live here. I wasn't thinking that far ahead when I booked my ticket. But now that you bring it up, I wonder if it's a possibility."

"Really?" I didn't expect her to admit that. Maybe there is some hope after all.

"I mean he's my dad, and I don't have many ties in America besides Brooke. I'm not saying I'd stay, but it's not exactly a no either. Does that make sense?"

It makes a hell of a lot of sense. All I need to do is convince someone who already wants to stay that she shouldn't leave in the first place.

Mission accepted.

CHAPTER THIRTY-THREE

SANTIAGO

"Please tell me you're joking."

"I wish I was." I press the button to start up the projector. The screen rolls down from the ceiling, and the lights dim on their own.

Money may not buy happiness, but it can buy moments like this with Chloe. I'll take domestic bliss in my at-home movie theater any day over the real deal. Crowds aren't my thing, and it's not like I can hide my celebrity status from the world and go on a normal date.

Chloe stands from her side of the couch. "You've never seen *Pretty in Pink*? Like ever?"

"No."

"Are you even human?"

"Unfortunately."

She laughs and snatches the controller straight from my hands. "We must fix this."

"Why?"

"Because that movie set my standards way too high for romance."

Now, she has my attention. "Tell me more."

"The whole reason I am obsessed with eighties movies in the first place is because my foster mom only had a VHS system—no cable TV."

Well, this is a depressing start to her story.

"Brooke and I binged every tape she had over and over again. We still have a yearly marathon to this day to commemorate our childhood."

"And what movies are your favorites?"

Her whole face lights up. "*Pretty in Pink,* no duh. And then *The Breakfast Club*, *Ferris Bueller's Day Off,* and *Say Anything*. I mean that scene with the boombox is one of my favorite movie scenes *ever*." Her enthusiasm grows as she explains different movies I have no clue about.

I ask her questions just to hear her talk. It's too much fun, watching her expressive face brighten every time I question something. Who knew being clueless about a topic could be this enjoyable? Chloe rolls her eyes when I make an obvious mistake and smiles when I remember a detail she shared a few minutes before.

Every damn second of the conversation is worth it.

I clear my throat. "We better get started if we ever plan on watching all these movies."

"You want to see them?"

"Of course. I'm curious to see how someone woos a woman with a boombox outside of her house."

"With a meaningful song, of course. Bonus points for nostalgia if you play 'In Your Eyes.'"

"I'm mentally noting all of this."

"Do you plan on wooing someone in the near future?"

"You never know. Someone told me wooing is important." I grin.

She smiles to herself as she settles back onto the opposite end of the couch.

"You're going to not only torture me with this movie but also by sitting far away? What kind of man do you take me for?"

"The kind who wants to make me happy?"

"What about my happiness?"

"Of course that's important."

I point to my empty side. "Then get your ass over here. I like to cuddle."

She lets out an exaggerated huff and scoots over toward me. I place my arm on the back of the couch, giving her room to lean into me.

"A smooth guy would've made a move rather than forced me over here."

"I'm crippled. Have pity on me."

She pinches my side. "Don't even try it."

I laugh. "Why bother making a move when I know I'll get what I want?"

That statement earns me a harder pinch right between two of my ribs.

"You're awfully cocky."

"Emphasis on the cock."

She lets out an obnoxious laugh that leaves her wheezing. "Please stop. My heart can't handle any more of this."

The movie starts, interrupting us with the intro to *Pretty in Pink*. Chloe cuddles up to my side and rests her head against my chest.

I wrap my arm around her.

Yeah, I could definitely get used to this, chick flicks and all.

Chloe has officially infiltrated my home. Having her around is like living with constant temptation in the form of short shorts and hints of cleavage. She scatters her items around the house, and while it should frustrate me, it only makes me smile like an idiot when I find them. And I mean it. Her shit is everywhere, but it surprisingly keeps me grounded in a good way. The kind of way I want to hold on to and relive day after day.

Chloe is working her way so deep into my heart that I'm struggling to remember how life was without having her around. But the best part of having her around is I have yet to fall into my dark place again. For the first time in a long time, I feel happy. Truly, unequivocally happy. I look forward to waking up earlier than her and cooking breakfast before she runs off to work.

In the past few months I've known her, Chloe Carter has banished the monsters making my days dark, and replaced them with everything that makes her days special.

It's not enough to have her here living under my roof. I want to cut a piece of my heart out and tuck Chloe inside, protecting her from the world.

She's like a rainbow after the storm, and I'll be damned if she fades away once the sun breaks through the clouds.

CHAPTER THIRTY-FOUR

Chloe

"I've been thinking about something…" I pass Santiago the wrench he asked for. Did I mention I love his car garage yet? No?

It would make grown men weep, it's that beautiful. Hell, I'd consider shedding a tear or two for the Bumblebee-lookalike Camaro in the corner.

He rolls half his body out from underneath his latest fix-up. "That's never a good idea."

I push my foot against his rolling device, attempting to shove him back under the car.

He laughs at my effort. "I was joking. What have you been thinking about?"

"Well, you going back to racing for one thing."

His penetrative gaze stays locked on mine. "What about it?"

"When are you planning on scheduling your test run?"

He rolls back underneath the car without answering me. The sounds of tools being used fills the silence, and a few bolts drop onto the cement floor.

"I scheduled it for next week."

"What?" I crouch down, trying to see his eyes. "You've been holding out on me!"

"I booked it for a day you're working."

"Why would you do that?" A throb I'm unaccustomed to blooms inside of my chest. I thought he wanted me to go with him. Did he change his mind?

"It's not because of you." He rolls back out from underneath the car. With more agility than I expect from him, he stands up.

"Do you not want me to go anymore?" Somehow I hide the hurt in my voice.

"It's not you, it's me."

Right. A classic brush-off. For some reason, it feels a lot different being on the receiving end.

"Then what?"

"I didn't want to disappoint you. I was afraid I'd chicken out and doing so would be a hell of a lot easier without you there."

"Because I wouldn't hold you accountable."

He shakes his head, stepping back into my personal bubble. "Because making you unhappy is the last thing I want."

He reaches out for my cheek. The roughness of his palm brushes against my skin, and everything inside of me aches for more. "I want to make you proud of me."

"Of course I'm proud of you. What roommate wouldn't be? You kicked my ass in Mario Kart earlier *and* completed a bunch of simulation laps." I jokingly shove his shoulder, but it comes off forced. My eyes flutter shut as his thumb trails across my lips.

"Roommates, huh?"

"The bestest. Like the show *Friends*."

"The one where they all get together? I couldn't have picked a better choice myself."

My eyes snap open. "That's not what I meant."

"You attempt with everything in you to resist us." He runs a finger across my clavicle, eliciting a shiver from me.

"I try hard to show you that certain things are more important than sex."

"That exists?"

This time I shove his shoulder harder. He budges an inch before standing his ground.

"You're hilarious. Really." Sarcasm weighs my words down. "And stop changing the subject."

"Then stop avoiding the one that matters. I'm changing, and if you haven't realized that, then you're not looking hard enough."

He's right. It's obvious that he is changing, little by little. Between his daily trainings in the simulation lab to his discussions on the phone with Noah, he really is attempting to get back out there. He even bought a second F1 simulator set so we could play Mario Kart together every day after I come home from work. Can I withhold what we both want when he is trying to be different?

I don't bother with a rebuttal once his lips touch mine. Whatever kiss I had on replay in my head from the elevator doesn't do the real deal justice. It's like comparing a single flame to a blowtorch.

His lips dominate, stealing away my thoughts. He traces the seam of my lips with his tongue, begging for entrance. I wrap my arms around his neck and let him take control. I can't help it. Kissing him is like eating dessert before dinner. I know it's bad for me, and it'll spoil my appetite for everything afterward, but I can't help wanting to do something forbidden.

His hands palm my ass before he lifts me up. I wrap my legs around his waist, holding on with dear life as he places me on the hood of his car. My hands search for any kind of purchase.

His lips never leave my body. My neck, my lips, the soft spot right behind my ear all fall victim to his touch. I ache, my lower half throbbing with need.

Nothing can stop him from his relentless torture. He fists the bottom of my shirt and tugs it off my body. His greedy hands explore every inch of my skin while his lips trail their way down my neck. "Tell me not to stop."

Is he crazy? My neck pulses rapidly, each breath becoming a chore.

"Don't stop," I whisper, my voice hoarse and desperate.

He pushes my body down against the hood of the car. Metal bends beneath our weight, but I can't find it in me to care. I can't find it in me to do anything but *feel*.

He leans down and presses his erection against my center.

My fingers dig into his shoulders as I moan. "If you're going any further, then you better have a condom on your person."

He abandons me for the rolling cart, finding his wallet in the mess of tools. I practically weep at the foil package in his hands.

"Been saving that for when you get lucky?" I smirk.

"I've been lucky ever since you stumbled into my life. This is an added bonus." He smiles. It's devilish, with a hint of something else in his eyes.

Oh my God. He did not just say that. My pulse quickens as he makes quick work of his sweatpants.

Everything seems promising until he freezes, his pants halfway down his legs. His body tenses as he exhales a deep breath.

That can't be good. I want to stop him before his brain gets going.

"Hey." I snap my fingers as I prop myself up on the hood of the car.

His eyes snap in my direction. He remains stoic, his face unreadable.

"Santiago, if you don't fuck me, I'll kill you. Leg be damned."

His forehead scrunches as he contemplates whatever demons threaten to take control of him. He clutches onto the condom with a death-grip. The foil crinkles under the added pressure, but he doesn't move an inch toward me.

Our moment is lost to whatever thought took over his lust. I release a tense breath as I scoot down the hood of the car. Making quick work of finding my clothes, I grab my shirt off the floor and throw it over my head.

I move toward him, helping lift the band of his sweatpants to cover himself. "It's okay. You're not ready yet."

His shoulders tense. He evades my gaze, his shoulders rising with each agitated breath he takes. "How can you say it's okay? How can you even want to be with me in the first place? I'm damag—"

I cut him off. "Because you're worth waiting for. Whether it's today, or weeks, or even months from now. This isn't about me. It's about you."

He shakes his head, turning away from me. He throws the condom on the cart and exits the garage without looking back.

I want to run after him. To stop him and explain how I see him. But something stops me.

I'm afraid. I've spent my entire life being rejected time and time again, and I don't know if I have it in me to go through it once more.

Darker thoughts threaten to take over, but I shove them away.

No. This isn't about me. This is about him battling the darkest part of himself and accepting who he is—leg or no leg.

I try my hardest to stay up for Santiago. The living room seems less warm without him, and no show can keep my attention. My efforts fail, and I give into the sleep begging to take hold.

Something jostles me awake. The thud of Santiago's iWalk pulls me from my sleep.

"What are you doing?" I whisper.

"Shh."

I snuggle into his chest, breathing in the fresh scent of fabric softener.

"I weigh a lot." And what about the extra pressure on his

leg? I couldn't bear the idea of causing him more pain.

He scoffs. "I could bench-press you on my worst day."

"Stop being so damn cocky. It's unattractive." I squeeze his bicep for good measure before yawning.

"Go back to sleep." The door to my room creaks open.

"I was sleeping until I was rudely interrupted."

"You talk way too much for someone who was sleeping as of three minutes ago."

Another yawn stops my reply. Santiago throws the comforter to the side and places me down in my bed. He tucks me back in, dragging the cover up to my chin.

He turns toward the door, but I call out his name.

"Will you stay?"

The moonlight seeping into my room highlights the bulging muscles of his back. "Why?"

"Because I want you here."

"Chloe, listen—"

"Don't give me the brush-off in my own bedroom. That's awful."

He grunts. "Don't force me to."

"I'm not asking for sex. I swear. I just want you here." *Because I miss you when you're gone.*

"No sex?"

"None. I'll be a saint. I promise." I offer him the sign of the cross, purposefully doing it wrong.

He corrects me like usual, a small smile gracing his lips. His hand brushes a loose strand of my hair away from my eyes. "You're hard to say no to."

"Then don't bother trying." I snuggle into my sheets.

It's obvious that I won this round and he knows it. His

iWalk thumps against the floor as he rounds the side of the bed. I smile at the rustling of my sheets on his end.

He goes through the motions of his routine, and I keep my eyes shut. The temperature in the room heats up as he settles beside me.

I take a peek in his direction. His body remains rigid as he stares up at the ceiling, his arms crossed over his chest. That will absolutely not do.

I roll over, throwing my leg over his without thinking. Every muscle in his body locks up as my thigh grazes his stump.

Shit, Chloe! "Oh, God. I'm so sorry, I wasn't thinking and—"

His arms remain plastered against his chest, unmoving as if he was carved of stone. "It's fine."

"But I just touched you and—" I attempt to move back to my side of the bed.

Santiago's hand stops me. He throws his palm across my thigh, securing me to his body. "Chloe. I mean it. It's fine."

"Like fine fine, or the fine your sister taught you."

He lets out a soft laugh. "Fine fine."

I snuggle into him, finding the perfect spot between his shoulder and neck to lay my head down on. My palm has a mind of its own, pressing against the cotton of his shirt.

I let out a sigh, finally content after a rough day.

"Chloe," Santiago calls out.

"Mmm." I fight to stay awake, but my body wants to drift back to that blissful resting place.

"Thank you for not running away, even when I give you every reason to," he whispers. His words hang around us, filling me with a warmth I didn't expect.

I run my palm across his chest in a soothing motion. "I'm

not going to run away because you don't feel comfortable enough to have sex with me. That's stupid and such a double standard."

"How so?"

"Because, if I felt similarly, I'd make you wait on purpose."

"Why's that?" Humor seeps into his voice.

"Because no man is worth my time if he isn't willing to battle my demons with me."

Santiago's hand tightens around my thigh. His other hand snakes around me, tugging me closer to his body. "I'd slay them all for you."

"Tickle dragons and all? Because those are some sly bastards."

He chuckles before placing a kiss against my forehead. "I really like you."

"If you like me, then promise me one thing."

The blades of the ceiling fan swoosh through the air, filling the silence.

He answers after what feels like hours. "What kind of promise?"

"Don't run away again. When things get hard, stick it out with me. I can't help you fight whatever holds you back if you retreat at the first sign of trouble."

"I will, but only if you promise the same."

"Deal."

We both fall into a comfortable quiet. Consciousness escapes me as I slip into a content sleep with Santiago by my side.

CHAPTER THIRTY-FIVE

SANTIAGO

I should've expected Chloe to join me on my trip to the racetrack. She didn't bother mentioning how she called Noah and asked for the information herself so she could take the day off of work. I underestimated her commitment to seeing this process through, and now that we are here, I appreciate it.

Her presence makes the experience lighter. More manageable. It holds me accountable to make it through today, no matter how hard it gets. I don't want to disappoint her. And most of all, I don't want to disappoint myself.

Today isn't about making my family happy, or even Chloe. It's about proving to myself that I can get back out there. I can have the comeback I dreamed of if I only commit to the hard work.

A skeleton crew hangs around the test track. Noah stands off to the side, running through sheets of paper with James. Seeing my old boss and Noah working together again hits me differently than before. This time, it's not about Noah's racing or his competition. It's about getting me in the damn car.

My eyes drop to the gray tarp with the Bandini logo. *This is it.*

A crew member drops a tire as my eyes land on them, and the wheel rotates in my direction.

Noah lifts his head at the noise and meets my gaze. "Look who finally showed up."

I told him he didn't have to come, but he said he wouldn't miss this moment. It's not as if I could tell him no, especially if he had a week off between races.

"I'm on time, asshole."

James crosses his arms over his massive chest. "If you're not early—"

"You're late," Noah and I reply at the same time.

"Some things never change." James smiles at the two of us. He walks up to me and offers his hand. "I'm happy to have you back here."

I swallow back the lump in my throat. "I know."

James nods before looking at Chloe. "Nice to see you again. When I met you at the Monza gala, I didn't realize how much power you had over our grumpy racer over here." James nudges his head in my direction.

Chloe shakes her head. "Power would insinuate I have control over him."

"Never underestimate yourself." James smiles.

"She's modest but she's been a big help." I smile down at her and wrap my arm around her waist. "And beating Noah in our hot-laps match was the real motivator."

"I let you win," Noah calls out with a smile.

"Spoken like a true loser."

Chloe muffles her laugh with her palm.

James's head snaps between the three of us. A crew member calls for him, and he turns back to me. "I'll be on the radio helping you with whatever you need. There's no need to rush anything about this process. You're here to test out a car and have a good time."

"I got it."

"I mean it. *No* pressure. Let's have some fun and burn some gas." He walks away once I give him one last nod of understanding.

Noah tugs at the tarp covering the Bandini car. The glossy red paint glistens under the afternoon sun, hitting me with a flood of memories. I take a hesitant step forward and run my hand across the sleek hood.

I take my time walking around the entire car, enjoying how it shines. My eyes mist as I assess the steering wheel Noah helped create. It's an exact replica of the one I've been practicing with at home. The car looks the same as my old one, except for the added throttle paddle bar on the steering wheel.

I take a deep breath and place a tentative hand on the wheel.

"I hope you like it. Be gentle on me these first couple of test runs. I have a different driving style than you, but I've studied enough of your tapes to know how you like your ride." Noah stands beside me.

"I can't believe you did all this."

"You're a brother to me." He places his hand on my shoulder and gives it a squeeze.

"I don't know what to say."

"Three years of silence is long enough, don't you think?"

"Yeah, it is," I whisper under my breath. "Thank you."

Noah tugs me in for a hug. "Thank me when you get on a real racetrack and compete against everyone else. Someone as talented as you shouldn't spend their prime racing years wasting away."

I nod my head. Crew members bring me gear to change into, and I take my time in the dressing room inside of the garage. I fumble through the motions, fighting the tremble in my hands as I zip up the fireproof suit.

What if I crash this car? Is there a spare wheel? Will James even want me back if I can't handle a simple test run?

I lean against the counter and hang my head.

A soft knock against the door pulls me away from my thoughts.

"Just a minute."

The doorknob rattles.

"I said to give me a minute."

"It's me." Chloe's voice is muffled by the door.

I unlock the door without thinking. If there is anyone who has seen me at my worst, it's her. What's the point of bringing her here if I don't let her help me when I need it most?

I turn my back toward her as she steps into the small space. She offers me a meek smile through the mirror.

"Wow. That's how you look when you're all dolled up." She bites her lip.

The way she says it has me throwing my head back and laughing.

"It's unfair, you know?" She walks up behind me, gesturing for me to turn around.

I do what she asks and lean my ass against the counter. "What's unfair?"

"How you can look that good in something so horrendous."

I tilt my head at her, fighting the smile begging to make an appearance. "Some women love the suit."

"That? How can they? It leaves nothing to the imagination!" She mockingly gasps. "Is that an outline of your...package?" she cups her mouth, leans in, and whispers.

"I don't know. Care to find out?" I wink.

"Oh, sure." She steps into my space.

I lean back against the counter and tug her into my body. The limited square footage of the bathroom doesn't give us much room. She tilts her head back, her eyes remaining locked on mine as her hand trails down the front of my race suit. My skin heats from her touch.

Her hand stops right above the area throbbing for her attention. "I'll wait until after you race to find out." She giggles and steps out of my grasp.

"What?" I sputter, trying to haul her back into my chest.

She shakes her head, evading my grasp. "No touching until after you test the car. Consider it collateral."

I grin at her reference. "Do I at least get a kiss for good luck?"

She looks up at the ceiling as if she needs to contemplate it.

I grab onto her hips and pull her flush against my body. My hand grips onto the back of her neck while my lips crush hers. Our kiss is a frenzy. Quick, energetic, and everything I needed to calm me down before getting out there.

It's as if this girl knows exactly what to do without ever having to ask me. I'm definitely falling for her, and instead of fearing it, I accept it wholeheartedly.

I only hope she feels the same way. If how she kisses me is any indication, I might be safe.

She pulls away from my hold. "That's it. No more kissing until after."

"I'm holding you to that."

Chloe smiles over her shoulder as she opens the door. The buzz from the garage echoes through the small space.

Damn. Chloe didn't just steal a piece of my heart. She carved her initials into it, branding me for life.

Entering the car, while awkward without my prosthetic, is easy. While I hate needing help, my safety is more important. My doctor recommended against driving with my prosthetic just in case another accident happens. It would become more of a liability than a help in that kind of circumstance, and more risk than it's worth.

Even the mechanics pulling me up to the checkered line and James prepping me over the team radio goes without a hitch. But pushing my mind to its breaking point in order to move past my trauma? Now *that* is hard as fuck.

The engine purrs behind my back, reminding me of old race day sensations I blocked from my mind. Before, memories of the past brought me pain, and pain caused depression. But now, with me sitting in the race car, everything feels real again.

There's a power about being behind the wheel. A mix of

adrenaline and a God complex, intertwined to create athletes who test their limits each and every day.

I want to be that guy again. I want to be that guy so damn badly, I'm willing to work through the bad memories and stress to get there. Because in the end, broken champions don't make history.

I look forward and focus on the road. The car rattles, and I'm sucked into a vortex. Images flood my brain. Tires squeal, and I rush to press my hands on my helmet. Something shudders against my back before metal scrapes. The humidity clings to my race suit, making my breathing heavy. Paved roads in front of me fade into rain-slick pavement.

Fuck. Not another flashback. I grab onto my stump and grind my teeth together. The motion grounds me, bringing me back to the present. Reminding me who and where I am.

This isn't the same track. This isn't that day. Breathe.

"Are you ready, Santi?" James speaks into the radio embedded in my ear.

I take a few deep breaths, regulating my heart rate. "About as ready as one can be after everything."

"Remember what I told you. No one is expecting you to be an all-star on day one. It took Noah months before he could get a handle on the wheel, and you know how much of a perfectionist he is."

I doubt it took Noah that long to master these controls, but I appreciate James's comment nonetheless. "Let's do this." I tighten my fists around the grips of the steering wheel.

The crew steps away from the car. I mess with the toggles, familiarizing myself with the feel of them in my hands.

"Start with the throttle. Take it easy and test it out. It's just like the sim lab."

I lightly pull on the throttle. The engine purrs behind my back, rumbling as the car pushes forward faster than anticipated. Before I lose control, I smash the brake pedal with my left foot. My body jolts and my helmet smacks into the headrest. Tires squeal in submission and metal shudders around me as the car halts its movement.

"I said take it easy. That is *not* easy!" James laughs into the mic.

"I'm glad you're enjoying yourself."

"Sorry, you reminded me of Marko trying out his first kart in the pit lane."

"Seriously, you're comparing my driving to my four-year-old nephew? Way to build my confidence."

James chuckles. "Okay, let's try that again. You just need to get a feel for the throttle paddle and trust your gut. The brakes are the same as the old left foot pedal."

"Okay, I got this," I whisper to myself.

I try the same motion, this time giving my car the ability to make it down the straight before hitting the brakes again. It's a slow start, but the wind rushing over the front wing has me smiling beneath my helmet.

"Much better! See, that's what I mean by easy. You're a natural out there," James offers.

I stare at the first corner, wondering how I can manipulate the wheel, the throttle, and the brake at once. Worried thoughts eat away at my budding confidence.

"Now this is where things get tricky. You're going to have to turn the wheel at the same time as you release the throttle, while monitoring the brake pedal beneath your foot. It's all mental."

I go through the motions in my head, attempting to

commit the move to muscle memory. It's not easy. Sweat drenches my back as I struggle to control the brake pedal and the throttle paddle simultaneously.

I tug on the throttle paddle, forcing the car to speed through the turn rather than slow down. My sneaker slams against the brake and my car spins. Tires shriek as the car halts.

Shit. Something in the car sputters as the steering wheel's lights flash before going out.

"Battery is dead. Good try with the turn. You'll get a handle on it eventually." James speaks with such sincerity.

All I can do is scowl at the wheel. The Bandini crew comes to secure my car and push me back toward the garage. I stew in my toxicity, allowing it to cloak the post-driving glow.

Chloe runs out into the pit lane with a huge grin plastered across her face. The sun shines down on her, highlighting the flush in her cheeks.

I don't understand the smile on her face. I failed. Plain and simple. She wouldn't be smiling if she saw what I used to be able to accomplish on the track.

"Oh my God. You did it!" She runs up to the cockpit and leans over the edge.

I pass the steering wheel to the mechanic and tug my helmet off my head. "Did what? Stall on the first turn?"

"No!" She laughs melodically as she grabs onto both my cheeks, forcing me to look at her. "You got in the car and drove. You. Did. It."

I soak in her positivity like the earth soaks up rain after a drought.

Noah strolls onto the track, assessing the car before

offering me his hand. "Nice work out there."

"You're both acting like I won a race rather than tested a car."

Noah shakes his head. "I kind of miss the old cocky you. He was a hell of a lot more fun than this self-deprecating version."

Chloe turns away, hiding her laugh.

I lift a brow. "You find this funny?"

"Who, me?" She presses a palm against her chest and flutters her lashes.

"Yes. Why are you laughing?"

She shrugs. "Because Noah's right. You kind of kill the vibes."

I frown. "You want me to be all self-love, now?"

"Honestly, yes. I think we owe it to ourselves to unapologetically love who we are no matter what. Because if you don't love yourself, then why do you expect anyone else to?"

I contemplate what she says. Noah pulls Chloe's attention away, talking to her about racing statistics and the secret behind the wheel he created.

If I don't love myself, then who will? And what kind of love am I asking for if I'm hell-bent on showing the worst version of myself, time and time again.

Is that who I want to be? The guy who gives up after one time because things got hard?

No. The opposite of a winner isn't a loser. It's the person who allows the loss to ruin any chance of trying again. The defeatist attitude needs to stop. Right here. Right now.

I clutch onto the wheel, running a finger across the

sensitive throttle paddle. "Hey, Noah?"

"What's up?"

"Do you have an extra battery in the garage?"

"Of course."

"What do you say about testing the car out again?"

Noah smirks. "I thought you'd never ask."

CHAPTER THIRTY-SIX

SANTIAGO

Something inside of me changed during my time on the racetrack. It's as if everything clicked into place for me the moment I drove an F1 race car again. No car in the world can match that kind of speed, and all the fancy cars I have are only cheap imitations of the real deal. I forgot what the high after the race felt like. To have my skin itching from the rush building underneath, begging to be let out.

Driving earlier today fed the part of my soul that was starving for attention. The same part that desperately wanted to feel useful again. To feel needed and wanted.

I struggle with disbelief as I shower and then meet with the crew to discuss test-track statistics. Chloe busies herself with embroidering while I spend time with Noah and James, reviewing tapes and strategies. Every smile she sends my way has my chest warming. Her presence keeps me grounded because my mind threatens to burst from all the information.

I drive us back home from the racetrack on autopilot, not

bothering to say a single word. Chloe keeps quiet, staring out of the window, giving me peace. I appreciate her for it. Hell, I appreciate her for *all* of it. Without her pushing me to be better, I wouldn't be in the position I am now. I wouldn't have been able to accomplish what I did without her because she makes life lighter. And it's about damn time I show her how thankful I am for her.

I pull into the garage and shut off the car. Neither one of us moves for minutes, both trapped in our own heads.

"That was fun." Chloe breaks the silence, looking over at me with her blue eyes.

I smile. "It was."

"Do you plan on doing it again sometime soon?"

"I already booked a testing session for tomorrow morning."

"Really?" Her lips gape apart.

I nod, my grin expanding. "Really."

She claps her hands together. "I knew you could do it! You only needed to believe in yourself!"

"You were right."

"Say it again."

"You were right. Are you happy?"

"Delighted!"

I step out of the car and walk around the hood to open Chloe's door. "I have something I want to show you."

She takes my hand, and I pull her out of the seat.

She follows me through the garage and into the house. I keep moving until we stop in front of a door I've kept locked for far too long.

She bites her lip. "If this isn't a Red Room of Pain, I'll riot."

"What?"

"Never mind." She scoffs.

I open the door with the key I haven't used in far too long. With a flip of the switch, all the lights turn on.

"Oh. My. God." Chloe steps around me and walks inside.

Trophies of all shapes and sizes line the shelves from floor to ceiling, shining under the spotlights. They're all the reminders of my past, dusty and neglected after years of abandonment. Pictures of my family, friends, and crew break up the space, displaying some of my proudest moments.

Chloe walks up to a brightly colored trophy resembling an alien spaceship. She runs a finger across the metal, swiping a line through the dust. "Wow. I knew you were good, but I didn't realize how good."

My chest puffs with pride. "This is a glimpse at what I did before."

She sneezes, making a plume of dust fly into the air.

I wince. "Sorry. It's a bit messy right now."

"Please don't apologize. This is amazing." She gives each trophy special attention, reading off the race and year.

I lean against the wall, enjoying her amazement. Any discomfort I used to feel whenever I entered this room is absent. For the first time in what feels like forever, it doesn't bother me to be surrounded by my past success. Instead, it fuels the beast inside of me that wants to return.

It's the reason I came in here today and invited Chloe along with me. Now is the time to consolidate the racer I was then with the man I am now. Rather than fight it, I want to accept every single part.

"Why are you showing me this?" She stops in front of

my first World Championship trophy. The massive piece still shines after years of abandonment. It's the trophy that started my entire journey—the one that not only changed my life path but my sister's as well.

"Because I wanted to show you the racer I was."

"That's all?" she whispers.

"And I wanted to remind myself why I'm worth fighting for. Why I shouldn't be afraid of the meeting I scheduled with the Formula Corp to defend my case."

"Really?" She turns on her heels and swallows the distance between us. "You're going to speak to them?"

"I'm going to fight for my right to race again, and there's no one I want there more than you."

Tears glisten in her eyes, but she blinks them away before they have a chance to trail down her cheeks. "I'm so proud of you. Like my chest hurts because I'm ridiculously proud."

"I couldn't have done this without you."

She offers me a watery smile. "You could've."

"Okay, let me amend my statement. I wouldn't have *wanted* to without you."

"Okay, you got me there." Chloe tips her head back and smiles up at me. She steps onto her toes and leaves a lingering kiss on my lips.

I deepen it, cradling her head in my palm as my tongue caresses hers. Chloe lets out the softest moan, and I take initiative. I move away from her lips and bend down. She screams as I hurtle her over my shoulder. There's a slight pinch from my prosthetic leg, but nothing I can't handle for a few minutes. Some things take precedent, and the way my dick throbs tells me I'm making the right choice.

"What are you doing?" she cries out.

"I have one last thing to show you."

"What?"

I clutch onto the backs of her thighs and carry her through the house. She pinches my butt cheeks and complains about the blood rushing to her head, but I ignore her. With my free hand, I rip her shoes off. They clatter to the ground.

I enter my bedroom. The sunset on the lake casts an orange glow across the walls. Chloe lets out an audible *oomph* as I throw her onto the bed.

I grab a few things out of a drawer and place them beside the nightstand.

"Newsflash: I've seen your bedroom. This isn't anything new or shocking here." She pushes her hair out of her eyes. The dark strands stand out against the white pillows.

I'm stuck in place, staring at her like a fool. She's perfect in every way. From her smile to the tiny freckles running across her nose. But most of all, I like the way she looks at me. Like I'm more than just a guy.

Like I matter to her as much as she does to me.

"Bueller," she calls out in the same voice as the movie we watched.

I crack a smile.

She pokes me in the chest with her foot. "What do you have to show me?"

"How much I care about you."

Now that shuts her up. Chloe remains mystified as I turn and crawl over her. I pause, unsure how to go about the next steps without making things awkward between us.

"Can you do something for me?" Chloe shifts beneath me.

"What?"

"Will you swap positions with me?"

I blink at her. Following her command, I press my back into the mattress. My head sinks into the soft pillows, and Chloe follows, covering my body with hers.

Chloe's lips press softly against mine. Her hands run over my shoulders before drifting down my abs. Every muscle she touches contracts, tightening until she moves on. Her hands lift the hem of my shirt, pulling it over my head. She kisses her way down my body. I'm addicted to the feel of her running her tongue across the rigid muscles.

My dick throbs painfully against the seam of my sweatpants. Her light caresses leave me straining for more. More of her. More of this. More of everything she has to offer.

"Keep your eyes shut. If you open them, then this is over." Her hot breath trails against my skin.

That's the last thing I want. I screw my eyes shut and grip onto the comforter. Instead of thinking, I focus on the feel of her lips against my body.

She grips onto the waistband of my sweatpants and briefs at the same time. Every muscle in my body tightens as she slides them down my legs, revealing the part of myself I keep hidden from the world.

Does she think my leg looks as awful as I do? Does the jagged scar and puckered skin freak her out? My body locks up at the onslaught of negative thoughts. I try to banish the idea of Chloe having an up-close and personal view of my stump and metal leg, but everything about the situation make me uncomfortable.

"Santiago. Stop thinking and focus on how I make you feel." Chloe runs her palms up my thighs. She settles between my legs, and her warmth erases some of the coldness seeping into my bones. Goosebumps pebble my skin as her palm runs up the length of my cock.

Blood roars in my ears at her touch. It's like static trailing across my skin, crackling from pressure and anticipation. Her lips replace her hand, leaving behind faint kisses across my length. Any scared thought I had melts away as her hot mouth wraps around my dick.

It's a mix of heaven and hell. Right and wrong. Desperation to make the moment last longer while craving my release from the torture of her mouth.

My cock twitches as she sucks me off, bringing me to the brink of pleasure before pulling away again. I grab a fistful of her hair and tug. "You're killing me."

Her lips pop as she releases my cock from her mouth. "Consider this payback for last time." She pumps my dick once for good measure.

"Enough," I hiss.

"Why?" she continues, moving her hand up and down.

My balls tighten, and the tingling sensation spreads up my spine. "That's it."

Chloe's wide eyes are the first thing I see when I open mine.

"I'm done with the games."

She smirks. "You're the one who broke the first rule."

"From now on, there's only one rule that matters and it's to make you come." I slide out from under her body and plant my feet on the floor.

She laughs as I drag her to the edge of the bed. With her help, I make quick work of her tank top and shorts. My movements are rushed and lack any kind of finesse. Her underwear and bra meet the same fate on the bedroom floor, and I finally soak up a vision of her naked.

Any worries about my prosthetic leave the room as I check her out. Sunset rays from the sliding door bask her skin in a golden glow. They bring out the navy in her hair, the wavy tendrils covering the white sheet behind her.

Everything about her is perfect. From her tits that fit in the palm of my hand to the tiny birthmark on her hip bone. But what stands out most is how she radiates beauty from the inside out.

"You're stunning, you know that?"

She bites her lip and looks away.

I grip her thighs, pushing them apart. "Now's not the time to get shy on me."

It was a stupid thing to say. I realize that, as I stare down at her, wondering how the fuck I can pull off pleasuring her in the way I'm used to. Would kneeling down kill the mood? It's not like getting back up is the quickest process.

"Santiago?" Chloe props herself up on her elbows.

"Hmm." I stare down at my leg.

"For fuck's sake. *I. Don't. Care.*"

I reply with a half-assed mumble.

"But I *will* care if you leave me high and dry, begging for your cock because you're too self-conscious to take what you want."

I smirk. "Bossy."

"I'll show you bossy. Kneel down before your queen, or else I'll get the job done myself."

I shake my head and lower myself down to the ground.

Chloe gasps as I trail kisses up the inner part of her thigh. My tongue traces the place I'm dying to taste, and Chloe's body jolts against the mattress. I switch between sucking on her clit and teasing her entrance.

I obsess over the noises Chloe makes. Every gasp, every moan, every damn sigh coming out of her mouth fuels the monster inside of me. She groans my name as her hands fist the sheets above her head. Her sighs become an anthem in my head I want to replay again and again.

My head grows cloudy as Chloe becomes more desperate for her release. She grinds against my face, and I smile. Her patience fades, and my confidence skyrockets as she latches onto my hair. There's a bite of pain, and I repay it by a hard suck on her clit.

Her body tenses and her toes curl as another breathy sigh escapes her. She comes apart as I lick her arousal away in tortuous circles, not stopping until her body relaxes under me.

This is something I could become addicted to. *Fuck, what am I saying?* I *am* addicted to her.

I don't know why I was so worried about kneeling. Chloe is incoherent as I speed through the process of rising from the floor.

"Roll to the center of the bed." I call over my shoulder as I roll the condom down my shaft.

Chloe follows my command. I get on the bed and crawl over her body. Her hand pressing against my shoulder stops me.

"Do you trust me?" She stares up at me.

Do I? I can't imagine having any reason not to. She's stood by me for months, supporting me at some of my lowest points. If there is anyone I should trust, it's her.

My throat tightens as I nod my head.

"Will you take it off then?" She looks down at my prosthetic.

"Take it off?" My voice is nothing but a whisper in the dark. Can I do that? Do I even want to?

"I promise it doesn't matter to me if you're missing a leg, or an arm, or anything else. It doesn't define the person you are." She places her palm against my heart. "This does. And you happen to have one of the prettiest ones."

My heart rate picks up speed as I look down at the one thing holding me back. Sex is supposed to be the most intimate two people can be, but this feels like more.

The last time was nothing short of a disaster, and I worry tonight might be similar.

But this is Chloe.

"You're beautiful to me no matter what. It doesn't matter," she whispers in a husky voice as she places her palm against my cheek.

"Beautiful?" My smirk wobbles.

"Don't let it go to your head." She rolls her eyes while smiling.

Something about her wipes away the fear threatening to take control.

I can do this for her.

I can do this for me.

I roll over and sit, giving her my back. With shaky fingers, I press the pin located at the bottom of my prosthetic. It slides off with ease and lands on the floor. The sock comes off next, and I place it on the nightstand.

This is it. This is the last thing in my way.

Using the strength in my arms and my one good leg, I move back over her body. The smile Chloe shoots up at me has my chest tightening. Not because of nerves, but because she truly is happy to be with me.

Shit. I never thought someone would look at me like *that* because of my leg.

"Thank you for being yourself with me." Her eyes shine, the moonlight emphasizing the unshed tears.

I bend down and kiss her with every emotion I feel inside of me. Fear, happiness, desire...excitement. The world fades away as it becomes just us.

I hold her gaze as I line myself up and slide into her, relying heavily on the strength in my arms and good knee to hold me up. My body shudders as I fill her to capacity. I shut my eyes, enjoying the moment of us becoming one.

Chloe feels like heaven, hell, and everything in between. It's ecstasy and poison. Lust and love. Everything I want while being everything I fear.

Chloe's back arches as I pull out to slam back into her. Her hands trace the divots of my spine, and my skin burns wherever her touch lingers.

My eyes don't know where to focus. Her face smiling up at me with every ounce of emotion I feel back. Her tits shaking with every thrust of my hips. Our bodies connecting in every single way. Physically. Emotionally. Like two hearts tethered together by fate's red string.

She claws at my back as my tempo changes from unhurried to desperate, growing sloppier by the minute. Sweat covers my skin as I expel every ounce of energy. She meets me with vigor, matching my strength with her own.

Our sex is just like her—wild and crazed.

Chloe milks my cock, swiveling her hips with every stroke. I grip onto her hair and tug, forcing her body closer to mine. There's not one trace of skin I don't lick and nip. She tastes like summertime, the salty taste of our exertion clinging to her skin.

Heat darts up my spine like flames licking my skin. The moans she makes as I change my position feed the desire growing within me.

Fuck. The experience with Chloe is like speeding down the track after winning a race. It's a rush I find more satisfying than any checkered flag or podium.

She falls apart as I place pressure on her clit with my thumb. My dick throbs as she tightens around me. I bellow as I pound into her a few more times, coming apart as I find my release.

Chloe Carter destroyed me in every way I needed. She broke me apart before gluing me back together, repairing me from the inside out.

I'm not letting this girl get away.

Not now and not ever.

CHAPTER THIRTY-SEVEN

Chloe

The faint sound of a strumming guitar wakes me up from my deep sleep. It's a haunted melody I can't place, but I find myself entranced anyway.

I peek with one eye, finding Santiago sitting on a chair by the large window. The glow of the moon highlights the guitar propped up on his thigh. One hand grips the neck, delicately pressing against the strings.

I can't believe he picked up his guitar again. After everything he said about avoiding music before, he is right here, playing in front of my very eyes.

Am I dreaming? I pinch my arm extra hard just in case. *Nope, he's still there.*

The music stops as he looks over at me.

I shut my eyes and feign sleep.

He laughs to himself. "You don't need to pretend. I can practically feel your eyes on me."

I pop one eye open and assess his face. A ghost of a smile

makes him seem youthful. Happy, even.

"Busted." I hold the sheet to my chest as I sit up.

He chuckles under his breath. His hands begin moving again, filling the room with music. "Any requests?"

My eyes expand to the point of pain. "What?"

"Do you have a favorite song?"

"Me?" The question comes out as a whisper.

He dramatically looks around the room for someone else.

I throw a pillow at his head. It flops on the ground in front of him with an unsatisfying thump.

"Do you know how to play 'XO' by John Mayer?"

He strums the beginning chords of the song.

"Impressive. It's like my own concert, right from the bed." I sink back into the mattress, smiling over at him as he gets lost in the music.

His eyes shut and his hands move in the most bewitching way. The significance of him playing again isn't lost on me. Santiago Alatorre reclaimed a part of his soul, and I never want him to lose it again.

"You first steam the milk, and then you pour it into the cup like this." Matteo shows off his impressive skill of creating a flower out of coffee foam.

"You make it look easy." I let out a huff.

He laughs. "Now you try." He passes me a cup.

I attempt to recreate the same flower, but my design ends up looking more like a cactus.

"You'll get it eventually." He knocks his shoulder into mine. "It took me months before I mastered different designs."

I step away and give him room to deposit our two cups of coffee in front of our only customers. He returns to the counter and starts cleaning the mess I made.

"I can do that. It's my job." I grab the rag from his hand.

"Oh, nonsense. I was cleaning long before you worked here, and I'll be doing it after."

I rear back. My sneakers squeak against the floor in my haste. "What?"

"Chloe"—he shakes his head—"you're dating Santiago Alatorre. The fact that you're working in this shop is shocking to begin with. If your dream is to own your own place, I'm sure he will set you up with whatever you want."

"Umm, but I'm not ready for that. I still have so much to learn from you."

"A baby bird never learns to fly if it's too scared to leave the nest."

Okay, Mr. Miyagi, settle down.

"Well, this baby bird still needs to learn some more from you. How can I start my own place if I still don't know how to make dainty flowers out of fancy foam?"

"Well, the fall season is coming soon, and everything tends to slow down here."

I stare around the empty shop, wondering what slow looks like.

Matteo smiles weakly. "And when it's slow, I tend to work here less. I travel a bit. Visit some old friends across Europe."

Oh, no. Is he seriously going to lay me off? He can't do that. I'm not ready to lose this connection with him. Not after everything I've been through to get to this point of comfort with him.

He seems to take my silence as approval. "I plan on taking some time off in two weeks and closing the shop for a month."

I choke on my sudden inhale of breath. "Two weeks? Closing shop?" Who can decide out of the blue to take a month off of work?

People who can pay their bills without skipping dinner for a week, Chloe.

He nods. "Don't worry. I'll still be around. And you always have a place to learn more from. But I wanted to tell you, that way you have time to find other arrangements. There's another shop on the opposite side of the lake with a great…" He continues speaking but none of his words resonate.

Frustration replaces my anxiety. I've spent the whole summer building up a relationship with him, hoping for the right moment to admit who I am. I can't let him disappear into the Italian sunset before I've had my chance to talk to him. To confront him and share what he means to me. Maybe if I reveal myself, he will decide to stay and get to know me. For real this time, minus the distractions and false apprenticeship.

Desperation makes me stupid.

I cut him off. "What do you think of having dinner together to celebrate the end of the busy season?"

Matteo smiles. "I'd love that. And we can celebrate you finding your stride, baby bird. You've spent a summer under my wing, and it's time for you to get out in the world."

I nod, finding it difficult to speak with the lump in my throat.

This baby bird is about to fly out of the nest. Let's hope I survive the fall because if I don't, a broken neck would be merciful.

I throw myself on the couch, covering my eyes with the crook of my elbow.

Santiago drags my arm away from my face. "What's wrong?"

I blink up at him, catching the frown on his face. "Matteo is firing me because the busy season is dying down; I haven't made any progress in our relationship." I spit out all the facts like word vomit.

"Maybe this is for the best."

I bolt up from my position. "How can you say that?"

Santiago takes a seat beside me. "Because you've been putting this off for months already."

I scowl. "Things like this take time."

"And things like this take courage."

"I'm courageous."

"Trust me, I'm well aware. Not many people would've accomplished what you did to begin with." He offers me a timid smile.

"Then what's your point?"

"Chloe…" He grabs onto my hand and laces our fingers together. "You've been helping me, and it's time I do the same."

My eyes dart to the opposite side of the living room, focusing on the painting hanging above the brick fireplace.

He squeezes my hand, forcing me to focus back on him. "You need to tell him."

"But what if he rejects me?"

"A wise and sassy woman taught me how things we fear the most are often worth overcoming because it's not about the risk. It's about the reward."

"Who is this wise woman and where can I find her?"

He cracks a smile. "Don't let the opportunity slip away. You'll end up regretting it, and that's not your style."

"Since when did you get all enlightened and stuff?"

"Since you came into my life."

That feeling inside of me? Where my heart races and my chest grows uncomfortably tight? It's not something I'll forget in this lifetime. It feels a lot like love, and I'm not sure what to make of it.

Dammit, Santiago Alatorre.

My fork rattles against the ceramic plate as I push my dinner around in circles. Our goodbye dinner has been nothing but pleasant. With good conversations and great food, thanks to Santiago, it should be amazing to sit with my father. No distractions, no son blabbing away. Santiago isn't even here vying for everyone's attention since he left the house earlier to give me privacy.

Everything was set up to make tonight perfect, but in reality, this dinner is an epic fail. I can't gather the courage to say what I need to. It's like my tongue loses the will to move every time I think about speaking out.

Matteo takes a swig of wine, not a care in the world. "This dinner was incredible, Chloe. I appreciate you taking the time to do this for me."

My stomach muscles clench. "Of course. I honestly couldn't have done it without Santiago though. He cooked half of this." *Okay, he cooked all of it, but whatever.*

"Well, you sure landed yourself a good man. If they can

cook, keep them."

"And if they can clean, marry them."

Matteo laughs. "I see you've picked up on a few things besides my coffee skills during our time together."

I struggle to smile. The tightness in my chest grows as I consider Matteo leaving me behind.

Matteo fumbles with his pocket. "And speaking of our time together...I think you deserve this after all you've done for the shop. I've never seen it look better." He slides an envelope over the wooden dining table.

A mist covers my eyes as I assess the sealed envelope. *Oh, God. Am I really going to cry because he is giving me money?*

No, you're going to cry because this is the first time a parent wants to take care of you rather than steal from you.

I blink away the tears in a rush, not wanting to scare Matteo. "I can't accept that."

"Of course you can. You barely made any money during the time you worked for me. And I've never had an employee work as hard as you. Not even my own son, and he owns part of the place."

Despite the shitstorm of emotions brewing inside of me, I can't neglect the sense of pride filling me up. Sibling rivalry at its finest. "I should be thanking you. Not many people would take a chance on teaching a random person their business secrets."

Matteo smiles. "It was my pleasure, truly. Even if you can only make smiley foam faces in your cappuccinos." He wipes his face and places his napkin on the table.

Is he leaving already? I eye the clock. *Shit. It's been an hour already.*

My heart pounds in my chest, the speed picking up as

Matteo rises from his chair.

This is it. The moment I've been waiting for. The very one I put off for months because I had no idea how to tell Matteo about myself.

"Matteo, wait." My voice croaks.

The chair scrapes as he halts his movement and looks over at me.

"I have something I've been meaning to tell you. It might sound shocking, but it's important."

Okay, that was *so* not what I practiced saying in front of the mirror this morning.

"Yes, *bambina*?" Color drains from his cheeks.

Fuck. I'm already messing up. Rule number one of telling someone a shocking secret: Don't warn them beforehand. "There's no easy way to say this…"

"There won't be if you say nothing." A faint smile crosses his lips.

My wobbly return of a smile lands somewhere between a scowl and a look of constipation. "I took a genetic test, and I found out you're my father."

Now's the moment Morgan Freeman drops the mic and exits my subconscious.

CHAPTER THIRTY-EIGHT

Chloe

The chair tumbles behind Matteo as he jumps backward. "What?"

Nothing could have prepared me for the absolute look of horror on his face. It tears my insides apart like a paper shredder.

I expected anything else. Shock, sadness, surprise. Anything but horror and outrage.

"There is a mistake. A big, big mistake." He steps backward and trips over his chair.

Oh my God. I move to help him, but he puts up his shaky hands.

"Stop." He grips onto the base of the chair with a shaky hand and stands.

"Please, let me explain."

"There is nothing to explain. There must've been a mix-up in the test. I'm not your father."

The man I spent the whole summer working with side by

side is gone. His grimace remains permanently etched onto his face, along with a sheen of sweat building across his brow.

My body is on autopilot, unable to let him go without getting a chance to explain what happened. I didn't go through all my shitty circumstances to back down at the first sign of trouble. "I assure you there isn't." I step toward him.

He prowls like a caged animal, inching closer toward the hall that leads to the main door. "You're not my child. There is absolutely no way."

"When you visited New York all those years ago...you slept with my mother. I'm not sure if you remember her but... well...she found out she was pregnant with me..." My voice drifts off. I let out a raspy laugh, hoping to lighten the mood.

Based on the way Matteo's eyes widen, I would say it didn't go as intended. It's as if I'm a ghost, haunting him with the truth. "We...I—I need to get to the bottom of this. This is a mistake. A big fucking mistake."

"Just listen to me. Maybe if I told you about my mother, you'd remember her—"

"I don't know who the fuck your mother is, but you are not my child," he bites out.

I shrink back.

He rubs his trembling palms across his face. "I'm sorry. Please forgive me. Just...let me figure out what is going on." He doesn't give me a chance to respond. His retreating form is the last thing I see before the door opening and closing echoes in the distance.

With shaky legs, I slide down the wall and sit on the marble floor, curling into a ball. Rejection settles deep into my bones. It fills me with a new sense of dread, erasing all the progress I made with Matteo.

It's not as if I thought Matteo would accept me with open arms. But the look of disgust on his face haunts my thoughts, reminding me of how another parent doesn't want me.

I forgot what it felt like to be abandoned. The cold feeling steals away my warmth, reminding me of past feelings about my mother. I was nothing but a hassle for her, and now I'm nothing but a regret for my dad. The product of an unmemorable one-night stand. Not even worth being listened to.

Tears run down my face as I swallow back my sobs. I place my forehead against my knees as I take a few deep breaths. I'm not sure how long I sit there, but it feels like hours before Santiago returns.

The usually calming thump of his iWalk does little to ease the emptiness inside my chest.

"Oh, Chloe." His voice cracks.

I look up at him, wiping at my tear-stained cheeks.

His forehead scrunches as his eyes scan my face. "Come on." He extends his hand out to me.

Not one grunt comes from him as I clutch onto it and stand.

Santiago pulls me into his body, basking me in his warmth. He doesn't speak as he leads me toward the living room. I'm in a daze, falling onto his lap as he lands on the couch.

"What happened?" He pushes my hair out of my face.

"He didn't take it well."

He makes a noise in the back of his throat. His arms secure themselves around me, holding me tight to his body. The way he cradles me reminds me of a child. It fills me with the same kind of feeling—security in my moment of distress.

I hide my head against his chest, muffling my sniffles. "It ended up being the worst-case scenario. He literally tripped over himself to get out the door. And he didn't even give me a chance to explain, let alone make sure he was okay."

"Maybe he needs some time to come to terms with it. It's a lot to take in, I'm sure."

I shake my head. "You didn't see his face. It was like I was this monster to him."

Santiago runs his hand up and down my back. "You're not a monster."

"It's hard not to feel that way when the people who should want me don't."

He pauses. "If they don't want you, then they aren't the people you need in your life, regardless if they're your parent or not."

"That's easy for you to say. You have a family. You have people who want to help you and make sure you're happy. I barely have anyone." I laugh to myself. The sound is shrill and bitter, making my flesh pebble. "All I have is Brooke. And she's not even here for me to vent to."

"Chloe." He tucks a finger under my chin and forces me to look at him.

His face catches me off guard, full of anguish as he stares me in the eyes. "You have me."

"Yeah, for how long?"

"As long as you want me." His arms tighten around me.

As long as you want me.

As long as you want me?!

What does someone say to that? How does someone even *feel* about that?

Santiago cups my chin with the gentlest touch. "I don't know why Matteo ran away. I can only assume he's in shock, and that he will come around sooner rather than later to the idea of you. But I promise you that you're not alone in this. You do have people who lov—care about you." His cheeks flush. "I care. Brooke cares. So it's not about the amount of people who do—but rather the quality of that care—that matters. I might be a bit biased, but whoever doesn't care about you is crazy, because you are single-handedly one of the best people I know. And I'm not the least bit sorry if they run away, because that means I can keep you all to myself. Because with you, I like being selfish."

My vision blurs. Something in the way Santiago looks at me has something in my chest coiling around my lungs, squeezing the oxygen straight out of me.

Santiago is everything I didn't realize I was missing in my life. Security. Friendship. *Love.* The tiny voice in my head whispers.

I'm growing dependent on a person and I can't deny the fear I have toward that. And cravings are bad. Cravings lead to destruction and heartache, and I'm not sure I can kick a bad habit like him. Everything about him sings to the broken part of my heart that desperately wants to be cared for. To be loved and cherished because I matter. To love someone else fully, and not let a day go by that they don't know it.

"I like you a lot," I whisper. It's not a declaration of love, but it's the most I can do for now.

He presses a soft kiss at the corner of my lips. "I like you a lot too. I like you a lot more than anyone else."

He runs his hand through my hair. It soothes me, easing

the ache in my chest.

"When do you know if you *like* versus *love* someone?" My hoarse voice breaks the silence between us.

"I can only speak from personal experience, but I think I can tell when it takes all my self-control not to stomp across my neighbor's yard and knock him out for making my girl cry."

Everything stops. My heart. My breathing. Santiago's hand brushing through my hair.

I blink up at him. "Personal experience?"

He nods.

"You love me?"

"I'd be insane not to."

I can't think, let alone speak. I wrap my arms around his neck and pull his lips to mine. Tears trickle down my cheeks, but I ignore them. Santiago kisses me back. It's a battle of tongues clashing and lips smashing together. I'm intoxicated, getting drunk on breathing in his life.

He pulls away. "I love you, Chloe. I love you so damn much, sometimes I ask myself if it's normal to have an uncomfortable feeling in my chest whenever you're not around."

"I don't even know what loving someone else feels like, let alone how to accept it from someone." I frown, hating how true the words are.

"Will you let me show you?"

His simple question steals my breath away. I nod my head, desperate to replace the ugliness Matteo left behind. There's nothing I want more than Santiago's love. I want to know what it feels like to be the center of someone's world, even if it's for a few hours.

Santiago rises from the couch and places me on my feet. He grabs my hand and drags me through the house toward his bedroom.

My pulse point throbs as he throws me on the bed. Heavy breaths leave my mouth, covering the clicking noises of Santiago removing his iWalk. A steady buzz takes over my body. My skin grows hot beneath my clothes, and I rip off all obstructions.

Santiago crawls over my body, chuckling. "You want to know what love feels like?" He cups the area begging for him. A single finger traces my arousal, spreading it.

"Yes." I nod my head up and down. *Do I ever. How can someone ever say no to him?* He looks at me in a way I've never recognized before.

"Loving you feels like I found a life raft in the middle of a raging ocean."

"Is that supposed to be romantic?" I tease.

He tugs on my hair, forcing me to arch my back. His lips trail down my neck before sucking on my nipple. Eager hands touch every inch of my skin as if he needs to commit my body to memory.

I groan as he inserts a finger and presses his thumb against my clit. His touch is electric. Thrilling. *Adoring.*

This is what love is. Being cherished and revered because the person wants to, not because they have to.

He leaves behind a faint kiss at my pulse point. "Loving you is like being stranded in a desert without food or water. Like I'm half delusional, wondering if this whole damn thing is a mirage, because nothing should feel or look this good." His slow torture takes a turn as he increases his tempo and inserts another finger inside of me.

His expert touch ignites every cell inside of me. Heat rushes across my skin as he strokes my most sensitive spot, forcing my back to arch off the mattress. All too soon, he leaves me panting as he makes quick work of the condom.

He returns, lining himself at my entrance. "And most of all, loving you is realizing heaven isn't a place, but a person."

I clutch onto his back as he slides into me. Waves of heat roll across my skin as I take every inch of him. The feeling is unlike anything I've experienced before, with a surge of emotions hitting me all at once. Santiago's words seep into the crushed part of me, reviving something I forgot existed in the first place. The part my mother broke. The part I hid from the world after years of anger and disappointment.

Tears leak out of my eyes, soaking the pillow underneath me. The way Santiago looks at me sets me ablaze from the inside out. I feel like a phoenix begging to rise again.

His thumb wipes away one of my tears. "I love you, Chloe. And it's okay if you don't know what it means to be loved by someone, let alone love someone else because I promise to love you enough for the two of us. To love you every day to make up for everyone else who failed miserably."

He really does love me. Deeply. Madly. Unconditionally.

I tighten my legs around his waist, pulling him as close as possible to my body. "I want that kind of love."

His lips clash against mine like lightning clapping through the stormy sky. It feeds the hunger building inside of me. His love surrounds us, healing me in the process.

He pulls me back into the moment, kissing me into a mindlessness. Together, we find our release.

This is bliss.

This is love.

This is us.

CHAPTER THIRTY-NINE

SANTIAGO

Sleep evades me as I consider everything Chloe shared about Matteo. Something about the situation doesn't sit right with me, and I can't shake it. I need him to understand why this is so important to Chloe. She deserves a chance to explain herself, and he needs to listen.

It takes an insane amount of willpower to crawl out of bed and leave Chloe behind. She looks peaceful, mindlessly grabbing a pillow in my absence. I'm tempted to stare at her for a few minutes but decide against it. I'll never leave if I keep it up.

After putting on my prosthetic and some clothes, I make my way toward Matteo's house. I press the ringer on his gate.

"*Chi è?*"

"Santiago Alatorre." I keep my voice neutral.

Nothing happens. Minutes pass, and not a single sound comes from the speaker. I move to press the button again but stop myself when the gates creak open.

Morning sunrays guide my walk up his long driveway. I barely pay attention to my surroundings, instead focusing on Matteo standing on his porch.

"Come inside." He sighs and ushers me through his front door.

I take in my surroundings, eyeing knickknacks and photos lining the walls.

"I know why you're here." He takes a seat on an old chair.

I follow suit, taking a seat across from him. "I need you to talk to Chloe. *Today*."

"I can't." He shakes his head.

"Why the fuck not?"

He pauses. His eyes move around the room, landing on a spot behind my head. "Because I'm not her father."

"She has a DNA test that says otherwise."

He visibly swallows as he avoids my gaze. "I heard. But the test is wrong. I'm not her father."

I can't believe this guy. "I'm curious to know who you think the fuck her father is then if it's not you."

He looks up at me with eyes that weren't glassy a second ago.

What the hell?

A single tear streaks down his cheek. "I can't be Chloe's father. I've never been with a woman from America, and I was faithful to my girlfriend—now ex-wife—at the time of Chloe's conception. She's not mine. She *can't* be mine."

"Are you denying this because you're afraid of your ex-wife or son finding out that you were unfaithful back then? Is that it?"

He shakes his head. "No. Not at all. My ex is the least

of my worries." He shuts his eyes. "It's just not possible. I'm being truthful, I swear it."

I try to wrap my head around the nonsense Matteo spews from his mouth but I struggle.

"The test linked Chloe to you. I don't care what fantasy you create to deal with this, but Chloe is your daughter.

He bolts out of his chair. "No. *You* need to understand. There's only one possible way Chloe is related to me."

Something about the wild look in his eye has me biting on my tongue.

He paces the small living room space, running his hands through his hair. "*Mio fratello mi sta fregando, persino dall'aldila.*"

"What?"

"My brother is still screwing me over."

My heart halts in my chest. I don't dare breathe. I don't dare move. I can't do anything but look at Matteo in silence.

Brother?

Matteo doesn't bother saying anything as he leaves the room.

I tap my fingers against my knee. The slamming of different drawers in the distance lets me know Matteo is still somewhere nearby. At least he hasn't run away from the property before he has a chance to clear up whatever the fuck is going on.

The longer I wait, the stronger my nausea grows. *What did he mean by his brother screwing him over?*

Matteo steps back into the room, clutching a picture frame. He wipes the glass with his sleeve before passing it to me.

Fuck. I couldn't have made up what I was seeing even if I wanted to. And damn, I want to because this is the last thing I expected.

The frame rattles as the shaking in my hands increases. There are two identical Matteos standing side by side. One Matteo beams at the camera while the other keeps a neutral face, looking rail thin and pale.

Matteo runs a finger across the face I stare at. "That's my twin brother. Dominic."

Thank God I'm sitting down because I don't think I would've made it to a chair before passing out.

Matteo returns to his seat across from me. "He's the only explanation for all of this. I never had sex with someone in New York...and my brother...he would get into all kinds of trouble when we visited my mom."

I don't care what his brother did as long as I can get his sorry ass here pronto. Chloe won't give a damn about Matteo's rejection if I can manage to secure her real father.

"Where is your brother? I need to find him. If I can convince him to come here, then he can get to know Chloe, and it'll solve all our problems." And then she will stay.

I can fix this. Sure, Chloe spent the whole summer getting to know Matteo instead of her real dad. But it's not exactly time lost. He is her uncle after all.

Matteo's reddened cheeks lose their coloring. "My brother can't come here."

"Why not? Where is he? I'll pay for anything he needs to get here."

Matteo's head hangs against his chest.

My stomach drops, and a chill spreads across my skin.

"Where is your brother, Matteo?" I bite out harsher than intended.

Matteo sits in silence, staring at his hands.

My patience wanes as Matteo fails to respond. "I'm going to need you to tell me how I can get in contact with Dominic. I don't care if he's a bad person or troubled, I just need to meet with him once to clear the air. I'll fix the rest."

He looks at me, pain etched into his face like permanent wrinkles. "You can't get in contact with my brother because he's dead."

CHAPTER FORTY

SANTIAGO

I choke on my breath of air.

Dead?

Dead?!

How the fuck am I supposed to fix this if the one man I need isn't alive to begin with? I wipe my sweaty palms down my pants.

What the hell is Chloe supposed to do if her father isn't even alive?

I settle on one question despite the flood of them filling my head. "What happened?"

Matteo places the picture frame facedown on the coffee table. "My brother had issues."

"What kind of issues?"

"The kind that end with an early death."

I can't say I'm exactly surprised. Based on the one interaction I had with Chloe's mom and the stories, it seems like she had a type.

"I'm sorry about your loss."

His head drops. "Me too. The pain gets easier, but then something like this happens to bring it all back again."

"I can't imagine what it's like to have a sibling who struggled and passed away. The thought of losing my sister alone makes me sick." I love Maya with everything in me. If she battled the same problems as Chloe's dad, a part of me would struggle with her.

"You have no idea the things I did to help him out. I'm not proud of half of them, but I didn't have a choice. He was my brother."

"I can tell you cared about him a lot."

"It wasn't enough in the end. I failed him. And now, he's not here, and Chloe… God, what am I going to do?" He runs both hands through his dark hair.

"You need to tell her the truth." I disguise the tremble in my voice. The idea of this makes me sick with nausea.

As much as I hate what happened to Chloe's father, avoiding the topic won't bring him back. Chloe deserves to know what happened to him before she invests more of her feelings into her relationship with Matteo.

"He's still getting me into trouble, even after all this time."

"If you don't mind me asking, what happened to him?"

"Drugs, alcohol, legal issues. You name it, he struggled with it. He was a mess up until the day he died, but I loved him despite it all. The summer before he passed, he got into some harder stuff, and his body couldn't keep up. He died of cardiac arrest in the middle of a rat-infested apartment in New York City. He wasn't even found until two days after he passed. My mother was absolutely destroyed. And me—" He clears his throat as he brushes away a single tear away from his cheek.

Shit. What an awful way to go. "I'm sorry for your loss. Truly I am."

"Losing a brother is hard. But losing a twin is like someone cut off my arm."

I cringe.

He swears something in Italian. "Sorry, that was a bad choice of words. It's just, when I lost my twin, it was like I lost a part of myself that I never got back. Even with all his problems, we were close. I mean, we were mirror copies of one another, and we loved it." A small smile spreads across Matteo's lips. "It got us in all kinds of situations growing up. But I was loyal to a fault, and I bailed him out way too many times in life. Maybe I was part of the problem, always saving him. It took me a decade to let go of my guilt about his death. I was consumed by the idea that maybe if I had gotten him help sooner, he could still be here today. Maybe he could've had this conversation with you after all. Maybe he could've met his daughter." His eyes fall to his lap. One tear slips down his face before landing on his clenched hands.

"I can't imagine how hard it was for you."

"How am I supposed to tell Chloe that I'm not her father and that her real dad is dead?" His voice cracks.

"I'm not sure there is an easy way to tell her."

He shakes his head. "I don't think I can do it. It would destroy her."

"What do you mean 'you don't think you can do it'? You *need* to tell her." I don't like the look on his face. I don't like it one bit.

"How do you tell someone their real father is dead? How can you expect me to do that?"

"I don't know how you should tell her, but you *will* do it. She deserves to hear it from you."

"What if you told her instead of me?"

I sputter. "What?" This man is absolutely psychotic.

"Yes. You're her boyfriend. She trusts you the most. It would be easiest coming from you than me—someone who is basically a stranger. You can soften the blow, and then I'll share who my brother was with her once she's ready."

I can't find the nerve to break her heart. Not when I worked the whole summer to gain it in the first place.

I shake my head from side to side aggressively. "No way. You're not putting this on me. She deserves to hear it from the person who was closest to her father. And that's *not* me. I can't answer any of the questions she might have." And the last thing I want to do is break her heart. I'd rather have Matteo be the one to do it.

I can't find it in me to rip someone's dream away from them. It's happened to me, and that kind of pain can be devastating.

"*Cazzo*." Matteo pinches the bridge of his nose.

I don't need a translator to draw my own conclusions about that phrase. His hesitation and dislike about the plan isn't my problem. To be honest, I don't give a fuck how upset this situation makes him. Chloe needs to hear this news from someone, and he's the best choice. He can help her mourn the loss of her father better than I can.

"I'm giving you a day to figure this shit out. I'll take Chloe somewhere, and you'll figure out the best way to break the news. Got it?"

"I can't believe this is happening. I don't know if a day is enough time to figure out what to do."

"A day is all you're going to get. She's going to want to see you again, and you can't pretend you're someone you're not."

His eyes dart away. It sets me on edge, and I need to gain control of this situation.

"You think this is easy for me? It's not. The last thing I want is for this situation to ruin her in a different way than ever before. You have no idea how excited she was to spend time with you, thinking you were her dad." Every muscle in my body locks up at the idea of Chloe finding out about all of this.

Matteo's eyes widen. "Does she even want to own a coffee shop?"

I shake my head from side to side.

"Wow." His eyes drop. "She spent the whole summer doing things she wasn't interested in to get to know me?"

"She'd do it all over again, just for the chance to spend time with you. She was desperate to be around you in whatever way she could get. And now..."

"Now I'm going to break her heart."

There's no use in denying Matteo's claim. I love Chloe, but I can't be the one to destroy her happiness. Not when she made it her mission to become mine. I'd rather help pick up the pieces of her broken heart once Matteo shatters her world into nothing but stolen wishes and missed chances.

I shut the bedroom door behind me without making a noise. Chloe is in the same spot I left her, looking peaceful as she holds on to the pillow. Something clenches in my chest at her vulnerability. A feeling of helplessness hits me as I consider everything I learned not even an hour ago.

Nothing in the world can fix what she's about to learn. All I can do is make the process as painless for her as possible.

Making quick work of my shoes, clothes, and prosthetic, I settle back into the bed. I pull Chloe into my body. She throws a leg over my body and nestles into the crook of my shoulder. I wrap my arms around her, holding her close to my chest. It's as if my conversation with Matteo never happened. Honestly, I wish I could go back in time and erase my memory of his confession.

I stay like that for an hour. I don't move an inch, afraid to wake her after the hellish night she had. And worse, I'm worried if I wake her up, the guilt will tear me apart. Guilt makes me stupid and reckless. She has a way of wanting me to be better, including telling her the truth no matter what. Even if it means hurting her.

I shake my head, nixing the idea. I'm doing this for her. Matteo needs to think of the best way to tell her, and I need to wait.

She startles awake, her body jolting against mine.

"Good morning." I brush her hair out of her face.

"Morning." A lazy smile graces her face.

"How are you feeling?

"Like I have the worst hangover, minus the alcohol."

"Because of last night?"

She nods. "Crying will do that to a girl."

"I'm sorry it happened that way." *And I'm sorry I have to lie to your face and pretend I don't know the truth. I'm so fucking sorry.*

She deserves much more than the shitty cards life has given her time and time again. Someone like her shouldn't be plagued by sadness and despair year after year.

She traces the divots in my chest with her fingers. "Out of all the ways I thought things would go down, I didn't expect him to run away, you know? I mean, I knew it was a possibility, but I stupidly hoped it would be way better than that."

Shit. I didn't expect to be tempted to break down and tell her after one minute. The nagging voice in my head forces me to stop and think of the consequences.

What if she freaks out and leaves? What if she realizes she doesn't love me after all, and Matteo's truth is the last thing holding her back from leaving for America? What if I'm the one to push her to that result?

I don't want to be the bad guy. There are too many unknown variables, and I need Matteo to be the one to figure this out.

I swallow back the words begging to be let out. "What do you want to do about it?"

Her eyes shift away from me. "I don't know. I thought about going over there and talking to him."

"When do you want to go over?" *Please, not today.*

"I was thinking of giving him the day to think everything over. If I go over there too soon, I'm scared he will flip out again, and I don't think I could handle that again."

I nod. *Thank God.* Matteo better pull his shit together over the next twenty-four hours. I'm not pretending I don't know for another day. This is torture.

"I've been thinking." I tuck a loose lock of her hair behind her ear.

"The world must be ending after all."

"That's quite rude of you." I roll on top of her body and tickle her.

"Stop! I'm sorry!" she wails as she thrashes against the sheets.

I take advantage of her distraction and plant a kiss on her lips.

She smiles up at me. "What were you thinking about?"

"How do you feel about doing something crazy today?"

"Crazy, you say? What do you have in mind?"

"Want to go somewhere special?"

"Somewhere special is exactly what the doctor ordered." Her grin expands.

God, she's gorgeous. The morning sun shines through the balcony, highlighting the icy shades of blue in her eyes. I wish I had a camera to photograph the moment.

I pull away, wanting to leave before I end up back in bed with her. "Get dressed in something that can get wet."

She sits up. "Wet? How naughty."

I shove her shoulder lightly, and she flops back on the bed. "Perv. I mean a swimsuit. We're going out on the boat."

"Yes! I've never been on a boat before!" She bolts out of bed and runs out of the room without a backward glance.

Experiencing life through Chloe's eyes is a new kind of thrill. The simplest things make her happy, and I find it infectious. I want to be the one to steal all her firsts and be all her lasts.

Despite her excitement, something in my chest pinches. I

check the clock on the nightstand.

Twenty-two hours and thirty minutes to go. I can do this.

I anchor the boat in the middle of the lake. Blue water glitters under the noon sun, resembling a sea of diamonds. The expansive valley surrounds us, setting up a beautiful backdrop of lush green forests. Our small town lines the edge of the shore. Buildings look like multicolored ants, scattered in front of the mountains.

The boat bobs. It's one of my smaller boats, with cushions in the front for lounging and a back meant for jumping off into the warm water.

"What do you think?" I shut off the motors.

"It's stunning. I could totally get used to this." She leans forward on the bow.

"Me too." I don't bother staring out at the vista because the only view I care about is her.

She looks over her shoulder at me and blushes. The unspoken meaning behind my words hangs between us.

I wish she would say something back about wanting to stay here. About wanting to explore our relationship more and see where things go if we give it a chance. I'd do just about anything to have her confirm what I can tell is growing between us.

She stays quiet like always. I can tell she likes my words, but a smile is the only confirmation I get.

"Are we going to get in the water or what?" She stands and brushes her hands down her ripped shorts.

I let out a deep breath, releasing the growing agitation inside of me. *Give her time. She wasn't surrounded by love growing up like you were.* "I'll race you to the water." I plaster a smile on my face.

"You're on." She fumbles with her clothing, making quick work of all the items.

Like an idiot, all I can do is stare at her once she reveals her damn bright pink bikini. It's nothing but two scraps of fabric poorly concealing her chest. She turns around to tuck her shorts into her backpack, and I'm hit with the perfect view of her ass.

Whoever made thong bikinis deserves a thank-you card signed by yours truly—a man who will be undoubtedly stuck with a permanent boner today.

"Fuck." My dick pulses to life in my swim trunks. The fabric tents in the front, and I do nothing to conceal it.

"Hello! You're not even trying. And that's saying something when you only need to take off your shirt." She waves her hands at my fully-clothed chest.

I grip onto my T-shirt and rip it off my head. "Happy now?"

"Elated!" She flashes me a grin before it drops. Her eyes bounce between me and the back of the boat.

Ah. I'm blocking her only way off. "And here you were, feeling confident about winning."

Her smile becomes something devious. "Oh, Santiago. When will you realize I'm not going to do what you expect of me?"

I don't have a chance to question what she means. Chloe turns and dashes toward the front of the boat. Her bouncing ass is the last thing I see as she dives off the bow.

Damn. This girl is nothing I'd expect, but everything I want. I won't stop until she's mine. No disability or shitty news about her dad can stop me from claiming her for myself.

If I have a say in things, Chloe Carter will never want for anything again.

"Hey, loser! Do you plan on staring at the view all day or are you actually going to get in the water?" Chloe calls out from the back of the boat.

I walk to the back platform. My eyes drop to my prosthetic leg, and a rush of emotion hits me. But it's not the usual negative thoughts. I'm not concerned with how Chloe views me because of my leg. I'm not worried about showing this part of myself and bracing for disgust.

I'm not worried. Period. End of story. But rather, I'm proud. The idea hits me out of nowhere, and I stumble. *Proud?*

I straighten my spine. *Yes, proud.* This is me, and this is the person Chloe has always accepted. Hell, this is the person I accept. None of it would've been possible to begin with without Chloe. Because of her and my push toward rejoining F1, I can finally embrace some confidence.

Chloe's head pops up from under the surface. Beads of water drip down her face, coating her lashes and cheeks, dripping into her smile lines. "Do you always check yourself out this much? I know you're sexy and all, but narcissism is only endearing to a certain extent."

I snort. "You're ridiculous."

"Ridiculously funny."

There goes that weird feeling in my chest again. The guilt from her situation sits heavy inside of me, eating away at my good mood.

I shake my head. *Stop it.*

I take a breath and jump into the water, splashing water all over Chloe. Her laugh is the last thing I hear before I sink beneath the surface.

She jumps on my back the moment I pop back up. I hold on to her and spin us around in circles, choosing to enjoy today. I'll worry about tomorrow once it gets here because there's nothing I can do about it now.

Some things are out of my control, and like Chloe says, it is what it is.

CHAPTER FORTY-ONE

Chloe

I wake up ready to take on the day. After spending yesterday with Santiago, I reminded myself that people take time to warm up. Santiago is the perfect example of that. A few short months ago, he wouldn't let me see his stump, let alone go on the boat with him. But yesterday, he let loose in the broad daylight and had fun with me. He was in full-on prosthetic mode and he didn't even so much as flinch at his leg.

I won't lie, a few tears of joy left my eyes. But it was a beautiful sight, with him not hiding his true self from me.

Santiago's big accomplishment reminded me how Matteo needs time too. How people need to process their feelings. I did tell Matteo I was his daughter after all, and it's not exactly something that can be easily digested after one day. So, I lowered my expectations after rethinking my situation.

"Are you sure you don't want me to go with you?" Santiago paces the front entryway of his house.

I double-knot the laces on my sneaker. "No. I appreciate the offer, but I think Matteo might do better if it's just me. You can be kind of distracting, no offense."

He doesn't laugh at my joke. "But I can be in another room. You know, just in case you need me like the other day."

The memory of Santiago helping me during my breakdown makes my smile wobble.

I take a deep breath, pushing back my worry. "You live next door. If anything goes wrong, I can walk here in under a minute. I promise if I need you, I'll call you."

He runs a hand through his hair, forcing the strands to stand in different directions. "You'll come back the moment things don't feel right, won't you?"

"*If* things don't feel right." *Why is he so nervous?* I'm not even that nervous, and I'm the one about to talk to Matteo after how everything went between us.

"Right. If." His voice lacks his usual confidence.

"Hey." I walk up to him and wrap my arms around his waist, forcing him to stop his pacing. "You don't have to be afraid. I accepted that this isn't going to be an easy process, and that's that."

His body tenses. "What do you mean?"

"I get that Matteo needs to warm up to the idea of me. It's not like he had any time to prepare for this like I did."

"Right," he whispers.

"Yes. It's okay if he freaks out once or twice. I would if I were in his position. It's to be expected."

"Nothing about this is expected," he grumbles under his breath.

I laugh. "I'll be back soon! Relax." I let go of him and walk toward the front door.

"Chloe," he calls out.

I grip the handle and look over my shoulder. "Yeah?"

"No matter what he says, remember that I care about you, okay? You'll always have a place here with me, and nothing he says will change that."

A warmth spreads through my chest as his words sink in. The sweetness Santiago shares with me is something I could definitely get used to. It's something I *want* to get used to, and that's a first for me. I crave the kind of stability he can offer me. I crave him, period.

I grin at him. "I like this version of you."

"And what version is that?"

"The one I'm falling in love with." I slip out of the house, leaving a slack-jawed Santiago behind me.

Matteo opens his gate the moment I press the buzzer. I powerwalk up the driveway and knock on his front door. The stucco walls reflect a well-loved house, weathered after years of lakeside winds.

Matteo opens the door. His eyes slowly move from the ground up to my face. "Hi, Chloe. It's nice to see you."

"Hi," I squeak.

"Why don't you come on in?" He pushes the door wider and I follow him inside.

"You have a nice home," I offer as I check out the framed pictures lining the walls. Countless photos of Giovanni over the years hang in a mindless pattern.

My eyes can't stay on anything for too long because I want to soak it all in. This is the most insight I've had into my father besides our conversations at work and during dinners.

"Why don't you have a seat?" Matteo motions to a couch across from an old leather chair. "Can I get you anything to drink?"

I shake my head, doubting my ability to keep anything down. My nerves eat away at my cool facade as Matteo settles into the leather chair.

Matteo remains quiet. The big hand on an old-school cuckoo clock ticks, filling the silence with its steady rhythm.

Neither one of us starts a conversation, and minutes pass us by. I find the awkward silence unbearable.

I take a deep breath, sucking up the last bits of courage I can muster up. "I want to start today off by saying I'm sorry for throwing everything on you like I did before. I realize it wasn't fair to you."

Matteo's eyes grow wide as he leans back in his chair. "You don't have to apologize."

"But I do. I freaked you out, and I didn't want that. I thought it would be easier if I spent all this time with you beforehand, but now I know that wasn't the case." I tuck a strand of my hair behind my ear, giving my hands something to do.

"It was shocking, to say the least."

"I know. I'm sorry again."

"Please stop apologizing. It's not your fault."

My cheeks heat. "Oh, okay."

He repeatedly taps his fingers against his knee. "What made you want to take the genetic test to begin with?"

"Well, um… Are you sure you want to know why?"

"Chloe, I'm not going to judge you. I don't think anything else you can say will surprise me."

His relaxed state sets me at ease.

"Okay…well, my life has never been easy. And I'm not telling you this for pity, but only because it's the truth and the whole reason why I took the test. I'm not ashamed of where I came from, but I don't want to shock you any more than I already have."

He shoots me a small smile. "Consider me unable to be shocked any more at this point."

I laugh. It feels good to release the tension from my body. "Okay. Well, my mother—not that I think it reflects on you or anything—is awful. Seriously, I can't believe I'm related to her or that she attracted someone as nice as you in the first place."

Matteo winces.

Shit, Chloe, be a little nicer, won't you? "She made my life miserable while I was growing up, and all I did was wish every year that I would find you. It's what kept me sane in a place that was anything but."

Matteo's cheeks lose their healthy coloring. *Oh, God, I'm botching this again.*

"No pressure or anything. I swear!" I raise my hands in a way to placate him. "I had hoped my father would be interested in developing a better relationship with me than my mother. And since she claimed she didn't remember who my dad was, I couldn't exactly find him. But then my roommate bought me an ancestry kit for my birthday and—"

"You found me."

"Yup. I couldn't believe it, to be honest. I mean—It was like something you see in a movie. But here I am, sitting with you."

He nods. "I took the test after someone gave it to me as a gift. I was curious to see where my ancestors were from, but I didn't expect it to connect me to anyone."

"I'm glad that you took it." I lace my fingers together in front of me.

Matteo's eyes soften. "What was it like growing up with your mother?"

"Are you sure you want to know?"

He nods, but he looks very unsure.

I settle with telling him the truth because I might as well rip the Band-Aid off now. "It's obvious she used me for the government payout. I hated living with her, but my first social worker kept trying to reunify us and give her a chance. That was until she started dating Ralph. Her boyfriend was creepy with me, and I caught him in my room on multiple occasions. I lived every day in fear, hoping there was something better for me in the world."

It's the rawest I've been with someone about my situation. I might have accepted my history, but it doesn't make the facts any easier to swallow. Instead of hiding the stirring emotions inside of me, I raise my chin and look Matteo in the eyes.

This is me. I rally. I fight. I make it through the day in hopes of a better tomorrow.

"I'm so sorry, Chloe. I hate to hear how awful you were treated. No child should ever grow up in a situation like that." His voice cracks.

"It's okay." I look away, unable to handle the weight of his sincere gaze. "I didn't have to live like that for too long. After an accident, I was reassigned to an amazing social worker who helped me get out of my house and into a good foster home. The foster care system took good care of me, and I met my best friend, Brooke, that way. I consider myself lucky in some ways."

"How can you make light of such traumatic experiences?"

"Because in the end, I'm here now. Yeah, the journey to get here wasn't the easiest one, but I have you and that's what matters. It's exactly what I wished for. The past is the past, but my future is brighter than ever." I beam.

Matteo's eyes drop to his lap again.

Did I come on too strong?

Matteo fists his palms in unison. Tension ripples up his arms at the gesture.

Yeah, definitely came on too strong.

Matteo lifts his head. His eyes shine, and wetness clings to his lashes. He clears his throat. "I know I can't take away the pain you went through, but will you let me try?"

My chest aches in the best kind of way. His acceptance is everything I wanted and wished for. I nod my head, happy to finally feel like I've found a home after so many years.

Santiago pounces on me the moment I unlock the front door.

I scream and jump back. My arms fly out to my sides as I lose my footing.

"Sorry!" He grabs onto my arm to prevent me from falling.

"What are you doing, creeping at the door like a freaking murderer?"

His wild eyes scan my face. "It's late."

"I didn't know I had a curfew, Dad."

"Why were you gone for so long?" He frowns.

"Because Matteo and I had a lot to talk about."

"And what did you two talk about?" Exasperation leaks into his voice.

"You're acting strange right now and it's weirding me out."

"Sorry, I've been dying to know how he reacted after everything." His voice seems hesitant as he lingers on the last word.

"Well, he seemed a lot more relaxed today. He asked me a lot of questions about myself."

"Oh."

Somehow one word carries the weight of Santiago's disappointment. Why is he acting like this? I thought he would be ecstatic about Matteo's sudden enthusiasm.

"Yeah…"

"I want to hear more about it." Santiago steers us toward the living room.

We settle into the couch, and I throw my legs over his lap. Despite his odd behavior, it's comforting knowing we have our little rituals. Especially this one where he gives me the best foot massage without me having to ask. If I was searching for a husband, he would be first on my list.

Seriously, what guy ever offers a foot massage?

The kind I want to date. I push the thought away for later tonight when I can stew in them properly. "Are you going to stop being weird now? I'll only share what happened if you stop acting like I'm about to bolt from the room any second or break down and cry. It went way better than last time. I swear."

He nods and looks down at my feet on his lap. "Yeah. Sorry about my reaction. I was just worried about you."

My heart throbs in my chest at his sincerity.

"Aw, that's sweet." I poke his chest with my foot.

"I'm glad to hear it went well." He looks up and smiles at me. Nothing about his voice sounds happy, but I let him be. He must've been pretty worried for his mood to be this awful even after I confirmed I was okay.

He clutches onto my foot and goes to work.

I sigh and sink into the cushions, enjoying his touch. "Did you know Matteo was arrested one time for running down the streets of Milan *naked*? And I mean *fully* naked."

He offers me the smallest smile known to man. "No, but I'm sure you'll tell me all about it."

And I do just that, sharing all the different stories Matteo told me during our day together. Everything feels like it's finally clicking into place, and I love every second of it. Not only is Matteo coming around, but everything with Santiago is perfect. *He's* perfect. I'd be stupid not to pursue a more serious relationship that he clearly wants.

Now that my relationship with Matteo is secure, I have an intense desire to embrace the second scariest thing I've ever done.

Fall in love.

CHAPTER FORTY-TWO

SANTIAGO

With an agitated finger, I press the buzzer on Matteo's gate for a third time. Patience is a thing of the past after spending the entire night pretending I didn't know about Matteo's secret.

He better pray for mercy because my mood hit new lows ever since Chloe fell asleep after last night. I barely slept, stuck overthinking everything she shared about her *father*.

This is what I get for trusting someone who didn't deserve it in the first place. The piece of shit told her a bunch of stories, and who the fuck knows if they are even true. And now, not only did I have to sneak out of the house for a second time in two days, but I had to do it to visit this idiot.

Matteo Accardi is on my shit list, and nothing and no one can convince me otherwise.

I press the button for the fourth time and pace the paved area. Sun rays peek through the early morning clouds, lighting up the area with a faint glow.

The old gears groan in protest as the gate opens. I stride toward the front door and knock three times. My teeth grind together as I wait minutes for Matteo to grace me with his presence.

Matteo doesn't bother looking me in the eyes when he opens the door. He doesn't even look rumpled in his pajamas. How charming. I'm here feeling like a mess from guilt-ridden insomnia while he looks fresh as a baby after a fat nap.

"What exactly did you not understand about telling Chloe the *truth*?" I snap.

He has the audacity to look surprised. "Listen, I can explain."

"By all means, please do, because I'm curious how the fuck you plan on getting us out of this motherfucking mess you created."

Matteo gestures for me to come inside. It's like I'm repeating this damn nightmare every day like a screwed-up remake of *Groundhog Day*.

Matteo leads me into his run-down kitchen. His hands shake as he grabs a pitcher of water and pours himself a glass.

"Matteo. I need you to get to the point of this story because I'm about two seconds from flipping my shit. And you really don't want that to happen."

He sips his water and places it back on the counter. "I couldn't do it."

"No fucking shit you couldn't do it. I was able to draw that conclusion myself when Chloe came back to my house looking like she floated in on a damn cloud."

"She shared her story and it was too much. I didn't expect her life story to be…"

"Tragic?"

He nods. "She has always been happy around me. I thought she was a normal girl, you know?"

"Her past doesn't change the fact that you're not her father. Nor does it mean you should keep the truth from her. I gave you a day to sort this out, and you didn't."

His eyes slide from me to his fisted hands. "I've been thinking."

A cold feeling sweeps through me. He can't be stupid enough to actually suggest what I think he wants to.

"What if—"

Yup. It's official. He downgraded from being an idiot to brain-dead. "No."

"Hear me out."

"*No. Hell fucking no.* That's wrong on so many levels, I wouldn't even know where to start."

"But what harm would it do? He was my twin, and she's my niece. She deserves to have someone take care of her. Her mother"—he shudders—"she's disgusting."

"I'm well aware of how awful that woman is. Trust me. I've had the pleasure of dealing with her myself. But she's not going to bother her anymore. And Matteo, you can't pretend to be someone's father! No. That's not an option." I can't believe his plan after all the trouble he gave me the other day about confessing his identity in the first place. How can a situation that was already terrible to begin with get progressively worse by the day?

Someone put an end to this nightmare. Either that or a bullet to my head would be merciful.

He clasps his hands together. "She wouldn't have to know."

"I couldn't live with myself if she didn't know the truth."

"Do you love her?"

I don't hesitate. "Of course I do. I wouldn't be here if I didn't."

"Then don't make me destroy her. Think about what the truth would do to her."

"That's all I've done. And it's the only reason I would say no to your idea in the first place. I love her too much to let you lie to her for the rest of her life."

He shakes his head. "You're making a mistake. You and I both know that an uncle can't replace what she has been desperately searching for."

"What people want isn't always what they need. She'll understand that eventually. But telling her the truth is non-negotiable. If you don't do it, then I will, and my version won't be as forgiving of your mistakes. You get me?"

His eyes darken. "Are you threatening me?"

"Read into it however you want. I'd do anything to protect her, even if it's from you. And you not telling her the truth and filling her head with false stories is not what we agreed on. You're doing more harm than good, and if you continue, I'll have no choice."

"The stories were all real. I just pretended they were from my perspective instead of my brother's."

My jaw ticks. "Matteo."

"Okay, okay. I get it." He focuses on his hands.

I stand. "Good. And I mean it, Matteo. You better tell her next time."

"I got it."

I nod my head, pleased with his submission. This isn't

about what either one of us wants. Chloe is old enough to make decisions on her own without either one of us playing God. There's only one man calling the shots from upstairs and he does a fine enough job screwing up everyone's life without us interfering.

My phone rings, interrupting my breakfast with Chloe. "Sorry, give me a second."

She nods and takes a sip of her juice.

I answer the call and pull the phone up to my ear. "Hello."

"Santiago, it's James."

"Hey, James. How are you?"

Chloe's eyebrows dart up.

"I have some good news and some news. Which one do you want to hear first?"

"Good or bad?" I grip the phone.

"Depends. How do you feel about meeting with the Formula Corp in two weeks?"

I choke on my sudden intake of breath. "Two weeks?"

"I pulled some strings so they could meet with us sooner. I didn't want to wait until January, and they were willing to compromise for you."

"Did you threaten them?"

"Only in a nice way."

I laugh, but the sound is off. *Holy shit. I'm going to finally defend my case after years of hiding.*

"You still there?"

"Yeah. I'm just shocked. You really want this to happen,

don't you?"

"Don't you?"

I look over at Chloe and imagine her cheering me on at a race. Her in a Bandini shirt with my name written across it, smiling and enjoying herself with my family. There's nothing I want more than to race again and have her be a part of the journey. Well, maybe to have her love me, but I don't doubt she does. She only needs to realize it too.

James coughs, gaining my attention again.

"Yes. I want it."

"Great. Then you better get ready for all the preparations we need to do. It's going to be a crash course of questions and answers. Noah and I will guide you through the process so that way the Corp has nothing to challenge."

"Sounds like a plan."

"Honestly, I'm very proud of you, Santiago. No matter what they decide, you're one of the strongest men I've had the pleasure of working with."

I clear my throat, trying to ease the tightness. "Oh, shucks. You're going to make me cry."

He laughs. "I'm just saying. You shocked me this summer. I didn't think you'd actually want to pursue this after everything you've been through, but you did. You have a way of surprising me lately."

I lean back in my chair and smile. "I like to keep you on your toes."

"Then how about I keep you on yours and offer you the best news. Bandini is willing to extend a racing contract to you. It's only for a year as a trial run because the investors are picky bastards, but if I have it my way, they'll see how successful you are next season and offer you a permanent deal. You could be in a Bandini race suit as early as two weeks if the Corp says yes."

The phone slips out of my hand and drops onto the floor.

Chloe looks up at me. "Are you okay?"

James continues speaking, but his voice comes out garbled because of the rug blocking the speaker. I remain seated, staring down at the floor.

Chloe stands and picks up my phone. She places it back in my trembling hand, wraps my fingers around it, and brings it to my ear.

"Did you get all that?" James continues.

"No. You're going to have to repeat everything after 'Bandini is willing to extend a racing contract.' I think I just had a heart attack."

James chuckles.

Bandini wants me back. Chloe takes a seat on my lap and wraps her arms around my neck. Her presence calms me, forcing my heart back into its normal pace.

James explains everything all over again, and Chloe remains by my side, running her hands through the hair at the nape of my neck.

James confirms all the information for the next two weeks. I'm on autopilot, speaking only when absolutely necessary. It's not until he hangs up the phone and Chloe tugs it out of my grasp that I finally move.

Chloe shifts on my lap, wrapping her arms back around my neck. "What happened?"

I bolt up from my chair, lifting Chloe up into the air and spinning us in a circle. Her scream turns into a laugh as I move round and round. The added weight bothers my stump, but I ignore it because who the hell cares right now.

"Bandini offered me a contract. They want me to race for them again!"

"WHAT?!"

I spin her around again, loving the way she laughs up to the ceiling. "James said it's only for a year, but they want me to be the driver who replaces Noah if the Formula Corp approve me joining again."

"Of course they're going to say yes! You should see yourself out on the track. You're absolutely incredible!" She peppers my face with a bunch of kisses.

"I couldn't have done it without you. I never thought I would get in a car again, but you pushed me to try."

"You pushed yourself. I only nagged you about it all."

I set her back on her feet. "No. That only added to my motivation. But it wouldn't have been there if it weren't for you forcing me in the best way to accept myself. So thank *you*." I place a lingering kiss against her lips.

She secures her arms around the back of my neck, holding me close. A sheen covers her eyes, but she blinks it away. "Do you know how stupidly proud of you I am?"

"No. But are you willing to show me?" I shoot her a wolfish grin.

"You, Santiago Alatorre, are a secret pervert. Your mother would be ashamed." She shoots me a breathtaking smile I can't resist kissing off her face. Damn. This girl has turned me into a lovesick idiot after only a few months. I confused her for something magical, but in reality she's a miracle.

"We have to celebrate!" She claps her hands together.

"We can after I meet with the Corp. I don't want to jinx it, just in case they say no."

She pauses her clapping and turns on her heel, leaving me behind.

"Where are you going?" I call out.

"Hold on!" Her voice echoes from somewhere in the house.

I pace the floor, considering what might happen if the Formula Corp denies the bill. My stomach churns at the idea. Now that I've had a taste of racing again, I'm not sure if I could ignore the pull toward the track anymore.

Being denied would destroy me before I had a chance to return to my former glory.

Chloe comes back into the room clutching a bubblegum pink notebook in her hand.

"What's that?" I point.

"I'm about to share a little magic with you."

That's all she has done up until this point. It's as if she sprinkles pixie dust wherever she goes, turning my life into something worth getting out of bed for. And most of all, turning me into someone that feels worthy of loving not only someone else, but also myself.

Chloe motions for me to sit in my chair. I follow her lead out of curiosity, and she pulls up another seat next to me.

She opens her journal to a blank page. "I want us to make a wish."

"This is your wish journal?"

She bites her lip and nods.

"You're sharing your wish journal with me?" My voice sounds as incredulous as I feel. "Why?"

"I think the phrase you're looking for is 'thank you.'" She bumps her shoulder into mine.

"I'm surprised."

"It's no big deal. Really." She rolls her eyes.

I look over at her with a raised brow.

"Okay, it's a slightly big deal." She pinches her fingers together, leaving a centimeter gap.

"You're going to let me steal a wish?"

"Stealing means you're taking without asking. In reality, I'm giving away one for free."

"Why?"

Chloe loves this journal, and I want to push her to realize why this is a big deal to her. To realize she cares more than basic infatuation or lust or friendship. I'm desperate for her to realize she *loves* me. Her actions scream it, yet the words never make it past her lips. I never thought I would crave this kind of affection from someone who does not give it willingly. But damn if it hasn't made Chloe all that more interesting, making me work for it.

Chloe runs a finger across the yellowed page. "I care a lot about you."

Okay…that's something at least.

She continues. "And you deserve to have your biggest wish granted." She grabs her pen and writes something across the page.

I wish that the Formula Corp lets Santiago Alatorre race again.

"Now it's settled. Obviously you're going to drive with Bandini next year. This journal doesn't fool around. I can promise you that."

"Can I write something too?" I blurt out.

Her lips form an O. She pauses before nodding and handing me the pen. I move to write on the page, but her hand covers mine.

"Wait." She flips the page to a blank one.

"Why did you do that?"

"New page, new wish. I don't make the rules."

I laugh to myself as I write down my wish. The one I've been thinking about for quite a while now.

I wish that Chloe Carter falls in love with someone worthy of her eighties-loving heart. That she finds that soul-crushing, heart-mending, passion-fueled love. A love that leaves her desperate for more because nothing that amazing should ever be done in moderation. The same love I found with her.

I drop the pen, and it rolls into the middle of the notebook.

Chloe looks down at the page, remaining silent.

"When you're quiet, it's never a good thing." I nudge her shoulder.

"That's your wish?"

"I wrote it, didn't I?"

She pinches my side, right in the spot that makes me wince. "Asshole."

"Aw, from you, I'll take it as a term of endearment."

She shakes her head. "You made a mistake."

"What do you mean?"

Her eyes slide from the journal to my face. The color of her irises looks more vibrant than ever, the blue flecks shifting from sapphire to aqua.

My heart pounds in my chest as I wait for her response.

"You can't wish for something I already have."

I never thought one sentence could carry this much meaning. It's like Chloe set off a serotonin bomb in my brain.

She smiles wider at whatever look I have on my face. "I love you. I'm so in love with you. The kind of love that does leave me desperate in a way that makes me think I'm going crazy."

I stand and pull her into me, landing a soft kiss against her lips. "Say it again."

"I love you, Santiago Alatorre."

"I'll never get used to you saying it."

Her smile drops a fraction. "I don't know whether to be afraid or happy."

"Stick with happy. Always happy."

"I am, but I also can't help being afraid," she whispers.

"Why?"

"Because there are two kinds of loves out there."

"Which are?"

"The love that flourishes and the love that kills."

Something inside me withers away at her words, forcing reality to crash back down around me. It erases the elation I felt from Chloe's admission of her love.

I desperately want to have the first kind of love with Chloe, but I can't help worrying about the latter. Not because I would intentionally hurt her. There is only one thing threatening whatever we have built with each other. And secrets have a way of destroying the loveliest things, and I wonder if mine is the most deadly of all.

CHAPTER FORTY-THREE

Chloe

Something about Matteo is off today. I can't put my finger on it, but he barely looks at me. It's as if he's not really here, even though I sit on the couch across from him. It was weird at first when he lacked any kind of enthusiasm as I showed him photos of me growing up. The notion stung, but I chalked it up to him not feeling well. But now, he doesn't even smile when he talks about Giovanni. And I know how much he *loves* Giovanni.

"Are you okay?" I fidget with my hands.

He shakes his head as if it can make whatever he is thinking about disappear. "No."

I freeze. "What's wrong?"

He sighs. His gaze penetrates me and pins me to my seat. "I have something to tell you."

Oh, God. This can't be good. The last time someone had *something to tell me*, I ended up in the back of a cop car because of Ralph.

"Yes?" I breathlessly whisper.

"I haven't been fully honest with you."

"What do you mean?" I somehow get the words out despite the tightness in my throat. Every muscle in my body locks up, and I find it difficult to breathe easily.

Matteo doesn't answer me. Instead, he lets out a sob as he breaks down. His body shakes as he hunches over and shields his face from me.

What the hell? With wobbly legs and a racing heart, I move to sit beside him on the couch and wrap my arm around his shoulder. I can't stand by and watch him lose it without offering some kind of support.

"What's the matter? You're scaring me."

He sniffles. "I'm sorry. I'm really fucking sorry. I didn't want to tell you, but Santiago told me it's the right thing, and he's probably right. But I still don't know how to do this, so give me a second."

"Santiago?" I hiss.

Something ugly and dark bubbles within me, begging to be let out. What is happening, and what the hell has Santiago been hiding from me?

Matteo nods, wiping away a stray tear.

"Are you talking about another Santiago by chance?"

He shakes his head from side to side.

My stomach churns, and acid crawls up my throat. I swallow it back.

I don't know what to ask about first. Why would Matteo and Santiago talk in the first place? What is upsetting Matteo enough to the point that he would cry?

Matteo doesn't give me a choice in the matter. He

steamrolls on, clearly gaining some kind of courage after his outburst. "Chloe, it kills me to do this to you. Shit, it kills me to have lied to you in the first place."

My body feels like all the warmth was sucked out of me, replacing blood with icy water. "What do you mean by you lied?"

"There's no easy way to tell you this, but...God. I'm not your father, Chloe."

I laugh in a way that says I'm everything but mentally okay. Are we seriously going through this cycle again? With Matteo, it's as if I take two steps forward before running a mile backward. "Yes, you are."

He moves away from me, giving him enough space to stare me straight in the eyes. "No. My identical twin brother was your father. I'm sorry to tell you this, but you're actually my niece. I can't be your dad. I swear on my son's and my lives."

I might not have a college degree, but it doesn't take a genius to understand twin genetics and DNA.

Like a dam bursting, tears spring free from my eyes, coating my lashes. "How can you be sure?" *Please, don't be sure. I can't handle this level of deception.*

The irony is not lost on me. I prefer the lie to the truth any day right now.

"I have only been with a handful of women in my life, and none of them were from America. I was faithful to my ex-wife—well girlfriend at the time. But my brother...he was different. Riskier." His voice cracks. "My brother would have loved you. You remind me of him with your humor and your smile. He even got the same look as you in his eyes when he had an idea or got overly excited."

Matteo continues to talk, but I struggle to process anything he says. Nothing matters except for that fact that he speaks about his brother in the past tense.

"Why are you talking about him like he's dead?"

Matteo looks down at his lap. "He passed away the summer after you were born."

The few tears I shed earlier become a waterfall, trickling down my face before landing on my lap. I can't believe it. I don't *want* to believe it. After all these years waiting and wishing... After Matteo pretended to be my father and told me stories. None of it matters. This whole damn trip was pointless. My father isn't even here, let alone *alive*.

God, how does my life continue to get worse as the years go by? I don't bother brushing away my tears. They fall in a continuous stream down my face, disappearing into the fabric of my custom embroidered jeans.

My father really is dead. Gone before I ever had a chance to meet him. My lungs burn as I inhale deep breaths, trying to ease the ache building inside of my chest.

"Say something. Please," Matteo's voice rasps.

"What do you want me to say? You *lied*."

Fuck, it hurts. And worse, I should've expected it. Instead, I let my guard down around the one person I expected to be there for me.

I let out a shrill laugh. Of course he let me down. It's as if I'm cursed, forever stuck surrounding myself with people who have no intention of building me up.

He winces. "I never wanted to lie to you. But I didn't know how to tell you the truth once I learned more about you. You have been through too many tragedies in your short life, and I didn't want to add to it."

"Nothing is more tragic or cruel than feeling like I gained a father only to lose him in the same week," I snap.

"I'm sorry."

"Sorry doesn't make it okay."

He nods his head. "You're right. I want to make it up to you."

I stand, unable to bear more of this conversation. I need time to process. To cry. To wrap my head around the fact that my father is *dead.* "You said Santiago told you that you needed to tell me the truth because it was the right thing. What did you mean by that?"

Matteo nods like a guilty bobblehead.

The thought of Santiago going along with this scheme for days makes me ill. "He knows about your true identity?"

More bobbing.

I want to scream. I want to throw up. I want to launch something fragile across the room and watch it shatter into a million pieces like my heart in my chest.

"He also willingly kept this from me?" I say the words more to myself than Matteo. My heart doesn't want to believe the words, but deep down, I know the truth.

How can Santiago tell me he loves me one minute and lie to me the next? That's not love, that's deception.

"Listen, he wanted me to tell you the instant he found out, but I told him to hold off until I coul—"

I raise my hand, halting Matteo's words. "You both were wrong. I don't care what excuse you want to come up with for him. Withholding information is a prettier kind of lie meant to make the liars feel better about their actions."

"He never wanted to lie."

"Then he shouldn't have done it in the first place." I exit the room, leaving a gobsmacked Matteo behind.

I open the front door and step onto the driveway. Tears continue to fall, and I brush them away with shaky fingers.

"Wait. Chloe! Wait!" Matteo calls out from behind. "Please, just please give me a chance to explain everything better. When you're calm, that is."

All I can do is nod my head. I want more answers, no matter how painful they are. It might not be easy but I need closure about my father, and that will never happen if I run away. But I can't deal with Matteo for the rest of today. If I do, I might break into a thousand pieces, and I'm not ready for that kind of devastating experience.

Heartbreak is better dealt with in private, away from those who made it happen in the first place.

CHAPTER FORTY-FOUR

Chloe

'm on a warpath by the time I get back to Santiago's house. My tears have dried on my cheeks, leaving behind streaks in my blush. Santiago isn't in the doorway when I return. I'm somewhat grateful because it gives me the ability to think over what he did.

I step into my bedroom and leave the door open, not caring if Santiago walks inside.

It doesn't take him long to find me. I'd pity him for the shitstorm he entered, but he is the cause of it after all.

"What's going on?" His eyebrows draw together as he assesses my luggage on the bed.

"I'm leaving." My voice is wooden.

The thump of his iWalk fills the silence. "What? Why?"

I shrug before throwing my clothes into my luggage, not caring how they land as long as they make it in there. I'm desperate to make this process as painless for me as possible. I'm no coward in the face of pain, but even I have my limits.

And this man right here is the ultimate test of them.

"Matteo told me about my dad." I throw a pair of sneakers with a little extra oomph into my luggage, and they smack against my clothes.

"What do you mean? Look at me." Santiago presses a tentative hand on my shoulder.

I wince at his touch, and he drops his hand. "Don't pretend you don't know. He told me *everything*, including how you knew for days about my real father and didn't tell me. If there is one thing I ask of you during this conversation, it's to not pretend anymore. I think I've had enough of your lies to last me a lifetime." My hoarse voice cracks. I blink back the tears threatening to leak out of my eyes.

I might have cried with Matteo, but I refuse to cry in front of Santiago. He is the last person who deserves my tears, especially when he's the reason for them in the first place.

"Chloe, please listen to me. I didn't lie to you."

I spin on my feet. "To me, withholding the truth is the same thing as lying; it doesn't matter how you want to validate it in your head. You knew Matteo's true identity and you said nothing. You let me go about my days like nothing happened. And worse, you let me believe my dad was really alive, and that's just cruel."

He recoils. "I didn't want to. I told him to tell the truth and he didn't listen. You have to believe me. When you went to his house for the first time, he was supposed to tell you. That was the plan."

Everything clicks together. "You knew. That's why you wanted to come with me."

He nods, becoming visibly uncomfortable as my scowl deepens.

"And that's why you pounced on me when I got back. And asked me a hundred questions. You knew, even then."

He lets out a deep breath. "Yes."

I place a hand on the bed, needing the stability. "And what did you do when you realized he didn't tell me the truth?"

"I went over there and told him that he had no choice but to tell you the real story. That you have the right to know that your dad passed away. The man wanted to pretend he was your father permanently for fuck's sake. Without me, who knows what he would've done. I was only doing what I thought was the best choice to make sure you heard it from the right person."

"You should've told me the moment you found out. I thought we were close. That we got one another." My voice breaks, matching the feeling inside of me. Everything hurts as I manage my thoughts.

"Of course we are close. *I love you.* There's nothing closer than that." He takes a step toward me.

I take one back, hitting the nightstand with my butt. "If you loved me, you wouldn't have pretended to my face that Matteo was my dad. I told you stories about him. We laughed about the craziness he shared with me. How did you sit there and act like you didn't know all this time?"

He throws his hands in the air. "I was trying to protect you! I thought it would be better to hear it from him rather than me."

"Why?"

"Because I was afraid to hurt you. I knew it would destroy you to learn about your dad from me."

"Well, it turns out your choice hurt me a hell of a lot more."

"Please, just give me a chance to explain my reasoning."

I shake my head. "No. I can't do this right now. I need space."

"You told me you wouldn't leave me."

"That was before I found out you could lie straight to my face and not even flinch while doing it. I feel like a fool for trusting you. Do you even know how hard that is for someone like me? Or how painful it is to admit I *love* someone? But I should've expected this. You grew up surrounded by love while I grew up being manipulated by it."

He starts to speak, but I cut him off. "I can't stay here anymore."

"You're going back to America?" Panic floods his voice.

"No. Not yet. I need to speak to Matteo more and learn about my dad."

He flinches.

Yeah, asshole, I'm not staying here because of you. "But just because I'm staying doesn't mean I want to live here after knowing what you did."

He fists his hands by his sides as if he needs to restrain himself. "Don't go. *Please.*"

I zip up my suitcase and tug it off the bed, ignoring him.

"Chloe, stop. Please." His voice croaks. "You should stay here. I'll go and stay somewhere else. I don't give a shit."

I halt, my hand frozen on the luggage handle. "What?" Why would he offer something like that?

"I want you to stay here. I know you don't entirely believe me right now, but I do love you and I don't want you staying in some hotel. This will always be your home if you want it. Plus, it gives you access to see Matteo at any time."

"I don't want that right now."

"But you might, and at least you'll be a short walk away. And it's free." He stumbles over his words, as if he needs to get them all out before I bolt for the exit.

I want to scream at him to stop being caring. It's the last thing my vulnerable heart needs, but I give in. He hooked me with the word *free*.

"Fine. I'm going to stay solely because I need to save the money for my return ticket back home. That's it."

His head drops, but he nods.

"You're actually not going to sleep here?" I still can't believe it.

"No. I'll go somewhere else."

I nod my head and turn back toward my luggage. "Okay."

He lets out a shaky breath. "Will you give me a chance to fix this?"

I don't bother looking in his direction. "People aren't like your cars. You can't repair what's too broken beyond repair."

"I would've said the same thing about myself, but then you came along. I'm not going to tell you I'm sorry. I'm going to show it."

I open my mouth to say something, but no words come out. A wave of exhaustion hits me and my shoulders drop. Staying strong is taking its toll.

He lets out a sigh. His footsteps fade away into the distance. It doesn't take long for the lock at the front door to turn. Instead of relief hitting me in Santiago's absence, a wave of sadness washes over me.

I crawl onto the bed and curl into a ball. Today's events weigh heavily inside of my chest. Just when I thought everything was going right in my life, God threw a bomb in my lap and expected me to disable it.

My dad is dead, Santiago knew and didn't say anything to me, and the whole reason I came to Italy in the first place is pointless.

I don't know what to do from here, but I do know one thing. I hate liars, and I somehow fell in love with the best one.

"Shut the fuck up! This can't be real," Brooke yells into her phone.

"*Ugh.*" I drop back onto my mattress, allowing the foam to swallow me whole. At least Brooke listened to the whole story before screaming. Down to the last detail, including everything about Santiago. From his deceit to him letting me stay in his home without him even living here.

"How is this even possible? The test can't be wrong."

I grip onto the loose thread of my raggedy pajama pants and pull. "They're twins. *Identical* twins. That means they share basically the same DNA. It's science."

"It's stupid."

"Doesn't make it any less true."

"Fuck." Brooke's voice becomes nothing but a hoarse whisper.

"Yup." I blink away the tears misting my eyes.

"What are you going to do now? Do you want to come back home?"

Thoughts flood my head. I can barely wrap my head

around everything Matteo revealed to me, let alone decide if I should leave. Any thought about leaving is instantly replaced by ones of Santiago and how he kept the truth from me. How can I trust someone who pretended in front of my face that he didn't know who Matteo really was?

Brooke sighs. "What are you going to do?"

"Pour wine into a baby bottle and cry myself to sleep?"

"And?"

"I don't know. I haven't had enough time to think up a plan. You're the first person I talked to after my life went from *Disney Channel Original Movie* to *Chernobyl Diaries*."

She snorts. "*Chernobyl Diaries* was a terrible movie."

"My point exactly."

"Do you want to FaceTime?"

"Do you even have to ask?"

"Grab your favorite wine and your laptop. Let's have ourselves a date night."

My throat tightens. "Brooke?"

"Hmm?"

"I appreciate you. Just so you know."

"Gross. Save the touchy-feely shit for the nine-inch dick you've fallen in love with."

"People don't fall in love with dicks." I let out my first laugh of the night despite the clenching sensation in my chest at her words. Brooke always has this way of erasing my pain, even if it's for a few hours.

"The person or the appendage? Because I have an argument for both."

My laugh turns into a full-blown fit of giggles.

Slowly the ache in my chest lessens at the thought of

Santiago deceiving me. Of course, I understand he didn't lie outright, but withholding the truth is still considered deception nonetheless.

But why don't I feel as angry or upset about Matteo doing the same exact thing? Is it because I'm too desperate for a connection with a father figure to care? Or is it because I willingly gave Santiago the opportunity to break down every single barrier left around my heart before he broke it?

God, I hate this back-and-forth argument going on inside of my head. No one warned me about what happens *after* two people fall in love. How once the credits roll, the rainbow disappears and the world is thrust back into the reality of rainstorms and ugly days.

But to be honest, what did I expect? I'm the one who fell in love with someone who built a relationship while deceiving others. There's no one I should be angry at besides myself. I'm basically the idiot piglet from the "Three Little Pigs" who thought life was good in a house made of straw before the big, bad wolf blew the house down and proved me wrong.

Angry at myself more than Santiago, I rip the covers off my body and climb out of bed to gather my video chat supplies. I skip grabbing a glass and pick a bottle of wine, shutting myself off from any kind of Santiago or Matteo-related thoughts.

And together, I get drunk with my best friend while saving my pain for another day.

CHAPTER FORTY-FIVE

SANTIAGO

I've never experienced a walk of shame quite like the one to a local hotel. I keep my head down, avoiding residents who might recognize me.

Leaving Chloe at my house alone was one of the hardest things I've had to do in a while, and I've done a lot of difficult things lately. Knowing she was hurt because of my actions made the task nearly impossible. But she deserves my respect, and that starts with giving her space to calm down. I don't blame her for feeling angry and needing room to process her life. She only found out her father is dead a few hours ago.

And rather than leaning on you for help like she should be able to, you fucked everything up. Good going, asshole.

I hate myself a bit more knowing she's alone, probably crying herself to sleep tonight about everything.

The hotel employee gives me a key to my room on the first floor. I enter the small space and let out a sigh, throwing my bag in the corner. Not bothering with the bedside lamp, I settle into the bed.

"You had to go about ruining the one thing that brought

you true happiness," I whisper up to the ceiling.

Sleeping without Chloe feels odd. Like something in the world is amiss, and nothing can fix it. The bed is too empty, the sheets too cold. No position feels comfortable enough, no matter how hard I try.

I readjust my pillow for the third time, smacking it to the point where a few feathers fly out of the pillowcase. I lay back down and look up at the ceiling.

Damn, I wish I could be cuddling with Chloe in my bed right now.

My chest tightens at the idea.

Is it terrible that I hope she misses me just as much?

I can only pray sleep comes easy for me because I can't handle another guilt-ridden, restless night.

I might have told Chloe I wouldn't sleep at my house, but she didn't say anything against visiting. Semantics are my friend. Semantics are what's going to get me the hell out of this mess I created for myself to begin with.

I use my key to unlock the back door. The early morning rays of sunshine peek through the windows, guiding me through the kitchen. No sounds alert me that Chloe is awake. She usually sleeps in on the weekends, until at least 10 in the morning, but I want to be safe. The last thing I need is for her to get mad because she found me lurking again. She trusted me to leave her alone here, and I plan on following through as much as I can.

After a few minutes of silence, I take the risk. With shaky

hands, I place a vase of wildflowers on the kitchen counter. I grab the accompanying note I wrote from my pocket and place it beside the bouquet. While my letter is more of an apologetic one, I still hope it carries the same feeling.

If everything goes according to plan, she will read the note and show up at the meet-up place I mentioned. I only need one chance to explain what happened and how much she means to me.

It takes a lot of self-control to step out of my home again. If Chloe doesn't forgive me soon, I'll be stuck making wishes to win her back.

I check the time on my phone for the third time in the last five minutes. Chloe is already half an hour late for our meeting, and I've already worked a path through the grass after all my pacing. I'd call her to check in, but I doubt that would go over well.

Did she actually stand me up?

Did you really believe she would show up in the first place?

I sigh to myself as I lean against the tree where I first found her climbing all those months ago. What do I do now? If this plan didn't work, what will? What if Chloe doesn't want to deal with me anymore, but doesn't know how to tell me?

I stare up at the branches as if they hold the answers.

A twig snaps, and I turn toward the sound. "Chloe?"

No one replies.

"If you're there, I want to start off with saying I'm sorry."

Crickets chirp in reply.

Great. My disappointment grows as minutes pass by and Chloe doesn't show herself. If she's not here, then what is she up to?

Curiosity gets the best of me. The idea of returning back to my hotel room without at least checking in on her doesn't sit right with me. My decision is made purely because of my need to ensure she is alive and well.

Right. You just miss her, you lying piece of shit.

I cling to the shadows, using them to disguise myself as I walk toward the back of the house. Each room of the house is dark except for the bright lights coming from the back.

I keep my distance, securing a good angle to see inside of the kitchen. *Note to self: Teach Chloe the importance of not leaving all the blinds open.* Any creeper could see what happens inside.

Chloe has her back to me. She opens the oven, and a cloud of smoke billows into her face. She uses an oven mitt to clear the air.

Fuck. I didn't consider how she's a safety risk to herself and the house. If she keeps this up, she's going to burn everything down before I have a chance to move back in.

Chloe clutches onto the pan. I wince at the black lump of something inedible crumbling in the center. She walks toward the trash bin and presses the pedal with her foot. The charred food drops into the bin, right on top of the flower stems poking out from the top.

Something cold seeps through my chest, replacing any warmth at seeing Chloe in the first place.

She threw away my flowers? What the hell?

Did she even bother reading my note or did it meet the same fate as the flowers?

Wow. I can't believe she threw them out.

Instead of accepting defeat by her dismissal of my gift, I use it to fuel me. I was a fool in the first place for thinking a vase of flowers and a note would get her to give me a chance. Flowers and sweet nothings aren't the way to her heart, and I should've known better. She's always been unexpected, and I went with the most basic idea.

I take today as the challenge it is. I'm not the type to back down from oppositional forces. If I was, I wouldn't have ever won a World Championship in the first place. Hell, I wouldn't have started racing again after my injury if I wasn't a fighter. Clearly, I underestimated my opponent.

Round one may have gone to Chloe, but I plan on winning the whole damn thing.

What do I get a girl who doesn't care much for presents? How do I express I love her and I'm sorry through actions rather than words?

I jolt from my bed as the idea hits me. Chloe loves eighties romances, and I'm here to deliver. It's time to channel my inner John Hughes and get to work.

The next idea takes an excruciatingly long time to complete. It frustrates me because I feel like I'm losing precious time getting her back. I don't know how the fuck Chloe makes these damn embroidery circles as quickly as she does, but what must take her minutes takes me hours. I've earned a new appreciation for the designs she creates because this is hard as fuck. Threads constantly get knotted together and I stab my fingers with the needles more times than I can count.

The whole process is worth it. Chloe seems like the girl who appreciates something handmade. And nothing says "I'm sorry" quite like an embroidered disaster-piece. Sure, the design looks a little wonky but it was made with love. I'm sure if Chloe closes her left eye and squints with the right, it will look pretty damn good.

Seriously, I might be biased, but I would forgive whoever made me something as atrocious as this. Anyone can tell the person has no shame and is so hopelessly in love, they would create it in the first place. I'm a simpering fool who has nothing to lose and everything to gain by fighting for Chloe's forgiveness.

I release a shaky breath.

Here goes nothing.

CHAPTER FORTY-SIX

Chloe

In a half-asleep daze, I reach out for Santiago, only to be met with empty, cold sheets.

He's not here because you told him not to be.

Yeah, well, he's not here because he lied again.

The voices in my head battle it out.

You're not being fair to him. At least hear him out. Would you have done something better than him if you were in that position?

Uh, I'd probably start with maybe not taking me out on a boat and pretending all is dandy in our little world. Sounds like a solid start.

I groan as I throw a pillow over my face and block out the world. Rationalizing Santiago's actions sucks because I have no idea what I would've done if I was in the same position as him. And it annoys me more than I care to admit.

An emptiness fills me as I wake up and get out of bed. The house is eerily quiet except for my feet slapping against the floor as I walk through the rooms.

Despite everything, Santiago was way too nice for letting

me stay here. It's not right for me to accept his offer and force him to sleep elsewhere.

But he did hurt you. So there's that.

Part of me is grateful for his absence. Besides him dropping off his present a few days ago, he hasn't shown up. He hasn't even texted me or grabbed an extra change of clothes. His silence surprises me more than I care to admit, and I don't know what to make of it. Just like I don't know what to make of his present the other day.

Did he think a vase of flowers would fix everything between us? It did the exact opposite. I spent the entire morning with a tightness in my chest every time I looked at them.

The visual reminder of us filled me with a different kind of sadness. And then I got mad that I was sad, and I stuck with anger because it seemed like a safer emotion.

During a flood of feelings, I ripped up the note and threw the bouquet away, only to instantly regret it. Beautiful things like flowers shouldn't be destroyed because of anger. I took my frustration at Santiago out on his gifts, and it's not right.

It's not that I don't want to forgive him. I wish my heart wasn't as vulnerable and forgiving as it is. And that weakness makes me frustrated because I want to forgive him despite everything, and I'm not sure how I feel about it.

Do I love him? Yes.

Am I angry at him for hiding the biggest secret of my life? Absolutely.

Could I forgive him after he promised not to lie anymore? I'm not too sure.

But in the end, is a love built on lies really love at all?

"When you told me stories about you in the past, was that really about you or my dad?" I choke on the last word. The idea that my dad isn't alive anymore takes some time to get used to. It's like I'm stuck in a weird limbo—mourning a man I never met.

Matteo sits down in his leather chair and takes a sip of his coffee. I decided it would be better if we met at his house. Santiago's home doesn't feel right without him, and I can't stand being there longer than I need to.

Is it fair that I forgave Matteo sooner than Santiago? Probably not. But some things take precedence, including learning whatever I can about my dad before I return to America. Because I *am* flying back soon. *Right?*

The tiny angel on my shoulder crosses her arms and pouts. *Yeah, yeah. Look where your good deeds got me.*

Matteo offers me a hesitant smile. "Everything I shared with you the other day was about him. I'm sorry I'm not cool enough to go streaking through Milan. My brother was the wild child while I was more reserved."

"A wild child you say?" Consider my interest piqued.

"Nothing could tame him. Whenever someone told him no, it was as if his brain rewired the word into a yes."

"I've been told I can be a bit wild myself." I smile at the connection to my dad.

"I don't doubt it one bit. Those kinds of genes don't skip a generation."

I clasp my hands together in my lap. "What else can you share about him?"

"Are you sure that you feel ready to hear about him? I don't want to upset you."

"Yeah. I want to know about him before I head back to America."

Matteo's brows raise. "You plan on going back? Why?"

"I came here to find my dad, and well, he's not exactly here anymore. There's nothing here for me."

"But what about Santiago?"

Shit. He's your boyfriend to the world, Chloe. Of course you need to think about how your decisions affect him. I rush to respond. "I think we could use a break."

He frowns. "Because of what happened between the three of us?"

I look away and nod. "Yes. It's hard for me to forgive liars. Not talking to you isn't an option for me because I want to learn about my father. But with Santiago…I've had plenty of bad experiences with people who manipulate the truth to last a lifetime."

"I can see where you're coming from. I really can, even though I haven't been through it myself. But you've been dating him for a year. That's a long time to just get up and leave when things get hard. Are you sure you can't sort it out?"

It's hard to not scoff at the idea of dating Santiago for a year. I haven't even had a relationship with my Netflix subscription for that long.

I choose my words wisely. "A break could give us some distance to figure things out."

"Distance doesn't fix things. Talking them out does."

"No offense, but the only reason I'm talking to you is because I want to know about my dad. I'm not exactly happy with you either."

"I know. And I appreciate you wanting to spend time

with me, even if it's for your own reasons. I promise I'll try harder to be a permanent person you can count on in your life because you are my niece. My brother would expect no less of me."

I swallow back the lump in my throat. "Okay."

"And as your uncle, I feel the need to apologize on Santiago's behalf."

Oh, God. I thought he had moved past this already.

He keeps going, ignoring the look on my face. "It's only right to explain what happened. See, he kept his cool when I told him the shocking truth. The poor man took it like a champ, repeatedly telling me that I needed to share the truth with you. I did ask him to tell you instead of me, but now I realize that wasn't fair to him. He was right that the news would have been better received if I told you. So, he was caught in the middle between wanting to protect you and wanting to tell you the truth. It's not like I made his job any easier by withholding the truth from you when you came over. It was wrong of me, and I'm very sorry for doing that to you. He came over the very next morning pissed as hell and told me to tell you the truth or else he would. And his version of the truth was undoubtedly a lot worse."

My throat tightens, limiting my ability to speak.

He takes a deep breath. "It wasn't fair, and you were right. It *was* cruel. And Chloe, I hope you forgive me one day. I understand honesty is extremely important to you, and I truly want to make it up to you. Not only because you're my niece, but because I do care for you. My brother would smack me if he were here right now for hurting you in the first place."

Unavoidable tears fill my eyes at the mention of my dad wanting to hurt someone for making me unhappy. It's a foreign concept to me when all I've done is get hurt by those who were supposed to defend me.

"You think so? That he would be angry at you?" My voice cracks.

"Absolutely. He would've kicked my ass outside for making you cry. He was aggressive like that. I'm telling you—wild child in all capital letters."

"I wish I could've gotten to know him."

"Me too. You remind me of him in the best ways."

"How so?"

"You have this kind of confidence I don't see often. He was similar. It always drew people to him no matter if they were strangers or old friends. And I get that same feeling from you. You're rather charming. It took you less than five minutes to get a job with me, and I never hire anyone."

My eyebrows raise. "Really?"

"Of course. I always have teens wanting to make a quick buck over the summer when it's the busy season. I always said no, but there was something in your eyes that told me you were worth the extra pay and effort."

What is it with this man and bringing on the waterworks? I'm like a leaky faucet around him. "Thank you."

"No. Thank you, Chloe. For giving me another connection to my brother again." His eyes shine, reflecting unshed tears.

"You have a way of making me cry, and I'm not much of a crier." I sniffle.

He chuckles. "You're very brave. Not many people would have the courage to confront someone about being their long-lost parent, but you did it. And now that I've had time to think about it, I can say that was incredibly courageous of you."

"Or stupid. Depends how you look at it."

Matteo chuckles. "You should be proud of yourself. I'm happy you shared who you were with me because it gives me a chance to reconnect with my brother in a different way now."

"Dammit, Matteo. You need to stop with all the nice words." I dab at the corner of my eyes before another tear escapes.

"I'm sorry."

"It's annoying because I'm trying freaking hard to stay mad at you."

"Then I'm not the least bit sorry about that."

I let out a genuine laugh. "Will you tell me a story about my dad?"

He nods. "Of course. What would you like to know?"

"Do you think he liked John Hughes's movies?"

"It's funny you say that. He always did have a thing for *The Breakfast Club*. Maybe it was his rebellious nature that made him resonate with the main guy."

I flash him a huge grin. "I love that movie too!"

"I'm telling you—you're more alike than you realize."

Matteo goes off, telling me stories about my father's past. I memorize every single word.

While I didn't get exactly what I wished for, I have the opportunity to learn about my father and who he was over the years he was alive. And to me, that's better than never having the chance to begin with.

I leave Matteo's house way later than expected. Silence greets me as I unlock the front door, opening it to find pure darkness.

I miss Santiago freaking me out the moment I walk through the front door.

I miss coming home to the smell of whatever he was cooking that day.

I miss *him*.

I miss him so damn much, I'm tempted to call him and break down.

But what if I forgive him, only to have the same thing happen again? Everything about our relationship was fake to the public. And what if the next time he lies, it's about cheating or something way worse? How does he expect me to believe anything he says again?

But are you being fair? You went along with some of his lies in the first place. And he was trying to protect you in the end. I can count on two fingers how many other people have tried to do the same.

Maybe it's time I acted like an adult and called him.

My stomach grumbles, forcing me to table my thoughts and head to the kitchen to attempt some kind of meal. If someone can count burnt charred remains as sustenance.

An embroidery circle takes up a spot in the middle of the counter. I rush toward it and pick it up.

My heart rate speeds up in my chest as I check out the most beautiful design I've ever seen. There's no mistaking who made this. Santiago crafted a field of wildflowers, making up every color of the rainbow. It's hands-down the best gift anyone has given me.

A wobbly looking quote takes up the top of the design.

Where most people see weeds, I only see you—my beautiful wildflower, untamed and free.

I flip over the embroidery circle to find a note taped on the back. His small yet elegant handwriting marks the page.

I called you a wildflower the moment you showed up at my house with a bouquet of them. That day, I asked myself what kind of person would go picking those crazy flowers in the first place. I thought they were just inconvenient weeds, but now I have my answer after all the time we spent together.

You might not realize it, but you're a wildflower. You grow in the most unexpected places, no matter who tramples on you or ignores your beauty. You can grow in a field, or through a crack in the sidewalk, but the result will always be the same. No one can stop you from flourishing in a world set on ignoring you. You have a way of turning any situation, good or bad, into something magnificent.

You taught me that life is stunning in its rawest form. That anyone can find happiness in the most unlikely places if they look hard enough. That life is about searching for the light, even if it means growing through broken places to get there.

I don't want to see the world through rose-colored glasses. I want to see it with a wildflower heart like yours, desperately chasing after what makes me happy, wild, and free. And most of all, I want to chase after it with you.

I love you, Chloe Carter. No matter the time, place, or circumstance, I'll always love you because you're my hidden beauty in a world of weeds.

I clutch onto the embroidery circle. Goddammit. Tears break free for the second time today, staining my cheeks.

I've never read something quite like that in my life. Especially not about me.

Definitely not about me.

Someone who writes something like that and creates a piece of art doesn't just love me. Santiago is *in* love with me, and I finally realize the difference. It's crazy, messy, beautifully imperfect. Everything comes at a cost and falling in love isn't exclusive to the rule. But the negatives are worth the one positive—finding someone who isn't just my lover, but the other half of my heart.

It doesn't matter about Santiago's lie at the end of the day. Of course it wasn't right. But I've been looking at it wrong too. Intentions matter. I've been stupid to ignore that for days because of my hurt feelings.

My whole life has been filled with people whose aims were always in the bad place. The difference with Santiago is all his decisions were made with me in mind. Even if it wasn't the right choice for me, it was the right choice to him, and I need to understand that. And most of all, growing up in a world of uncaring people shows me that it's not okay to punish someone for caring too much.

I run out of the room to find my phone because I'm done holding back from him anymore. How can I when he writes me a poetic letter and makes me my own embroidered gift?

The sound of Peter Gabriel's "In Your Eyes" playing outside has me halting at the front door.

"Shut the fuck up."

No way.

There's just no freaking way.

I pull at the handle, throwing the front door open.

I cover my mouth with my palm.

Oh yeah, there's a fucking way.

CHAPTER FORTY-SEVEN

SANTIAGO

Chloe stares at me, wide-eyed and unmoving as her eyes bounce between my trench coat, the stereo above my head, and my face.

Yeah, I'm a fool in love. A big fool who can't help recreating one of her favorite movie scenes just to get her back. The biggest idiot for searching high and low all over the internet for an eighties stereo like the film.

Did I need to do this? Probably not. But I wasn't taking any risks in case my artwork didn't win her over. Chloe is worth the sacrifice to my self-esteem.

Her feet remain planted on the front porch. I didn't expect some grand display of affection from her, but anything is better than the silence right now. Peter Gabriel croons above my head and fills the void between us.

I shoot her a hesitant smile. *Any day now.*

She snaps out of her daze and runs full throttle at me. I barely have enough time to put the stereo down on the ground before she launches herself into my arms. I stumble before catching my balance.

It's bliss, having her back with me. Her arms wrap around my neck right before her lips crash against mine. Our kiss is like two cars colliding. Uncontrolled with sparks flying and the world grinding to a halt around us. I run my fingers through her hair and lock her in place, enjoying the feel of her closeness.

God, I missed her. I missed her in my arms and the way she releases a breathy sigh when I stroke my tongue against hers.

Everything about her calls to me.

The wildness of her touch, both greedy and reverent.

The way her body molds to mine in all the right places, like she was destined to be my match.

The way she whispers my name under her breath when I run my hands down her body.

How did I survive a week without her? Scratch that. How did I make it through most of my life not knowing she existed? I could spend forever with her, and it still wouldn't be long enough.

She breaks away from the kiss first and steps out of my embrace.

I tuck a lock of her hair behind her ear. "I'm so sorry for hiding the truth from you. It was terrible, knowing what I did about Matteo and your dad. Keeping it a secret was one of the hardest things I've had to do, and I've done a lot of difficult things in my life. But I swear, I thought I was doing the right thing. I didn't know what to say, and I thought Matteo would be better at explaining everything. But then he—"

She presses her index finger against my lips, stopping me. "I know. It's not fair to hold it against you when you were put in an impossible situation to begin with. I realize that."

My body warms at her words. "I swear from here on out that I will always tell you the truth. No matter the consequence. No matter the situation. No matter how much it could hurt me or you."

"You promise?"

I nod.

"Even when I ask you if I look fat in a pair of jeans?"

"Is that a trick question?"

She pinches me in the ribs.

I grin, loving the smile on her face. "I'll tell you, *especially* if you look fat in your jeans. The more curves, the better." I wiggle my brows.

She throws herself back into my arms and wraps her arms around my neck.

I lean back against my car, easing some of the weight off my leg. "Am I forgiven?"

"You were forgiven the moment I read your letter on the back of your design. While your executions sucked, I realize you had good intentions, and that's what matters most. I can't fault you anymore for wanting to save me from a painful experience."

I stare at her wide-eyed in disbelief. "I promise not to lie anymore. No matter what my reasoning is, you always deserve the truth."

She chuckles under her breath and cradles my face. "Even when I ask what you think of my cooking?"

"Especially when you ask about your cooking. Dying

from food poisoning isn't on my current agenda."

She laughs in the most beautiful way.

"I love you, Chloe."

"I love you too."

I place a soft kiss against her forehead before taking a deep breath of her flowery scent.

"So I'm you're wildflower, huh?"

My cheeks heat. I might have gone a little overboard with my writing. I'm no Robert Frost, but I can get inspired too.

"I love when you get all shy on me. It's cute."

"I'm not shy."

She lifts a brow. "I thought we said no more lies."

"Is it too late to cancel this connection?"

She throws her head back and laughs. "I'm not a cellphone data plan. You can't just cancel me whenever you feel like it. Plus, you can't write a love letter like that and expect me to disappear. That's what every girl dreams of."

"Did it make your closet-romantic heart happy?"

"No. It made my heart whole."

I follow her into my house. The massive front door clicks shut behind us. Chloe turns on her heel and pushes me against the door. I barely have a moment to recover before her lips crash against mine, her tongue tracing the seam of my mouth. My body shudders as her hands latch onto my T-shirt. With a huff, she pulls away from our kiss to give herself room to pull my shirt off.

Her eyes match a stormy ocean, endless and dark as her

pupils dilate. She licks her lips, tracing the scar I love.

I want to fuck her so badly, to erase the last week from our memories. The time we spent apart might as well have been a year based on the way my cock pulses to life in my jeans.

My shirt falls to the ground and Chloe's lips return to my neck. I groan as her right hand presses against my erection.

My hand covers hers, halting the movement. "Wait."

"Are you really going to stop me right now?"

"No."

Her lips find the sensitive spot on my neck, but I pull back, smacking my head into the door. "Yes. Wait."

"What's wrong?" She pulls away and steps out of my personal circle. Her brows draw together.

I don't blame her for being confused. Hell, even my dick is siding with Chloe on this one.

"I need to tell you one last thing before we move onto that part of making up."

"What?" She takes another step back, adding to the growing distance between us.

"There's one more thing I need to tell you."

She blinks. Once. Twice. Three times.

The silence is deafening as she says nothing.

I stare her in the eyes despite the urge to look away. "I did something you probably won't be happy with."

"Don't leave me hanging in suspense. My heart can't handle it."

"I should preface this with the fact that the only reason I did this in the first place was because I wanted to protect you."

"Thanks for the prologue. What is it?" Her voice comes

out wooden.

"Your mom called Noah, who called me."

"WHAT?!"

"Let me explain the whole thing before you interrupt okay? Please?"

Her frown becomes more pronounced. "Don't skimp on one detail, or else I swear to God..."

Okay, I can work with that. "So, I called her after Noah told me that she spoke to his personal assistant. She threatened to release some story about you and an assault charge because of Ralph. The whole phone call was disgusting. I didn't expect her to be obvious about how little she cares about you. After that, I paid her off because I just wanted her out of your life permanently. And to be clear, I didn't do it because I was afraid of what something like that could do for my reputation. Any decision I made about her was solely to save you from any additional pain. I want you to know that first and foremost."

Chloe nods but doesn't say anything.

My heart beats faster in my chest. Is she pissed I withheld this too?

Of course she is. You keep fucking up over and over against with her. I ramble on, desperate for her to understand. "The story...I was afraid how it could hurt you if it got out. She was threatening to take your story to the reporters, and if I've learned anything, it's that they love drama like that. And she only wanted money, and I have plenty of it, so I didn't think she was worth it. I've been broken by the media, and I didn't want the same for you."

"You paid her off because you wanted to make sure I wasn't hurt in the process?"

I nod my head up and down. "I swear. The kind of money she was asking for has such little value to me. It's laughable how she could've asked for *way* more, and I wouldn't have hesitated because you're more important. I was trying to free you of ever having to deal with her again. After everything you shared, I was only trying to help. If that's what you want, that is."

"Right," she mumbles under her breath.

What is she thinking? Her blank face reveals nothing, and I'm not sure how to gauge her reaction.

I cup her chin and force her to look at me. "God, I don't know how you came out pure-hearted after being raised by someone like her."

"Because she didn't raise me to begin with. Locking me in rooms and forcing me to fend for myself year after year barely counts as being human, let alone a parent."

My chest tightens at her words. I'd do anything to replace all her memories with new ones. No child deserves to have gone through what she did. While I can't change Chloe's past, I can be part of a better future. One that includes endless laughs and the best adventures.

She runs her hand down my chest. Heat rushes down my spine from her touch.

Her hand stops, lingering over my beating heart. "You had the choice to keep this from me and I wouldn't have found out—if what you said is true about paying her off forever. You risked me getting upset again and potentially leaving you for good. Why would you do that?"

"Because I made a promise to you earlier to always tell the truth, and I plan on keeping it. Forever."

"Forever?" Her lips part as she sucks in a breath.

"Forever." I pull her body against mine.

I kiss her with everything I have in me. Every unspoken promise I plan on holding myself to as long as I'm with her.

Chloe didn't just bring back a part of me that was missing. She helped me grow into someone better than ever before, and for that, she has my loyalty and love.

CHAPTER FORTY-EIGHT

Chloe

"**K**eep your eyes closed."

I spread my fingers apart a fraction of an inch, only for Santiago to smack them lightly.

"Do you ever listen?"

"I don't know. I listened pretty well last night." I smirk.

I'm not naming names, but *someone* is mighty confident in the bedroom now. And with his boosted self-esteem comes a lot of new experiences. And I mean *new*. Things *Cosmo* magazine would blush about. Hell, I'm blushing just thinking about it.

"If you keep this up, you'll never see your surprise."

I groan. "Surprise? I thought we agreed those are the worst! Right up there with gender reveal parties still being a thing."

His breath tickles my ear as he releases a hoarse laugh. "But I promise you'll like this one. Trust me."

A door creaks open, and Santiago shuffles me inside. I

keep my fingers secured over my eyes. Deep down I don't want to ruin whatever he's planned, even if it is a surprise.

"Did you finally add a Red Room of Pain to this creepy castle?"

"No. And Mr. Grey will not see you now or ever." He halts, forcing me to stop.

"You're kind of sexy when you get jealous."

His lips press against mine. It's brief, and I yearn for more the moment he pulls away.

"Do you ever stop talking?"

"Only when your cock is in my mouth."

He lets out a howl of laughter.

I drop my hands, wanting to see his smile. What I find is so much better.

"Oh my God." I stare wide-eyed at the room.

Can someone please scoop my jaw up off the floor and return it back to its rightful place?

Santiago remains silent as I take it all in.

Huge bay windows allow for the afternoon sun to light the room. A massive white table and comfy chair is set up in the middle. Empty embroidery hoops of every size line one wall, making a pretty cool design. Clear drawers filled with supplies line another wall.

I walk toward one of the drawers and pull it open. T-shirts of every color and material are lined up perfectly. The next drawer reveals threads from the entire rainbow. Other drawers house jeans of all sizes, hats, and sweaters. You name it, he bought it.

It's a crafting paradise. I couldn't have dreamed up this design even if I wanted to.

I turn toward the man who made this all possible and run into his arms.

He lifts me up and spins me in a circle. "Do you like it?"

I cradle his face and place a bunch of kisses all over it. "*Do I like it*? I *love* it!"

"Now you have no excuse not to chase after your dream. There's an Etsy shop waiting for you."

"Thank you! Thank you! Thank you!" I say between kisses.

"No. Thank *you* for reminding me what it means to have a passion. This is only the start of returning that favor."

"Is this your way of getting me to come over every single day once I get my own apartment in town?"

He smirks. "No. This is my way of getting you to stay. Permanently. I don't want you to move out."

"We can't live together. We're not even married!"

He laughs. "Is that a necessity? Because I can amend that problem very fast."

I smack his arm. "Don't joke."

"Who said anything about joking?"

"You want me to move in with you? Like forever?"

"Unless you have somewhere else to go, I think that's what *permanently* means."

I roll my eyes. "You can't be serious."

"I am."

"You're crazy."

"So are you."

"I don't cook."

He laughs. "I do."

I tick off another finger on my hand. "I don't clean very much."

"There's a maid for that."

"I leave my makeup all over the counter, and my clothes never make it into the hamper."

"I've yet to hear a real negative in all this rambling of yours."

I grin up at him. "You really want this?"

"More than anything else."

"That can't be true. There has to be something else you want."

"There is. But some things take time and even you aren't ready for that."

What on Earth does that mean?!

He leans down and kisses me. It's an electric storm growing between us, morphing into something uncontrollable. Like lightning could be crashing down around us and we wouldn't even notice.

I'd be a fool to say no after a declaration of love like that. It looks like I'm staying in Italy after all.

"I have somewhere I want to take you." Santiago grabs my hand and pulls me up from the couch.

"Is it an art store?"

"No."

"The grocery store?"

"God, no. Why would I want to take you there?"

"Because I ate the last couple of Oreos last night after you fell asleep."

"Seriously? You didn't bother saving one?"

I shrug. "Do crumbs count?"

He shakes his head as if he can't believe he was lucky enough to score someone as thoughtful as me. I know. I'm such a catch, even the Oreos couldn't resist me.

An idea hits me. "Oh, I know! We're going to the junk yard to search for your next restoration job."

He grunts. "No. I'm taking you on our first official date as a real couple. Are you happy now?"

"Even better!" I bounce off the couch and into his arms.

He cradles my face and places a soft kiss on my lips.

I lean into his touch, silently begging for more.

"If you keep this up, we will never leave."

"Is that the worst thing?"

He sighs. "I'd say no, but I put a little something together and I don't want it to go to waste."

Aw, how sweet. I step away, stopping my torture.

I look down at my T-shirt and skirt full of tiny daisies. "Am I dressed okay?"

"You look beautiful."

"That was the best evasion technique I've ever heard."

He laughs under his breath. "We better get going. It's getting late."

"It's ten in the morning."

"If you're not early…"

"You're late. *Ugh.* You're getting predictable."

"You won't be saying that in an hour."

Oh, shit.

"What are we doing in the middle of nowhere?"

Santiago parks the car off to the side of the dirt road we traveled down.

"I thought it was a good place for no one to hear your screams."

A cold chill spreads across my skin. "Back to plotting my murder? I thought we moved past that plan once we started fake dating."

"To be fair, you *did* eat the last Oreos." He exits the car and grabs something from the trunk.

I clutch onto the door handle to open the door, but Santiago beats me to it. Whoever said chivalry was dead clearly hasn't met the right man.

My eyes drop to the basket and the backpack Santiago carries in his hand. "A picnic?"

"Hmm."

I squeal like a freaking schoolgirl because my boyfriend went out of his way to plan a picnic for me. "Oh my God. You're such a softy."

"My abs beg to differ."

I snort. "You planned a picnic! That's romantic. I thought that was only a thing in movies."

"I'm committed to recreating some of the movies you love and making them better."

I almost fall out of my seat from swooning too hard.

Santiago ushers me out of the car. He puts on the backpack and transfers the basket to one hand so he can grab onto mine.

We hike together through a short trail. It's something out of a fairy tale, with a little creek and trees as far as the eye can see. The trail spits us out into a field.

"Whoa," I whisper under my breath.

A field of wildflowers stretches on forever. Flowers of every color dance in the wind, swaying together in perfect harmony. There's not a single soul nearby except for the birds chirping in the distance.

It's absolutely stunning, and all I want to do is run through them. I resist the urge. "How did you find this place?"

"I have my ways."

"It's gorgeous."

"It's how I see you." He looks down at me, his eyes reflecting an array of emotions.

Tears prick my eyes. Never in my life have I felt this loved and cherished. It's a blessing to feel so damn important to someone, to the point that they make sure I know it every single day. Santiago Alatorre loves me in a way that most people spend their whole lives chasing. And I love him equally as much.

Santiago taught me how there's a difference between want and need. I need him. Like the trees need sunlight or the ocean needs the tide. Being around him is becoming something fundamental for me.

He plucks a dandelion from the field and holds it up to me. "It might not be your journal, but the wish works just the same."

My smile wobbles.

I shut my eyes and suck in a breath.

I wish Santiago achieves all his dreams because no one deserves it more than him.

I blow and open my eyes to find the hundreds of dandelion

parts floating away. It's a beautiful sight, like magic spreading across the land.

"Is it illegal for me to ask what you wished for?"

I laugh. "Yes, and don't bother trying. Did you pack a blanket in that bag?"

He nods his head up and down. "It wouldn't be a picnic without one according to my friends."

If he continues to shock me, he might need to nail my jaw shut.

"You asked your friends about what supplies to bring?" I ask incredulously.

"No. They wouldn't shut up when I told them what my plan was for today. Liam—you haven't met him yet—was especially vocal, going off about all the supplies to make it special."

I'm so proud of him for branching out again and talking more with his family and friends. He seems happier—lighter even.

Santiago sets everything up. He moves to grab our lunch out of the basket, but I place my hand over his.

"What is it?" He looks up at me.

I lean over and place a kiss on his pouty lips. "I want to show you something."

"What?" His voice takes on a husky tone.

"It's time I repaid a favor you did a while ago."

His brows dart up. "You've got my attention. What do you want to show me?"

"How much I love you." I push at his shoulders.

He follows my lead and lays down. I crawl over his body and cup one of his cheeks with my hand.

I kiss him with everything in me. Every emotion. Every memory of us. Every ounce of love I feel towards him. I'm desperate to show him how I feel like he did.

I sit up. His erection presses into my ass. With desperate hands and his help, I tug his shirt over his head and throw it toward the edge of the blanket. My clothing and underwear meet the same discarded fate. Santiago makes quick work of unbuttoning his shorts and tugging them down his legs.

Our lips crash together again, the need between us growing as our hands memorize each other's bodies again. His touch is tender and adoring as his hands run down my back. They heat my skin like a brand.

I brush my hand across his throbbing cock. Santiago hisses at the touch, and his kiss becomes more punishing as I wrap a hand around him and pump.

My desperation pushes him over the edge. His touch becomes more purposeful as he strokes the place between my legs begging for his attention. A sky of shooting stars bursts behind my eyelids as his touch brings me alive.

I cherish every minute, our kisses saying things words can't.

Santiago grabs a condom from the backpack pocket and passes it to me. I roll it over his thick erection and line our bodies together.

I place a soft kiss against his lips and lean back again. "Loving you is like the first day of spring after a harsh winter."

He smiles up at me, clearly recognizing my attempt to recreate the moment he shared with me all those weeks ago when I asked him about love.

"Loving you is like the ocean. Infinite. Fierce. Breathtaking."

He sits up on his elbows and cups my face.

I lean into his touch, allowing his warmth to seep through my body. "Loving you feels like seeing a rainbow for the first time. It's so amazing, you can't help wondering if it was created by magic." I slide down his shaft, connecting us in more ways than one.

There is an understated beauty in intimacy. It binds us together, making a wonderful blend of lust and love. With Santiago, it's unlike anything I've ever experienced before.

I place my hands against his chest and rise, only to slide back down.

He groans at the motion, and I grin from ear to ear. Everything about him makes me happy. From the sweet things he says to the devious look he gets in his eyes when we make love.

I lean over and press a soft kiss against his lips. I whisper low, our breaths mingling together, "And most of all, loving you is realizing I don't have to make a wish ever again because I already have everything I could ever want."

CHAPTER FORTY-NINE

SANTIAGO

Chloe and I walk hand in hand into the boardroom, following Noah and Maya. It reminds me of a law courtroom with the panelists sitting in a row of seats where a judge usually resides.

I halt, and Chloe stumbles from the momentum of being pulled back. She looks back over her shoulder. I can barely focus on her because of the sight in front of me.

Every seat in the room is filled with people of my racing past. Maya takes a seat beside Sophie and Liam, who both wave at me from the front row. Beside Liam sits Jax, who has his arm wrapped around Elena. He offers me a chin tip before turning his attention back to Elena and Elías.

Countless Bandini crew members sit in the rows behind them, all chatting or smiling at one another. There isn't one face I don't recognize. The sight assaults me, forcing ragged breaths from my lungs.

All these people are here for me?

James waves me over from the table in the front meant for lawyers.

Chloe squeezes my hand, gaining my attention. "Ready?"

I swallow back the lump in my throat. "I'd say no, but I'm supposed to act calm, cool, and collected according to Noah, or else he'll kick my ass."

She laughs under her breath. "You've got this. No one has prepared more than you have for something like this."

"It's hard to compete against no one. It's not like many racers have been in this position before."

She stands on her toes and places a kiss on my cheek. "There's no one better suited to do this than you. You already showed that you can get behind the wheel and race as well as the rest of them. During your last test, you even broke your old record. There's no one else meant for driving more than you."

Nodding my head, I lead Chloe toward her seat beside Maya. I press a kiss against the top of her head before heading toward Noah and James.

"Ready?" Noah slaps a hand against my back.

"About as ready as I'll ever be." My eyes dart across the panel.

It's a bunch of suits, staring down at me with stoic faces. A cool sweat breaks out across my brow, and I swipe it away with the sleeve of my suit.

"Relax. They'd be foolish to say no. You're a legend, and everyone is a sucker for a good comeback story." James smiles at me.

The head of the panel introduces himself and starts the meeting. Noah and James present my race statistics at the test track and discuss the steering wheel Bandini designed that allows me to race like everyone else.

I hide my shaking hands beneath the table the entire meeting. My heart remains permanently lodged inside of my throat as everyone speaks.

The head of the meeting looks over at me and calls my name.

"Yes, sir." I stand.

"Are you afraid of going back out there?"

I look over my shoulder at Chloe. She throws her two thumbs up and shoots me a goofy grin, making me smile back.

Am I afraid? Only an idiot wouldn't be.

I turn back toward the main speaker. "Fear isn't always a bad thing."

His brows lift. "How so?"

"Fear motivates me. It reminds me how the best things in life will always make us afraid, but that shouldn't stop us from pursuing them anyway. I spent three years of my life allowing fear to guide my decisions and look where that got me. I'd rather be afraid and drive anyway than be afraid and watch life pass me by. Because in the end, nothing is more fearful than realizing life goes on, with or without you."

All the people on the panel nod their heads.

A woman at the end of the row raises her hand to speak. "Santiago, I want to ask how you plan on approaching your injury with the public."

"By being upfront about it. Someone taught me honesty takes strength." My eyes slide from the panel to Chloe. Her eyes gain a sheen in them as she stares at me.

I return my focus back on the panel. "I want to be a

champion for those like me. I want to show them that—
no matter what they want to achieve in life—no injury or
obstacle should stop them. But I also want to be a model for
those who have been broken by their circumstances because
they deserve hope too."

The leader asks if anyone else has any questions. The
panel remains silent, and everyone in the room is asked to
leave during the deliberation.

We all exit like cattle. Noah and I turn toward a corner
while James excuses himself to talk to a colleague.

Chloe finds me and wraps her arms around my waist.
"You did amazing! I'm beyond impressed by your answers."

I kiss her temple. "Thank you."

"I loved all your answers! And to think you thought them
up on the go. Wow," Maya chimes in.

"Hey, man. Long time, no see. I'm digging your new
look." Liam wraps his arm around my shoulder.

"It beats the *Duck Dynasty* thing you had going for
yourself. Did you even bother using the beard lube I got you
for Christmas last year?" Jax offers me his fist to pound.

I frown. "I thought it was a joke."

"No, man. Sophie loves that shit, especially during certain
activities." Liam winks.

Sophie hides her face in his chest, only giving me a peek
at her blonde hair.

Some things never change. I forgot how much I missed
the easygoingness of our friendships. A surge of shame hits
me at neglecting them during my time of darkness. But like
Chloe says, I can't change the past. I can only make up for it
now.

"I'm surprised you all came." Something squeezes in my chest.

"We can't miss the beginning of your comeback story. This is how legends are made, after all." Elena beams at me.

I cough and look down at my shoes.

"And I'm guessing this is Chloe? I've heard quite a lot about you from Noah and Maya." Jax smiles at Chloe.

"Oh." Chloe's cheeks flush.

"I'd like you all to formally meet Chloe, my girlfriend."

Her arms tighten around my waist as everyone assesses her.

She's pretty. Sophie mouths before winking at me.

"It's nice meeting you all." Chloe grins.

"Is it really?" Noah smirks. "Don't lie. The four of them are way less cool than Maya and me."

"Wait, has Maya hung out with you and not said anything?" Sophie's blue eyes bounce between her best friend and Chloe.

Chloe nods her head in all four directions, not giving anyone a clear answer.

I crack up at her anxiousness. "Don't mind Sophie. She tends to get jealous."

"Of what? Being kept secrets from? You have a girlfriend. You've *never* had a girlfriend besides that one girl from grade school," Sophie sputters.

"Honestly, I thought you were gay for about point five seconds, but then Maya told me that wasn't true." Elena raises her hand.

"You thought I was gay?" My mouth drops open.

Elena nods.

I groan. "Is it too late to hide again? Chloe, are you in favor?"

Her body shakes from silent laughter. "Nope. I think you're right where you belong."

"Aw, how cute," Sophie coos at us. "Look at Santiago in love. Someone grab me a camera before the moment disappears."

Liam tugs her into him. "Why bother? If he's in love with her, he's never letting go in the first place."

Damn right.

I look over at the wild girl who captured my heart. She belongs by my side, smiling at my friends and laughing at their jokes. It fills me with warmth to find her enjoying herself around the people I consider family. I want to give this to her. To show her family isn't about blood, but the bond between people who care enough to stick around, even during the hardest times.

"Santiago Alatorre, you came today to present your case, with the assistance of Noah Slade and James Mitchell." The head speaker stands.

The rest of us follow, rising to our feet. Noah and James nod their heads. The three of us stand shoulder to shoulder in front of the panel.

I tuck my trembling hands into the pockets of my slacks.

"We find everything you have done thus far to be incredibly brave. It's no easy feat to get back in a race car after what you went through, and we couldn't imagine a racer better suited to tackle his life circumstances more than you. I've had the pleasure to watch you since you began racing in Formula 3. Even as a teenager, you overcame all the odds stacked against you, time and time again. Whether it was a lack of finances or working with a teammate who was your rival"—he shoots a tight smile at Noah—"you challenged adversity head-on and came out winning."

Every deep breath I take makes my lungs burn. Is he giving me this whole walk down memory lane to let me down softly?

He continues. "We worry that your circumstances are too severe for Formula 1's racing circuit. The conditions are grueling, as you are well aware, and the crashes are menacing. It's of great importance to note that we considered the consequences of you racing again and the potential injuries you might sustain that may worsen your condition."

Fuck. The panel doesn't want to take a risk on me. The rush of adrenaline from earlier escapes me, replaced by a wave of melancholy. I drop my eyes, focusing on the wooden stand the speaker talks behind.

"But…"

My eyes snap up. His grin grows as he assesses my face. "There's no one we think is more deserving and more ready to take on the challenges thrown his way than you. It is with great pleasure that we are approving the bill that will allow you to race again with the modifications Noah Slade designed with the help of James Mitchell. We want to welcome all drivers— no matter their disability—to race if they are talented enough. As the leaders of the Formula Corp, we are looking forward to cheering you on during the next season. Welcome back to the grid, Santiago. It's good to have you back."

The room goes crazy with hooting and clapping hands.

Noah turns toward me. "You did it."

I shake my head. "There's no *me* without *you*." I pull him into a hug. I tuck my head into his shoulder and let out the few tears I was holding back.

I can't believe I'm going back. I never imagined this day would happen in my lifetime. Not when I recovered after rehab. Not after I spent year after year away from the track. Not until someone barged into my life and turned it around.

Noah smacks my back. "The racing world isn't the same without you. I'm so proud of you for giving this and me a chance because everything he said was true. There's no one who should be racing more than you."

I pull away and look him in the eyes. "Thank you. For creating the wheel. For pushing me to realize the mistakes I was making. And thank you for never giving up on me, even when I gave up on myself."

"That's what brothers are for." He smiles.

Chloe barrels through the swinging gate. She tackles me for a hug. "You're going to race again! In a race car! With those sexy suits and champagne podiums!"

I chuckle into her hair. "Sexy suits?"

"Only on you. No offense, Noah." She looks over at him sheepishly.

"None taken. I'm retiring in a few months anyway." He winks.

Maya and my parents join us to celebrate. Everyone wishes me congratulations. I keep Chloe by my side, never letting her step away.

I smile the entire time I chat with old friends and family. All the weight from the years I lived in isolation lifts from my shoulders. It's as if the darkness was never there, trapping me with negative thoughts and hopelessness.

I can finally breathe easily, knowing I can achieve my dreams again with Chloe by my side.

CHAPTER FIFTY

Chloe

Santiago and I have fallen into the best kind of routine together ever since he asked me to move in. While he busies himself with practice rounds at the racetrack with Bandini, I spend my days with Matteo and work on my latest designs for my Etsy shop. I already have a few orders after Maya helped me take photos of the different pieces of clothing I made.

Somehow while searching for my father, I found a man to love and a job that makes me happy to wake up every morning. It's as if every last piece clicked into place for me.

Well, almost every last piece. I never thought I'd truly find out what would make me happy in life, but it seems like everything I could possibly want has fallen into my lap when I least expected it.

Even Brooke shipped over all my belongings, with Santiago's help. What once was a house devoid of emotion now bursts with colorful blankets and plants on windowsills.

We turned his house into a home, and it's somewhere I wouldn't mind spending many years of my life sprucing up.

Santiago preps dinner while I sip wine and stare.

He pauses his chopping to look up at me. "Are you happy?"

"*Moi?*" I lift a brow.

He smirks. "Yes."

"Of course! What kind of question is that?"

He shrugs, resuming his cutting of tonight's vegetables. "Yesterday you were kind of mopey."

"That's because I'm on my period, you dufus. I can't always be the type to throw confetti around wherever I go."

He frowns. "Is that why you cried while watching *Bridesmaids?*"

I cringe. Did I really cry during a comedy? Okay, maybe I was a bit emotionally reactive yesterday. "It made me emotional."

"Because?"

"Because it's Brooke's favorite movie and it made me miss her. I haven't seen her in forever and she's so far away that even our usual phone calls aren't enough."

"I gathered that after you fell asleep with your laptop while video chatting with her last week."

"I'm not cut out for long-distance relationships. They suck."

"Thank God for that." He smirks.

"Are you seriously smiling? You're evil."

"Only in the ways that count." He winks.

I throw my hands up. "What does that even mean?"

Santiago looks over at the clock on the oven. "3...2...1..."

Nothing happens. A bird chirps from outside, adding to

the awkward silence between us.

I somehow found someone about as crazy as me. What a feat to accomplish. "Are you feeling okay? That was anticlimactic, to say the least."

He rolls his eyes. "I expect too much out of people. It seems that being on time is a thing of the past."

"What are you going off ab—"

The front door bangs open in the distance. "When you told me that you were staying in a castle that had a Transylvania vibe, you were not kidding!"

The sound of Brooke's voice has me screaming as I run through the halls to meet her.

I hurl myself into her arms, forcing her to drop her luggage on the ground. "Oh my fucking God! You're here! You're really here! How did you even get here?!"

She lets out a huff of air. "God you weigh a lot more. What have they been feeding you over here? Cookies for breakfast, lunch, and dinner?"

I cackle, letting go of her. "What are you even doing here?"

"Santiago asked me to come visit you." She beams.

I look over my shoulder, catching Santiago smiling at us. He waves at Brooke and introduces himself.

"Seriously? Are you always going to be this perfect or will it wear off like a car's warranty?" My eyes slide from Santiago to my best friend, ensuring I didn't make any of this up.

All Santiago does is smile at me. It's one that beams from the inside out, practically lighting up the damn entryway with his positivity.

"The dynamic duo is back." Brooke does a little dance around me.

"You're actually going to be visiting us for a while? I can't believe it!" I wrap my arms around her again and give her a squeeze.

She matches my hug with one of her own. "Well…"

I release her and take a step back. "What?"

She bites her lip. "Since I now am a proud graduate with a degree under my belt, and we are in the land of designer royalty…"

"*No.*" My mouth pops open. *Is she saying what I think she is saying?*

"Yes!" she squeals. "I applied to a bunch of jobs here. London, Paris, Milan. If there's a country with a fashion magazine, I'm attempting it."

"You're going to live in Europe? Like permanently?"

She beams. "It depends where I get hired, but it'll be somewhere on this side of the world, that's for sure. I can't let my best friend move to Europe without me. We're like a pair of kidneys."

"Better off together than ever apart." I smile.

Santiago walks up to my side and throws his arm over my shoulder. "We have a guest room set up for you upstairs. I can imagine you want to relax and take a shower after that long flight."

I look up at the man who repaired my cracked heart with superglue and sheer willpower. "Are you sure that you want to sign yourself up for another roommate?"

"For a little while, at least until she gets on her feet and lands herself a job. Not to mention when she suggested staying at the same place you did, I told her I couldn't allow that. I wouldn't wish that on my worst enemy… Well, maybe

Noah, but only because it would be a humbling experience for our Royal Highness."

I struggle to hold back my laugh.

"Speaking of Noah Slade... Does he have any friends? Any *single* friends, that is." Brooke waggles her brows.

Santiago shakes his head. "Unfortunately, all of us are taken."

"Do you hear that?" Brooke leans in and whispers.

"What?" I raise a brow at her.

"I thought I heard all the women in the world sobbing, but maybe I'm just going crazy."

Santiago and I both laugh. He looks at her with a bit of wonder. "I see why Chloe loves you."

Brooke preens like a damn show-off. "Oh, do tell. I love compliments."

"You've got the same kind of magic she has."

I blush.

"Is it possible for me to vicariously fall in love with you too? Asking for a friend?" Brooke speaks with her most serious face even though I can tell she wants to burst into a fit of laughter.

I laugh up to the ceiling. My chest fills with a new kind of warmth at the idea of having my best friend living on the same continent as me.

I didn't even need to make a wish for it to come true. All I needed was Santiago—a man set on proving the magic isn't the wish itself, but the people who make the dream come true.

CHAPTER FIFTY-ONE

SANTIAGO

SEVEN MONTHS LATER

"The kids are ready for you." Chloe walks into my Bandini suite.

I smile up at her as I zip up my race suit. "They're all out there?"

She nods and offers me her hand. "Ready to watch their favorite guy race in his first Grand Prix."

I finish strapping on my iWalk before standing up from the couch. Together Chloe and I exit the Bandini motorhome where I get ready and relax before races.

We walk down the main road toward the series of stages where racers and sponsors meet fans.

Chloe swings our hands between us. "Are you ready for your first season back?"

"Yes."

People stop and stare. Some openly gape at my iWalk

while others avoid direct eye contact with me. It should make me uncomfortable, but one look at Chloe's grinning face has me ignoring them.

Who cares about the rest of the world when mine revolves around this girl?

She leads me toward the stage. "Are you nervous?"

"Surprisingly no."

"How do you feel about the car?"

"Are you sure you want the answer to that? You might get jealous."

Her shoulders shake as she laughs to herself. "*Me*? Jealous of a car?"

"I loved her before you," I tease.

She sticks her tongue out at me. "She might be your first love, but she won't be your last."

"Someone is cocky."

"I've earned my place." She winks.

A rush of laughter erupts out of me.

We stop at the entrance to the stage. I tug her into my body and place a kiss on her head. Wanting to soak in the moment, I take a few deep breaths.

Chloe fiddles with the zipper on my suit. "Just a fair warning. I might have done something extra special for today."

"I'm almost afraid to ask you."

"Why don't I show you instead?" Chloe's devious smile sets me on alert.

Hand in hand, we walk up the steps of the stage. Hundreds of kids scream at the top of their lungs as I enter the massive stage. They're not wearing the Bandini gear I sent them as part of the charity welcome package.

No.

Every child, from little babies to teens with smug grins, wear variations of Iron Man clothing. Some wave their prosthetic arms in the air, holding up posters with my name. While everyone looks different, from their ethnicities to their ages, they all have one thing in common.

They're all like me.

I blink at their costumes, which was definitely not part of the plan.

"Surprise?" Chloe looks at me in a way that seems like she wants to gauge my reaction.

The crowd screams as my family walks out onto the stage. Noah holds on to Marko who is decked out in his own Iron Man costume. Maya and my parents join him, smiling at me in their Bandini shirts. My mom brushes away a tear running down her cheek while my dad hugs her close to his side.

I look down at the woman I love. "You planned all this?"

"Well, you did ask me to help you set up today's event."

The crowd begins to chant *Iron Man* louder and louder. I walk up to the edge of the stage, completely mystified.

Chloe places something in my hands, and I look down at it. It's a new custom race helmet. Iron Man's arc reactor symbol is centered at the top, surrounded by the Spanish flag. I flip it around and check out the back. A custom sticker with Chloe's dainty writing is located at the bottom of the helmet.

You might be the hero in my story, but you're the legend in theirs.

This is one of the best gifts someone has given me.

With one hand, I grab Chloe and pull her into my body. I place a soft kiss against her lips. "Thank you."

"Oh, please! You're the one who started this charity. I only brought them all here."

"There wouldn't be a charity, let alone an event, without you to begin with. You and your crazy plan to trespass on private property."

She laughs to herself. "Maybe there was a cat who needed saving."

"Or maybe there was a *man* who needed saving." I look out at the crowd of kids who all have prosthetics because of the foundation I started. All it took was one video of a kid crying as he looked at his stump to show me that I had a different purpose besides racing. Parents struggle to afford the prosthetics to begin with, but add children's growth spurts into the mix, and they have whopping medical bills. With Chloe's help, I created my foundation in the hopes of setting an example.

I'm not only racing for me anymore. I'm racing for *them*. For the people who need someone to look up to who can show them that they're bigger than a disability. To show them that we are the new normal.

Their chants grow louder as I raise the helmet in the air and smile.

Time to race.

Engine vibrations tickle my spine. The smell of fresh rubber taints the air, blowing into the tiny gap I left open in my visor. My third-place spot on the grid is behind my Bandini teammate and Elías, the race leader.

I'm back. I make a sign of the cross and say a quick favor. With two gloved hands, I clutch onto my steering wheel. There's a slight tremble in my hands.

Relax. You've practiced for months with Noah. You've got this.

Crew scatter away from the pavement. Five red lights turn on, one by one. My heart lurches in my chest as all five shut off simultaneously.

I tug on the throttle pad. My tires screech as my car speeds through the grid. The rush builds inside of me as I make it through the first straight unscathed. Somehow, I hold on to third place, right behind Elías and my teammate, Finn.

I smile behind my helmet as James comes onto the mic.

"Great start, Santiago. Keep a steady pace and show these bastards what a podium winner looks like." He rattles off some statistics to watch.

I use the throttle pad and brakes interchangeably, making it through the first lap without a problem.

I love the way my heart races in my chest. Love the feel of the tires shuddering beneath me, shredding apart as I complete each lap. It's addictive to pass by the roaring Grandstands.

I love it all. Every ragged breath escaping my lungs, every curve of the track, every time my teammate gives me a hard time about passing him.

Lap after lap, I hold my third place while fighting off other drivers behind me. None get past me, but it's not good enough.

I want more. For the kids who came to support me and for the woman who stood by my side through it all.

I inch up to my teammate. We drive in tandem through the long road before I go around the outside of his car and speed in front of his.

"Amazing! That's what I'm talking about!" James hoots.

Adrenaline is my drug of choice. The rush is instant, and the feeling is unparalleled.

The engine rattles as I increase my speed. The throttle paddle works like a dream, and after all my practices, it's second nature to me.

Elías remains the race leader in his gray McCoy car. He hugs the curves at every turn and centers himself during every straight.

I pull on the throttle, and my car speeds up behind him. His rear bumper is close, to the point where I can practically touch it with the tip of my front wing.

"Take it easy," James adds through the team radio.

Everything about this is easy, and that's what makes it all the more fun. I don't care about landing on a podium anymore or becoming the best. All I care about is having fun and living my life.

Winning isn't about a Championship title anymore. It's about making me proud, no matter the outcome. Other people's praise is only an added bonus now. Because in the end, I spent way too many lost years focusing on the opinions of people who didn't matter.

Elías doesn't hold back during the last few laps. I drive by his side, only to be pushed back into second place when we reach the next turn. He's talented and a natural at defending. I can honestly learn a thing or two from his skills.

He passes the finish line less than a second before me. I raise my fist in the air and drive up to the Grandstand housing all the kids from earlier. Their screams grow louder as my car gets closer.

I force my car to do donuts on the track in front of them.

Smoke rises from the burning tires, and the crowd goes wild. My smile doesn't drop the entire time.

I don't need my leg to race. All I needed was a dream, the courage, and a badass girlfriend who called me out on my shit time and time again. I needed someone to teach me how to accept that I wasn't broken but lost.

Life isn't about chasing the rush anymore. It's about wanting to slow time down and enjoy every single second because I don't want to miss a thing.

It took one chance encounter with a stranger to change my life. One person to make me realize that I can't love someone else until I love myself. One dreamer who makes me want to wish in journals or on lucky stars or on damn dandelions for all I care.

One girl. One love. One forever.

EPILOGUE

Chloe

Two pink lines. That's all it takes to change my life.

I shake the stick, as if it can make one of the lines fade away. "This isn't a freaking Etch A Sketch, Chloe."

No, it's just a positive pregnancy test.

Me. Pregnant.

"Holy shit."

Wait, I can't say shit *anymore.*

Oh my God. I'm pregnant. Like really, actually, ninety-nine percent pregnant, if the statistics on the drugstore pregnancy test are accurate. I instantly regret purchasing the test in advance and storing it in my bathroom because now I have no way to deny the facts.

I'm going to have a child with Santiago. I sink onto the cool tile of the bathroom because I don't trust my legs at the moment.

How did this happen?

When two people have sex without—

Okay, obviously I know *how* it happened. But how did it happen so fast? Santiago and I just agreed to stop using condoms less than a few months ago. I mean, shit, we only got married this year. And after hearing Maya's struggles about having kids, I anticipated it might take some time for us. But this? Seriously, what kind of magic sperm does Santiago have?

The hand that clutches the pregnancy test trembles. Shit. I'm really going to be a mom. Like I'm about to go from sex marathons and lazy Sundays to changing diapers, breast-feeding, and complaining to Brooke about how much it sucks to put a stroller in the trunk of a car while managing an infant.

But what if I'm a terrible mother? What if they hate me because I mess up or think that I'm not as good as all the other moms in their class because I can't cook, or bake, or even do much without fumbling—"

"Chloe, are you feeling okay? You left the dinner table in a rush." Santiago's voice carries through the closed door.

I left because my phone sent me an alert right in the middle of our dinner about missing my period two weeks in a row. Clearly, my tracking app has it more put together than me at the moment.

"Sure." My voice croaks.

"Do you need any help?"

"Define what you mean by help?"

He coughs. "Well, umm, is there enough toilet paper in there?"

I'm tempted to open the door only to slam it in his face after.

"Just so you know, bathroom jokes are *so* not welcome in this marriage."

"That didn't make you laugh? Now I know something really is wrong with you." The doorknob rattles, but the lock stays in place.

"Go away," I mumble.

"What's wrong? Talk to me."

I crawl to the door and turn the lock. It opens with a soft click, and Santiago enters the space. His eyes bounce between the test in my hand and my face.

"Because thanks to you and your magic sperm, I'm pregnant."

His face leeches of color. He drops ungracefully onto the floor and pulls me into his body. "Holy shit. You're pregnant."

"It's 'holy shirt' now. No cursing in front of the child, please."

Santiago throws his head back and laughs. I crack a smile, but no laughter escapes me.

His brows draw together as he assesses my face. "What's the matter? I thought this was what you wanted?"

The arms I love tighten around me, securing me to his body. God, I'll miss him being able to hug me like this. It'll never be the same once I become the size of a human beach ball.

"Chloe?" He places a soft kiss at the crook of my neck.

A few tears leak out of my eyes. "I'm happy. I promise I am." And I really am, but it's a lot to process right now, and my mind struggles to keep up.

"Then why are you crying?"

"Because I'm afraid I'll never be good enough for our child."

He squeezes me tighter before turning me around in his

lap, forcing me to face him. His hand tucks a loose lock of my hair behind my ear. "You'll be the best mother."

"Of course you have to say that. You knocked me up, after all."

He shakes his head. "No. I'm saying it because I truly believe you will be. The kind of love you share with those closest to you is the most precious gift, and I'm somewhat jealous I have to share it with—"

"Jellybean."

"Jellybean." He smiles wide, the brown color of his eyes lightening. "So, yeah, I'm jealous Jellybean will steal part of your love away from me, but I'll manage."

"How gracious of you."

He places a soft kiss against my lips. "I mean it. You'll be the most incredible mother. You're generous and kind. Forgiving yet strong. The best kind of role model and the best kind of friend. Whether we only have one child or a horde of them—"

I hold out my hand. "Okay, whoa. Let's start with Jellybean and see how it goes because the word *horde* just had my vagina clench in fear."

Santiago roars with laughter, and I join him. Together on the bathroom floor, we discuss ideas related to our future horde, from ridiculous gender reveal party ideas to outrageous baby names.

But in all the craziness, there is one thing Santiago and I settle on. Together, we will raise this baby with every ounce of love we have in us.

And while Santiago has had his chance to redeem himself with racing, this is mine.

It's time to let go of my past and actually mean it.

"Do you think he really has a chance of winning?" I look over at Noah.

The pit crew stays seated on one side of the garage, prepped and ready to go if Santiago needs a change of tires. Maya entertains Marko with a coloring book in a corner near the entrance to the suites.

James stands by the computers, calling out orders while feeding Santiago information through the team radio.

"If he lands on the podium this race, then he solidifies his first-place standing. He'll be a World Champion again."

Wow. I knew Santiago was good. Hell, I knew he was great. He's spent the last two seasons working his ass off to make it on podiums. But World Championship material after his accident? Now that speaks to his talent more than my words can.

It hasn't been an easy road to get here. Phantom pains still flare up occasionally, and he struggles some days more than others. But Santiago fights every single day to be the best at everything he can.

At racing. At marriage. At preparing to be the best father for our baby boy.

I rub my bulging belly. The diamond on my ring shines under the pit lights, reflecting a rainbow of colors on the ceiling.

I look up at the screens broadcasting the race from Santiago's dashboard camera. He's in second place right now, and while that will secure him points to land on the podium, it won't make him a World Champion.

This is the last race of the season. It's now or never for him to earn the title he has been chasing after since he came back.

Santiago hangs behind Elías, one of McCoy's best drivers. Every move my husband makes to get around Elías's gray car is met with resistance by the McCoy driver.

"Come on." Noah runs a hand through his hair.

Santiago presses on the throttle. His car shoots down the straight, driving up to Elías's side. They drive in tandem down the narrow road.

The turn comes up, and Santiago breaks a second later than Elías, giving him more speed through the turn.

Santiago pulls in front of Elías, securing the first-place spot. The garage cheers as Santiago rushes through the next straight. Elías stays in his rearview, unable to get the upper hand.

A kick in my stomach has me clutching onto Noah's arm for stability.

"Are you okay?"

"Oh my God. The baby just kicked! For real this time, not that usual bubble feeling or fluttering." I grab Noah's hand and shove it against my stomach. I don't bother asking for permission because I need someone to confirm it's not just my imagination.

"Oh, wow. You've got a little fighter." Noah chuckles.

"Maya! Come here. The baby is kicking like he's kung fu

fighting!"

She runs over and replaces Noah's hand with her own. "Ahh! He's a strong one."

I cringe when another kick lands somewhere near my bladder. "Are they always this active?"

"This is only the beginning. Santiago's going to freak out when he realizes he missed this." Maya frowns.

My eyes focus back on the TV. I rub my belly in a circular motion, hoping to ease the baby. "Are you excited for your daddy too, little guy?"

I take the next kick to my stomach as a yes.

Santiago doesn't let his guard down for the rest of the race. He sails past the finish line, and the crew goes wild.

"He did it!" I jump into Maya's arms. We cry together, the matching tears streaming down our faces as Santiago parks his car in his first-place spot.

We walk, even though my heart wishes I could run. My baby has other plans like throwing a private party in my belly.

Someone passes Santiago his iWalk as soon as he lifts himself out of the car. He straps it on and stands, ripping off his helmet in the process. He turns toward us and shoots us a huge smile.

"You won! You're officially a World Champion!" I walk straight into his waiting arms and breathe in his scent of sweat and gasoline.

Is it healthy? No.

Is it slightly addictive and reminds me solely of him? You betcha.

"I already was a World Champion before this."

I punch him lightly in the arm. "Now's not the time to

be cocky."

"You're right. How rude of me. I'll refrain, seeing as I have the perfect evidence of my cockiness right in front of me." He places his gloved hands against my belly.

"Hold on. Take your gloves off."

He follows my request and bites the tips, successfully ripping them off.

Who knew glove removal could be this sexy? Sign me up for a replay, please.

"You're daydreaming again." He smiles.

"Sorry. Look!" I place his hands against the spot that was active not a minute before.

"Am I supposed to rub your belly and make a wish?"

I narrow my eyes at him. "Asshole. Just wait."

It doesn't take more than a minute for our little guy to return with a vengeance.

"*Ay Dios*," Santiago whispers under his breath. "Is that what I think it is?"

"He's happy Daddy won the Championship!"

Santiago keeps his hands on my stomach as he leans down and captures my lips with his. He deepens the kiss, stroking his tongue against mine. People clapping forces us apart.

His eyes glitter with happiness. "I won more than a Championship. I won a woman who makes me appreciate every day how lucky I am to have survived that crash in the first place. Because I couldn't imagine never meeting the one person who completes me. I never believed in soulmates before you, but I'll be damned if you didn't make me a dreamer with your wishes and wildflowers and smile that could make any bad day instantly better."

My hormones take over, and the tears make an encore appearance.

"I love you."

There's no doubt in my mind that I love this fearless man with everything in me. The man who taught me love isn't something to be feared but revered. The very one who spends every single day of his life showing me how much he loves me—with his words, with his actions, with every breath he takes to support our family.

I'll love Santiago Alatorre for as long as the wildflowers keep growing in beautiful chaos.

EXTENDED EPILOGUE

SANTIAGO

A German rendition of a Christmas song plays from the speakers hidden within the walls of Liam and Sophie's house. Each of our families sit at our individual round table with our gingerbread house supplies strewn across the surface. It looks like someone set off a bomb in Santa's village.

The only two successful houses out of the bunch are Marko's and Stella's. It's the same thing every year, with both of them competing in all the Christmas games the Zanders plan. I'm half convinced Liam and Sophie keep coming up with outrageous ideas just to see what the two kids come up with. It borders on ridiculous, but we let Marko and Stella get away with it because it entertains everyone too much.

All the families are dressed in ridiculous matching Christmas pajamas that Sophie picked out. This has been a tradition ever since we all got married and decided we would rather spend the holidays together than apart.

Jax, Elena, and Lennox, their son, sit together, trying to

keep the walls of their house up. Sol, their younger daughter, steals a candy cane off the roof while no one is looking. While both of their kids are adopted, no one could tell based on all their matching dark locks and range of golden skin tones.

Maya takes a photo of Noah balancing my little niece on his lap. It took them plenty of years of healing and enjoying life before they wanted to try again, but with the help of a doctor and in vitro fertilization, my sister got her wish of another child. She's already inching toward three years old and getting bigger by the day. Marko, now old enough to have a little stubble on his chin and a shirt to fill out with muscles, sits next to them in his matching PJs. With all his F2 traveling, I feel like I've missed out on the last year of his life. He's a lot grumpier than I remember. I thought it would make him happy to finally achieve what he has worked so hard for over the years, but his scowl the entire weekend has told a different story.

Marko's eyes remain glued on Stella, who argues with Leo, her twin brother. Their PJs are covered in candy and icing of all different colors. Based on the gumdrops stuck in Stella's blonde hair and the crumbles of gingerbread in her brother's, they got into a food war.

Nothing changes.

"Teddy, do you mind taking a photo of us? Since you're not part of the family and all." Liam beams at Stella's first boyfriend ever, Theodore.

"Dad! His name is *Theodore*." Stella shakes her head.

Oh, Stella, what did you expect? We're a bunch of protective assholes.

Theodore rocks a normal pair of clothes because he wasn't

offered a pair of the Zanders' matching PJs. He attempts to hide his scowl at his new nickname, but I don't miss it. To be honest, Theodore hasn't been having the best night after Liam dubbed him Teddy in front of everyone.

"Like the damn chipmunk. How cute." Marko huffs at the table next to mine.

Now that I look at Theodore, he does kind of look like one with his full cheeks, brown hair, and almond-colored eyes.

"Good eye." I wink at him.

Stella's electric blue eyes slide from her boyfriend to Marko's. "Or Theodore Roosevelt."

"Who also goes by Teddy." Marko's grin widens as Stella focuses all her attention on my nephew.

Teddy stands there with his mouth gaping, a bystander to Stella and Marko's battle. I half expected the newbie to run out the door after Liam grilled him earlier with Noah and Jax's help, but he stuck it out.

"Don't worry about it, babe. Nicknames are always welcome." Teddy throws his arm around Stella's shoulder.

Marko's jaw twitches. Maybe it's time for me to have a talk with my nephew about his little crush on Stella. It's been years, and he has yet to make a move. It's not right for him to get annoyed when he has barely spoken a word to her except when handing over a Christmas gift from the Slades. But now that I think about it, maybe it was from him based on the half-assed wrapping paper job. My sister would never wrap something like that.

Interesting. Very interesting.

"No one calls my daughter 'babe' in front of me. Try again when you're both not teenagers." Liam matches Marko's death stares as he plucks Teddy's arm off his daughter's shoulders. He shoves his phone into Teddy's waiting hands and tugs Stella into his body.

"Dad, we are sixteen." Stella rolls her eyes.

Liam rubs Stella's head. "Did I say teenager? I meant try again when you're a senior citizen. At least I'll be gone from this planet by then."

Jax cackles in a corner with Elena while Noah smiles. Even after all these years, we are still a bunch of clowns who pick on the next generation instead of each other.

Chloe steals my attention as she leans over my shoulder and whispers in my ear, "I finally finished wrapping the last present. Operation North Pole is a go." She places her cup of eggnog on the table before sliding onto my lap.

I wrap my arms around her. "Why didn't you accept my offer to help?"

"Because you can't wrap a present to save your life."

Ah, like nephew, like uncle.

She wiggles her hands in front of my face. "There's enough presents in the attic to rival a toy store, and my fingers are shredded to bits. I feel like I deserved a disclaimer about this. I didn't expect you to want to create your own army of children."

"Well, you do love having sex." I wink.

"I can't be held accountable for my hormones. I should've married someone less attractive. My vagina would have thanked me in the long run."

"I'm slightly insulted, yet also amused."

"Mommy, my tummy hurts." A small voice whines next to us.

"Speaking of our army." I chuckle.

We both look over at Olivia, the youngest out of our three children. She looks up at us with big brown eyes framed by dark lashes. She somehow managed to get green icing all over her PJs. The real crime scene is her mouth, which is tinted green like the Grinch.

"Oh, God. That's going to be a pain to clean before the pictures." Chloe groans.

"Maybe we can sit her next to the tree and pretend she's a decoration?"

Chloe snorts. She passes Olivia a cup of water to drink.

"Daddy! I think we saw Santa Claus!" Serena, our middle child, throws herself onto my lap, replacing Chloe's spot.

I give her a squeeze. "Oh, did you? Were you nice enough to offer him cookies?"

"No! We got nervous," Camilo, our eldest, yells out.

"Ho, ho, ho." James Mitchell calls out from behind us. I turn, assessing his premium Santa Claus suit. Every damn year he puts the suit on with a smile. I'm surprised the younger ones don't guess who he is. Even though Marko, Stella, Leo, and Lennox are older and seem unfazed by the arrival, the little ones go wild.

The living room becomes a mosh pit of screaming kids waving their icing-coated hands in the air.

"Look who it is!" Liam claps his hands together after throwing on his elf hat. Damn, he really enjoys hosting the holiday festivities. He rolls out a list in a dramatic fashion. "So, who has been naughty this year?"

"Not me!" My little niece smiles.

"Nope!" Olivia and Serena speak up.

"I only stole an extra cookie one time," Camilo chimes in.

Liam's eyes meet mine. He fails to hide his massive smile.

I shrug. *Well, at least my kid is honest.* I better soak up one of his last Christmases actually thinking Santa still exists.

"Who's ready for presents?" Sophie calls out, wrapping her arm around Liam's waist.

"Me!" Our Alatorre army jumps up and down, screaming in unison.

Chloe presses a soft kiss against the crook of my neck. "Now's our chance to run for it while the kids are distracted. I honestly doubt they'll miss us. What do you think?"

"Why would I run? I have everything I could possibly ever want."

"Including kids who eat every pack of icing instead of making a gingerbread house?"

"Especially that. It's practically tradition by now." I grab her cup and take a sip. Despite my disgust, I swallow the contents. "Why the hell would you drink eggnog without alcohol? That's sacrilegious here."

She lifts her shoulders in faux innocence and looks up at me from under her thick lashes. "Alcohol isn't going to be on the menu for a while."

My heart stops. *No fucking way.* "What?"

"When you say you have everything you could possibly want, do you have a little more room for one more Alatorre?" Her smile widens as she finishes speaking.

I ditch the eggnog. The cup clatters against the table, spilling all over the Christmas themed tablecloth. "You're joking."

She shakes her head and giggles. "I asked the doctor

the same thing. Turns out your little swimmers are quite the overachievers."

Holy shit. I smack a bunch of kisses on her face, not leaving an inch of skin untouched. "Oh my God. We're having another kid."

"Suit up, Iron Man. It's going to be a wild one. I thought three was a lot, but four? That's minivan material."

We both look over at our three kids. My arms tighten around Chloe as I place a kiss on her neck. "Thank you for the best presents ever, including this one." I place my palm against her flat stomach.

"And thank you for showing me how life is a gift in the first place," she whispers back.

I kiss the love of my life with every ounce of affection I feel. Somehow, the worst accident of my life led to the best surprise. A life full of love, happiness, and laughter.

A life I plan on making the most of, up until my very last breath.

THANK YOU!

If you enjoyed *Redeemed*, please consider leaving a review!
Support from readers like you means so much to me and
helps other readers find books.

Join my Bandini Babes Facebook group for all the grid
gossip about the Bandini and McCoy racers.

SCAN THE CODE TO JOIN THE GROUP

ALSO BY LAUREN ASHER

Throttled
Read Noah and Maya's forbidden romance.

Collided
The Dirty Air series continues with
Sophie and Liam's story.

Wrecked
Don't miss out on Jax's enemies-to-lovers story.

SCAN THE CODE TO READ THE BOOKS

ACKNOWLEDGEMENTS

To all the readers who fell in love with Santiago—Thank you for loving Santiago as much as you have. He was originally set to be a side character but your push for his story drove me to create this new world.

To my ride or die—It might seem silly to thank someone for believing in me, but I can't go without speaking the truth. Your constant support has kept me going on the hardest days. And thanks for letting me bounce plots off you. My books wouldn't be the same without you telling me how evil I am for the things I do to my characters.

To Julie, the best kind of friend and PR badass—I offer my endless thanks for all you do. You not only organize my life, but you're the best kind of friend (and plot buddy)! I couldn't do this without you, and while this is the end of a series (and era), I can't wait to explore the future with you.

To my editor, Erica—Thanks for always being the best of the best! There's no one else I would want by my side to help my characters and stories come to life.

To Mary at Books and Moods—Thank you for convincing me to change my cover a year ago. I never thought I would make such a great friend out of this experience, and I appreciate all you do! Seriously, graphics, formatting, covers. You are unstoppable!

To my teams—I appreciate every single thing you share related to my books. You all hold such a special place in my heart, and I am thankful for all your kind words. I only hope to create another world you fall in love with soon.

To Emilia—I am beyond thankful for your unwavering

support and love for this series. Thank you for believing in my dream, and I only hope to keep creating characters and worlds you want to be a part of.

To Billy Monger—You are an incredible role model to so many individuals. Your perseverance to compete in racing despite your crash is inspirational, and I only wanted to create a character with as much heart and drive as you.

To my dog, Theodore—You really shouldn't have made me angry on the day I was writing that extended epilogue LOL. Now you'll be remembered as the guy everyone wants to hate.

Milton Keynes UK
Ingram Content Group UK Ltd.
UKHW020621250524
443091UK00016B/129